the STRUGGLE

WANDA & BRUNSTETTER

BARBOUR
PUBLISHING

Print ISBN 978-1-61626-089-7

eBook Editions:
Adobe Digital Edition (.epub) 978-1-60742-002-6
Kindle and MobiPocket Edition (.prc) 978-1-60742-023-1

All scripture quotations are taken from the King James Version of the Bible.

All German-Dutch words are taken from the *Revised Pennsylvania German Dictionary* found in Lancaster County, Pennsylvania.

This book is a work of fiction. Names, characters, places, and incidents are either products of the author's imagination or used fictitiously. Any similarity to actual people, organizations, and/or events is purely coincidental.

For more information about Wanda E. Brunstetter, please access the author's website at the following Internet address: www.wandabrunstetter.com

Cover design: Faceout Studio, www.faceoutstudio.com
Cover photography: Steve Gardner, Pixelworks Studios

Published by Barbour Publishing, Inc., P.O. Box 719, Uhrichsville, OH 44683, www.barbourbooks.com

Our mission is to publish and distribute inspirational products offering exceptional value and biblical encouragement to the masses.

 Member of the
Evangelical Christian
Publishers Association

Printed in the United States of America.

DEDICATION/ACKNOWLEDGMENT

To Richard and Betty Miller, our dear Amish friends
who know what it's like to deal with the adjustment
of having family members move away.

If ye forgive men their trespasses,
your heavenly Father will also forgive you.
MATTHEW 6:14

Fisher Family Tree

Abraham and Sarah (deceased) Fisher's Children

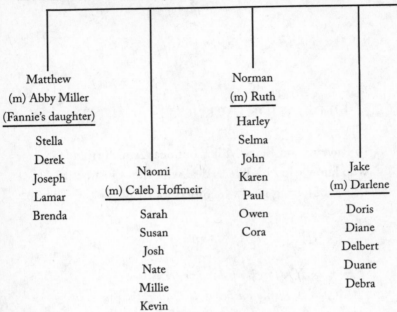

Matthew
(m) Abby Miller
(Fannie's daughter)

Stella
Derek
Joseph
Lamar
Brenda

Naomi
(m) Caleb Hoffmeir

Sarah
Susan
Josh
Nate
Millie
Kevin

Norman
(m) Ruth

Harley
Selma
John
Karen
Paul
Owen
Cora

Jake
(m) Darlene

Doris
Diane
Delbert
Duane
Debra

Abraham and Fannie Fisher's Children

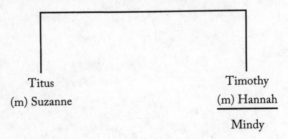

Titus
(m) Suzanne

Timothy
(m) Hannah

Mindy

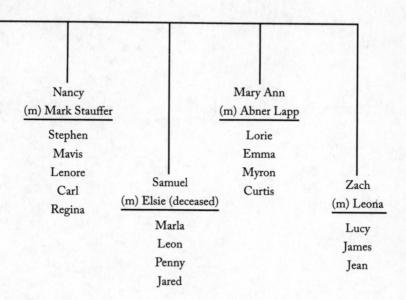

Nancy
(m) Mark Stauffer

Stephen
Mavis
Lenore
Carl
Regina

Samuel
(m) Elsie (deceased)

Marla
Leon
Penny
Jared

Mary Ann
(m) Abner Lapp

Lorie
Emma
Myron
Curtis

Zach
(m) Leona

Lucy
James
Jean

Fannie's Children from Her First Marriage

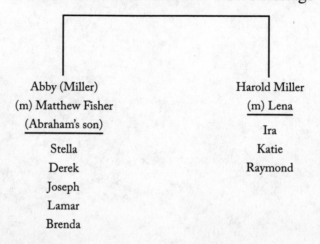

Abby (Miller)
(m) Matthew Fisher
(Abraham's son)

Stella
Derek
Joseph
Lamar
Brenda

Harold Miller
(m) Lena

Ira
Katie
Raymond

CHAPTER 1

Paradise, Pennsylvania

Timothy Fisher approached his parents' home with a feeling of dread. Good-byes never came easy, and knowing Mom disapproved of his decision to move to Kentucky made this good-bye even harder.

He stepped onto his parents' porch and turned, trying to memorize the scene before him. He liked the rolling hills and rich, fertile land here in Pennsylvania. As much as he hated to admit it, he did have a few misgivings about this move. He would miss working with Dad in the fields. And just thinking about the aroma of Mom's sticky buns made his mouth water. But it was time for a change, and Christian County, Kentucky, seemed like the place to go. After all, his twin brother, Titus, and half brother Samuel were doing quite well in Kentucky. He just hoped things would work out for him, too.

Shrugging his thoughts aside, Timothy opened the back door and stepped inside. Mom and Dad were sitting at the kitchen table, drinking coffee and eating sticky buns.

"Guder Mariye," he said with a smile, trying to ignore his throbbing headache.

"Mornin'." Dad motioned to the coffeepot on the stove. "Help yourself to a cup of coffee. Oh, and don't forget some of these," he added, pushing the plate of sticky buns to the end of the table.

"I'll get the coffee for you." Mom started to rise from her seat, but Timothy shook his head.

"I can get the coffee, Mom, but I can't stay long because I have some last-minute packing to do. Just wanted to see if there's anything either of you needs me to do before I leave."

Tears welled in Mom's brown eyes. "Oh Timothy, I really wish you weren't going. Isn't there anything we can do to make you stay?"

Timothy poured himself a cup of coffee and took a seat at the table. "I've made up my mind about this, Mom. Samuel's gotten really busy working for Allen Walters, and he's finding a lot of paint jobs on his own, so he has enough work to hire me."

"But you had work right here, helping your *daed* and painting for Zach."

"I realize that, but Dad's already hired someone else to work the fields, and Zach has other people working for him." Timothy blew on his coffee and took a sip. "Besides, I'm not moving to Kentucky because I need a job. I'm moving to save my marriage."

"Save your marriage?" Mom's eyebrows furrowed. "If you ask me, taking Hannah away from her *mamm* is more likely to ruin your marriage than save it! Hannah and Sally are very close, and Hannah's bound to resent you for separating them."

"Calm down, Fannie." Dad's thick gray eyebrows pulled together as he placed his hand on Mom's arm. "You're gettin' yourself all worked up, and it's not good for your health."

Her face flamed. "There's nothing wrong with my health, Abraham."

"*Jah*, well, you may be healthy right now, but with you gettin' so riled about Timothy moving, your blood pressure's likely to go up." He gave her arm a little pat. "Besides, if he thinks it's best for them to move to Kentucky, then we should accept that and give him our blessing."

Mom's chin quivered. "B–but we've already lost two sons to Kentucky, and if Timothy goes, too, you never can tell who might be next. At the rate things are going, our whole family will be living in Kentucky, and we'll be here all alone."

Timothy's gaze went to the ceiling. "You're exaggerating, Mom. No one else has even mentioned moving to Kentucky."

"That's right," Dad agreed. "They're all involved in their businesses, most have their own homes, and everyone seems pretty well settled right here."

"I thought Titus and Samuel were settled, too, but they ran off to Kentucky, and now they've talked Timothy into moving." Mom sniffed, and Timothy knew she was struggling not to cry.

"They didn't talk me into moving," Timothy said, rubbing his forehead. "I made the decision myself because I'm sick of Hannah clinging to her mamm and ignoring me." He huffed. "I'm hoping things will be better between us once we get moved and settled into a place of our own. Hannah will need a bit of time to adjust, of course, but once she does, I'm sure she'll see that the move was a good thing." He smiled at Mom, hoping to reassure her. "After we get a place of our own, you and Dad can come visit us. Please, Mom, it would mean a lot to know you understand my need to do this."

Mom sighed. "If you're determined to go, I guess I can't stop you, but I don't have to like it."

Timothy smiled when Dad gave him a wink. Mom would eventually come to grips with the move—especially when she saw how much happier he and Hannah would be. He just hoped Hannah would see that, too.

———

Hannah stood at the kitchen sink, hands shaking and eyes brimming with tears. She could hardly believe her husband was making them move to Kentucky. She couldn't stand the thought of leaving her family—especially Mom. Hannah and her mother had always been close, but Timothy was jealous of the time they spent together. He wanted her all to himself— that's why he'd decided they should move to Kentucky. She wished she could convince Timothy to change his mind, but he wouldn't budge.

She sniffed and swiped at the tears running down her cheeks. "It's not fair! I shouldn't be forced to move from my home that I love to a place I'm sure I will hate! I can't believe my own husband is putting me through this!"

Hannah jumped when the back door banged shut. She grabbed a dish towel and quickly dried her tears. If it was Timothy, she couldn't let him know she'd been crying. It would only cause another disagreement like the one they'd had earlier this morning, and they sure didn't need any more of those. Timothy didn't like it when she cried and had often accused her of using her tears to get what she wanted.

When Hannah was sure all traces of tears were gone, she turned and was surprised to see her mother standing near the kitchen table. Hannah breathed a sigh of relief. "Oh Mom, it's you. I'm so glad it's not Timothy."

"Are you okay? Your eyes look red and puffy." Mom's pale blue eyes revealed the depth of her concern.

Hannah swallowed a couple of times, unsure of her voice.

"I...I don't want to move. Just the thought of it makes me feel ill. I want to stay right here in Lancaster County."

Mom stepped up to Hannah and gathered her into her arms. "I wish you didn't have to move, either, but Timothy's your husband, which means your place is with him." She gently patted Hannah's back. "Your daed and I will miss you, but we'll come to visit as soon as you get settled in."

"But that probably won't be for some time." Hannah nearly choked on the sob rising in her throat. "We'll be staying with Timothy's brother Samuel until we get a place of our own, and I–I'm not sure how that's going to work out."

"I understand your concerns. From what you've told me, Samuel has a lot on his hands, having four *kinner* to raise and all. He'll no doubt appreciate your help."

Hannah stiffened. "Do you think Samuel will expect me to watch the children while he's at work?"

"Maybe. It would mean he wouldn't have to pay anyone else to watch them—unless, of course, he decides to pay you."

"It's my understanding that Esther Beiler's been watching them, but I suppose that could change with me living there."

Mom pulled out a chair at the table and took a seat. "You'll just have to wait and see, but hopefully it'll all work out."

Hannah wasn't sure about that. She hadn't planned on taking care of four more children. "Moving to a strange place and being around people she isn't used to seeing will be difficult for Mindy. My little girl is going to need my attention more than ever."

"That's true. It will be an adjustment. But Mindy's young, and I'm sure she'll quickly adapt to her new surroundings," Mom said.

Hannah sighed. She didn't think anything about their

move to Kentucky would work, and to be honest, she hoped it wouldn't, because if things went badly, Timothy might see the light and move back to Pennsylvania where they belonged.

CHAPTER 2

Lexington, Kentucky

Hannah shifted on the seat, trying to find a comfortable position. After tearful good-byes to their families last night, she, Timothy, and Mindy had left home at four this morning and spent the last ten hours on the road. The few hours of sleep Hannah had managed to get while riding in Charles Thomas's van had done little to relieve her fatigue and nothing to soften the pain of leaving Pennsylvania.

Why couldn't Timothy understand the closeness she and Mom felt? Didn't he care about anyone's needs but his own? When they'd first gotten married, he'd said he loved her and wanted to spend the rest of his life making her happy. Apparently he'd lied about that. Maybe he'd told her what she wanted to hear so she would agree to marry him. He probably only wanted a wife to cook, clean, and give him children, because he sure didn't seem to care about her wants or needs—or for that matter, what was important to her. Hannah's inner voice told her this wasn't true, but somehow it just felt better to think so.

She glanced at her precious daughter sleeping peacefully in the car seat beside her. Mindy resembled Hannah's mother in some ways. She had the same blond hair and pale blue eyes, but she had her daddy's nose and her mama's mouth. If they had more children, Hannah wondered what they would look like. Oh, how she wished for another baby. A little brother or sister for Mindy would be so nice. She thought about the miscarriage she'd had last year and wished once more that the baby had lived.

Seems like I never get what I want, Hannah thought bitterly. *Makes me wonder why I even bother to pray.*

Hannah's inner voice told her again that she shouldn't feel this way. Looking at Mindy, she knew how blessed she was to have such a special little girl.

She glanced toward the front of the van where Timothy sat talking to their driver. It made her feel sick to hear the excitement in Timothy's voice as he told Charles about the phone call he'd had with his twin brother, Titus, last night. Titus was married to Suzanne now, and Samuel and Esther would probably be married soon, as well. Both Samuel and Titus were happy living in Kentucky, but Hannah was certain she would never be happy there.

Hannah leaned her head against the window and closed her eyes as the need for sleep overtook her. She wished she could wake up and discover that this was all just a bad dream and find herself home in her own bed. But of course, that was just wishful thinking. At least for now, sleep was her only means to escape the dread that kept mounting the closer they got to their destination.

—⁂—

Timothy glanced at the backseat and was pleased to see that his wife and daughter were both sound asleep. They'd pushed hard all day, only stopping to get gas, eat, and take bathroom breaks. If all went well, they should be in Pembroke by this evening.

A sense of excitement welled in Timothy's soul. It would be good to see his brothers again, and he could hardly wait to start a new life in Kentucky, where he'd been told that land was cheaper and more abundant. Since their house in Pennsylvania had already sold, he had the money to begin building a home. The problem would be finding the time to build it, since he'd only be able to work on it when he wasn't painting with Samuel. Of course, it might be better if he could find a home that had already been built—maybe a place that needed some work and he could fix up in his spare time. Well, he'd decide about that once he'd had a chance to look around.

"How are you holding up?" Charles asked, running his fingers through his slightly thinning gray hair, while glancing over at Timothy. "Do you need to take a break?"

"Naw, I'm fine. Just anxious to get there is all."

Charles nodded. "I'm sure. It's been a long day, but we're making good time. According to my GPS, we should be in Pembroke by six-thirty or so, barring anything unforeseen."

"That sounds good. If I can borrow your cell phone, I'll call and leave a message for Samuel so he knows what time to expect us."

"Sure, no problem." Charles handed Timothy his phone.

Timothy dialed Samuel's number and was surprised when a young boy answered the phone. He hadn't expected anyone to be in the phone shanty.

"Hello. Who's this?" he asked.

"It's Leon. Who's this, and who are ya callin' for?"

"It's your uncle Timothy, and I'm calling to let your daed know that we're in Kentucky and should be at your place around six thirty."

"Oh, good. Should I tell Esther to have supper ready then?"

"Is Esther there now?"

"Jah. *Daadi*'s still at work, and Esther's here with me, Marla, Penny, and Jared."

"Okay, will you let your daed know when he gets home from work what time to expect us? Oh, and if Esther doesn't mind holding supper till we get there, we'd surely appreciate it. It'll save us some time if we don't have to stop and eat somewhere."

"Sure, no problem. I'll tell 'em both what you said."

"*Danki*, Leon. See you soon." Timothy hung up and put the phone back in the tray. "I think Esther will have supper waiting for us when we get there," he said to Charles. "So we shouldn't have to stop again except if you need gas or someone needs a bathroom break."

"Sounds good. Nothing like a good home-cooked meal to look forward to. Would you mind letting the other drivers know?"

"Don't mind a'tall." Timothy called each of their drivers, who were transporting his family's belongings, then settled back and closed his eyes. If he slept awhile, the time would pass more quickly.

Just think, he told himself, *in a few more hours, I'll be sitting in my brother's kitchen, sharing a meal and catching up on all his news. Sure hope I get to see Titus and Suzanne this evening, too. I can't wait to find out how they're doing.*

CHAPTER 3

Pembroke, Kentucky

We're here, Hannah! Better wake Mindy up so we can greet Samuel and his family."

Hannah's eyes snapped open, and she bolted upright in her seat. The moment she'd been dreading was finally here. She could see by his expression that Timothy was excited. Too bad she didn't share his enthusiasm.

Hannah fiddled with her head covering to be sure it was on straight then gently nudged her rosy-cheeked daughter's arm. "Wake up, Mindy," she said softly, so as not to frighten the child. Ever since Mindy had been a baby, she'd been a hard sleeper, and if she was awakened too abruptly, she either cried or became grumpy. It was better if she was allowed the freedom to wake up on her own, but right now that wasn't possible.

"Let's get out and stretch our legs before we go inside." Timothy had the van door open before Hannah could even unbuckle the seat belt holding Mindy in her car seat. They'd no more than stepped out of the van when Samuel rushed out the door to greet them. "It's mighty good to see you, brother!" he said, giving Timothy a big bear hug.

"It's good to see you, too." Timothy's smile stretched ear to ear as he pounded Samuel's back.

"It's nice to see you, as well," Samuel said, turning to Hannah and giving her a quick hug. "How was your trip?"

"It was long, and I'm stiff and tired." Hannah knew her voice sounded strained, and probably a bit testy, but she couldn't help it. She didn't want to be here, and there was no point in pretending she did. Life was perfect back home in Pennsylvania—at least, she thought so.

Samuel nodded with a look of understanding. "I remember how tired the Kinner and I felt when we got here last year." He smiled at Mindy and reached his hand out to her, but she quickly hid behind Hannah.

"She's a little shy—especially since she hasn't seen you in a while," Timothy said. "I think she just needs some time to get reacquainted."

Woof! Woof! A black lab bounded out of the barn and headed straight for Mindy. When Mindy screamed, Timothy quickly scooped her into his arms.

"Sorry about that." Samuel grabbed the dog's collar. "Lucky gets excited when he sees someone new to play with," he said.

Hannah frowned. "Mindy's too little to play with a dog that big. She's obviously afraid of it."

"I'll put the dog away. Come on, boy." Samuel led the dog back to the barn.

I don't think our daughter wants to be here any more than I do, Hannah thought. *Why can't you see that, Timothy? Why couldn't we have stayed in Pennsylvania? How can you expect Mindy or me to like it here? I'll never consider Kentucky my home.*

Samuel had just returned from the barn when his four

children rushed out of the house, followed by a pretty, young Amish woman with dark hair and milk-chocolate-brown eyes.

"Esther, you remember Timothy when he came for Titus and Suzanne's wedding, and I'd like you to meet his wife, Hannah, and their daughter, Mindy," Samuel said. It was obvious from his smiling face that he loved her deeply.

Esther smiled warmly and gave Hannah a hug.

"It's nice to meet you," Hannah said, forcing a smile.

"It's real good to see you again," Timothy said, shaking Esther's hand.

Samuel smiled down at his children. "So what do you think, Timothy? Have the kinner grown much since you last saw 'em?"

Timothy nodded. "They sure have. I hardly recognize Leon, he's gotten so tall, and when I called earlier, I didn't realize at first it was him on the phone. And would you look at Marla, Penny, and Jared? They've all grown a lot, too!"

Charles stepped out of the van, and Timothy introduced him to Samuel and Esther.

"The trucks with all of Timothy and Hannah's things aren't far behind," Charles said. "Should we start unloading as soon as they get here?"

"Maybe we could eat supper first," Esther said. "It's almost ready, and it won't be good if it gets cold. Believe me, there's plenty of food for everyone, even the drivers, so make sure you tell them to stay and eat with us."

"That sounds good to me." Timothy patted his stomach. "With all the work we have ahead of us yet tonight, I'll need some nourishment to give me the strength to do it."

"I'd suggest that we wait till tomorrow, but since it'll be Sunday, that won't work," Samuel said.

Sunday. Hannah groaned inwardly. If this was the week

Samuel's church district had church, she'd be forced to go and try to put on a happy face when she met a bunch of people she didn't want to know.

"Where are we going to put everything?" Timothy asked his brother. "Will there be room enough in your barn?"

"I think so," Samuel said with a nod. "And if there isn't, we can always put some of your things in Titus's barn."

"Speaking of my twin, where is he?" Timothy questioned, looking back toward the house. "I figured he might be here waiting for us."

"He and Suzanne are coming, and I'm sure they'll be here soon. Titus probably had to work a little later than usual this evening."

Esther touched Hannah's arm. "You look tired. Why don't you come inside and rest while I get supper on the table?"

Resting sounded good, but Hannah didn't want to appear impolite, so she forced another smile and said, "I appreciate the offer, but I should help you with supper."

"There really isn't that much left to do. Marla set the table awhile ago, and the chicken's staying warm in the oven. But if you really want to help, you can cut up the veggies for a tossed salad while I mash the potatoes."

"Sure, I can do that."

Hannah reached for Mindy, and when Timothy handed the child over, Hannah followed Esther into the house.

While Mindy played with her cousins in the living room, Hannah helped Esther in the kitchen.

"How long have you and Samuel been courting?" Hannah asked, feeling the need to find something to talk about.

"We started courting this past summer, but then Samuel broke things off for a while because he was afraid of being untrue to his wife's memory. Since he'd promised Elsie before she died that he'd always love her, he felt as if he was betraying her memory when he fell in love with me. But something miraculously changed his mind, and Samuel renewed his relationship with me." Esther smiled brightly. "We hope to be married sometime next year."

I wonder if Timothy would find someone else if something happened to me, Hannah mused as she washed and patted the lettuce dry. *With the way things have been between us lately, he might be glad if I was gone. He might find another wife right away.*

Hannah knew she couldn't continue with these negative thoughts, so she watched out the window as the two big trucks pulled into the yard. Timothy greeted the drivers and unloaded their two horses, Dusty and Lilly, from the trailer that had been pulled behind one of the trucks. All their furniture and household items were in those trucks, along with the buggy they used for transportation and all of Timothy's tools and farming equipment. Nothing had been left in Pennsylvania except their empty house, which would soon have new owners living in it. Everything seemed so final, and it was hard to even think about someone else living in their house.

"It's so nice that you and Timothy are here," Esther said. "I know Samuel's pleased that Timothy has made the move. And of course, Titus will be happy to have his twin brother living nearby. He's often mentioned all the fun times he and Timothy had growing up together."

Hannah was about to comment when she spotted a horse and buggy pull into the yard. A few minutes later, Titus and Suzanne climbed down, and Timothy and his twin brother embraced. When they pulled apart, Titus snatched Timothy's straw hat and tossed it into the air. When the two brothers started whooping and hollering, Hannah wondered if they would ever settle down. They acted like a couple of kids—the way they had during their running-around years. Timothy and Titus looked so much alike, and they'd always been very close. They had the same thick, dark brown hair and brown eyes; although Titus's left eye was slightly larger than his right eye. That was the only way some folks were able to tell them apart. They were obviously happy to be together again.

But I'm not happy, and nobody seems to care. Hannah fought the urge to give in to the tears stinging the backs of her eyes. They'd been in Pembroke less than an hour, and already she hated it. Pennsylvania was where her heart remained, and Kentucky would never replace it. No matter how long they lived here, Pennsylvania was the only place she'd ever call home.

CHAPTER 4

As Timothy sat in church on Sunday morning, he looked across the room and noticed that Hannah wasn't paying attention to the message being preached by one of the ministers. Ever since they'd taken their seats on the backless wooden benches inside Suzanne's mother's home almost three hours ago, she'd either stared out the window or fussed with Mindy, whom she held on her lap. Fortunately, Mindy had recently fallen asleep, so Hannah should have been paying attention, but she seemed completely bored, as though her mind was elsewhere. When they lived in Pennsylvania, Hannah had always appeared interested during church. Was her disinterest now because she hadn't enjoyed any of the messages, or was it simply because she didn't want to be here at all? Timothy guessed the latter, because so far, Hannah had made it clear that she didn't like anything about moving to Kentucky. He'd hoped that once she accepted the idea that this was their new home, she would learn to fit in and end up actually liking the area.

When Timothy realized that he, too, wasn't paying attention to the message, he pulled his thoughts aside and, for the rest of the service, concentrated on what was being said.

When church was over, the men and women ate the noon meal in shifts, so Timothy wasn't sure how Hannah was doing or if she'd met any of the women. Once everyone had eaten, a few people went home, but most gathered in groups to visit.

Timothy meandered around the yard for a bit then stopped for a spell to lean against the fence. Behind him he could hear cows mooing in the distance, but he preferred to watch the activities around him. He glanced at the big maple tree nearby, now barren with the approach of winter, and noticed his wife sitting on a chair with Mindy in her lap, looking more forlorn than ever. He'd seen some of the women try to talk to Hannah, but then a short time later, they would leave and join the others who were visiting on the opposite side of the yard. This caused him even more concern, wondering if his wife may have given these women the cold shoulder.

Hannah had been quiet and moody ever since they'd left Pennsylvania, and even during the time they'd spent with family last night, she'd remained aloof—as if her thoughts were someplace else. *Probably back in Pennsylvania with her mamm,* Timothy thought with regret. Keeping to herself so much was not a good thing. Worse yet, she was hovering over Mindy again, not letting her play with the other children. Timothy had hoped that by coming to Kentucky, Hannah would want to make some friends. But if she continued to remain aloof, making new friends probably wouldn't happen. He worried that people might get the impression that his wife was standoffish. But then how could they think otherwise with the way she'd acted so far?

Maybe she just needs a bit more time, Timothy told himself. *Once Hannah gets better acquainted with Suzanne and Esther, she'll fit right in. At least, I hope that's the case, because I sure wouldn't want her to mope around all the time. It could have a negative effect on Mindy, and it won't do any good for our marriage either. I'm probably rushing things and need to be more patient.*

"You look like you're somewhere far-off. What are you thinkin' about, brother?" Titus asked, bumping Timothy's arm as he joined him at the fence.

"Oh, nothing much."

"Come on now." Titus nudged Timothy's arm a second time. "This is your twin *bruder* you're talkin' to, so you may as well say what's on your mind."

Timothy smiled, knowing how it had always been between him and his twin. They could sense things about each other, good or bad. It was as if they knew what the other one was thinking. "I'm worried about Hannah," he admitted. "I'm afraid she may never adjust to living so far away from her mamm."

"I wouldn't worry too much. I'm sure she'll get used to it. But if you're really concerned, I'll speak to Suzanne and ask her to make sure Hannah feels welcome. Maybe they can hire a driver and go shopping in Hopkinsville soon or just get together for lunch or something."

"Danki. I'd appreciate that. At this point, anything's worth a try."

"You know, Timothy, you might be rushing things a bit. Maybe you just need to relax and let Hannah work through it all," Titus added. "You've only been here for one day."

"I was just thinking the same thing. You and I always did think alike."

"Jah. So changing the subject," Titus said, "have you had a chance to talk to Samuel about working with him?"

Timothy nodded. "He said he's been really busy lately, doing a lot of jobs for Allen, plus some he's lined up on his own. Starting tomorrow, I'll be working with both Allen and Samuel on a job in Crittenden County." He shifted, feeling uncomfortable all of a sudden. "You know, with this being the Lord's Day and all, guess we really shouldn't be talkin' about work."

Titus gave a nod. "You're right, so why don't we go find Samuel and some of the other men here and see if we can get a game of horseshoes started?"

Timothy smiled. "Sounds good to me. Let's go!"

—∞—

"Everything looks so different here," Hannah said after they left the Yoders' place and were heading down the tree-lined road in their horse and buggy toward Samuel's house. "The grass in the fields is an ugly brown, and from what I can tell, there aren't many houses or places of business nearby. Christian County is nothing like Lancaster County at all."

"That's true," Timothy agreed, "but it's peaceful and much quieter here, and there aren't nearly so many cars or tourists."

"I've gotten used to the tourists. In fact, if it weren't for the tourists, my daed's bulk food store wouldn't do nearly as well as it does."

"Guess you're right about that, but I still think it's nice to be here where the pace is slower."

Hannah grimaced when Mindy, who was asleep in her lap, stirred restlessly as their buggy bounced over the numerous ruts in the road. She turned in her seat a bit to look at Timothy and frowned. "The pace may be slower here, but the roads in Christian County need some work, don't you think?"

"I suppose, but there are some rough roads around Lancaster, too."

Hannah knew her husband was trying to look on the positive side of things, but so far she didn't like one thing about being here. In fact, Timothy's bright outlook actually irritated her. Every time she complained, he had some way of twisting things around to make it all sound good.

"See that driveway over there?" Timothy pointed to the right. "It leads to the bed-and-breakfast I told you about. It's run by a young English woman, Bonnie Taylor." He gave Hannah a dimpled smile. "I met Bonnie when I came here for Titus and Suzanne's wedding, and she seemed very nice. Samuel and Allen did some work on her house before she opened the B&B, and Esther's been working for her part-time ever since. She helps Bonnie in the mornings before heading to Samuel's to keep house and watch the kinner. Then she goes back to help at the B&B again in the evenings after Samuel gets home from work."

Hannah grunted in response. She wasn't interested in hearing about the B&B or the woman who owned it. She wished Timothy hadn't gone to his brother's wedding, because it wasn't long after that he'd come up with the crazy notion to move here.

Maybe I should have gone with him to the wedding, she thought. *Then I could have discouraged him from the very beginning.*

"So what did you think of the church service today?" he asked, moving their conversation in a different direction.

She sighed. "It was okay, I guess."

"Did you hear what the bishop said in his message about remembering to count our blessings and learning to be content?"

"I. . .I don't really remember."

"Well, he said contentment helps to keep one's heart free from worry. It also teaches us to live simply and think of others more than ourselves. I think his message was a good reminder for us, don't you?"

Hannah stiffened. "What are you trying to say, Timothy? Do you think I'm supposed to be thankful and content that you forced me to leave the home I loved and come here to a place I already hate? How can you even accept that someone else will be living in our house in Pennsylvania?"

Timothy gripped the reins a bit tighter. "You only think you hate it here because you didn't want to move, but if you'll give it half a chance, I think you might change your mind. Besides, the house in Pennsylvania is not ours anymore, remember?"

"Jah, you made sure of that, didn't you? And I doubt I'll ever like it here. I mean, what's to like? We're stuck living with Samuel and his kinner, and—"

"We won't be living with him forever," Timothy interrupted. "As soon as we find some suitable property, I can start building a house."

"But it's the middle of November, Timothy. Even if we could find the perfect property right away, you'd never get a house built for us before winter sets in."

"You're right, but spring will come sooner than we think."

"I can't imagine us being cooped up with Samuel and his rowdy kinner throughout the winter months." Hannah frowned. "If we have to live here, I'd really like to have a place of our own."

"And we will—just as soon as I can get one built."

"Can't we see about buying a house that's already built? We could move in quicker, and our stay with Samuel would be brief."

He shrugged. "Samuel said there's not much for sale in this area right now. He feels fortunate to be renting the house owned by Esther's folks."

"What's going to happen after he and Esther are married?" Hannah asked. "Will they continue renting the place from her folks, or will they end up buying it?'

"I'm not sure. Samuel hasn't said anything about that. And as far as I know, he and Esther aren't officially engaged yet."

"I'll bet they will be soon. Samuel needs a *mudder* for his kinner, and it's pretty obvious that he's smitten with Esther."

"I don't think *smitten* is the right word for what my bruder feels for Esther," Timothy said. "All ya have to do is watch how they interact to see that they're obviously in love with each other."

Hannah looked down at Mindy and stroked her soft cheek. *Well, at least I have you,* she thought. *That's something to be thankful for. Mindy, you are my one constant blessing.*

CHAPTER 5

W ake up, sleepyhead." Timothy shook his wife's shoulder.

"I'm tired. It can't be time to get up already." Hannah moaned and pulled the quilt over her head.

Timothy nudged her arm through the covers. "It's Monday morning, and Samuel and I need to get an early start because we'll be working out of the area today. Allen will be coming by to pick us up soon."

Hannah just lay there, unmoving.

"Hannah, please get up. I was hoping you'd fix us some breakfast and pack lunches for us to take to the job."

She pulled the covers aside and yawned noisily as she sat up. "Oh, all right." Her long, tawny-brown hair hung around her shoulders in an array of tangled curls. Hannah's thick hair had always been naturally curly—which meant she had to work hard at getting it parted down the middle, twisted on the sides, and pulled back into a bun. When she took it down at night, she spent several minutes brushing it out. During the first year of their marriage Timothy had often brushed Hannah's hair. That had been a special time for him, when he felt really close to her. He hoped they could bring those days back again now that they were making a new start.

Timothy leaned down and kissed Hannah's cheek. It was warm and soft, and he was tempted to forget about going to work with Samuel and stay here with Hannah. But he knew he couldn't do that. He had to earn a living and provide for them.

"I'll see you downstairs in the kitchen," he said, before giving her another quick kiss. Then he moved away from the bed and stopped for a minute to gaze at Mindy, sleeping peacefully on a cot across the room, her golden curls fanned out across the pillow. She looked like an angel, lying there so sweet. Mindy could have shared a room with Penny, of course, but Hannah had insisted that their daughter needed to be close to them—at least until she felt more familiar with this new place. Timothy figured it was just an excuse. Hannah, following in her mother's footsteps, was too clingy and overprotective where their little girl was concerned.

Mindy's so sweet and innocent, he thought. *She's always smiling and full of curiosity.* Timothy hoped in the years ahead that he and Hannah would have a few more children, whom he was sure would be equally special. His stomach clenched as he thought about the baby Hannah had lost last year and how hard she'd grieved after the miscarriage. It had taken some time for her to pull out of her depression, but with the help and encouragement of several family members, she'd finally come to accept the baby's death, although he didn't think she had ever fully understood why God had allowed it.

Of course, God's ways aren't our ways. Sometimes it's better if we don't try and figure things out—just accept life's disappointments and trust God to help us through them, because He's in control of every situation anyhow, Timothy reminded himself as he slipped quietly out of the room.

—w—

After fixing breakfast for Timothy and Samuel and packing them both a lunch, Hannah, still feeling tired, was tempted to go back to bed. But she knew she couldn't do that because Samuel's children would be up soon, and then she'd have to fix them breakfast and see that the two oldest were off to school. Esther had been caring for Samuel's children, but since Samuel hadn't mentioned Esther coming over, Hannah assumed she'd be watching them. She'd been worried that it might be expected of her, but now that she was here, she'd changed her mind. Truth was, she thought she could do a better job with the kids than Esther, not to mention with keeping the house running smoother. Good habits began at an early age, and as far as Hannah was concerned, Samuel's children needed more structure.

After Leon and Marla left for school, she would find something for the little ones to do while she unpacked some of her and Timothy's clothes and got things organized in the bedroom they shared with Mindy. Hannah had suggested that Mindy sleep in the bed with her and Timothy for a few nights, but he'd put his foot down and insisted that she sleep on the cot. Didn't he care that Mindy was being forced to adjust to new surroundings and needed the comfort of her mother?

With determination, Hannah forced her thoughts aside, knowing if she didn't keep busy she would feel even more depressed. "Maybe I should organize around here today," she muttered as she put away the bread. The whole house, while clean enough, seemed quite cluttered—not nearly as tidy as she'd kept their home in Pennsylvania.

"Who ya talkin' to?" a small voice asked.

Startled, Hannah whirled around. Seven-year-old Leon,

still in his pajamas and barefoot, stared up at her, blinking his brown eyes rapidly.

"No one. I mean, I was talking to myself." She suppressed a yawn.

"Are ya bored? Is that why you were talkin' to yourself?"

"No, I'm not bored, I was just. . . . Oh, never mind." Hannah motioned to the table, where the box of cold cereal she'd served the men for breakfast still sat. "Would you like some cereal?"

He shook his head.

"Would you rather have eggs?"

"Don't want no *oier*. I was hopin' for some *pannekuche*."

"I don't have time to make pancakes this morning."

"Esther fixes us pannekuche whenever we want 'em." Leon, who had his father's light brown hair, made a sweeping glance of the entire room. "Where is Esther, anyways? She's usually here before we get up."

"I don't think she'll be here today."

He tipped his head and looked at her curiously. "How come?"

"Because I'm here, and I'll be fixing your breakfast this morning."

Leon studied her a few more seconds then shrugged. "So can we have pannekuche?"

Hannah shook her head. "I said no. I don't have time for that this morning." *This child is certainly persistent*, she thought.

He pointed to the battery-operated clock on the far wall. "It's still early. Marla, Penny, and Jared ain't even outa bed yet."

"The correct word is *aren't*, and I'm not going to fix pancakes this morning, so you may as well go back upstairs and get dressed. By the time you come down, I'll have a bowl of cereal and a hard-boiled egg ready for you to eat."

"Don't want an *oi*," Leon mumbled, shuffling toward the door leading to the stairs.

"Make sure you wake Marla," Hannah called after him. "I don't want either of you to be late for school."

Leon tromped up the stairs.

Hannah cringed. She hoped he didn't wake Mindy. Like Hannah, Mindy wasn't a morning person, and if she got woken out of a sound sleep, she was bound to be cranky.

She listened for a few minutes, and when she didn't hear her daughter, she went to the refrigerator and took out a carton of eggs. She'd just gotten them boiling on the stove when both Leon and Marla showed up.

"Leon said Esther's not comin' today. Is that true?" Blond-haired, nine-year-old Marla, asked, casting curious brown eyes on Hannah.

Hannah nodded. "I'm sure that's the case, because if she was coming, she would have been here by now." She motioned to the table. "Have a seat. You can eat your cereal while the eggs are boiling."

"I told ya before—I don't want no boiled oi," Leon said. "It'll get stuck in my throat."

Hannah grimaced. Was there no pleasing this child?

"Just eat your cereal, then," she said, placing two bowls on the table.

The kids took a seat and bowed their heads for silent prayer. Hannah waited quietly until they were finished; then she poured cereal into the bowls and gave them each a glass of milk. She'd just turned off the stove when she heard Mindy crying upstairs. "I'll be right back," she said to Marla before hurrying up the stairs.

Hannah was about to enter the bedroom she and Timothy shared with Mindy when three-year-old Jared and Penny, who was five, padded down the hall.

"*Wu is* Daadi?" Penny asked. Her long, sandy-brown hair hung down her back in gentle waves, and she blinked her brown eyes as she looked up at Hannah curiously.

"Your daddy went to work," Hannah said. "Now go downstairs to the kitchen. I'll be there as soon as I get Mindy."

"*Kumme*, Jared," Penny said, taking her blond-haired little brother's hand.

As the children plodded down the stairs, Hannah went to see about Mindy. She found the child curled up on the cot sobbing. No doubt she was confused by her surroundings. After all, they'd only been here two nights, and waking up and finding herself alone in the room probably frightened her.

"It's okay, my precious little girl. Mama's here." Hannah bent down and gathered Mindy into her arms. Truth was, she felt like crying, too. Only there was no time to give in to her tears right now. She had to feed the little ones and get Marla and Leon off to school.

—⁊⁊⁊—

When Esther stepped into Samuel's kitchen, she was surprised to see Marla and Leon at the table eating cereal.

"Where's your daed?" she asked, looking at Marla.

"He and Uncle Timothy went to work."

Esther glanced at the clock. She knew she was running a little behind but didn't think she was that late.

"Daadi left early this mornin'," Leon explained. "Had a paint job to do up in Marion."

"Oh, I see." Esther smiled. "So did you two fix your own breakfast?"

Marla shook her head. "Aunt Hannah fixed it for us."

"I guess that makes sense. Where is Hannah?"

"Went upstairs 'cause Mindy was cryin'," Leon answered around a mouthful of cereal.

Just then, Jared and Penny entered the kitchen, both wearing their nightclothes. As soon as Penny caught sight of Esther, she grinned and held up her arms.

Esther bent down and scooped the little girl up, giving her a kiss on the cheek. Penny was such a sweet child—easygoing and so compliant. Her little brother, on the other hand, could be a handful at times, but he was still a dear. Esther loved him, as well as all of Samuel's children, as if they were her own. After she and Samuel got married, these little ones would be hers to help raise, and she could hardly wait. It would be wonderful to leave the guesthouse where she'd been staying on Bonnie's property and move back here to the home where she used to live with her parents. The best part of moving back would be that she would finally be Samuel's wife.

Esther had missed her folks dearly after they'd moved to Pennsylvania to help care for her brother, Dan, who had multiple sclerosis. Her family was never far from her thoughts.

Esther removed her shawl and black outer bonnet, placing them on a wall peg near the back door. Then she returned to the kitchen to fix Jared and Penny's breakfast. She'd just gotten them situated at the table when Hannah, carrying Mindy, stepped into the room.

Hannah blinked her eyes rapidly. "*Ach*, you scared me, Esther! I didn't expect to see you here."

"I come over every morning to watch the kinner while Samuel's at work. I assumed you knew."

"I did hear that, but since we'll be living here until we have a home of our own, I figured I would be watching the children." Hannah shifted Mindy to the other hip. "It only makes sense, don't you think?"

Esther couldn't think clearly enough to say anything. It probably didn't make sense for them both to care for the children, but Samuel had been paying her to watch them, and she enjoyed being here. Besides, some of the money Esther earned went toward her brother's medical expenses, so it was important that she keep working right now. Should she speak up and say so, or let Hannah take over? Maybe it would be best to wait until Samuel got home and let him decide who would watch the children. In the meantime, she was here now, and she planned to stay.

CHAPTER 6

Marion, Kentucky

This is my first time in Marion," Samuel said as he, Allen, and Timothy worked on a storefront Allen had been contracted to remodel. "It's really a nice little town."

"Yep, and there's a lot of interesting history here," Allen said while sanding around one of the large window casings.

Timothy listened with interest as Allen talked about the Crittenden County Historical Museum, which had been built in 1881 and was originally a church. "It's the oldest church building in Marion, and the interior includes original wood floors, pulpit, balcony, and stained-glass windows," Allen said, pushing his dark brown hair under his baseball cap. "The church held on for over 120 years, until it was finally forced to close its doors due to a lack of membership. Soon after that, the building was donated to the historical society. Now it houses a really nice collection of memorabilia, pictures, and many other things related to the history of Marion and the surrounding communities that make up Crittenden County." Allen looked over at Timothy and grinned. "Guess that's probably a bit more than you wanted to know, huh?"

Timothy smiled as he opened a fresh bucket of paint. "Actually, I thought it was quite interesting. Anything that has to do with history captures my attention."

"My brother's not kidding about that," Samuel chimed in. "I'm anxious to show him the Jefferson Davis Monument, because I'm sure he'll be interested in that."

"Titus told me all about it," Timothy said. "He said the view from inside the monument is really something to see."

"He's right about that," Samuel said with a nod. "Maybe in the spring, we can go there and take our kids. I think they'd get a kick out of riding the elevator and being up so high."

"I'd sure like to go," Timothy said, "but I don't know about Mindy. She's pretty young to enjoy something like that, and Hannah might not go for the idea either." He paused long enough to grab a paint stick and stir the paint in the can. "As you probably know, my *fraa* tends to be pretty protective of our daughter."

"*Fraa* means *wife*, right?" Allen questioned.

Timothy nodded. "How'd you know that?"

Allen motioned to Samuel. "Between him and Esther, they've taught me several Pennsylvania-Dutch words." His face sobered. "There was a time when Samuel thought I was interested in Esther because I talked to her so much."

"But you set me straight on that real quick," Samuel said, winking at Allen. "And now everyone knows Bonnie's the love of your life."

Allen's face reddened. "I hope it's not that obvious, because I haven't actually told Bonnie the way I feel about her yet."

Samuel snickered. "Well, you'd better do it quick, 'cause if you don't, someone else is likely to snatch her away."

Allen's dark eyebrows furrowed. "You really think so?"

Samuel shrugged. "You never can tell, but I sure wouldn't chance it if I were you."

Timothy grinned as he continued to paint while listening to Samuel and Allen kibitzing back and forth. The two men had obviously become really good friends.

I like working with both of them, he decided. In fact, so far, Timothy liked everything about being in Kentucky. The countryside where Samuel lived, as well as here in Crittenden County, was nice, and the land was fertile—just right for farming. *Now if Hannah will just catch on to the idea, we might make a good life for ourselves here,* he thought.

"How does Zach feel about you moving to the Bluegrass State?" Allen asked, looking at Timothy. "I know you used to work for him."

"Zach's fine with it. Since I only painted part-time and mostly farmed with my dad, I don't think Zach will miss having me work for him that much. Besides, he's employed several Amish men."

Allen smiled. "Zach's been my good friend since we were kids. I was hoping he might move his family here, too, but I guess that's not likely to happen."

"I'd be surprised if he ever did move," Samuel said. "After being taken from our family when he was a baby and then spending the next twenty years living in Washington State without even knowing his real name or who his Amish family was, once Zach got back to Pennsylvania, he vowed he'd never leave."

"I can't blame him for that," Allen agreed.

"I know our folks are glad Zach's staying put," Timothy said, "because Mom hasn't taken it well that three of their other sons have moved out of state."

—ᘑ—

Paradise, Pennsylvania

Fannie had just entered Naomi and Caleb's general store when she spotted Hannah's mother, Sally, looking at some new rubber stamps.

"Wie geht's?" Fannie asked, noticing the dark circles under Sally's pale blue eyes.

Sally sighed and pushed a wisp of her graying blond hair back under her white head covering. "I wish I could say that I'm doing well, but to tell you the truth, I'm really tired."

"That's too bad. Haven't you been sleeping well?"

Sally shook her head. "Not since Hannah and Timothy left. I'm concerned about how my daughter is doing."

"How come? Is Hannah *grank?*"

"She's not physically sick, but when I spoke to her on the phone Saturday evening, she said she already doesn't like Kentucky and wishes she could come home. I'm not sure that's ever going to change."

Fannie wasn't sure what to say. She wasn't any happier about Timothy leaving Pennsylvania, but it was what her son wanted, and if getting Hannah away from her mother strengthened their marriage, then it probably was for the best. Hannah and her mother were too close, and Fannie knew from some of the things Timothy had shared with her that Hannah's unhealthy relationship with her mother had put a wedge between the young couple. It was a shame, too, because Timothy really loved his wife and wanted her to put him first, the way a loving wife should.

"Don't you miss your son?" Sally asked. "Don't you wish he would have stayed in Pennsylvania?"

Fannie glanced at her stepdaughter, Naomi, who stood behind the counter, and wondered if she was listening to this conversation. She had to be careful what she said, because if Naomi repeated it to her father, he'd probably lecture Fannie about letting their children live their own lives and tell her not to discuss Timothy and Hannah with Sally.

Sally touched Fannie's arm. "Is everything okay? You look *umgerrent.*"

"I'm not upset." Fannie lowered her voice to a near whisper. "You know, Sally, I haven't lost just one son to Kentucky; I've lost three. And if I can deal with it, then I think you can, too."

Sally's forehead wrinkled. "Are you saying you're okay with the fact that three of your boys live two states away?"

"I'm not saying that at all. I've just learned to accept it because it's a fact, and short of a miracle, none of my sons will ever move back to Pennsylvania."

Sally tapped her chin, looking deep in thought. "Then I guess we ought to pray for a miracle, because I really want Hannah to come home."

CHAPTER 7

Pembroke, Kentucky

How would you like to go over to the B&B and meet Bonnie?" Esther asked Hannah after Leon and Marla had left for school.

Hannah shrugged. "I suppose that would be okay." Truth be told, she didn't really care about meeting Bonnie but guessed it would be better than sitting around Samuel's house all day, trying to keep Mindy occupied and making idle conversation with Esther, whom she barely knew. *Of course, I don't know Bonnie either,* she reasoned. *But it'll be good to get out of the house and go for a buggy ride.*

"We can take my horse and buggy," Hannah said. "After being confined in the trailer with Timothy's horse on the trip here, Lilly's probably ready for a good ride."

Esther hesitated a minute then finally nodded. "I'll get the kinner ready to go while you hitch your horse to the buggy."

Hannah wasn't sure she wanted Esther to do anything with Mindy, so she quickly said, "On second thought, maybe we should take your horse and buggy, because I'm not used to

43

the roads here yet, and neither is Lilly."

"If that's what you'd prefer." Esther went over to Jared and Penny, who sat beside Mindy playing with some pots and pans, and explained that Hannah would help them wash up and get their jackets on because they were all going to Bonnie's.

Samuel's children leaped to their feet and started jumping up and down. Following suit, Mindy did the same.

"*Ruhich*, Mindy," Hannah said, putting her fingers to her lips. "You need to calm down." She looked sternly at Penny and Jared. "You need to be quiet, too."

The children looked at Hannah and blinked several times as tears welled in their eyes.

"Now don't start crying," Hannah said.

"They're just excited." Esther spoke in a defensive tone. "They love going over to Bonnie's and playing with her dog, Cody."

"Well, they're getting Mindy all worked up, and it's hard for me to get her settled down once that happens."

"Be still now," Esther said, placing her hands on Penny and Jared's heads. "Listen to Hannah and do what she says while I go out and hitch Ginger to my buggy."

The children calmed down right away, and so did Mindy. Then as Esther went out the door, Hannah led the three of them down the hallway to the bathroom to wash up. When that was done, she took their jackets down from the wall pegs in the utility room and helped the children put them on.

By the time they stepped onto the back porch, Esther had her horse hitched to the buggy. When she motioned for them to come, Hannah ushered the children across the yard. Once they were seated in the back of the buggy, she took her seat up front on the passenger's side.

"Everyone, stay in your seats now," Hannah called over her

shoulder as Esther directed the horse and buggy down the driveway. "This road is bumpy."

"You're right, the driveway is full of ruts right now," Esther said, looking over at Hannah. "That's because we've had so much rain this fall."

Hannah grimaced. She knew the damage too much rain could cause. A few years ago, they'd had so much rain in Lancaster County that many of the roads had flooded. She wondered if that ever happened here.

After they turned onto the main road and had traveled a ways, Esther pointed out various church members' homes. "Oh, and there's the store my folks used to own before they moved to Strasburg to help care for my brother, Dan."

"Who owns the store now?" Hannah asked.

"Aaron and Nettie Martin. They're a Mennonite couple, and they're fairly new to the area."

"I see. Is that where you do most of your shopping?"

"Jah, but when we're able to go into Hopkinsville, I shop at Walmart."

They rode silently for a while; then Hannah turned to Esther and said, "I understand that your brother has MS."

Esther nodded. "The disease has progressed to the point that he has to use a wheelchair most of the time."

"That's too bad. I can't imagine how I would feel if something like that happened to Timothy."

"It's been hard on his wife, Sarah, because she has a lot more responsibility now, but with my mamm and daed there to help, it makes things a bit easier."

"Easier? How could anything be easy if you have someone in your family in a wheelchair or with a severe disability?"

"Mom and Dad don't see it as a burden, and neither does Sarah. They love Dan very much, and there isn't anything they wouldn't do for him."

Hannah nodded. Some people might be able to sacrifice that much, but she wasn't sure she could. And she hoped she'd never have to find out.

Someone tapped Hannah's shoulder, and she turned around to see Penny. "What is it?" she asked, trying to keep the edge out of her voice.

Penny pointed at Mindy and said, "*Schuck.*"

Hannah looked at Mindy and noticed that she'd taken one of her shoes off. "It's fine. Don't be a *retschbeddi,*" she said, frowning at Penny.

"I don't think she means to be a tattletale," Esther said, jumping to Penny's defense. "She was probably concerned that Mindy might lose her shoe."

"Well, it's not her place to worry about Mindy—especially when she wasn't doing anything wrong."

Hannah couldn't help but notice Esther's icy stare. *She obviously doesn't like me, but I don't care. I don't care if anyone here in Christian County likes me.* She swallowed around the lump in her throat. *But if nobody likes me, I'll never fit in. Maybe I should try a little harder to be nice.*

"Just look at those maple trees," Esther said, bringing Hannah's thoughts to a halt. "It's hard to believe that just a few short weeks ago they were a brilliant reddish gold, and now they've lost most of their leaves." She sniffed the air. "That pungent odor tells me that someone in the area is burning leaves."

"It sure is chilly today," Hannah said. "I wonder if we'll have a cold winter."

"I wouldn't be surprised. A few years ago we had a terrible ice storm that left many Englishers without power. A lot of us Amish pitched in to help out wherever we could."

"I'm sure everyone needed help during that time," Hannah said.

Esther nodded. "They sure did."

They rode a little farther, and then Esther guided the horse and buggy up a long, graveled driveway. "See that big house at the end of the drive?" she said, pointing out the front buggy window. "That's Bonnie's bed-and-breakfast."

Hannah studied the stately old home. On one end of the long front porch was a swing, and two wicker chairs sat on the other end. A small table was positioned between them, holding a pot of yellow mums. The place looked warm and inviting. Even the yard was neat, with bushes well trimmed and weed-free flower beds in front of the house. "The outside of the home looks quite nice," Hannah said. "Where's the guesthouse you stay in?"

"Over there." Esther pointed to a smaller building that was set back from the house. It didn't look like it had more than a couple of rooms, but Hannah figured it was probably big enough for Esther's needs. Since she spent most of her time helping out at the B&B or watching Samuel's kids, she really only needed a place to sleep.

Just then a little brown-and-white mixed terrier bounded up to the buggy, barking and leaping into the air like it had springs on its legs.

"That's Bonnie's dog, Cody," Esther said. "He gets excited as soon as he sees my horse and buggy."

"*Hundli!* Hundli!" Mindy shouted from the backseat.

"No, Mindy," Esther said. "Cody's a full-grown dog, not a puppy."

"All dogs are puppies to her," Hannah said in Mindy's defense.

Esther silently guided her horse up to the hitching rail and climbed down from the buggy. After securing the horse, she came around to help Penny and Jared down, while Hannah put Mindy's shoe back on and lifted her out of the buggy.

Then, with the dog barking and running beside them, they made their way up to the house.

When they stepped inside, Hannah sniffed at the scent of apples and cinnamon. She figured Bonnie must have been baking. A few seconds later, a young woman with dark, curly hair and brown eyes stepped into the hallway. "Oh Esther, it's you," she said with a look of surprise. "I didn't expect to see you again until this evening."

"I came by because I wanted you to meet Samuel's sister-in-law, Hannah. They've moved here from Pennsylvania." Esther motioned to Mindy, who clung to Hannah's hand. "This is their daughter, Mindy; she's three."

"It's nice to meet you, Hannah. I'm Bonnie Taylor." Bonnie shook Hannah's hand; then she bent down so she was eye level with Mindy and said, "*Brauchscht kichlin?*"

"Why would you ask if my daughter needed cookies?" Hannah questioned.

"Oh my!" Bonnie's cheeks flamed as she straightened to her full height. "I've learned a few Pennsylvania-Dutch words from Esther and Samuel and thought I knew what I was saying. What I meant to ask was if Mindy would *like* some cookies." She looked down at Jared and Penny, who were smiling up at her with eager expressions, then motioned for them to follow her into the kitchen.

"What's that delicious smell?" Hannah asked, sniffing the air.

"Oh, you must smell my new apple-pie fragrance candle." Bonnie pointed to the candle on the table. "I bought it the other day at Walmart in Hopkinsville."

"I hope I'll get to go there soon," Hannah said. "I could use a few things that I probably can't find at the Mennonite store in this area."

"I'd be happy to drive you to Hopkinsville whenever you want to go." Bonnie motioned to the table. "If you'd all like to take a seat, I'll give the children a glass of milk and some of the peanut butter cookies I made yesterday, and we ladies can enjoy a cup of tea."

"Can we have a few cookies, too?" Esther asked, wiggling her eyebrows playfully while smiling at Bonnie. It was obvious that the two women were good friends, and Hannah felt a bit envious.

After the children finished their cookies and milk, Penny asked if she and Jared could take Mindy outside to play with the dog and see Bonnie's chickens.

"I don't think so," Hannah was quick to say. "Mindy's never been here before, and she might wander off. I'd feel better if she stayed inside with me."

Esther instructed Penny to keep an eye on her little brother and told Jared to stay close to his sister and remain in the yard. The children nodded, and after being helped into their jackets, they skipped happily out the back door.

Hannah gathered Mindy into her arms. She couldn't believe Esther would send two small children into the yard to play by themselves. She wondered what Samuel would think if he knew how careless Esther was with his children.

—⁓—

Bonnie took a seat at the table, and as she visited with Hannah and Esther, she couldn't help but notice the look of sadness on Hannah's face. The young woman was polite enough and appeared to be interested in hearing how Bonnie had acquired the bed-and-breakfast, but her voice seemed flat, almost forced, like she was making herself join in the conversation. Bonnie remembered when Timothy had come for Titus and Suzanne's wedding, she'd been surprised that his wife hadn't been with him. He'd said Hannah stayed home to take care of her mother, who'd sprained her ankle, but Bonnie had a feeling it was more than that. She was pretty intuitive and had a hunch that Hannah didn't like it here. Probably hadn't wanted to leave Pennsylvania at all.

"It's so nice to just sit and visit like this, with a warm cup of tea and some delicious cookies," Esther said. "I enjoy such simple pleasures."

Bonnie nodded. "I remember when I was a girl visiting my grandparents here, Grandma once said to me, 'Whatever your simple pleasures may be, enjoy them and share them with someone else.' She also said that we sometimes take for granted the everyday things that give us a sense of joy and well-being. These simple things are often forgotten when problems occur in our lives." She lifted her cup of tea and smiled. "Since I've moved here I've been trying to savor all the down-to-earth pleasures I possibly can."

Hannah smiled and nodded. At least she was responding a bit more.

Bonnie was about to ask if either Esther or Hannah would like another cookie when the back door bounced open and Penny and Jared rushed in.

Penny dashed across the room and clutched Bonnie's hand. "Eloise is *dot!*"

"Eloise is dead?" Bonnie looked over at Esther for confirmation. "Is that what she said?"

"I'm afraid so," Esther said with a nod.

"Oh my! I'd better go see about this!" Bonnie jumped up and hurried out the door.

CHAPTER 8

Hannah shuddered at the thought of someone lying dead in Bonnie's yard. "Wh–who is Eloise?" she asked in a shaky voice.

"She's one of Bonnie's laying hens," Esther replied. "If you don't mind keeping the kinner in here with you, I think I'll go outside and have a look myself."

"No, I don't mind." Hannah said with a shake of her head. Truth was, she had no desire to see a dead chicken, and she didn't think the children needed to be staring at it either.

Esther leaned down and gave Jared a kiss on the cheek. "Be a good boy now."

After Esther went out the door, Hannah seated the children at the table and gave them each a piece of paper and some crayons she had brought along in her oversized purse.

While they colored, she studied her surroundings some more. The kitchen was cozy, with pretty yellow curtains at the window. There was a mix of modern appliances—a microwave, portable dishwasher, and electric coffeemaker, along with an older-looking stove and refrigerator on one side of the room. Several older items—a butter churn, a metal bread box, some

51

antique canning jars, and an old pie cupboard that looked like it had been restored—added character to the room. Everything in the kitchen looked neat and orderly, much the way Hannah had kept her kitchen back home. It was nice that Bonnie had been able to use her grandparents' place as a bed-and-breakfast so others could enjoy it. Hannah hoped when Bonnie came in that she might show her the rest of the house.

Being here, in this place so warm and inviting, made Hannah miss her home all the more. She felt like a bird without a tree to land in, and it just wasn't right. She knew, according to the Bible, that she needed to be in subjection to her husband, but it was hard when she felt he'd been wrong in insisting they move to Kentucky.

I mustn't dwell on this, Hannah told herself. *It's not going to change the fact that I'm stuck in a place I don't want to be, so I need to try and make the best of my situation—at least until Timothy wakes up and realizes we were better off in Pennsylvania.*

———

"What do you think killed Eloise?" Bonnie asked after she and Esther had dug a hole and buried the chicken.

"I'm pretty sure she died from old age, because her neck wasn't broken and there were no tears in her skin or any feathers missing. You can be glad it wasn't a fox, because they can really wreak havoc in a chicken coop. In fact, a fox probably would have killed every one of your chickens," Esther said.

Bonnie breathed a sigh of relief. Taking care of chickens kept her busy enough; she sure didn't need the worry of keeping some predator away.

"Shall we go back inside and give Hannah a tour of the B&B?" Esther asked once they were done.

Bonnie shrugged as she jammed the shovel into the ground

and leaned on it. "Do you think she'd be interested? She seems kind of distant."

"I believe so. She did comment on the outside of your house when we first pulled into your yard. In fact, she seemed impressed by what she saw."

"Well, she wouldn't have been if she'd seen the way it looked before Samuel and Allen did all the repairs on this place."

"It just goes to show that there's hope for almost any home, even those that are really run down," Esther said with a chuckle.

Bonnie laughed, too. "This old house was definitely rundown. I think if my grandparents were still alive, they'd be pleased with the way it looks now. And I know they'd appreciate their home being put to good use."

"I believe you're right, and I'm glad your business is doing well."

"You get the credit for some of that, because if you hadn't taught me how to cook, I couldn't offer my patrons a decent breakfast as part of their stay."

Esther smiled. "I'm glad I was able to help, and I'm appreciative for the job you've given me."

"You'll have it for as long as you like, because I have no plans to go anywhere." Bonnie gave Esther's arm a gentle squeeze. "You, on the other hand, might have other plans that don't include the B&B."

Esther tipped her head. "What other plans?"

"Marrying Samuel, of course. Once you two are married, I'm sure you'll want to be a full-time mother to his children and any other children you may have in the future."

Esther's cheeks flushed to a deep pink. "Samuel and I haven't set a date to be married yet, but I hope it'll be soon."

"Well, whenever it happens, once you're married, your first obligation will be to him and his children."

Esther smiled. "What about you and Allen?"

"What about us?"

"Has he hinted at marriage yet?"

"No, but if he had, I would have avoided the subject."

"How come?"

"You know why, Esther."

"So you haven't told him yet about the baby you had when you were sixteen?"

Bonnie shook her head. "No, and I'm not sure I ever will. I'm afraid it might ruin our relationship."

"You can't have an honest relationship if you're not truthful with him about your past." Esther's sincere expression was enough to make Bonnie tear up.

"I know I should tell him, but I need to be sure our bond is strong enough before I do."

"How long do you think that will be?"

Bonnie shrugged. "I don't know. I'll have to play it by ear." She started walking toward the house. "Now changing the subject, after I give Hannah a tour of my house, would you all like to stay for lunch?"

"That'd be nice, but we wouldn't want to impose."

"It wouldn't be any trouble, and I'd enjoy not having to eat alone."

"If it's okay with Hannah, then it's fine with me," Esther said.

When they stepped back into the house, they found Hannah watching as the children colored pictures while seated at the table.

"I was wondering if you'd like to stay for lunch," Bonnie said.

Hannah looked at Esther, as though seeking her approval.

When Esther nodded, Hannah smiled and said, "That'd be nice."

"Before we eat, though, would you like a tour of my bed-and-breakfast?"

"Yes, I would," Hannah replied. "I've been admiring some of the things you have here in the kitchen, and I'd enjoy seeing what the rest of the house looks like."

Bonnie found a game for the kids to play and situated them on the living-room floor; then she motioned for Esther and Hannah to follow her upstairs.

"I've seen all the rooms many times, so I think I'll stay down here with the children," Esther said.

"That's fine. Since you're up there cleaning every morning, you probably get tired of looking at the rooms."

Esther shook her head. "Not really. I enjoy my work, but I think it's best if I stay with the children."

"I agree," Hannah spoke up. "They might end up coloring everything in Bonnie's kitchen." A hint of a smile crossed her face, and Bonnie was pleased. It was the first time Hannah had seemed this relaxed. Maybe as Bonnie got to know Hannah better, they might even become friends.

CHAPTER 9

When Hannah and Esther returned from Bonnie's that afternoon, the first thing they did was put the kids down for their naps. All three of them were tired and cranky. Jared and Mindy had screamed and fussed so much on the way home that Hannah thought she would go insane. She'd figured the ride home would lull them to sleep, but it apparently had the opposite effect. They were probably full of sugar from the cookies they'd eaten. Hannah would have to watch Mindy a little closer from now on and make sure she ate properly. She didn't like it when her daughter became hyper.

"I'm going out to the phone shanty to make a call," Hannah told Esther after she'd put Mindy down and made sure she was asleep.

"That's fine." Esther smiled. "While you're doing that, I'll start cutting up the vegetables for the stew I'm going to make for supper this evening."

Hannah frowned. "Actually, I was planning to fix a meat loaf for supper. I saw some ground beef in the refrigerator and thought I'd use it for that."

"Oh, well, Samuel really likes stew, and that's what I told

56

him I'd make for supper tonight."

Hannah's jaw clenched. Esther and Samuel weren't even married, but she acted like she was in charge of his kitchen. For that matter, she acted like she was in charge of everything in this house, including Samuel's children.

"Will you be staying here to eat supper with us?" Hannah asked.

Esther nodded. "I usually eat supper and then do the dishes before I head back to Bonnie's."

"Now that I'm living here, you won't need to stay."

"Oh, but I want to. I enjoy eating supper with Samuel and the kinner." Esther's cheeks colored. "Unless you'd rather that I didn't join you for supper. If that's the case, I can just fix the meal and be on my way."

Hannah folded her arms. "It's not that I don't want you to stay. I just don't see the need for you to fix supper when I'm perfectly capable of doing it."

"I'm sure you are, but. . ." Esther's voice trailed off. "If you'd prefer to fix meat loaf, that's fine with me."

Hannah nodded in reply then scooted out the back door. She was anxious to call Mom and tell her about Bonnie's B&B. Seeing the antiques there had given her an idea about how she might earn some money. She was eager to tell Timothy about it as well.

When Hannah stepped into the phone shanty, she was pleased to discover a message from her mother. But as Hannah listened to Mom talk about going shopping at Naomi and Caleb's store in Paradise and then eating at Bird-in-Hand Family Restaurant, a wave of homesickness rolled over her. She sat for several minutes, fighting the urge to cry, then finally laid her head on the table and gave in to her tears.

When the tears finally subsided, Hannah dried her face on her apron and headed back to the house, not bothering to return Mom's call. When she stepped inside, she was surprised to see Esther standing in front of the kitchen sink. "Oh, you're still here?"

Esther nodded. "I'll leave as soon as Marla and Leon get home from school."

"Since I'm here to greet them, there's really no need for you to wait."

Esther, looking more than a bit hurt, nodded. "I'll see you tomorrow then."

Not if Samuel agrees to let me watch the kinner, Hannah thought.

—✺—

Bonnie had just taken a pan of cinnamon rolls from the oven, when she heard the distinctive *clip-clop* of horse's hooves. She set the pan on the cooling rack and looked out the kitchen window, surprised to see Esther's horse and buggy coming up the driveway.

"I wonder what she's doing here at this time of the day. I hope nothing's wrong."

Bonnie slipped into a sweater and hurried outside, just as Esther was tying her horse to the hitching rail. "I didn't expect to see you until later this evening. Is something wrong?" she asked.

"Yes, I'm afraid so."

Bonnie felt immediate concern. "What is it?"

Esther's chin trembled as tears welled in her brown eyes. "Hannah doesn't like me, Bonnie. I'm sure of it."

"Did you two have a disagreement?"

"Not exactly. She pretty much told me how it's going to be."

"What do you mean?"

"Hannah let it be known that she'd rather I not stay for supper, and she didn't want me to fix the stew I'd promised Samuel I would make." Esther stroked Ginger's velvety nose, as though needing the horse's comfort. "She thinks my services aren't needed now that she and Timothy are living in Samuel's house."

"That's ridiculous! Samuel hired you to watch the kids, cook meals, clean the house, and do the laundry."

"I know, but now that Hannah's there, I feel like I'm in the way. I'm sure she's quite capable of doing everything I've been doing, and it would save Samuel some money if he didn't have to pay me."

"Have you talked to him about this?" Bonnie questioned.

"Not yet. I was hoping to speak with him this evening, but that was before Hannah practically pushed me out the door."

Bonnie put her arm around Esther and gave her a hug. "Now, don't you give in so easily. You need to talk to him soon, because Hannah has no right to just come in and take over like that."

Esther sniffed and slowly nodded. "I'll go over there a little early tomorrow morning. Hopefully, I can discuss things with him before he leaves for work."

"That's a good idea. In the meantime, you can come up to the house and have supper with me."

Esther smiled. "Thank you, Bonnie. I don't know what I'd do without your friendship."

"You've been a good friend to me, as well." Bonnie shivered, feeling a sudden chill. She hoped Hannah wouldn't do anything to mess things up between Esther and Samuel. They'd already had their share of struggles, and if anyone deserved some peace and happiness, it was them.

CHAPTER 10

"W here's Esther?" Marla asked when she and Leon arrived home from school.

"She went home." Hannah motioned to the stairs. "You'd better go up to your rooms and change out of your school clothes so you can get your chores done before it's time to eat supper. Oh, and go quietly, please, because the little ones are napping."

Leon looked up at Hannah with a wide-eyed expression. "Esther went home?"

"That's what I said." Didn't the child believe her, or was he hard of hearing?

"But Esther never goes home till after supper." Leon's brows furrowed; he looked downright perplexed.

"That's right," Marla put in. "And after supper, Esther and I always do the dishes together before she goes back to Bonnie's."

Hannah looked directly at Marla. "From now on, I'll be fixing supper, and you can help *me* do the dishes."

Marla opened her mouth as if to say something more, but Leon spoke first. "But what about Esther?"

Hannah sighed. "I just told you. Esther won't be here for supper."

Leon's forehead wrinkled. "But she'll still be comin' in the morning to fix our breakfast and take care of Penny and Jared while we're in school, right?"

"That hasn't been decided yet. I'll be talking to your daed about it when he gets home from work," Hannah said, her irritation mounting. "Since your uncle Timothy and I will be living here until we get our own home, there's no reason I can't watch your brother and sister during the day while you're at school and your daed's at work."

"But Jared and Penny like Esther, and so do we." Marla looked over at Leon, who agreeably bobbed his head.

"I'm sure you do, and you'll have plenty of time to spend with her once she and your daed get married."

Leon's mouth opened wide. "Daadi and Esther are gettin' married? How come nobody told us about it?"

Hannah flinched. *Oh great. Now I've said something I shouldn't have said.* "What I meant to say was that if your daed keeps courting Esther, then I'm sure in time he'll ask her to marry him."

A smile stretched across Leon's face as he hopped up and down and clapped his hands. "That's really good news! I'm gonna ask Daadi to marry Esther right away!"

"That's not a good idea," Hannah was quick to say. "I'm sure your daed will let everyone know once he and Esther have set a date."

"But he might do it quicker if we ask him to." Marla grabbed Leon's hand and gave it a squeeze. "Won't it be *wunderbaar* when Esther's our mamm?"

He nodded vigorously.

"Well, it hasn't happened yet, so you need to keep quiet

about it." Hannah wished she'd never brought the subject up. And she certainly hoped that by the time Samuel married Esther, she and Timothy would be living in their own place, because two women in the same house, each trying to do things her own way, would never work.

—⁂—

Hannah had just finished making a tossed green salad when she heard the rumble of a truck coming up the driveway. Looking out the window and seeing Timothy and Samuel climb out of Allen's truck, she hurried to set the table.

A few minutes later, Samuel and Timothy entered the kitchen.

"Mmm. . .it smells good in here, but it doesn't smell like stew," Samuel said, sniffing in the air. "Esther said she'd fix my favorite stew for supper this evening." He glanced around. "Where is Esther anyway? Is she in the living room?"

"No, uh. . .Esther went home, and we're having meat loaf."

Samuel's eyebrows furrowed, and even Timothy shot Hannah a questioning look. "Why'd she go home? Was she feeling grank?" Samuel asked.

"No, she's not sick. I just told her that since I was here she wouldn't need to help with supper and could go home."

"You sent Esther home?" Samuel's eyebrows lifted high, and his voice raised nearly an octave.

Hannah looked at Timothy, hoping he would come to her rescue, but he just stared at her as though in disbelief.

"Well. . .uh, I didn't send her home exactly. I just told her that I could fix supper and that her help wasn't needed."

"What gives you the right to be tellin' Esther that?" A vein on the side of Samuel's neck bulged just a bit.

"That ain't all, Daadi," Leon said, rushing into the room.

63

"Aunt Hannah said she didn't think Esther would be comin' here in the mornings no more. Least not till the two of you get married."

"Is that so?" Samuel's sharp intake of breath and his pinched expression let Hannah know he was quite upset.

"I. . .I didn't actually say Esther wouldn't be coming over. I just said I'd need to talk to you about it, because I really don't see a need for her to be here when I'm perfectly capable of taking care of your kinner, cleaning the house, and cooking the meals." Hannah's cheeks warmed. "And I mistakenly mentioned that you might marry Esther."

"I do plan to marry her," Samuel said. "But it's not official yet, and I haven't talked to her about a wedding date." He leveled Hannah with a look that could have stopped a runaway horse. "I'd appreciate it if from now on you don't tell my kinner anything they should be hearin' directly from me." Samuel turned and started for the door.

"Where are you going?" Timothy called to him.

"Over to the B&B to speak with Esther!" Samuel let the door slam behind him.

"We need to talk about this," Timothy said, taking hold of Hannah's arm and leading her toward the door.

"What about supper?" She motioned to the stove. "The meat loaf's ready, and I really think we should eat."

"The meal can wait awhile. Let's go out on the porch where we can speak in private."

Before Hannah could offer a word of protest, he grabbed her jacket from the wall peg, slung it across her shoulders, and ushered her out the door.

"Now what gives you the right to send Esther away when you know she's been watching Samuel's kinner?" Timothy asked, guiding her to one end of the porch. "Do I need to remind you that this is Samuel's home, and he's been kind enough to let us live here?"

"You don't need to talk to me so harshly." Hannah's voice whined with the threat of tears.

"I'm sorry, but surely you could see how upset Samuel was. He loves Esther very much and wants her to care for his kinner when he's not at home." Timothy's voice softened some but remained unyielding. "Things shouldn't have to change just because we're living here right now."

Hannah stiffened and started to snivel. "Well, they've changed for me! But I guess you don't care about that."

"I do care, and I hope we can either build or find a place of our own really soon so we can feel settled here in Kentucky," Timothy said. "And Hannah, please turn off the waterworks. There's no reason for you to be whimpering about this. There's no question that what you said to Esther was wrong—especially when those arrangements had been worked out between Samuel and Esther long before we moved here."

"I didn't suggest that Esther leave because I was trying to change anything. I just thought it wasn't necessary for both of us to take care of the house and kinner, and I figured Samuel would appreciate me helping out." Hannah folded her arms and glared at him, wiping tears of frustration away. "And I doubt that I'll ever feel settled living here, because my home is in Pennsylvania, not Kentucky!"

"You've said that before, Hannah, and it's gettin' kind of old." He placed his hand on her shoulder. "Life is what we make it, and unless you're willing to at least try to accept this change and make the best of it, you'll never be happy. I'm tired of our constant bickering, and I'm worn-out from trying to keep the peace between us. You need to focus on something positive for a change."

Hannah stared at the wooden floorboards on the porch; then she lifted her gaze to meet his. "I think I know something that might make me happy—or at least, it would give me something meaningful to do."

"What's that?"

"Esther and I took the little ones over to see Bonnie Taylor this morning, and while we were there, I was impressed with all the antiques Bonnie has."

His forehead wrinkled. "I'm confused. What's that got to do with anything?"

"I was thinking maybe I could start my own business, buying and selling antiques. It would help our finances, and—"

He held up his hand. "You can stop right there, Hannah, because your idea won't work."

"Why not?"

"For one thing, Samuel's barn is full of our furniture, so you wouldn't even have a place to store any antiques. Second, most antiques can be quite expensive, and we don't have any extra money to spend on something that might not sell. Third, I seriously doubt that antiques would sell very well around here."

"What makes you say that?"

"There are no tourists here—at least not like we had in Lancaster County, and there aren't nearly as many people living in this area." Timothy slowly shook his head. "You need to find something else to keep yourself busy, because selling antiques is definitely out—at least for right now. It would be too big of a risk. Now let's get inside and eat supper."

Resentment welled in Hannah's soul. She was getting tired of Timothy telling her what to do all the time, and it didn't surprise her that he'd been against her idea right from the start. He didn't even want to consider it. Was there anything they could agree on, or was this a warning of how things were going to be from now on?

—⁊⁊—

Samuel fumed all the way to Bonnie's. *Just who does Hannah think she is, sending Esther home when she should have been taking care of the kinner and sharing supper with us? Hannah has a lot of nerve coming into my house and trying to take things over!* Samuel wondered how his brother put up with a wife like that. Of course, Hannah, being the youngest child and only girl in her family, had always been a bit spoiled. Even back when she was a girl growing up in their community, he'd noticed it. And it didn't help that she was under her mother's thumb, which he knew was why she'd been opposed to the idea of moving to Kentucky in the first place.

I wonder what made Timothy decide to marry Hannah, Samuel thought as he gripped the horse's reins a bit tighter. *It must have been her pretty face and the fact that she could cook fairly well, because Timothy was sure blinded to the reality that Hannah's tied to her mamm's apron strings.*

Samuel drew in a couple of deep breaths, knowing he needed to calm down before he spoke to Esther. He sent up a quick prayer, asking God for wisdom.

By the time he pulled up to the hitching rail in Bonnie's yard, he felt a bit more relaxed. He climbed down from the buggy, secured his horse, and sprinted across the lawn to the guesthouse, where he rapped on the door and called, "Esther, are you there?"

No response.

He knocked again, but when Esther didn't answer, he figured she might be up at the main house with Bonnie.

Hurrying across the lawn, he took the steps two at a time

and knocked on Bonnie's door. Several seconds went by before Bonnie answered the door. "I came to see Esther. Is she here?" Samuel asked.

Bonnie nodded. "We were about to have supper."

"I'm sorry to interrupt, but I need to talk to Esther for a few minutes, if you don't mind."

Bonnie smiled. "Come in. I'll wait in the living room while you two visit."

"Thanks, I appreciate that."

Bonnie turned toward the living room, and Samuel headed for the kitchen.

"Samuel, I'm surprised to see you here. I figured you'd be at home having supper with your family," Esther said when Samuel stepped into the room.

He frowned. "I figured that's where you'd be, too, but when Timothy and I got home, Hannah said you'd come here."

Esther nodded. "I think my being there made her feel uncomfortable. I sensed a bit of tension between us all day."

Samuel pulled out a chair and joined her at the table. "When I go back home, I plan to tell Hannah in no uncertain terms that I want you to keep watching the kinner, and that includes bein' there for supper."

"But Samuel, if it's going to cause trouble with Hannah, maybe it might be best if—"

Samuel shook his head. "It won't be best for the kinner, and it sure won't be best for me." He reached for Esther's hand. "I know it won't be easy for you to deal with Hannah, but I'm asking you to keep working for me and to try and get along with Hannah." He smiled and gently squeezed her fingers. "I'd set a date to marry you right now so you could be with us all the time, but I think we'd better wait till Timothy and Hannah find a place of their own. We have to keep reminding ourselves that these arrangements are only temporary."

Esther's eyes sparkled with unshed tears. "Oh Samuel, let's pray it won't be too long."

—⁓—

Timothy stepped outside after the evening meal was finished, while Hannah cleaned up and occupied the children. It felt good to breathe in the fresh air, especially when things had gone downhill after arriving home. He didn't blame Samuel for being upset with Hannah, and he hoped it didn't put a further strain on their living arrangements until they had a place of their own.

Timothy thought about Hannah's desire to sell antiques. He had to admit her eyes had been shining when she'd shared her thoughts with him about it. It was the first time since they'd arrived in Kentucky that Hannah had showed any kind of enthusiasm.

Was I wrong to discourage her? he wondered. *Maybe something like that would help Hannah adjust to her new surroundings. Guess I was wrong for not listening more to what she had to say. I'll think about it more once we're able to get a place of our own. By then, I'll have a better idea of what our expenses will be like.*

For now, though, he should go out to the barn to make sure everything was secured for the evening. He'd wait for his brother and hope he could smooth things over with him, because the last thing he needed was for Samuel to ask them to leave. If he did, where would they go? They sure couldn't move in with Titus and Suzanne in their small place.

Now, don't borrow any trouble, he told himself. *Things will work out. They have to.*

CHAPTER 11

Leaves swirled around the yard, and the wind howled eerily under the eaves of the porch as Hannah stood waiting for Bonnie to pick her and Mindy up. She gazed at the gray-blue sky and the empty fields next to Samuel's place and wished it was spring instead of fall. They were going into Hopkinsville today to do some shopping, so maybe that would lift her spirits. Hannah looked forward to the outing because it had rained every day last week and she was tired of being cooped up in the house with Esther and the children. She'd had to learn how to deal with Esther coming over every day to watch Samuel's children, but it wasn't easy. Esther did things a lot differently than Hannah, but she found if she kept busy writing letters to Mom and cleaning house, the days were bearable. It wasn't that Esther didn't keep the house clean—she just wasn't as structured and organized as Hannah had always been. Many times Esther had tried to engage Hannah in conversation, but since they really didn't have much in common, there wasn't a lot to talk about. They'd worked out an agreement to take turns fixing supper, so at least that gave Hannah a chance to do some cooking, which she enjoyed.

Hannah watched as Esther hung some clothes on the line, using the pulley that ran from the porch to the barn. Mindy must have seen her, too, because she left Hannah's side, darted across the porch, and tugged on Esther's skirt. Esther stopped what she was doing, bent down, picked Mindy up, and swung her around. Hannah cringed as Mindy squealed with delight. It really bothered Hannah to see how Mindy had warmed up to Esther. It seemed like she was always hanging on Esther, wanting to crawl up into her lap to listen to a story, or just sitting beside Esther at the table. This was one more reason Hannah hoped she and Timothy could find a place of their own soon, where she and Mindy could spend more quality time together without Esther's influence. Everyone seemed to love Esther.

Hannah looked away, her thoughts going to Timothy. He'd been keeping very busy helping Samuel. They'd had several indoor paint jobs, which was a good thing on account of the rain. The downside was that most of the jobs were out of town, and by the time the men came home each evening, Timothy was tired and didn't want to talk with Hannah or even spend a few minutes playing with Mindy before she was put to bed. He often went to bed early and was asleep by the time Hannah got Mindy down and crawled into bed herself. Where had the closeness they'd once felt for each other gone? What had happened to Timothy's promise that everything would be better once they had moved? So many things had gotten in the way of what had brought them together in the first place.

When Esther went back inside, Hannah glanced at Mindy, now frolicking back and forth across the porch, amusing herself as she pretended to be a horse. *Your daadi hardly spends any time with you anymore, either. Will we ever be like a real family again?*

Hannah's musings were halted when Bonnie's car pulled into the yard and she tooted her horn. Grabbing Mindy's car seat from the porch, Hannah took Mindy's hand and hurried out to the car.

"Where's Esther?" Bonnie asked when Hannah opened the car door. "Aren't she and Samuel's little ones coming with us today?"

Hannah shook her head. "Jared and Penny have the beginning of a cold, and she thought it'd be best if she kept them in today."

"I guess that makes sense. Is everyone else well?"

"So far, and I hope it stays that way, because I sure don't want Mindy coming down with a cold." Hannah put Mindy's car seat in the back and lifted Mindy into it, making sure her seat belt was securely buckled. Then she stepped into the front seat and buckled her own seat belt.

Bonnie smiled. "I appreciate the fact that you use the seat belts without me having to ask. I know that the Amish don't have seat belts in their buggies, so I sometimes have to remind my passengers to use them when they're riding in my car."

"I've sometimes wished we did have seat belts," Hannah said, "because when someone's in a buggy accident, they're often seriously injured."

Bonnie nodded with a look of understanding. "Getting to know my Amish neighbors has been one of the biggest blessings in my life, and I don't like hearing about accidents of any kind. I pray often for my Amish and English friends, asking God to keep everyone safe."

"Esther mentioned that you're a Christian and that you go

to a small church in Fairview," Hannah said.

"Yes, that's right." Bonnie pulled out of Samuel's yard and headed down the road in the direction of Hopkinsville. "It's a very nice church, and I enjoy attending the services. When my grandma was alive, she and Grandpa used to go to that church."

"Have you ever attended an Amish church service?" Hannah asked.

"Not a Sunday service, but I did go to Titus and Suzanne's wedding, which I understand was similar to one of your regular preaching services."

Hannah nodded. "So what did you think of the wedding?"

"It was nice. Quite a bit different from the weddings we Englishers have, though."

"When you and Allen get married, will it be at the church in Fairview?"

Bonnie's mouth dropped open. "Where did you get the idea that Allen and I will be getting married?"

"Samuel said so. I heard him talking to Timothy about it during supper a few nights ago."

"What did he say?"

"Just that he knew Allen was planning to marry you, and he hoped it'd be soon."

Bonnie gave the steering wheel a sharp rap. "That's interesting—especially since Allen hasn't even asked me to marry him."

"He hasn't?"

"No, but he has dropped a couple of hints along the way."

"Maybe he's waiting for just the right time."

Bonnie kept her focus on the road.

Did I do it again and say something I shouldn't have? Hannah wondered. *Maybe Bonnie doesn't love Allen enough to marry him.*

—⁂—

Oak Grove, Kentucky

"Samuel, I wanted to tell you again how much I appreciate your understanding after we had our little talk concerning Hannah and Esther," Timothy said before hauling one of their paint cans across the living room of the older home they were painting.

"Hey, it's okay. I'm glad we had the chance to talk things out." Samuel smiled. "We're family, and it's important that we all get along, for our sake, as well as the kinners'. It's not good having unspoken tension between us."

"I don't want that either," Timothy said. "Hannah has seemed a little more content this past week, now that she and Esther are taking turns with the cooking. I'm hoping maybe with Hannah getting into some sort of a routine while getting better acquainted with life in Kentucky she'll learn to like it here as much as I do."

"I hope so, too," Samuel said, "because I'm really glad you're here."

"How are things going for you two?" Allen asked Samuel when he entered the house, interrupting their conversation.

"Real well," Samuel replied. "We should have it done before the week is out." He motioned to Timothy, who was kneeling on the floor, painting the baseboard an oyster shell white. "With all the work we've had lately, it's sure good to have my brother's help. Even though Timothy only worked part-time for Zach, he learned some pretty good painting skills."

"I can see that he's doing a fine job." Allen moved closer to

74

where Samuel stood on a ladder. "I'm sure the folks who live here will be glad to hear that all the painting will be finished before Thanksgiving."

"Speaking of Thanksgiving, what are you doing for the holiday?" Samuel asked.

"I'm going over to Bonnie's."

"That's good to hear. I was going to invite you to join us at Titus's house if you didn't have plans."

"I appreciate the offer," Allen said, "but I'm really looking forward to spending the day with Bonnie. We've both been keeping so busy and haven't seen much of each other lately."

Samuel chuckled. "You'll never get her to agree to marry you if you don't spend some time with her."

"I know. That's why I accepted her invitation for Thanksgiving dinner. And if everything goes well, I'll ask her to marry me before the day is out."

Samuel grinned. "Well now, isn't that something? Be sure and let me know how it goes."

"I'd like to hear that news myself," Timothy called from across the room.

Allen nodded. "You two will be the first ones I tell—after my folks, of course. Oh, and I'll also tell your brother Zach, because I'm sure he'll be happy to hear I'm finally willing to give up the single life and have found a woman I want to marry."

—⁓⁓—

Paradise, Pennsylvania

"Johnny, are you sure you don't need my help at the store today?" Sally asked her husband as they sat at the kitchen table eating breakfast. "Since Hannah's been gone, I've been bored and really need something to occupy my time and thoughts."

"Our niece, Anna, and her friend, Phoebe Stoltzfus, are working out really well. I'm not needed there all the time, so you wouldn't find much to do either." Johnny pulled his fingers through the ends of his nearly gray beard. "Makes me wonder if I ought to retire and buy a little place for us in Sarasota. We could live in the community of Pinecraft, where so many Plain folks retire or vacation."

Sally frowned as she shook her head. "Then we'd be living even farther from Hannah. Unless Timothy brought his family down to Florida for a vacation, which I doubt, we'd rarely see them."

He patted her arm. "Now don't look so worried. It was only wishful thinking on my part. I'm not really ready to retire just yet, but when the time comes for me to sell the store, I'd like to move to a place where it's warm and sunny all year."

Sally felt a huge sense of relief. At least she didn't have to worry about that for a while. She picked up her cup of tea and took a drink. "I've been wondering about something."

"What's that?"

"Thanksgiving's just a week away, and I was hoping we could go to Kentucky for the holiday. It would be nice to see Hannah and find out for ourselves how she, Timothy, and Mindy are doing."

Johnny shook his head. "I don't think so."

"Why not?"

"It's too soon for us to pay them a visit. Hannah needs to adjust to living in Kentucky, and seeing us right now might make it harder on her."

"But Johnny, our daughter's miserable. Every time she calls, I can hear by the tone of her voice how distressed she is. And the letter I got from her the other day made me feel so sad, reading how much she misses us and wishes she could come home."

"Just give her more time. She'll get over her homesickness after a while." Johnny gulped down the rest of his coffee, scooted his chair away from the table, and stood.

"I'm not so sure about that. Hannah liked it here in Pennsylvania, and she doesn't like much of anything about living in Kentucky."

"I don't have time to debate this with you right now. I need to get my horse and buggy ready so I can get to the store."

"But you said you weren't needed there."

"I said I wasn't needed as much as before, but there are still some things I need to do. I may have some boxes to unpack and move if the newest shipment came in yesterday afternoon when I left Anna in charge." Johnny grabbed his straw hat, slipped into his jacket, and hurried out the door like he couldn't get out of there soon enough.

Tears welled in Sally's eyes. *I don't think he cares how miserable our daughter is or even how much I miss her. If I thought for one minute that Johnny wouldn't get angry with me, I'd catch a bus to Kentucky and go there for Thanksgiving myself!*

CHAPTER 12

Fresno, California

Trisha Chandler sat at the head of her small dining-room table, hands folded in her lap, and lips pursed with determination. She'd just shared a delicious noon Thanksgiving meal with her two closest friends, Shirley and Margo, whom she'd met at a widow's support group after her husband died of a heart attack two years ago. As soon as they'd finished eating, she'd given them some news that hadn't been well received. But she wasn't going to let them talk her into changing her mind. No, she'd waited a long time to do something fun and adventurous, and their negative comments were not going to stop her from fulfilling a dream she'd had for several years.

"I've always wanted to travel, and now that the restaurant where I've worked since Dave passed away has closed its doors, I think it's time for me and my trusty little car to go out on the road," Trisha said.

"But it's not safe for a woman your age to be out on her own," Margo argued. "What if something happened to you?"

Trisha grunted. "Nothing's going to happen, and I'm

not that old. I just turned fifty-eight last month, remember? Besides, it doesn't matter how old I am. In this crazy world, there's no guarantee that any of us are ever really safe."

Tears welled in Shirley's blue eyes. Always tenderhearted, Shirley had joined their widow's group six months ago when her husband lost his battle with colon cancer. "After thinking it through a bit more, maybe it's not such a bad idea after all. Truthfully, I wish I could be brave enough to venture out on my own," she said. "We're going to miss you, Trisha, that's for sure."

Trisha gave Shirley's hand a gentle squeeze. "Why don't you come with me? Just think of all the wonderful things we can see."

Shirley shook her head. "I can't be gone for six months, the way you plan to do; my children would never allow it. Besides, I really don't like being too far from home."

Trisha nodded in understanding. "Since I don't have any children, there's really nothing to keep me here."

"Does that mean you plan to sell your condo and be gone for good?" Margo asked, her dark eyes widening.

"Oh no. I'm sure I'll be back."

"You know this really isn't a good time of the year to be driving across the United States," Margo pointed out. "You could run into all kinds of foul weather."

"I've thought about that, but I'll start out in the southern states, and then as the weather warms up in the spring, I'll head up the East Coast and see some of the historical sights."

Shirley took a drink of water. "What about the expense? A trip like that could cost plenty. I don't mean to pry, but can you afford the gas and hotels you'll need along the way?"

"Dave had a pretty good-sized life insurance policy, and I'm sure it'll be more than enough to provide for my needs on this trip I've always dreamed about taking."

Margo leaned forward and leveled Trisha with one of her most serious looks. "And there's nothing we can do to talk you out of it?"

Trisha shook her head determinedly. "I've made up my mind, and I'm confident that God will be with me as I venture out to see some of the beautiful country He created."

—⟆⟆—

Pembroke, Kentucky

"Let's see now. . . . The turkey is in the oven, green beans and potatoes are staying warm on the stove, a pumpkin and an apple pie are in the refrigerator, and the table is set." Bonnie smiled as she surveyed her dining-room table. She'd used a lace tablecloth her grandmother had made many years ago, set the table with Grandma's best china, and placed a pot of yellow mums from Suzanne's garden in the center of the table with pale orange taper candles on either side. Everything was perfect and looked very festive. Now all she had to do was wait patiently for Allen to arrive.

Bonnie moved over to the window and pulled the lace curtains aside. The morning had started out with some fog, but then the fog had lifted and revealed a beautiful day with blue skies and white, puffy clouds, with no rain in sight. It was quite a contrast from the last few weeks when they'd had nothing but gray skies and too many rainy days.

She stepped into the hall to look in the mirror and check her appearance. She'd chosen a pretty green dress to wear today, and her dark, naturally curly hair framed her oval face. Bonnie also wore a cameo pin, one of the few pieces of jewelry that had belonged to her grandmother. She kept the brooch safely tucked away in her jewelry box except for special occasions such as this. A touch of lipstick, a little blush, and some pale green eye shadow completed her look. She'd always been told that she was attractive and didn't need makeup, so she'd never worn much. But it wasn't her natural beauty she hoped Allen was attracted to. She wanted him to see and appreciate her inner beauty as well.

Should I share my past with him today? Bonnie wondered. *Or would it be best to wait for another time? I wish I could just tell him right out, but I'm so afraid of his reaction.* Since she didn't know how he would deal with hearing she'd once had a child, she didn't want to chance spoiling the day—or worse, their relationship.

The closer Bonnie and Allen had become, the more she struggled with her insecurities and fears. Her thoughts and reality seemed to be at odds with each other these days. It was unnerving at times. She would talk herself into telling him, but then her fears got in the way and she'd chicken out.

The sound of a vehicle rumbling up the driveway put an end to Bonnie's musings. She looked through the peephole in the front door and saw Allen's truck pull up to her garage. With a sense of excitement, she waited until Allen stepped onto the porch before she opened the door.

"Happy Thanksgiving!" they said at the same time.

He grinned. "Wow, you look absolutely beautiful!"

"Thanks. You look pretty good yourself," Bonnie said, admiring his neatly pressed gray slacks, light blue shirt, and black leather jacket.

Allen followed her into the house and paused in the hall to sniff the air. "Mmm. . . Something sure smells good."

She smiled. "Everything's ready, so it's just a matter of putting the turkey on the platter, carving it, and serving things up. Then we can eat."

He handed her his jacket. "I'm starving! If you'll hang this up for me, I'd be happy to cut the bird for you."

"That would be great. I don't know about you, but I've always loved seeing the Thanksgiving turkey sitting in the center of the table. You know, like one of those Norman Rockwell paintings." Bonnie hung Allen's jacket on the coat tree in the hall and followed him to the kitchen. While he carved the turkey, she put the potatoes and green beans into bowls and took them out to the dining-room table, along with some olives, pickles, and the whole-wheat rolls Esther had made for her the day before. She laid a serving spoon next to the spot for the turkey platter. That way they could scoop the hot stuffing right out of the bird and onto their plates.

Oops! Guess I'd better make more room for the turkey, Bonnie thought, as she moved the yellow mums to the far end of the table. Then she returned to the kitchen to make the gravy while Allen finished up with the turkey.

"I think we're all set," Allen said, rubbing his hands briskly together. "For now, I think I've carved off enough meat for the both of us."

"Yes, it looks wonderful, and I'm right behind you with the gravy," Bonnie replied as they started for the dining room.

Once they were seated, Allen took hold of her hand. Bowing his head, he prayed, "Heavenly Father, I thank You for this wonderful meal that's set before us. Bless it to the needs of our bodies, and bless the hands that prepared it. Be with our family and friends on this special Thanksgiving Day, and keep them all safe. Thank You for the many blessings You've given to us. Amen."

Allen opened his eyes, looked at Bonnie, and winked. "As our Amish friends often say, 'Now, let's eat ourselves full!'"

"You carved the turkey, and you're my guest, so you go first," she said, pointing to the golden brown bird. "If you want some stuffing, you can use the large spoon to scoop some onto your plate."

Allen forked a few pieces of turkey onto his plate and got some stuffing as well. Then they served themselves the side dishes. As they ate, they visited about various things that had happened in the area lately. Bonnie noticed that one minute Allen seemed very relaxed and the next minute he seemed kind of nervous and fidgety and would lose his train of thought. She knew he'd been working long hours lately and figured he might be tired or uptight. Hopefully, after he finished eating, he'd feel more relaxed.

"I'm surprised you didn't go to Washington to spend Thanksgiving with your folks," Bonnie said when the conversation began to lag.

"I'd thought about it, but Mom and Dad aren't home right now. Their thirty-fifth wedding anniversary is tomorrow, so they're on a two-week vacation in Kauai."

"I'm sure they must be having a good time." Bonnie sighed. "I've always wanted to visit one of the Hawaiian islands, but I guess it's not likely to happen. At least not anytime soon."

"How do you know?"

"I'm too busy running the B&B. Besides, I'm sure a trip like that would be expensive."

"You never know. You might make it there someday. Maybe sooner than you think." Allen fiddled with his spoon. "What about you? How come you didn't go to Oregon to spend the holiday with your dad?"

"For one thing, I have some guests checking into the B&B on Saturday. Besides, my dad is coming to Kentucky for Christmas, so it's only a month before I get to see him."

Allen smiled, seeming to relax a bit. "That's good to hear. I'm anxious to meet your dad."

"I'm eager for you to meet him, and I'm sure he'll enjoy getting to know you as well."

They sat in companionable silence awhile, finishing the last of their meal. Then Bonnie pushed back her chair and stood. "As much as I hate to say it, I think it's time to clear the table and do the dishes." She motioned to the adjoining room. "If you'd like to make yourself comfortable in the living room, I'll join you for pie and coffee as soon as my kitchen chores are done."

Allen shook his head. "I wouldn't think of letting you do all the work while I kick back and let my dinner settle." He stood. "If we both clear the table and do the dishes together, we'll be done in half the time. Then we can spend the rest of the day relaxing."

"That sounds nice, and I'll appreciate your help in the kitchen."

An hour later, when the food had all been put away and the dishes were done, Bonnie gave Allen a cup of coffee and told him to go relax in the living room while she got out the pies.

"This time I won't argue," he said, offering her a tender smile. He really was a very nice man, and as hard as Bonnie had fought it, she'd fallen hopelessly in love with him.

Allen took the cup of coffee, gave her a kiss on the cheek, and headed for the living room.

Bonnie went to the refrigerator and took out the pumpkin pie and whipped cream. She was on her way to the dining room when she heard Cody barking outside.

"Would you mind checking to see what Cody's yapping about?" she called to Allen. "Sounds like he's in the backyard."

"Sure, no problem." Allen went through the kitchen and opened the back door.

Woof! Woof! Cody rushed in and darted right in front of Bonnie, causing her to stumble. The pie slipped out of her hands and landed on the floor with a *splat*, and the can of whipped cream went rolling across the room, stopping at Allen's feet.

Cody didn't hesitate to lick up the pie, and Bonnie didn't know whether to laugh or cry.

When Allen started laughing, she gave in to the urge, too. "I hope you like apple pie," she said, "because that's the only kind I have left."

"Apple's my favorite anyway, and since the whipped cream came right to me, I can just spray some on," he added, leaning over to pick up the can.

Bonnie didn't know if apple really was Allen's favorite or if he was just trying to make her feel better, but the easygoing way he'd handled the situation helped a lot. Gazing at the pie splattered all over the floor, they both gave in to hysterical giggles.

At last, Bonnie put the dog outside and, with Allen's help, cleaned up the mess on the floor.

"This might not be the most romantic place to say it," Allen said, taking Bonnie into his arms, "but I'd like to spend the rest of my life with you—cooking, cleaning, and getting after the dog."

Bonnie tipped her head and looked up him. "Wh–what exactly do you mean?"

"I mean that I love you very much, and if you'll have me, I want to make you my wife."

Bonnie felt like all the air had been squeezed out of her lungs, and she leaned against Allen for support.

"Can I take that as a yes?" he asked, kissing the top of her head.

"No. Yes. I mean, maybe." She pulled away. "What I really mean is I'd like to think about it a few weeks, if you don't mind."

Allen's forehead wrinkled. "In all honesty, I was hoping you'd say you love me, too, and that you'd be happy to be my wife."

"I. . .I do love you, Allen, but marriage is a lifelong commitment, and I—well, I don't want to make a hasty decision. I'd really like a little time to think and pray about it before I give you my answer."

He nodded slowly. "I guess that makes sense. When do you think you'll have an answer?"

Noticing his disappointment, she searched for the right words as she moistened her lips with the tip of her tongue. "Umm. . . How about Christmas Eve? Would that be soon enough?"

"That's only a month away, so I guess I can hold out that long." Allen lowered his head and kissed her gently.

Dear Lord, Bonnie prayed when the kiss ended. *Help me to have the courage to tell Allen about my past. I'm just not ready to do it today.*

CHAPTER 13

Paradise, Pennsylvania

What can I do to help?" Fannie asked when she entered her daughter-in-law Leona's kitchen on Thanksgiving Day.

Leona, red-faced and looking a bit anxious, smiled and said, "I appreciate the offer, because you and Abraham are the first ones here, and I really could use some help." Her metal-framed glasses had slipped to the middle of her nose, and she quickly pushed them back in place. "Would you mind basting the turkey while I peel and cut the potatoes?"

"I don't mind at all." Fannie grabbed a pot holder and opened the oven door of the propane stove, releasing the delicious aroma of the Thanksgiving turkey that was nicely browning. "Mmm. . . Just the smell of this big bird makes me *hungerich*," she said, while reaching for the basting brush lying on the counter to her right.

Leona nodded. "I know what you mean. The smell of turkey has been driving me crazy ever since it started roasting."

"Where are the kinner?" Fannie asked after she'd covered the turkey again and shut the oven door.

"James is out in the barn helping Zach clean out a few of the stalls so the rest of our guests will have a place to put their horses if they'd rather not use the corral."

"That's where Abraham went, too, so he'll probably end up helping them," Fannie said. "Now, where are the girls hiding themselves? I didn't see any sign of them when I came into the house."

Leona pointed to the door leading upstairs. "They're tidying up their rooms so their cousins won't see how messy they can be."

Fannie chuckled. "I guess that's what you can expect with most kinner. Of course, my Abby wasn't like that at all. Even when she was little, she kept her room neat."

"Maybe I should ask her to have a little talk with Lucy and Jean. They might be more inclined to listen to their aunt than they are to me."

"I know what you mean. Someone else usually has a better chance of getting through to our kinner than we do ourselves. And that doesn't change, even when they're grown with families of their own." Fannie motioned to the variety of vegetables on the table. "Would you like me to make a salad from those?"

"I'd appreciate that." Leona placed the cut-up potatoes in a kettle of water and set it on the stove. "Now that I've finished that chore, I can help you cut up the vegetables. Have you heard anything from Timothy lately? I was wondering what he and Hannah will be doing for Thanksgiving."

"I talked to him a few days ago," Fannie replied, reaching for a head of lettuce. "He said they'd be having dinner at Titus and Suzanne's place today."

"Who else will be there?"

"Samuel and his kinner and Esther, as well as Suzanne's

mother, grandfather, brothers, and sisters."

"None of Suzanne's siblings are married yet, right?"

Fannie shook her head. "Nelson's the oldest, and from what Titus has said, Nelson used to court a young woman from their community, but they broke up some time ago because they weren't compatible."

Leona reached for a tomato and cubed it into several small pieces. "If he was thinking about marriage at all, then it's good that he realized before it was too late that she wasn't the right girl for him."

Fannie sighed deeply. "I worry about Timothy, because I don't think he and Hannah are compatible. They've struggled in their marriage almost from the beginning."

"A lot of that has to do with Hannah's mamm, don't you think?"

"I'm afraid so. Sally King is a very possessive woman, and she's clung to Hannah ever since she was born. Hannah's always turned to her mamm when she should've been turning to her husband."

"Moving to Kentucky has put some distance between mother and daughter, so maybe things will improve for Hannah and Timothy with Sally out of the picture."

"I certainly hope so." Fannie stopped talking long enough to shred some purple cabbage. "I saw Sally at the health food store the other day, and she was really depressed because Johnny said they couldn't go to Kentucky for Thanksgiving."

"Did he give a reason?"

"Said he thought it was too soon—that they needed to give Hannah and Timothy some time to adjust to their new surroundings before making a trip there."

"Did Sally accept his decision?" Leona asked.

"I guess so. She said they'd be having Thanksgiving at one

of their son's homes, but I could see that she was pining for Hannah."

Leona reached for a stalk of celery. "I hope I never interfere in my girls' lives once they get married. I wouldn't want my future son-in-law to move away because he felt that I was coming between him and his wife."

Fannie shook her head. "I doubt that would ever happen, Leona. You and Zach are raising your kinner well, and you're not clingy with them the way Sally is to Hannah."

Leona smiled. "Danki. I appreciate hearing that."

The sounds of horses' hooves and buggy wheels crunching on the gravel interrupted their conversation.

"Looks like more of the family has arrived," Leona said, looking out the window. "I see Naomi and Caleb's buggy pulling in, and behind them is Nancy and Mark's rig."

Fannie smiled. It would be good to spend the holiday with some of their family. The only thing that would make it any better would be if Samuel, Titus, Timothy, and their families could join them.

Maybe next year we can all be together, she thought. *And when Esther and Samuel get married, I'm sure most of us will go for the wedding, so that's something to look forward to.*

—⊸⊸—

Pembroke, Kentucky

"If everything tastes as good as it smells, I think we're in for a real treat," Timothy said as he and the rest of the family gathered around the two tables that had been set up in Suzanne and Titus's living room. Even though their double-wide manufactured home was short on space, Suzanne had wanted to host the meal, and it was kind of cozy being together in such a crowded room. Fortunately, it was a crisp but sunny fall day, and the kids could go outside to play after the meal. That would leave enough room for the adults to sit around visiting or playing board games.

"You're right about everything smelling good," Titus said. "I think the women who prepared all this food should be thanked in advance."

All the men bobbed their heads in agreement.

"And now, let us thank the Lord for this food so we can eat," Suzanne's grandfather said.

The room became quiet as everyone bowed their heads for silent prayer. Timothy recited the Lord's Prayer; then he thanked God for the meal they were about to eat and for all his family in Kentucky, as well as in Pennsylvania.

When the prayers were finished and all of the food had been passed, everyone dug in.

"Yum. This turkey is so moist and flavorful," Suzanne's mother, Verna, said. She smiled at Esther. "You did a good job teaching my daughter to cook, and we all thank you for it."

Suzanne's cheeks colored, and Titus chuckled as he nudged her arm. "That's right, and my fraa feeds me so well I have to work twice as hard in the woodshop to keep from getting fat."

Everyone laughed—everyone but Hannah. She sat staring at the food on her plate with a placid look on her face. Timothy was tempted to say something to her but decided it would be best not to draw attention to his wife's sullen mood. No doubt she was upset that her folks didn't come for Thanksgiving, but she should have put on a happy face today, if only for the sake of appearances. It embarrassed Timothy to have Hannah pouting so much of the time. Just when he thought she might begin to adjust, something would happen, and she'd be fretful again. He worried that some people might think he wasn't a good husband because he couldn't make his wife happy. Well, it wasn't because he hadn't tried, but nothing he did ever seemed to be good enough for Hannah. He worried that it never would. What if he'd made a mistake forcing her to move? What if she never adjusted to living in Kentucky and remained angry and out of sorts? Was moving back to Pennsylvania the only way to make his wife happy?

But if we did that, we'd be right back where we were before we left. Hannah would be over at her mamm's all the time, and I'd be fending for myself. If we could just find a place of our own, maybe that would make a difference. Hannah might be happier if we weren't living at Samuel's, and if we weren't taking up space in Samuel's house, he and Esther could get married and start a life of their own.

"Hey, brother, did ya hear what I said?"

Timothy jumped at the sound of Titus's voice. "Huh? What was that?"

"I asked you to pass me the gravy."

"Oh, sure." Timothy took a little gravy for himself and then handed it over to Titus.

"I thought about inviting Bonnie to join us for dinner," Suzanne spoke up, "but Esther said Bonnie had invited Allen to eat at her place today."

"Allen could have joined us here, too," Titus said. "He knows he's always welcome in our home."

Samuel cleared his throat. "Well, I probably shouldn't be broadcasting this, but I happen to know that Allen had plans to propose to Bonnie today."

"Oh, that's wunderbaar," Esther said. "I can hardly wait until I see Bonnie tomorrow morning and find out what she said."

"She'll say yes, of course." Titus grinned. "I mean, why

wouldn't she want to marry a nice guy like Allen?"

"Speaking of Allen," Samuel said, looking at Timothy, "did he say anything to you about the house that's for sale over in Trigg County, near Cadiz?"

Timothy shook his head. "What house is that?"

"It's a small one, but I think it could be added on to. Allen went over to look at it the other day because the owners were thinking of remodeling the kitchen before they put it up for sale, and they wanted him to give them a bid."

Timothy looked at Hannah. "What do you think? Should we talk to Allen about this and see if he can arrange for us to look at the place?"

Hannah shrugged, although he did notice a glimmer of interest in her eyes. Maybe this was God's answer to his prayers. While he wasn't particularly fond of the idea of living thirty-seven miles from his brothers, he was anxious for them to find a place they could call home.

"All right, then," Timothy said. "Tomorrow morning I'll talk to Allen about showing us the house."

Hannah said nothing, but she did pick up her fork and eat a piece of meat, and that made Timothy feel much better about the day.

Chapter 14

Esther woke up early on Friday morning and hurried to get dressed so she could get up to the main house and speak to Bonnie. She found her friend sitting at the kitchen table with a cup of tea.

"I wasn't sure if I'd see you this morning," Bonnie said, looking up at Esther. "Since I don't have any guests checking into the B&B until tomorrow, I figured I wouldn't see you until this evening."

"I wanted to find out how your Thanksgiving dinner with Allen went."

Bonnie smiled. "It was nice. At least I didn't burn anything."

"I didn't think you would. You've gotten pretty efficient in the kitchen."

"Yes, but I'll probably never be as good a cook as you." Bonnie's face sobered. "The pumpkin pie I made got ruined."

"Oh no! What happened?"

"Cody was outside barking, and when Allen opened the door to see what the dog was yapping about, Cody came running in." Bonnie chuckled. "After that, it was like watching a comedy act. I tripped, the pie went flying, and the can of whipped cream rolled across the room and landed at Allen's feet. Afterward, we just stood there, laughing like fools. Fortunately, I'd also made an apple pie, or we wouldn't have had any dessert at all."

"Oh my. I can almost picture it." Esther laughed. "That sounds terrible and funny at the same time."

Bonnie nodded. "But the day ended on a good note, because Allen asked me to marry him."

Esther clapped her hands. "Oh, that's such good news. I hope you said yes."

Bonnie shook her head. "I told him I needed to think about it for a few weeks."

"What's there to think about? You love Allen, and he loves you. I think you'll be very happy together."

"I still haven't told him about my past, and I'm not sure I can do it."

"Of course you can. Allen's a good man; he'll understand."

"Maybe, but I'm afraid to take the chance."

"What are you going to do?"

"I'm not sure. I told Allen I'd have an answer for him by Christmas Eve, so if I'm going to tell him about the baby I adopted out when I was a teenager, I'll need to do it before I agree to marry him." She groaned. "It wouldn't be right to wait until after we're married and then spring the truth on him."

"No, and it wouldn't be right to keep the truth from him indefinitely either."

"Guess I need to pray a little more about this and ask the Lord to give me the courage to tell Allen the truth," Bonnie said, while warming her hands on the teacup.

Esther smiled. "I'll be praying for you, too."

"Thanks, I appreciate that." Bonnie motioned to the teapot.

"I don't know where my manners are. Would you like to have a cup of tea?"

"That sounds nice. Since we don't have to do any baking this morning, there's plenty of time for me to sit and visit awhile."

"How was your Thanksgiving?" Bonnie asked after Esther had poured herself a cup of tea and taken a seat.

"The food was delicious." Esther frowned. "But Hannah was in a sullen mood most of the day, and that made us all a bit uncomfortable."

"I'm not surprised," Bonnie said. "With this being the first holiday she's spent away from her family, she probably felt sad."

"I suppose so, but I dread going over to Samuel's today, because Hannah might still be in a bad mood. I realize that she misses her family in Pennsylvania, but I wonder if the family she has right here will ever be good enough for her."

"I'm sure she'll adjust eventually," Bonnie said. "Time heals all wounds, and it will help if we all try to make her feel welcome. Right now I think what Hannah needs most is friends."

Esther nodded. "That's what I think, too, and I've been trying, but I don't think Hannah likes me. Even though she seems to have accepted the idea of me coming over every day to watch Samuel's children and cook supper every other evening, I think she still resents me. It's like she's turned this into some sort of competition or something."

"Just give her a bit more time, Esther. Once Hannah gets to know you better, she'll come to love you and treasure your friendship as much as I do."

Esther forced a smile. "I hope you're right, because if we're going to be sisters-in-law, I wouldn't want any hard feelings between us."

—◌—

Hannah glanced at the battery-operated clock on the far kitchen wall and frowned. The men had left early this morning for a job in Elkton, which meant she'd had to get up early in order to fix breakfast and pack their lunches. In a few minutes, the children would be getting up, and then she'd have to fix their breakfast as well. Why was it that Esther always seemed to be late on the days she was needed the most?

Not that I really want her to be here, Hannah thought as she reached for her cup of coffee and took a sip. *It's just not fair that I should have to be responsible for two men and five children—four who aren't even my own.*

She tapped her fingers along the edge of the table. *If I wasn't here right now, and Esther was late, I wonder what Samuel would think about that. Was she ever late before we came to live here? Should he really be thinking of making her his wife?*

"For goodness' sake," she said aloud. "I don't even know what I think anymore. It wasn't long ago that I didn't want Esther here at all. Now I'm complaining that she's not here to help me."

Hannah got up from the table and moved over to the window, letting her thoughts focus on yesterday and the close friendship she'd noticed between Suzanne and Esther. It seemed like they had their heads together, laughing and talking, most of the day. Again, she found herself wishing for a friend—someone with whom she could share her deepest feelings and who wouldn't criticize her for the things she said or did—someone she could be close to the way she had been with Mom.

Oh, how she wished her folks could have joined them for Thanksgiving, but maybe they could come for Christmas. She hoped she, Timothy, and Mindy would be living in their own place by then. The house Allen had mentioned to Timothy might be the one. Hannah hoped they could look at it soon, because she really wanted to be moved out of Samuel's house before Christmas.

CHAPTER 15

W hat time will Allen be here?" Hannah asked as she, Timothy, and Samuel sat at the kitchen table drinking coffee on Saturday morning.

"Said he'd be here by nine o'clock." Timothy glanced at the clock. "So we have about ten more minutes to wait."

Hannah rose from her chair. "I'd better get Mindy's coat on so we can be ready to go as soon as he arrives."

Timothy shook his head. "I don't think taking Mindy with us to look at the house is a good idea."

Hannah quirked an eyebrow. "Why not?"

"We need to concentrate on checking out the house that Allen's found, and having Mindy along would be a distraction. You know how active she can be sometimes."

Hannah pursed her lips. "We can't expect Samuel to watch her. He'll have enough on his hands watching his own kinner today."

"I don't mind," Samuel spoke up. "Penny and Marla will keep Mindy entertained, and she shouldn't be a problem at all. The kids are all playing upstairs right now, so they'll probably keep right on playing till they're called down for lunch."

Hannah tapped her foot as she contemplated what Samuel

had said. He was pretty good with his children, so maybe Mindy would be okay left in his care. "Well, if you're sure you don't mind. . ."

Samuel shook his head. "Don't mind a bit."

"Okay, we'll leave Mindy here." Hannah glanced at the clock again. It was almost nine, and still no Allen. She really wished he'd show up so they could be on their way. And oh how she hoped the house he'd be taking them to see was the right one for them.

"Take a seat and have some more coffee," Timothy said, motioning to her empty chair. "Allen's probably running a little late this morning. I'm sure he'll be here soon."

With a sigh, Hannah reluctantly sat down. She'd only taken a few sips of coffee when she heard Allen's truck pull in. "Oh good, he's here," she said, jumping up and peeking out the kitchen window. "I'll get my shawl."

"Guess I'd better wear a jacket," Timothy said, rising from his seat. "When I went out before breakfast to help Samuel and Leon with the chores, I realized just how cold it is out there."

"Jah," Samuel said with a nod. "Wouldn't surprise me if we got some snow pretty soon."

Hannah wrinkled her nose. "I hope not. I'm not ready for snow."

"Well, the kinner might not agree with you on that." Samuel chuckled. "I think they'd be happy if we had snow on the ground all year long."

Hannah wrapped her shawl around her shoulders, set her black outer bonnet on her head, and hurried outside without saying another word. She had thought about going upstairs to tell Mindy good-bye but decided it would be best if she snuck out the back door. If she'd gone upstairs and Mindy started crying, she would have felt compelled to take her with them, which, of course, might have caused dissension between her and Timothy.

"Are you sure you don't mind driving us all the way to Cadiz?" Timothy asked Allen after they'd gotten into his truck.

Allen shook his head. "I don't mind a bit, and it's really not that far. Maybe when we're done looking at the house we can stop in Hopkinsville for some lunch."

"That sounds nice," Hannah was quick to say, "but Samuel might need some help fixing lunch for the kinner, and since today is Esther's day off, he'd probably appreciate me being there to help." Truth was, Hannah doubted Samuel's ability to fix a nutritious lunch for the children. He'd probably give them whatever they asked for instead of what they needed.

"Eating lunch at a restaurant sounds good to me," Timothy spoke up, looking straight at Hannah. "And I'm sure Samuel can manage to fix something for the kinner just fine."

Hannah was tempted to argue the point but didn't want to make a scene in front of Allen. "Okay, whatever," she said with a nod. She supposed it wouldn't hurt Mindy to have an unhealthy lunch once in a while. Forcing herself to relax, Hannah focused on the passing scenery as they headed for Trigg County.

Sometime later, Allen turned off the main road and onto a dirt road—more of a path, really. "The house is just up ahead," he said, pointing in that direction.

A few minutes later, a small house came into view. *It's too small for our needs,* Hannah thought at first glance, *but I suppose it could be added on to. Well, I'll give it the benefit of the doubt—at least until we've seen the inside of the place.*

—⁓—

As Tom Donnelson, the real estate agent, showed them through each room of the house, all Timothy could think was, *This place is way too small.* The kitchen, while it had been recently remodeled, didn't have a lot of cupboard space. He didn't see any sign of a pantry, either, which would have helped, since the cabinet area was so sparse. The living room and dining room were both small, too, and there were only three bedrooms. If he and Hannah had more children, which he hoped they would someday, a three-bedroom house wouldn't be large enough—especially if any overnight guests came to visit. They would definitely have to add more bedrooms to the house, as well as enlarge the living room and kitchen. And of course, since this was an Englisher's home, they would have to take out all the electrical connections.

The other thing that bothered Timothy was the distance between Trigg and Christian Counties. If they moved here, they'd have to hire a driver every time they wanted to see Samuel, Titus, and their families. And how would that work with him working with Samuel? It would be inconvenient and costly to hire a driver every day for such a distance, not to mention the miles his brothers would have to travel if they helped him with renovations on the small house. It would be expensive for Titus and Samuel to get someone to bring them here whenever they came to visit, too, and he wouldn't feel right about putting that burden on his brothers.

Timothy glanced at Hannah, hoping to gauge her reaction to the place. She'd commented on how nice it was to see new cupboards in the kitchen and bathroom and even said how convenient it would be to have everything on one floor. If she liked it here, it would be hard to say no to buying it, because keeping Hannah happy in Kentucky would mean she'd be less likely to hound him about moving back to Pennsylvania. *Is this a sacrifice I'd be willing to make?* he asked himself.

"The owners are motivated to sell," Tom said. "So I'm sure

they'd be willing to consider any reasonable offer."

Timothy looked at Hannah, but she said nothing. It wasn't like her not to give her opinion—especially on something as important as buying a house.

Timothy cleared his throat, searching for the right words. "I. . .uh. . .think my wife and I need to talk about this, but we appreciate you taking the time to show us the place."

Tom rubbed the top of his bald head. "Sure, no problem. Just don't take too much time making a decision, because as nice as this place is, I don't think it'll be on the market very long."

"We'll get back to you as soon as we can." Timothy ushered Hannah out the door and into Allen's truck, where he'd been waiting for them.

"That didn't take too long," Allen said. "So, what'd you think of the house?"

Timothy glanced at Hannah, but she didn't say a word— just sat with her hands folded in her lap, looking straight ahead.

"Well, uh. . . It's a nice little house, but I'm not sure it's the right one for us," Timothy said. "I can see we'd be sinking a lot of money into the place just to enlarge it for our needs."

Hannah released a lingering sigh. "Oh, Timothy, I totally agree."

"You do?"

She nodded vigorously. "The place is way too small, and it's so isolated out here. I wouldn't think you'd want to be this far from your brothers either."

A sense of relief flooded over Timothy. She was as disappointed in the place as he was. Even so, she was probably unhappy that they would have to continue living with Samuel for who knew how much longer.

"It's okay," he said, whispering in Hannah's ear. "I'm sure

some other place will come up for sale, and hopefully it'll be closer to home."

"Home?" She tipped her head and looked at him curiously.

"What I meant to say was, closer to Samuel and Titus's homes."

"It'll need to be a much larger house and not so isolated." Her lips compressed, and tiny wrinkles formed across her forehead. "I think I'd go crazy if we moved way out here."

"Not to worry," he said, resting his hand on her arm. "We'll wait till we find just the right place. Anyway, we can consider this as a practice run in knowing what we need to look for. Live and learn, right?"

Hannah gave a quick nod; then she leaned her head against the seat and closed her eyes. Was she still hoping he'd give up on the idea of living in Kentucky and move back to Pennsylvania? Well, if she was, she could forget that notion.

CHAPTER 16

Hannah glanced out the kitchen window and grimaced. It had started snowing last night and hadn't let up at all. Christmas was just two weeks away, and if the weather turned bad, it could affect her folks' plan to come for the holiday. Timothy's parents were planning to come, too. In fact, their folks planned to hire a driver and travel together. Andy Paulsen, the driver they'd asked, was single, owned a nice-sized van, and had some friends who lived in Hopkinsville, so it was the perfect arrangement.

Hannah wondered if Timothy was as anxious to see his folks as she was hers. It was different for Timothy; he had family here. She didn't. He never talked about home the way she did either, so maybe he was happy just being here, where he could see his twin brother and Samuel whenever he wanted. Despite a bit of competition between Timothy and Titus, they'd always been very close. Hannah remembered one evening when she and Timothy were courting that Titus, who liked to play pranks, had taken her home from a singing, pretending to be Timothy. Since it was dark and she couldn't see his face well, he'd managed to fool her until they got to her house and one of the barn cats had rubbed against his leg when he was helping Hannah out of the buggy. He'd hollered at the cat and called it a stupid *katz,* something Timothy would never have done. Hannah knew right away that she'd ridden home with the wrong brother.

She chuckled as she thought about how she'd decided to play along with the joke awhile and had picked up the cat and thrust it into Titus's arms. When the cat stuck its claws into Titus's chest, the joke ended.

"What's so funny?"

Hannah whirled around. "Ach, Esther, you shouldn't sneak up on me like that."

"I didn't mean to frighten you," Esther said apologetically. "I just came into the kitchen to check on the soup I've got cooking and saw you standing in front of the window laughing. I thought something amusing must be going on outside."

Hannah shook her head. "The only thing going on out there is a lot of snow coming down."

Esther stepped up to the window. "It doesn't seem to be letting up, does it?"

"Do you get much snow in this part of Kentucky?" Hannah asked.

"Some years we do. Other times we hardly get any at all." Esther motioned to the window. "If this is an indication of what's to come, we might be in for a bad winter this year."

Hannah frowned. "I hope not. The weather needs to be nice so Timothy's folks and mine can get here for Christmas."

Esther smiled. "From what Samuel's told me, his folks are really excited about coming, so it would probably have to be something bad like a blizzard to keep them at home. Maybe the snow will stick around, if it stays cold enough, and give us a white Christmas."

"My parents are looking forward to coming here, too, and

I guess if this is the only snow we get until they arrive, it would be nice to have it around for Christmas."

"Can we go outside and play in the *schnee*?" Penny asked as she, Jared, and Mindy raced into the kitchen.

"That sounds like fun," Esther said. "And when you're done playing in the snow, you can come inside for a warm bowl of chicken noodle soup."

Jared and Penny squealed, jumping eagerly up and down.

"Schnee! Schnee!" Mindy hollered, joining her cousins in their eagerness to play in the snow.

Hannah put her finger to her lips. "Calm down." She looked at Esther. "I'm sure it's frigid out there, and I don't think any of them should go outside to play."

"They'll come in if they get too cold," Esther said.

Hannah shook her head. "I don't want my daughter getting cold and wet."

"I understand that, but I don't think a few minutes in the snow will hurt her any. I'm sure when you were little you loved the snow. Didn't you?"

"Jah, but I was never allowed to play in it very long because my mamm always worried about me getting chilled."

"Please. . .please. . .can Mindy go outside with us to play?" Penny pleaded.

All three children continued to jump up and down, hollering so loudly that Hannah had to cover her ears. "Oh, all right," she finally agreed. "But I'm going outside with you, because I want to make sure Mindy doesn't wander off or slip in the wet snow and get hurt."

"I think I'll turn down the stove and join you," Esther said. "It's been awhile since I frolicked in the snow."

—⁓—

After all the fuss, Esther was surprised to actually see Hannah laughing and romping around in the snow like a schoolgirl.

She even showed the children how she liked to open her mouth and catch snowflakes on the end of her tongue.

"This is *schpass!*" Penny shouted as she raced past Esther, slipping and sliding in the snow.

"Jah, it's a lot of fun!" Esther tweaked the end of Penny's cold nose. "Should we see if there's enough snow on the ground to make a snowman?"

All three children nodded enthusiastically, and even Hannah said it sounded like fun.

Hannah helped Mindy form a snowball, and they began rolling it across the lawn while Esther helped Jared roll another snowball. Since Penny was a bit older, she was able to get a snowball started on her own.

As the children worked, they giggled, caught more snowflakes on their tongues, and huffed and puffed as their snowballs grew bigger. Esther was pleased to see Hannah actually enjoying herself. It was the first time she'd seen this side of Hannah. Maybe she was warming up to the idea of living here. There might even be a possibility that the two of them could become friends. It wasn't that Esther needed more friends; she had Suzanne and Bonnie. But Hannah needed a friend, and if she could act happy and carefree like she was doing now, she'd probably make a lot of friends in this community. Unfortunately, though, since Hannah had arrived in Kentucky, her actions had made her appear standoffish.

After they finished building the snowman, Esther suggested they look for some small rocks to use for the snowman's eyes and buttons for his chest.

The children squatted down in an area where some dirt was showing and started looking for rocks, and Esther joined them.

"Maybe I should run inside and check on the soup,"

Hannah said. "Just to be sure it's not boiling over."

"I turned the stove down, so I'm sure it's fine." Esther reached for a small stone she thought would be perfect for one of the snowman's eyes. "And Hannah, I just thought of something."

"What's that?"

"I was wondering what your thoughts are on the two desserts I'm hoping to make for Christmas."

"What did you have in mind?" Hannah asked.

"One of the things I wanted to make is pumpkin cookies, because I know Samuel and the kinner like them. I also found a recipe for Kentucky chocolate chip pie, and I was thinking of trying that, too. I've never made it before, but it sounds really good."

"I could make the pie if you like," Hannah said. "I'm always looking for new recipes to try."

"That'd be great." Esther was glad Hannah had made the offer. It was what she'd been hoping for. Maybe baking together would bridge the gap that still seemed to be between them.

Hannah smiled. "Timothy loves anything with chocolate chips in it, so I know at least one person who'll be eager to try out the pie. That is, if it turns out okay."

"You're a good cook, so I'm sure it'll turn out fine." Esther felt hopeful. She was glad today had been going so well.

"I can only hope so. Now, I think somebody ought to check on that soup," Hannah said. "So, if you'll keep a close eye on Mindy, I'll go do that."

"Sure, no problem." Esther glanced up at Hannah to make sure she'd heard her, and when Hannah turned and headed into the house, she continued to look for more rocks.

Esther was only vaguely aware that Jared and Mindy had

begun chasing each other around the yard, until she heard a bloodcurdling scream.

Dropping the rock she'd just found, she hurried across the yard, where Mindy stood holding her nose. Blood oozed between Mindy's gloved fingers and trickled down the sleeve of her jacket. The children had obviously collided. So much for fun in the snow!

Just then, Hannah rushed out of the house. Seeing Mindy's bloody nose, she glared at Esther. "What happened?"

"The children were running, and I think Jared and Mindy collided with each other," Esther said.

Hannah knelt down to take a look at her daughter's nose. "I thought you promised to keep an eye on Mindy for me," she said, taking a tissue from her jacket pocket and holding it against Mindy's nose. "If you'd been watching her, Esther, this wouldn't have happened!"

"I'm sorry," Esther said above Mindy's sobbing.

Hannah grabbed Mindy's hand and ushered her into the house.

That's just great, Esther thought. *Things were going so well between Hannah and me. Now this is one more thing for Hannah to complain to Samuel about when he gets home from work tonight. If Hannah and Timothy don't move into a place of their own soon, Hannah will probably have Samuel convinced that I'm not fit to be his wife or the kinner's stepmother.*

CHAPTER 17

Branson, Missouri

I s this your first time here?" an elderly woman with silver-gray hair asked Trisha as she took her seat in one of the most elaborate theaters in Branson. She'd gone to the women's restroom before entering the theater and was surprised to see that even it was ornately decorated.

Trisha nodded, feeling rather self-conscious. "Does it show?"

The woman chuckled. "Just a little. I couldn't help but notice the look of awe on your face as you surveyed your surroundings. It is quite beautiful, isn't it?"

"It is a magnificent theater," Trisha said. "I've never seen anything quite like this before."

"You know the old saying, 'You ain't seen nothin' yet'? Well, you just wait until you see this show. The star attraction is a violinist, and his Christmas show is absolutely incredible. I've seen him perform before, and I guarantee you won't be disappointed."

Trisha smiled in anticipation. "I'm looking forward to it."

111

"So, are you here alone?"

Trisha nodded. "I'm from California, and I'm making a trip across the country to take in some sights I've always wanted to see. After I spend a few days here, I'll be heading to Nashville. From there, I'm going to Bowling Green, Kentucky, to see an old friend."

Just then the show started, ending their conversation. As the curtain went up, Trisha turned her attention to the stage, listening with rapt attention to the beautiful violin music that began the show. So far this trip was turning out well, and she looked forward to spending Christmas with her friend Carla.

—❦—

Hopkinsville, Kentucky

"I'm so glad the weather's improved and there's no snow on the ground," Hannah said as she and Suzanne pushed their carts into Walmart's produce section. Since it was Saturday, and Samuel and Timothy had volunteered to watch the children, Hannah and Suzanne had hired a driver to take them to town so they could do some grocery shopping and buy a few Christmas gifts.

"It would be nice to have a white Christmas," Suzanne said wistfully, "like the ones I remember from my childhood."

"Esther said the same thing about having a white Christmas. Maybe so, but snowy weather makes it harder to travel, and I don't want anything to stand in the way of my folks coming for Christmas."

"I'm sure their driver will have either snow tires or chains for his van, so driving in the snow shouldn't be a problem. Unless, of course, it became a blizzard."

Hannah nodded. "That's what worries me. I'd be so

disappointed if my folks couldn't come, and I'm sure Timothy and his brothers would feel bad if their folks couldn't make it either."

Suzanne patted Hannah's arm. "Not to worry. I'm sure everything will be fine and we'll all have a really nice Christmas, with or without the snow."

—⁂—

Pembroke, Kentucky

"I've got some good news and some bad news," Timothy said when he returned to the house after checking the messages in Samuel's phone shanty.

"Let's have the good news first," Samuel said, placing his coffee cup on the kitchen table.

"Mom and Dad's message said they're still planning to come for Christmas and they can stay until New Year's."

Samuel grinned. "That is good news. It'll be great to see our folks again, and we'll have plenty of time to visit and catch up on things." He picked up his cup and took a drink. "So, what's the bad news?"

"Hannah's mother left a message saying she and Johnny won't be coming after all." Timothy groaned. "I sure dread telling Hannah about it, because I know she's gonna be very upset. She's been looking forward to her parents' visit for weeks now."

"Why can't Sally and Johnny come?" Samuel asked.

"Johnny injured his back picking up a heavy box at the store. He's flat in bed, taking pain pills and muscle relaxers. Sally has to wait on him hand and foot because he can't do much of anything right now and was advised by his doctor to stay in bed for the time being."

"That's too bad. I remember last year when Allen hurt his back after falling down some stairs. He was cranky as a bear with sore paws and none too happy about his mom coming to take care of him."

"Doesn't he get along well with her?" Timothy asked, taking a seat beside Samuel.

"They get along okay, but from what I could tell, his mom tried to baby him, and Allen didn't go for that at all."

"I guess most men don't like to be babied. We want to know that our women love us, but we don't want 'em treatin' us like we're little boys."

"That's for sure." Samuel reached for one of the cinnamon rolls Esther had baked the day before and took a bite. "So how are you gonna break the news to Hannah?".

"Guess I'll just have to tell her the facts, but I'm sure not looking forward to it." Timothy grimaced. "Hannah's been in a better mood here of late, but I'm afraid that'll change once she hears about her folks."

—w—

Later that night after Hannah had put Mindy to bed, she and Timothy retired to their room, and she told him what a good time she'd had shopping. "Suzanne and I found all of the Christmas gifts we had on our lists." Hannah smiled, realizing how good it felt to tell Timothy the events of her day. The outing with Suzanne had been just what she needed to vanish some of the tension she'd felt since arriving in Kentucky.

"Oh Timothy, I'm so excited about my folks coming for Christmas. It will be wunderbaar to have all of our parents here for the holidays. I think I actually feel some of that special holiday spirit." Hannah plumped up their pillows, feeling a sense of lightheartedness she hadn't experienced in some time.

But then she noticed a strange look on her husband's face.

"Hannah, I'm really glad you had such a nice day with Suzanne," Timothy said, "but there's something I need to tell you."

"What is it?"

"I wanted us to be alone when I told you this, and there's no easy way to soften the blow, so I may as well just come right out and say it. Your parents won't be able to make it for Christmas."

She hoped she'd heard him wrong. "What do you mean? Why aren't they coming?"

"Your daed hurt his back and won't be able to travel for a while."

"Oh no." She groaned, plopping down on the bed. "I just can't believe it."

"I'm sorry," Timothy said. "I know how disappointed you must be."

Hannah sniffed, trying to hold back the tears that threatened to spill over. "Jah." Her hands shook as she stood and pulled the covers back on the bed. Changing into her nightgown and climbing under the covers, she could almost feel Timothy watching her. Yet he remained quiet as he slid into bed next to her. After a few minutes, she heard his steady, even breathing and figured he must have fallen asleep.

Hannah knew it had probably been hard for Timothy to break the news about her folks not coming, and she was grateful he'd waited until they were alone to do it. But couldn't he have at least given her a hug instead of turning his back on her and falling asleep? Staring at the ceiling and feeling worse by the minute, Hannah realized there was nothing she could do but accept the fact that her folks weren't coming, but that didn't make it any easier.

Poor Dad, she thought as tears slipped from her eyes. *He must be in terrible pain, and both he and Mom are probably just as disappointed as I am that they can't come here for Christmas.*

Hannah rolled over and punched her pillow. *I'll accept it, but I don't have to like it! If I wasn't so far from home, I'd be able to help Mom and Dad right now. If. . . If. . . If. . .* She buried her face in the pillow, trying to muffle her sobs. *Why do things like this always happen to me?*

CHAPTER 18

J ust look at all that snow coming down. I think it's safe to say that we're gonna have a white Christmas," Timothy said as he and Samuel headed out to the barn to do their morning chores on Christmas Eve. "Sure hope Mom and Dad make it before this weather gets any worse."

"I hope so, too." Samuel's boots crunched through the snow. "This could mean we're in for a bad winter."

"If the snow and wind keep up like this, it could also mean Mom and Dad might have to stay longer than they planned." Timothy glanced toward the road. "I wonder if the snowplows will come out our way today."

"It's hard to say. Guess it all depends on how busy they are in other places."

When Samuel opened the barn door, the pungent aroma of horse manure hit Timothy full in the face. "Phew! There's no denying that the horses' stalls need a good cleaning."

"You're right about that. Guess we should have done them last night, but since we got home so late from that paint job in Hopkinsville, I was too tired to tackle it."

"Same here."

As they stepped into the first stall, Samuel asked, "Do you think Hannah and Esther are getting along any better these days?"

Timothy shrugged. "I don't know. Why do you ask?"

"I was thinking if they were, maybe Esther and I could get married sometime after the first of the year, even if you and Hannah haven't found a house by then."

"I have no objections to that, but I think it's something you and Esther will need to decide." Timothy reached for a shovel. "I know I've said this before, but I really do appreciate you letting us stay with you and giving me a job. You've helped to make things a lot easier for us, which has given me a few less things to worry about."

Samuel thumped Timothy's back. "That's what families are for. I'm sure if the tables were turned, you'd do the same for me."

Timothy gave a nod, although he wasn't sure his wife would be so agreeable about Samuel and his kids staying with them. Hannah was more desperate to find a place of their own than he was, and he figured it was because she wanted to have the run of the house and didn't want to answer to Esther. Of course, if they'd been living with Hannah's folks all this time, Hannah wouldn't have a problem with her mother telling her what to do. And if Sally and Johnny needed a place to live, Hannah would welcome them with open arms.

Ever since he'd given her the news that her folks wouldn't be coming for Christmas, she'd gone around looking depressed and had even refused to do any baking with Esther, saying she wasn't in the mood. Timothy was fairly certain that Hannah didn't know that he'd lain awake for at least an hour after she'd cried herself to sleep that night, not knowing what to say that would make her feel better. He felt even worse because, before he'd given her the news about her folks, she'd seemed upbeat about her day with Suzanne. Had it not been for the bad news, Hannah's day of Christmas shopping might have been a turning point in helping her to be more comfortable with living in Kentucky. Instead, her Christmas spirit had disappeared.

Sure hope Hannah's able to put on a happy face while my folks are here, Timothy thought, gripping the shovel a little tighter. *I don't need to hear any disapproving comments about my wife from Mom. And Hannah's negative attitude won't help Mom any, since she is already none too thrilled about any of her sons living here.*

The whole idea of moving had been to improve their marriage, and if Timothy's mother didn't see any sign of that, he'd probably have more explaining to do. Instead of getting easier, things seemed to be getting harder.

Timothy directed his thoughts back to the job at hand, and after he and Samuel finished cleaning the stalls, they left the barn.

"We must have gotten at least another two inches of snow since we started shoveling the manure," Samuel mentioned as they tromped back to the house.

"I'll say!" Timothy jumped back when a snowball hit him square on the forehead. "Hey! Who did that?" he asked, looking around as he wiped the snow off his head.

"There's your culprit!" Samuel pointed to Leon, sprinting for the back porch. "Come on. Let's get him!"

Leon squealed as Timothy and Samuel pelted him with snowballs.

"That ain't fair! It's two against one!" Leon jumped off the porch, scooped some snow into a ball, and slung it hard. This one landed on Samuel's back.

In response, Samuel turned and pitched a snowball at

Timothy. Pretty soon snowballs were flying every which way, and no one seemed to care who they were throwing them at.

"This has been a lot of fun," Samuel finally said, "but we'd better go into the house and get warmed up."

Timothy, gasping for breath, nodded, but he was grinning as he headed for the house. He felt like a kid again and was sure from the look on his brother's face that Samuel did, too. It had been good to set his worries aside for a few minutes and do something fun. He'd forgotten that playing in the snow could be such a good stress reliever. He'd also forgotten the enjoyment he and Hannah had in the earlier years of their marriage when the first big snowstorm hit Lancaster County. It had only been a few years, yet it seemed so long ago.

Peeking into the oven at the pumpkin cookies, Esther was pleased to see that they were almost done. She planned to serve them this evening, along with hot apple cider. Since Hannah hadn't made the Kentucky chocolate chip pie like she'd planned, Esther had also baked an apple and a pumpkin pie to serve for dessert on Christmas Day.

Esther looked forward to spending Christmas Eve with Samuel and his family, and was glad she could be here at Samuel's all day to help with the cooking and cleaning. She felt sorry for Hannah, though, knowing how disappointed she was over her folks not being able to come. Yet despite Hannah's sullen mood, she was upstairs right now, putting clean sheets on the bed in the guest room. Fannie and Abraham would stay here for a few nights, and since they didn't plan to return home until New Year's Day, they would spend a few nights with Titus and Suzanne. Esther knew Titus, Timothy, and Samuel were looking forward to seeing their folks. She'd hoped her own folks might be able to come for Christmas, but they'd decided it was best to stay in Pennsylvania to be with Sarah and Dan. Esther hoped they'd be able to come for her wedding—whenever that would take place. At the rate things were going, she was beginning to wonder if she'd ever become Samuel's wife.

Esther had been relieved that Hannah hadn't said anything to Samuel about Jared causing Mindy's nose to bleed the other day. If Hannah had mentioned it, then Samuel hadn't brought it up to Esther, which probably meant he either didn't know or didn't blame her. She hoped that was the case, because she didn't want anything to come between her and Samuel.

Esther had just taken the last batch of pumpkin cookies from the oven when Samuel, Timothy, and Leon entered the kitchen laughing and kidding each other.

"Brr. . . It's mighty cold out there," Samuel said, rubbing his hands briskly together.

"And it's snowing even harder now." Timothy rubbed a wet spot on the bridge of his nose. "Sure hope our folks make it here soon, 'cause I can't help but be concerned about them."

"Worrying won't change a thing," Samuel said.

"Your brother's right," Esther agreed. "Whenever I find myself worrying, I just get busy doing something, and that seems to help. It makes the time go by faster, too."

"Guess you're right. While we were out in the snow chasing each other with snowballs, I didn't even think about my worries. But now that I'm back inside, I have a nagging feeling that the weather is going to cause some problems on the roads."

"Well, I don't think it'll bother Mom and Dad," Samuel said with an air of confidence. "They've hired an experienced driver with a reliable van, and I'm trusting God to keep them all safe."

"I need to trust Him, too." Timothy moved across the room toward Esther. "Any chance I might have one of those Kichlin?"

"The cookies are really for this evening, but since I baked plenty, it's fine if you have a few. I'm sure you guys must have worked up an appetite playing out there in the snow. You can let me know if they're any good."

"If they taste as good as they smell, you don't need to worry." Timothy grabbed two cookies. "So, where's my Fraa and *dochder*?"

"Hannah's upstairs making the bed in the guest room," Esther replied. "And Mindy's playing with Samuel's kinner up in Penny's room. I think I heard Leon running up the stairs to join them. No doubt he wants to tell them about that snowball fight you all had."

"Think I'll go up and see how Hannah's doing," Timothy said, holding up one of the cookies. "I know she's feeling pretty down today, so maybe I can cheer her up with one of these." He ate the other cookie he'd taken. "Mmm. . . This is really good, Esther. Think I may need to have a couple more when I come back downstairs."

Esther chuckled. "Just don't eat too many or you'll spoil your appetite for supper."

He wiggled his eyebrows playfully. "After that snowball battle, not a chance."

When Timothy left the room, Esther turned to Samuel and said, "I doubt that one of my cookies will help Hannah. I think she'll be down in the dumps tonight and tomorrow as well."

"You're probably right." Samuel, his hair still wet from the snow, moved to stand beside Esther. "I've been thinking about something," he said, slipping his arm around her waist.

"What's that?" Esther asked as Samuel wiped a drip of water that had splashed from his hair onto her cheek.

"I was wondering how you'd feel about us getting married right after the first of the year."

Esther drew in a sharp breath. The thought of marrying Samuel so soon made her feel giddy. "Oh Samuel, I'd love to marry you as soon as possible, but Timothy and Hannah haven't found a home of their own yet."

"I realize that, but I was hoping we could get married anyway."

"You mean two families living under the same roof?"

He nodded.

"I don't think it would work, Samuel. Hannah and I do things so differently—especially concerning the kinner. It's been hard enough for us to get along with me here just a few hours each day. If I was here all the time, I'm afraid Hannah would resent me even more than she does already. Sometimes things are fine, and other times I can feel the tension between us. It's uncomfortable being constantly on edge."

Samuel nuzzled her cheek with his nose, where the drip of snow had just been. "So would you prefer to wait to get married till after Timothy and Hannah find a place of their own?"

Esther's heart fluttered at his touch. "Jah. As difficult as it will be to wait even longer, I think that would be best."

—⁂—

Hannah had just finished putting the quilt back on the guest bed when Timothy entered the room. "What's that you have behind your back?" she asked, blowing a strand of hair out of her eyes.

Timothy held up the cookie. "Thought you'd like to try one of Esther's pumpkin kichlin. They're sure good." He smacked his lips and handed her the treat.

As much as Hannah disliked hearing her husband rave about Esther's cookies, her stomach growled at the prospect of eating one. The whole house smelled like pumpkin, and she had to admit when she bit into the cookie that it was really good.

"You should have seen the snowball battle Samuel and I just had with Leon. Foolin' around in the snow like that made me feel like a kid again." Timothy grinned and kicked off his boots. "Remember when we first got married, how we enjoyed doing things like that?"

"I did see you three down there in the yard," she said, ignoring his comment. "I was watching out the window and thinking how nice it would be if you spent more time with Mindy and played games with her like you did with Leon." Hannah tromped across the room and picked up Timothy's boots. "You should have taken these off downstairs. I hope you didn't track water all the way up the stairs," she grumbled. "Now please take them over to our room and put them on the throw rug. I just got this room all nice and clean for your parents, and now you're dripping water all over the floor."

Hannah watched as Timothy picked up his boots and did as she asked, not saying a word as he walked across the hall to their room. She knew his good mood had evaporated once she'd started lecturing him. But it irritated her to see Timothy have fun with Samuel's son instead of their own daughter. And couldn't he see that the room for his parents was all nice and clean?

"I guess not," Hannah muttered. "Timothy and I just don't see things the same way anymore. Maybe we never did, but it seems like it's gotten worse since we moved to Kentucky."

—⁓—

Nashville, Tennessee

"It sure is good to see you," Bonnie said as she and her dad left the airport terminal and headed for her car.

He grinned and squeezed her hand. "It's good to see you, too, and I appreciate you coming all this way to pick me up."

"It's not that far, Dad. Besides, this is the closest airport to where I live. I just wish you could stay longer than a few days," she said, opening her trunk so he could put his suitcase inside.

"I do, too, but I need to be back at work by next Monday."

"I'd hoped you might have put in for a few more days' vacation than that."

"Maybe I can come and stay longer sometime this spring or summer." He climbed into the passenger's side and buckled his seat belt.

As they drove toward Kentucky, they got caught up with one another's lives. "I'm really anxious to show you all the changes that have been made to your folks' old house," Bonnie said. "I think Grandma and Grandpa's place makes the perfect bed-and-breakfast."

He smiled. "I'm looking forward to seeing it, too."

As they neared Clarksville, it began to snow, so Bonnie turned on the windshield wipers and slowed down a bit. "It started snowing in Pembroke last night," she said. "And when I left to come to the airport, it was still snowing, but as I got closer to Nashville, it quit."

"I sure didn't expect to see snow on this trip," Dad said. "We haven't had any in Oregon yet."

Bonnie frowned as she stared out the front window. If

125

the snow kept coming down like it was right now, by this evening it could be a lot worse. She hoped Samuel's folks would make it safely and said a mental prayer for everyone who might be driving in the snow throughout the day.

CHAPTER 19

O ut of politeness, Hannah stood on the front porch, watching as Timothy and Samuel greeted their parents. From the joyous expressions on the brothers' faces, she knew they were happy to see their folks. Fannie and Abraham were equally delighted to be here.

Hannah couldn't deny them that pleasure, but it was hard to be joyful when she missed her own parents so much. Her chin quivered just thinking that at this very moment she could have been greeting her parents as well. She looked away, trying to regain her composure and knowing she'd have to put on a happy face. She'd make every attempt to do it, if for no other reason than for Mindy's sake, because she wanted her daughter to have a nice Christmas with at least one set of grandparents. But she'd only be going through the motions, because inside she was absolutely miserable.

When Fannie finished greeting her sons, she turned to Hannah and gave her a hug. "Wie geht's?" she asked.

"I'm doing okay. How about you?"

Fannie smiled. "I'm real good now that we're here safe and sound."

"That's right," Abraham said, nodding. "The roads on this side of Kentucky are terrible, and we saw several accidents. Fortunately, none of 'em appeared to be serious."

"Let's go inside where it's warmer." Samuel opened the door for his parents. Everyone followed, including Fannie and Abraham's driver, who said he could really use a cup of coffee before heading to his friend's house on the other side of Hopkinsville.

Esther greeted Fannie and Abraham as soon as they entered the kitchen; then she and Hannah served everyone steaming cups of coffee.

"I made plenty of cookies for our dessert tonight, so we may as well have some of them now." Esther smiled as she placed a plate of pumpkin cookies on the table.

"Those look *appenditlich*," Fannie said, reaching for one.

"You're gonna enjoy 'em." Timothy grinned at his mother. "I already sampled a few, and they are delicious."

"I can vouch for that," Samuel agreed. " 'Course, everything Esther bakes is really good." He smiled at Esther, and the look of adoration on his face put a lump in Hannah's throat. It had been such a long time since Timothy had looked at her that way or complimented her on her baking.

Maybe he doesn't love me anymore, she thought. *If he did, then why'd he force me to move here?* Hannah's mood couldn't get much lower. *Just listen to them. Everybody loves Esther's cookies.* It made her want to escape upstairs to her room. They'd probably be enjoying that Kentucky chocolate chip pie she'd volunteered to make if she hadn't changed her mind about it. But her heart just wasn't in it. Without her parents coming to celebrate Christmas with them, Hannah wasn't in the mood for much of anything. She might try making the pie some other time. Maybe after she and Timothy had a place of their own. If she baked something Timothy really liked, he might compliment her for a change.

Hannah's thoughts were quickly pushed aside when five young children darted into the room. With smiling faces, Fannie and Abraham set their coffee cups down and gathered the children into their arms.

"Ach, my!" said Fannie, eyes glistening. "We've missed you all so much."

"We've missed you, too," Marla said, hugging her grandma around the neck. The other children nodded in agreement.

After all the hugs and kisses had been given out, the children found seats at the table, and Esther gave them each a glass of milk and two cookies.

"That's plenty for Mindy," Hannah said. "If she eats too many kichlin, it'll spoil her supper."

"We won't be eating the evening meal for a few hours yet," Timothy said. "So I don't think a couple more cookies will hurt her any."

Hannah, though irritated, said nothing, preferring not to argue with her husband in front of his parents.

"I'm sorry your folks weren't able to make it." Fannie offered Hannah a sympathetic smile. "We stopped by their place before we left town to pick up the gifts they asked us to bring, and your daed seemed to be in a lot of pain."

"That's what Mom said when I spoke with her on the phone this morning." Hannah blinked against the tears pricking the back of her eyes. Not only was she sad about her folks being unable to come, but she still felt bad that Dad had injured his back, and she wished she could be there to help Mom take care of him.

"I know your mamm was really looking forward to coming here," Fannie said, "but I'm sure they'll make the trip as soon as your daed is feeling better."

"It probably won't be until spring," Hannah said, her mood plummeting even lower. "I'm sure they won't travel when the roads are bad, and I wouldn't want them to."

"Speaking of the roads," their driver, Andy, spoke up, "I'd better head to my friend's house now, before this weather gets any worse."

Timothy and Samuel both jumped up from the table. "We'll get Mom and Dad's stuff out of your van so you can be on your way," Timothy said.

"I'll come with you." Abraham pushed his chair aside and stood.

After the men went outside, the children headed back upstairs to play. "I think I'll go out to the phone shanty and call Bonnie," Esther said. "Her dad is supposed to arrive today, so I want to see if he made it okay." She slipped on her jacket and hurried out the door.

Thinking this might be the only time she'd have to speak with Fannie alone, as soon as everyone else had left, Hannah moved over to sit next to her mother-in-law.

"I know how close you've always been to your twins," she said, carefully choosing her words, "and I'm sure having them both move to Kentucky has been really hard for you."

Fannie nodded slowly. "I never thought any of our kinner would leave Pennsylvania."

"I didn't think they would either—especially not Timothy. I thought he enjoyed painting for Zach and farming with his daed."

"I believe he did," Fannie said, "but Timothy wanted a new start, as did Samuel and Titus."

"I don't like it here," Hannah blurted out, wanting to get her point across. "I want to go back to Pennsylvania, and I was hoping you might talk Timothy into moving back home."

Fannie sat quietly, staring at her cup of coffee. With tears shimmering in her eyes, she said, "I can't do that, Hannah. I've already expressed the way I feel to Timothy, and if I say anything more, it would probably make him even more determined to stay in Kentucky. It could drive a wedge between us that might never be repaired."

Hannah lowered her gaze, struggling not to cry. "Then I guess I'll have to spend the rest of my life being miserable."

Fannie placed her hand on Hannah's arm. "Happiness is not about the place you live. It's about being with your family—the people you love."

"That's right, and my family lives in Pennsylvania."

Fannie shook her head. "When you married my son, you agreed to leave your mother and father and cleave to your husband. You must let go of your life in Pennsylvania and make a new life here with your husband and daughter."

Hannah knew Fannie was right. When she'd said her vows to Timothy on their wedding day, she'd agreed to cleave only unto him. But she'd never expected that would mean moving away from her mother and father and coming to a place where she didn't even have her own home. Maybe if they could find a house to buy soon, she would feel differently, but that remained to be seen.

—⁊⁊⁊—

"It's nice to meet you, Ken," Allen said when Bonnie introduced him to her father.

"Nice to meet you, too. Bonnie's told me a lot about you." Ken grinned at Bonnie and gave her a wink.

"I hope it was all good," Allen said, taking a seat in the living room next to the Christmas tree.

"Of course it was all good," Bonnie said before her father could reply. She looked over at Ken and added, "Allen's never been anything but kind to me."

Allen smiled. Hearing her say that made him think she might be ready to accept his marriage proposal. The only problem was, he couldn't bring it up in front of her dad. He'd have to wait and hope he had the chance to speak with Bonnie alone at some point this evening. He had even gone over in his mind what he wanted to say when he finally did pop the question.

His gaze went to the stately tree he'd helped her pick out a week ago. It looked so beautiful with all the old-fashioned decorations and even a few bubble lights mixed in with the other colored lights. He wished he'd brought the subject of marriage up to her that day when they'd been alone and in festive moods. But since he'd promised to wait until Christmas Eve, he hadn't said anything.

Tonight Bonnie seemed a bit tense. Maybe she was nervous about her dad being here. It was the first time he'd come to visit since Bonnie had left Oregon and turned her grandparents' home into a bed-and-breakfast. Allen knew from what Bonnie had told him that her dad had lived here with his folks during his teenage years but had hated it. It wasn't the house or even the area he hated, though; it was the fact that he'd been forced to leave his girlfriend in Oregon. When she'd broken up with Ken, he'd blamed his folks for forcing him to move, and once he graduated from high school, he'd joined the army and never returned to Kentucky.

"I have some open-faced sandwiches and tomato soup heating on the stove, so if you're ready to eat, why don't we go into the dining room?" Bonnie suggested.

"Sounds good to me." Allen rose from his chair, and her

dad did the same.

After they were seated at the dining-room table, Bonnie led in prayer and then dished them each a bowl of soup, while Allen helped himself to an open-faced egg-salad sandwich. "These really look good," he said, passing the platter to Ken.

"They sure do. When Bonnie's mother was alive, she used to make sandwiches like these every Christmas Eve. It was part of her Norwegian heritage to make the sandwiches open-faced and garnish them with tomatoes, pickles, and olives."

Bonnie smiled. "And don't forget the fancy squiggles of mustard and mayonnaise Mom always put on the sandwiches."

Allen took a bite. "Boy, this tastes as good as it looks."

"The soup's good, too," Ken said, after he'd eaten his first spoonful. "Bonnie, you've turned into a real good cook."

"I owe it all to Esther," she said. "She's an excellent cook and taught me well. Without her help, I'd never have been able to come up with decent breakfast foods to serve my B&B guests."

"Esther's your Amish friend, right?" Ken asked.

Bonnie nodded. "I'm anxious for you to meet her, but she's with Samuel's family this evening, so you won't get the chance until tomorrow morning."

"Will she join us for breakfast?" Ken asked.

"I think so. Then she'll be going back to Samuel's to spend Christmas Day."

"I hope you intend to join us tomorrow for Christmas dinner," Ken said, looking at Allen.

"Most definitely." Allen grinned at Bonnie. "I wouldn't miss the chance to eat some of that delicious turkey you're planning to roast. The meal you fixed on Thanksgiving was great, so I'm sure Christmas dinner will be as well."

Bonnie smiled. "Thank you, Allen."

As they continued their meal, Allen got better acquainted with Ken. When he wasn't talking, he was thinking about whether he'd get the chance to speak with Bonnie alone. It made him a little nervous, hoping he'd remember what he'd practiced saying all week. Allen thought he was about to get that chance when Bonnie excused herself to get their dessert.

"Would you like some help?" he offered.

"That's okay. Just sit and relax while you visit with Dad." Bonnie disappeared into the kitchen. Allen hoped he'd get a chance to speak to her before the evening was out.

"I hear you're in the construction business," Ken said after he'd taken a drink of coffee.

"Yes, that's right." Allen glanced at the kitchen door, wishing he could be in there with Bonnie. Not that he didn't enjoy her dad's company; he just really wanted to know if she'd made a decision about marrying him.

"How do you like what Bonnie's done with the house?" Allen asked, looking back at Ken. "She's really turned this place into a nice bed-and-breakfast, don't you think?"

"Yes, it's amazing the transformation that's taken place," Ken agreed. "Not that I didn't have faith in my daughter's abilities, but to tell you the truth, this house was pretty run-down, even when I lived here, so I really didn't know what to expect."

Allen smiled. "Your daughter's pretty remarkable."

"Bonnie says you want to marry her," Ken blurted out.

Allen nearly choked. "Well, uh. . .yes, but I didn't realize she'd mentioned it to you."

Ken gave a nod. "Yep. Said she's supposed to have an answer for you soon."

"That's right. Tonight, to be exact."

"Are you planning to start a family right away?"

"I don't know. That's something Bonnie and I will have to discuss—if she agrees to marry me, that is."

"She'll make a good mother, I think. She's older and ready for that now. Not like when she was an immature sixteen-year-old and had to give her baby up."

"Wh–what was that?" Allen thought he must have misunderstood what Ken just said. *Baby? What baby?*

"She was too young to raise a child back then, and with my job at the bank and trying to raise Bonnie alone, I sure couldn't help take care of a baby. So I insisted that she give the child up for adoption."

Allen's spine went rigid. Bonnie had given birth to a baby when she was sixteen, and she hadn't said a word to him about it? What other secrets did she have?

He leaned forward and rubbed his head, trying to come to grips with this news.

"Are you okay?" Ken asked.

"Uh—no. I have a sudden headache." Allen pushed his chair aside. "And I think I'd better go before the weather gets any worse." He rushed into the hall, grabbed his jacket from the coat tree, and hurried out the door. He couldn't get out of there fast enough.

CHAPTER 20

Bonnie had just placed some slices of chocolate cheesecake on a platter, when she heard the rumble of a vehicle starting up. She went to the window and peered out. It was snowing pretty hard, but under the light on the end of her garage she could see Allen's truck pulling out of the yard.

Now where in the world is he going?

Bonnie hurried into the dining room. Dad sat at the table, head down and shoulders slumped. "I just saw Allen's truck pull out of the yard. Did he say where he was going?"

Dad looked up at her and gave a slow nod. "He's going home."

Bonnie frowned. "Why? What happened?"

"Said he had a headache, but I think it had more to do with me and my big mouth."

"What are you talking about, Dad? Did you say something to upset Allen?"

Dad rubbed the bridge of his nose. "I'm afraid so."

"What'd you say?"

"We were talking about his desire to marry you, and I asked if he wanted children." Dad paused and took a sip of water. "Then I. . .uh. . .mentioned the child you'd given up for adoption."

Bonnie gasped and sank into a chair with a moan. "Oh Dad, you didn't! How could you have told Allen that? It was my place to tell him about my past, not yours."

"I know that, but I figured it was something you had already told him. I mean, if you're thinking of marrying the guy, then you should have told him about the baby."

"I was planning to, but I couldn't work up the nerve, and there just never seemed to be the right time. I would have told him before I'd given an answer to his proposal though."

"Good grief, Bonnie, you can't wait to spring something like that on a man right before you agree to become his wife. What in the world were you thinking?"

Bonnie stiffened. She didn't like the way Dad was talking to her right now—as though she was still a little girl in need of a lecture.

"I'm sorry, honey," Dad said before she could offer a retort. "I wasn't thinking when I blabbed to Allen. I was wrong in assuming you had already told him. I'm sure when he comes here for dinner tomorrow you'll be able to talk things out."

Tears welled in Bonnie's eyes, and she blinked to keep them from spilling over. "I hope so, Dad, because I really want things to work out for us. I love Allen so much."

"Does that mean you're going to accept his proposal?"

She gave a slow nod. "If he'll have me now that he knows the truth about my past."

"I'm sure he just needs some time to process all of this. He loves you, Bonnie. I'm certain of it." Dad pushed his chair aside and stood. "You know, I'm really bushed, so if you don't mind, I think I'll head upstairs to bed."

"That's fine. I'll just clear things up in here, and then I'll probably go to bed, too."

"Things will work out for you and Allen. Just pray about it, honey." Dad gave her a hug. Before he headed up the stairs, he turned and looked back at her. "As I said before, I'm really sorry I blurted all that out to Allen."

Noticing her dad's remorseful expression, Bonnie said, "What's done is done, Dad. I should have told Allen sooner, and it's too late now for regrets."

"It'll work out, honey. You'll see. Allen probably just needs some time to think about it."

"I hope so. Good night, Dad. Sleep well."

"You, too."

After Dad went upstairs, Bonnie remained in her chair, staring at the lights on the Christmas tree. It had helped to hear Dad's reassuring words. Now if she could only believe them. *Does Allen really have a headache, and if so, why didn't he come to the kitchen and tell me himself? Did he leave because he couldn't deal with the truth about my past? Will he be back for Christmas dinner tomorrow? Should I give him a call or just wait and find out?*

—w—

Trisha squinted as she tried to keep her focus on the road. With the snow coming down so hard, it was difficult to see where she was. This was so nerve-wracking, especially since she didn't have a lot of experience driving in the snow. She figured she should be getting close to Hopkinsville though, where she could get a hotel room and call her friend in Bowling Green to let her know she wouldn't arrive tonight after all but would try to get there tomorrow. At the rate the wind was blowing the snow all around, she began to question where she was. She'd lost service on her GPS and wasn't sure if she was supposed to go straight ahead or turn at the next crossroad.

Maybe Margo was right, she thought. *It might have been a mistake to venture out on my own.*

When a truck swooshed past Trisha's car, throwing snow all over the windshield, she swerved to the right and nearly hit a telephone pole. Heart pounding and hands so sweaty she could barely hold on to the steering wheel, Trisha sent up a prayer as she made a right turn. *Please, Lord, let this be the way to Hopkinsville.*

Driving slowly, with her windshield wipers going at full speed, she proceeded up the road. There were no streetlights on this stretch of road, and she had a sinking feeling she'd taken a wrong turn.

Should I turn around and head back to the road I was on or keep going? she asked herself. *Maybe I'll go just a little farther.*

Trisha saw a pair of red blinking lights up ahead. She slowed her car even more as she strained to see out the window. Then, as she approached the blinking lights, she realized the vehicle in front of her was an Amish buggy. While doing some online research of the area before making this trip, Trisha had learned that there were Amish and Mennonite families living in Christian County, Kentucky. Apparently the Amish in this buggy had been out somewhere on Christmas Eve and were probably on their way home.

Afraid to pass for fear of frightening the horse, Trisha followed the buggy until it turned onto a graveled driveway. It was then that she noticed a sign that read: BONNIE'S BED-AND-BREAKFAST.

Maybe there's a vacancy and I can spend the night, she thought, hope welling in her soul. *Then in the morning, I'll ask for directions to Bowling Green and be on my way.*

Trisha turned in the driveway and stopped her car several

feet from where the horse and buggy had pulled up to a hitching rail. When a young Amish woman climbed down from the buggy, Trisha got out of her car.

"Excuse me," she hollered against the howling wind, "but are you the owner of this bed-and-breakfast?"

The woman shook her head. "I just work here part-time, and I live over there in the guesthouse." She pointed across the yard, but due to the swirling snow, Trisha could barely make out the small building. She could, however, see the large house in front of her, which was well lit and looked very inviting right now. It was obviously the B&B.

"Is the owner of the bed-and-breakfast here right now?" Trisha asked, pulling her scarf tighter around her neck to block out the cold wet flakes that were now blowing sideways from the storm.

"I'm sure she is, but—"

"Thanks." Being careful with each step she took, Trisha made her way across the slippery, snowy yard and up the stairs leading to a massive front porch. As she lifted her hand to knock on the door, a sense of peace settled over her. She had a feeling God had directed her to this place tonight, and for that she was grateful. She just hoped she wouldn't be turned away.

Bonnie had just put away the last of the dishes she'd washed when she heard a knock on the front door. Hoping Allen might have come back or that maybe it was Esther returning from Samuel's, she hurried to the foyer. When she opened the door, she was surprised to see a middle-aged English woman with snow-covered, faded blond hair on the porch.

"May I help you?" Bonnie asked.

"My name is Mrs. Chandler, and I was wondering if you

might have a room available for the night." The woman pushed a lock of damp hair away from her face. The poor thing looked exhausted.

"The B&B isn't open during Christmas," Bonnie said.

"Oh, I see." The woman's pale blue eyes revealed her obvious disappointment, and she turned to go.

Bonnie's conscience pricked her. Like the innkeeper on the first Christmas Eve, could she really fail to offer this person a room? Thankfully, she could provide something much better than a lowly stable.

"Don't go; I've changed my mind," Bonnie called as the woman walked toward the stairs. "I have a room you can rent. This weather isn't fit for anyone to be out there—especially if you aren't familiar with the area. Come on in and warm up."

The woman turned back, and a look of relief spread across her face as she shook the snow out of her hair and entered the house. "Oh, thank you. I appreciate it so much. You're right. The roads are horrible, and I didn't want to get stuck. I could hardly see where I was going with all the snow coming down. I hate to keep rambling on about this, but this storm is a bit scary, and I had no idea where I was."

"It's not a problem." *After all,* Bonnie thought, *it's Christmas Eve, and I can't send a stranger out into the cold.*

CHAPTER 21

Bonnie awoke early on Christmas morning and, seeing that Mrs. Chandler was still in her room, made her way quietly into the kitchen. Once she had a pot of coffee going, she slipped into her coat and went out the back door. She was glad it wasn't snowing at the moment, even though there was more than a foot of the powdery stuff on the ground. From the way the sky looked, Bonnie figured more snow was probably on the way.

She paused on the porch to breathe in the wintry fresh air. The sight before her looked like a beautiful Christmas card, and she couldn't take her eyes off the wintry scene. Except for a few bird tracks under the feeders, the snow was untouched. Nothing had escaped the blanket of snow. In every direction was a sea of white. The mums that had long lost their autumn color were covered with snow, forming a pretty design. The pine branches were decorated with fluffs of powder, and the pinecones were like nature's ornaments.

Bonnie stepped off the porch, turned, and looked up. The rooftop on the house was covered with heavy snow, giving it an almost whimsical look. Bonnie was glad for a white Christmas.

It was what all kids, young and old, dreamed of having.

Glancing at the place where Allen's truck had been parked the night before, she noticed that the snow was so deep that it had erased all signs his vehicle had ever been there. Her heart was heavy after what had happened last night, but the beautiful white snow helped to lighten her spirits a bit. Besides, it was Christmas—a time for joy, hope, love, and a miracle. Bonnie felt it would take a miracle for Allen to understand why she hadn't told him about her past and to forgive her for holding out on that important part of her life.

Forcing her thoughts aside, she carefully made her way out to the guesthouse, knowing Esther was usually up by now. She rapped on the door, and a few seconds later, Esther, bundled in her shawl and black outer bonnet, opened the door.

"I was just on my way up to the house to see you," Esther said. "I wanted to wish you a merry Christmas and let you know that I'm heading over to Samuel's to watch the children open their gifts."

"So you won't be joining us for breakfast?" Bonnie asked, feeling a bit disappointed. "I was hoping you could meet my dad."

"How about if I stop by this evening after I get back from Samuel's?"

"That's fine. Your place is with Samuel and his children this morning." She nodded toward the road, which hadn't been plowed. "I'm a little concerned about the weather and the road conditions, though. Do you think you can make it to Samuel's okay?"

Esther nodded. "Ginger's always been good in the snow, and it's much easier for our buggies to get around in this kind of weather than it is for a car. Since I'm leaving early, there shouldn't be many vehicles on the road yet."

"You're probably right." Bonnie hesitated a moment, wondering if she should tell Esther what had happened last night between her dad and Allen.

"You look as if you might be troubled about something," Esther said, as though reading Bonnie's mind. "Is everything all right?"

"I don't know."

Esther opened the door wider. "Come inside where it's warm, and tell me what's wrong."

"Are you sure you have the time? I don't want you to be late getting to Samuel's."

"It's okay. I'm sure they won't start opening presents until I get there."

"All right, thanks. I really do need to talk."

Esther removed her shawl and outer bonnet as she led the way to her small kitchen. "Let's take a seat at the table and have a cup of tea," she said, placing her garments over the back of a chair.

"I really don't need any tea, but if we could just spend a few minutes talking, it might help me sort out my feelings."

Bonnie told Esther all that had transpired between her dad and Allen, and how Allen had told Dad he had a headache and gone home without even saying good-bye.

"But I thought you were planning to tell Allen about your past," Esther said.

"I was, and I would have done it before I gave him an answer to his proposal, but I had no idea Dad would blurt it out like that before I had a chance to explain things to Allen." Tears welled in Bonnie's eyes. "I'm afraid the reason Allen left is because he's upset with me for not telling him the truth before this. He probably thinks I'm a terrible person for what I did when I was sixteen. I doubt that he'd want to marry me now."

"Even if Allen was upset about it, I'm sure that after you talk to him, he'll understand why it was hard for you to share this part of your past with him. You can explain things when he comes over for dinner this afternoon," Esther said, placing her hand gently on Bonnie's arm.

"*If* he comes for dinner." Bonnie fought back tears of frustration. "I'm afraid the special relationship Allen and I had might be spoiled now."

"I'm sure it's not, Bonnie, and I'm almost positive he'll come for dinner. Allen's too polite not to show up when he's been invited to someone's house for a meal. I'm equally sure he'll want to talk with you about all of this."

"I hope you're right, because we really do need to talk, although if he does come for dinner, we won't be able to say much in front of my dad or Mrs. Chandler."

"Mrs. Chandler?"

"My B&B guest."

"Oh, that must be the woman I met last night when I got back from Samuel's."

"You did?"

"Yes, and she asked if I was the owner of the bed-and-breakfast. When I told her I work for you part-time and that you were probably at home, she took off for the house before I could explain that you weren't open for business on Christmas. The poor woman looked pretty desperate."

"It's okay," Bonnie said. "After Mrs. Chandler explained her need for a room, I didn't have the heart to say no. There was no way I could have made her go back out in that blizzard last night."

Esther smiled. "I figured that might be the case." She got up and gave Bonnie a hug. "You're always so kind to others. No wonder you've become such a good friend."

Bonnie smiled. "You've been a good friend to me, as well."

"I do hope everything will work out for you and Allen."

"Me, too," Bonnie murmured. "I've waited a long time for love to come my way, and if things don't work out, I'll never allow myself to fall in love again."

—⁂—

"*Guder mariye. En hallicher Grischtdaag*," Timothy said, joining Hannah at the bedroom window, where she stared out at the snow.

"Good morning, and Merry Christmas to you, too," she said, in a less than enthusiastic tone.

Timothy's heart went out to her. This was the first Christmas she'd spent away from her parents, and he knew she was hurting. *I hope the gift I made for Hannah will make her feel a little happier.*

"I have something for you," he said, reaching under the bed and pulling out a cardboard box.

She tipped her head and stared at it curiously. "What's in there?"

"Open it and see."

Hannah set the box on the bed and opened the flaps. As she withdrew the bird feeder he'd made, tears welled in her eyes. "Oh Timothy, you made it to look like the covered bridge not far from our home in Pennsylvania."

"That's right. Do you like it, Hannah?" he asked.

"Jah, very much."

"I know how much you enjoy feeding the birds, so I decided to make you a different kind of feeder. See here," he said, lifting the roof on the bridge. "The food goes in there, and then it falls out the ends and underneath the bridge, where the birds sit and eat."

Hannah smiled. "Danki, Timothy. As soon as we find a house of our own, I'll put the feeder to good use."

"You don't have to wait till then," he said. "I can put the feeder up for you in Samuel's backyard. With all this snow, I'm sure the birds, and even the squirrels, will appreciate the unexpected treat."

She shook her head. "I don't want to put it here at Samuel's place."

"Why not?"

"I just don't, that's all." Hannah hurried across the room and opened the bottom dresser drawer. "I have a Christmas present for you, too," she said, handing him a box wrapped in white tissue paper.

Timothy took a seat on the bed and opened the gift. He was a little hurt that Hannah didn't want to use the bird feeder right away, but he hid his feelings, not wanting anything to ruin the day. Inside the package he found a pale blue shirt and a pair of black suspenders.

"Danki," he said. "These are both items I can surely use."

Excited voices coming from outside drew Timothy back over to the window. "Looks like Esther just arrived, so Samuel will soon present his kinner with the new pony he bought them for Christmas," he said. "Let's get Mindy up and go outside and join them."

"You go ahead," Hannah said. "Mindy needs her sleep. Besides, I don't want her getting all excited over the pony. She might think she should have one, too."

"In a few years, maybe we ought to get her one," Timothy said.

Hannah shook her head vigorously. "Ponies are a lot of work, and I don't want our daughter thinking she can take a pony cart out on the road. That would be too dangerous."

She frowned. "If you want my opinion, Samuel shouldn't be giving his kinner a pony, either. They're all too young and irresponsible."

"What Samuel does for his kinner is none of our business, and since Mindy's too young for a pony right now, there's no point in talking about this anymore." Timothy turned toward the bedroom door. "You can stay here if you want to, but I'm going outside to see the look of joy on my nieces' and nephews' faces when they see that new pony for the first time." Timothy hurried out the door.

Arguing with Hannah was not a good way to begin the day—especially when it was Christmas. But he wasn't going to let her ruin his good mood. Why couldn't things stay positive between them, the way they had been when he'd given her the bird feeder? Would they ever see eye to eye on anything that concerned raising Mindy? Was he foolish to hope that at least Christmas would be a tension-free day?

—◊◊◊—

Allen sat at his kitchen table drinking coffee and stewing over what Bonnie's dad had told him last night. Now he wasn't sure what to do. Should he go over to Bonnie's for dinner this afternoon or call her and say he'd decided to stay home? He could probably use the weather as an excuse. The roads had been terrible last night, and from the looks of the weather outside, they most likely weren't any better today. Besides, with it being Christmas, the state and county road workers were probably stretched pretty thin, with only a skeleton crew filling in on the holiday. But blaming the weather for his absence would be the coward's way out, and running from a problem wasn't how he handled things. Of course, he'd never asked a woman to marry him, only to find out from her father that she'd given birth to a baby and given it up for adoption. It might not have been such a shock if Bonnie had told him herself. But the fact that she'd kept it from him made Allen feel as if she didn't love or trust him enough to share her past. Was she afraid he would judge her? Did she think he would condemn her for something that had taken place when she was young and impressionable?

How do I really feel about the fact that the woman I love had a baby out of wedlock? Allen set his cup down and made little circles across his forehead with his fingers, hoping to stave off another headache. *Is that what really bothers me, or is it the fact that she didn't tell me about the baby? If we'd gotten married, would she ever have told me the truth? Do I really want to marry her now?* There were so many questions, yet no answers would come.

Allen sat for several minutes thinking, praying, and meditating on things. The words of Matthew 6:14 popped into his head: *"If ye forgive men their trespasses, your heavenly Father will also forgive you."*

He groaned. *I know I'm not perfect, and I've done things I shouldn't have in the past. It's not my place to judge Bonnie or anyone else. The least I can do is give her a call and talk about this—let her explain why she didn't tell me about the baby.*

Allen was about to reach for the phone, when the lights flickered and then went out. "Oh great, now the power's down. Someone must have hit a pole, or it's due to the weather. Guess I'll have to use my cell phone."

Allen went to the counter where he usually placed the cell phone to be charged and discovered that it wasn't there. "Now what'd I do with the stupid thing?" he mumbled.

He checked each room, looking in all the usual places. He also searched the jacket he'd worn last night, but there was no sign of his cell phone.

Maybe I left it at Bonnie's, he thought. *If I could use the phone and call her, I could find out. Guess I'd better drive over there now and hope she has power at her place, because if I stay here with no heat and no way to cook anything, I'll not only be cold, but hungry besides.*

Allen grabbed his jacket and headed out the door. When he stepped into his truck and tried to start it, he got no response. Either he'd left the lights on last night, or the cold weather had zapped the battery, because it was dead.

"This day just keeps getting better and better. That settles that," he muttered as he tromped through the snow and back to the house. "Looks like I'll be spending my Christmas alone in a cold, dark house and nothing will be resolved with Bonnie today."

CHAPTER 22

That's a mighty cute pony Samuel bought for the kinner, isn't it?" Fannie said as she, Hannah, and Esther worked in the kitchen to get dinner ready.

"Jah, it certainly is." Esther smiled. "And I think the name Shadow is perfect for the pony, because it sure likes to follow the kinner around."

"Looks like they all took to the pony rather quickly, too," Fannie added.

Hannah rolled her eyes. "If you ask me, Samuel's kinner are too young for a pony. They can barely take care of their dog."

"They're not too young," Fannie said with a shake of her head. "Marla and Leon are plenty old enough to take care of the pony."

"I agree with Fannie," Esther said, reaching for a bowl to put the potatoes in. "Having a pony to care for will teach the children responsibility."

Hannah made no comment. Obviously her opinion didn't matter to either of these women. She picked up a stack of plates and was about to take them to the dining room when

Esther said to Fannie, "When Suzanne and Titus were here last night, she mentioned that she's been feeling sick to her stomach for the last several weeks. I was wondering if she said anything to you about that."

"No, but it sounds like she might be expecting my next *kinskind*." Fannie grinned. "And if that's the case, I think it would be wunderbaar, because Abraham and I would surely welcome a new grandchild."

Hannah swallowed hard. She couldn't help but feel a bit envious—not only because she wanted to have another baby and hadn't been able to get pregnant again, but because she saw a closeness developing between Esther and Fannie.

It's not right that Fannie's nicer to Esther than she is to me. I'm her daughter-in-law, after all. Esther isn't even part of this family yet. Hannah wished, yet again, that her parents could have been here for Christmas. It would help so much if she and Mom could sit down and have a good long talk. Hannah's mother had always been there for her and would surely understand how she felt about things.

—⁂—

Trisha yawned, stretched, and pulled the covers aside. She couldn't remember when she'd slept so well. "Oh my, it's so late," she murmured after looking at her watch and realizing it was almost noon.

She sat up and swung her legs over the edge of the bed, just as her cell phone rang. "Hello," she said, suppressing a yawn.

"Trisha, this is Carla."

"It's good to hear from you! Merry Christmas."

"I wish it was a merry Christmas. Jason and I just received some bad news."

"I'm sorry to hear that. What's wrong?"

"Jason's mother was taken to the hospital this morning, so we'll be heading to Ohio right away."

"That's too bad. I hope it's nothing serious."

"They think she had a stroke."

"I'll be praying for her, and for you and Jason as you travel."

"Thanks, we appreciate that." There was a pause. "I'm sorry we won't be here to have Christmas dinner with you."

"That's okay. I understand. Now be safe, and I'll talk to you again soon."

When Trisha hung up, she hurried to take a shower and get dressed. She probably should have checked out by now and might even be holding things up for the owner of the bed-and-breakfast if she had Christmas plans, which she probably did. Most everyone had plans for Christmas—everyone but her, that is.

Maybe I should have stayed in Fresno instead of taking off on this trip, she thought. *At least there I could have spent Christmas with Margo and Shirley. Well, it's too late to cry about that now. I'm not in Fresno, and I need to get back on the road. With any luck, I may be able to find a restaurant in Hopkinsville that's open on Christmas Day. That is, if I can even find Hopkinsville.*

Trisha picked up her suitcase and went downstairs, where a tantalizing aroma drew her into the kitchen.

"I apologize for sleeping so late," she said to Bonnie, who stood in front of the oven, checking on a luscious-looking turkey. "I was snuggled down under that quilt, feeling so toasty and warm, and I didn't want to wake up."

Bonnie closed the oven door, turned to Trisha, and smiled. "That's okay. I'm glad you slept well. I figured you must be tired after your drive here last night. I know from experience that driving in such bad conditions can really exhaust a person, especially when they are unfamiliar with the roads." She motioned to a tray of cinnamon rolls on the counter. "Would you like a cup of coffee and some of those?"

Trisha's mouth watered. "That sounds so good. I'll just eat one and be on my way."

"Do you have any plans for today?" Bonnie asked.

"Not anymore." Trisha told Bonnie about the call she'd had from Carla. "So, if you'll be kind enough to tell me how to get to Hopkinsville, I'll see if any restaurants are open there. After I eat, I'll probably head on down the road."

"I doubt that any restaurants will be open today. And if you did find a restaurant, what fun would it be to eat alone?"

"It's never fun to eat alone," Trisha admitted, "but I've gotten used to it since my husband passed away."

"Why don't you stay here and join me and my dad for Christmas dinner?" Bonnie offered.

"It's kind of you to offer, but I wouldn't want to impose."

"It's not an imposition. There's plenty of food, and if you'd like to spend another night here, that's fine, too."

"Really? You wouldn't mind?"

"Not at all."

"Thanks, I think I'll take you up on that." Truth was, this charming B&B had captivated Trisha—not to mention that it would be much nicer to have a home-cooked meal in the company of Bonnie and her dad than to sit alone in some restaurant to eat.

Trisha glanced around the room. "Is there anything I can do to help you with dinner?"

"I appreciate the offer, but there's nothing that needs to be done until closer to dinnertime. So why don't you just relax for now?"

"Maybe I'll take my coffee and cinnamon roll upstairs. I really should call a few of my friends from California and wish them a merry Christmas."

—∽—

A few minutes after Trisha left the kitchen, Bonnie's dad came in.

"Did you meet my B&B guest out in the hall?" Bonnie asked. During breakfast she'd told him about Mrs. Chandler.

"Nope. I came from the living room, but I did hear footsteps on the stairs, so I guess that must have been her."

"I hope you don't mind, but I invited Mrs. Chandler to join us for dinner today. Oh, and she'll be staying one more night, too."

Dad smiled. "You're sure accommodating, Bonnie. Most people running a business that is supposed to be closed for the holiday wouldn't have welcomed a guest at the last minute the way you did."

"I couldn't very well send her out into the cold. Besides, the poor woman looked tired and lonely. And she's not from around here."

"How do you know?"

"When she was filling out the paperwork to check into the B&B last night she said she was from California."

"She's a long ways from home then."

"Yes, and she could have easily gotten lost in that blinding snow."

"Have you heard anything from Allen today?" Dad asked.

Bonnie shook her head. "I tried calling him at home awhile ago, but the phone just rang and rang."

"Maybe he's on his way here. Did you try his cell phone?"

"No, I didn't. Even if he was coming for dinner, I didn't think he would have left already, so I only called his home phone."

"Why don't you give his cell phone a try?" Dad suggested.

"Good idea." Bonnie picked up the phone and dialed Allen's cell number. She was surprised when she heard a phone ringing somewhere else in the house. It sounded like it was coming from the dining room.

"What in the world?" Moving quickly into the dining room, she discovered Allen's cell phone lying in the chair where he'd been sitting last evening.

"It must have fallen out of his pocket," Bonnie told Dad when he followed her into the dining room. "I guess now all we can do is wait and see if Allen shows up for dinner."

"I hope he does," Dad said with a nod. "I owe him an apology for what I blurted out last night, and I know you're anxious to talk to him, too."

"Yes, I am, although I'm feeling nervous about it." Hearing the wind howling outside, Bonnie glanced out the window and saw that it was snowing again. "I hope if Allen is on his way over that he'll be safe. Whatever roads have been plowed will probably drift shut again since the wind has picked up."

"Try not to worry; I'm sure he'll be fine," Dad said.

"You're right. Worry won't change a thing, so I'll pray and trust God to bring Allen here safely today."

"Good idea." Dad moved toward the living room. "If you don't need me for anything, I think I'll go relax in front of the fire for a while. Since I don't have a fireplace in my house, I'd forgotten how nice one can be."

Bonnie noticed a faraway look in his eyes. He'd obviously had some good memories from living in this place.

"I remember how my mom used to sit in front of the fireplace humming while she knitted," Dad continued. "I can still almost hear the click of her knitting needles, as though keeping time to her music."

"Yes, I recall her doing that when I came here to visit

sometimes." Bonnie patted Dad's arm. "You go ahead and relax. I'll call you when dinner's ready."

"Thanks, honey."

When Dad left the room, Bonnie said a prayer for Allen; then she picked up his cell phone and returned to the kitchen to check on the meal. By the time she had everything on the dining-room table, it was two o'clock, and still no Allen. She was sure he wasn't coming.

Bonnie was about to call Mrs. Chandler for dinner when the lights went out. Fortunately, she was done cooking, so at least they wouldn't have to worry about eating cold food.

While Dad added more wood to the fireplace, Bonnie lit some candles, grabbed a flashlight, and headed upstairs to the room she had rented to Mrs. Chandler.

She knocked on the door, and a few seconds later, Mrs. Chandler, looking half-asleep, answered. "Oh, I'm so sorry. After I made my phone calls, I laid down on the bed to rest and must have fallen asleep." She yawned and stretched her arms over her head. "I can't believe with all the sleep I had last night that I could still be so tired. I slept like a baby, though. It's so peaceful and quiet here, and as soon as I reclined on the bed and pulled that beautiful quilt over me, I was out like a light."

"That's okay. You must have needed the extra rest, and you know, I think there's something about being wrapped up in a quilt that makes a person feel safe and comforted."

"You're so right. I was asleep almost before my head hit the pillow. If you'll give me a minute to freshen up, I'll be right down."

Bonnie explained that the power was out and gave Mrs. Chandler the flashlight, because there were no windows in the hall. Then she carefully made her way down the stairs, where she opened all the curtains to let what little outside light there was into the house.

A short time later, Bonnie's guest came down and joined them in the dining room. Bonnie introduced Dad to Mrs. Chandler, and they all took their seats. Even though she'd opened the curtains, the room was quite dark, but the flickering candles helped. Bonnie thought the candlelight made it seem more relaxing and festive—sort of like back in the days of old.

After Bonnie prayed, giving thanks for the meal, she passed the food around.

Dad looked over at her and said, "It doesn't look like Allen's coming, does it?"

"No, I'm afraid not. Once the lights come back on, I'll try calling him again. He needs to know that his cell phone is here, because I'm sure he's going to need it when he goes to work tomorrow morning."

"You mean, *if* he goes to work," Dad said. "With the way the snow's been coming down, the roads might not be passable by morning."

The conversation changed as Bonnie asked Mrs. Chandler a few questions about herself, including her first name.

"Oh, it's Trisha. My husband and I used to live in Portland, Oregon, but we moved to Fresno, California, shortly after we got married."

"What was your maiden name?" Dad asked with a peculiar expression.

"It was Hammond."

Bonnie heard Dad's sharp intake of breath and wondered if he'd choked on something. Just then, the lights came back on, and Bonnie worried more, because Dad's face looked as white as Grandma's tablecloth.

"Dad, are you all right?"

He just sat staring at Trisha as if he'd seen a ghost.

Trisha studied him for several seconds, and then she gasped. "Kenny Taylor? Is that you?"

Dad nodded. "What are you doing here in Kentucky? Did you know I'd be here at my folks' old house?" His eyes narrowed and deep wrinkles formed across his forehead.

Trisha shook her head vigorously. "Of course not. I had no way of knowing you were here, or that this was where you used to live. How would I have known that?"

"You sent me a letter after I moved here, remember? Or did you forget about that?"

Trisha's brows furrowed as she slowly nodded. "I'd almost forgotten about that, and I sure didn't remember your address after all these years. When I pulled in here last night, I had no idea this used to be where you lived."

"So what are you saying—that it was just a twist of fate that brought you here?"

"Maybe; I don't know. The snow was really bad, and I had to get off the road. I didn't even know where I was. Thankfully, I saw the blinking lights on a horse-drawn buggy and followed it here." Trisha paused, and her voice lowered as she looked at him and said, "Maybe it was God, and not the weather, who led me here."

Dad grunted. "Yeah, right."

Bonnie, feeling as shocked as Dad obviously was, could almost feel the tension between him and Trisha. She wished there was something she could do. What a stressful Christmas this had turned out to be. It was bad enough that the man she loved was so upset with her that he didn't want to join them for Christmas dinner. Now, as fate would have it, Dad's old girlfriend had shown up out of the blue, and Dad's Christmas had been ruined, too. How much worse could it get?

CHAPTER 23

I'm sorry about what happened between me and your dad yesterday. I'm sure it ruined your Christmas," Trisha said the following morning when she entered the kitchen and found Bonnie sitting at the table reading her Bible.

Bonnie looked up and smiled. "It's not your fault. Dad should be the one apologizing—and mostly to you, because you had no way of knowing he was here."

Trisha sank into a chair with a sigh. "I'm glad you realize that, but even after all these years, I believe he's still angry with me for breaking up with him. I don't understand it, though. It's not like we were engaged to be married or anything. We were just teenagers back then and thought we were in love."

"I think the reason Dad was so upset is because when you broke up with him, he believed it was due to the fact that he was moving to Kentucky. So he was upset with his parents and blamed them for the breakup."

"But I sent him a letter telling him I'd fallen in love with Dave, and that was the only reason I broke up with him shortly before he moved. After reading my letter, Kenny should have realized that our breakup had nothing to do with him moving, and most of all, that it wasn't his parents' fault."

Bonnie shook her head. "Dad never got your letter."

"How do you know that?"

"Soon after I moved here, I found the letter stuck between some papers in an old pie cupboard in the basement. The letter was unopened," Bonnie explained. "Then later, when I went to Portland to take care of Dad after he'd been in a car accident, I showed him the letter."

"What'd he say about that?"

"He was stunned and said he'd never seen the letter before. After he read it, he regretted having blamed his parents for making him move to Kentucky and wished he could tell them how sorry he was. But since they'd both passed away, it was too late for that," Bonnie added.

"So Ken's more upset about how our breakup affected his relationship with his folks than he is with me for choosing Dave over him?"

"I think so. Although I know from the few things Dad's told me that he really did care about you. I believe it was a long time before he got over you breaking up with him." Bonnie motioned to her Bible. "Dad's a Christian now, and he needs to remember what God says about forgiveness."

"I'm a Christian, too," Trisha said. "I found the Lord soon after Dave and I moved to Fresno and started going to a neighborhood church."

"Since you and Dad are both Christians, you ought to be able to work this out." Bonnie rose from her seat and pointed out the window, where huge snowflakes swirled around the yard. "And from the looks of this weather that's set in, I'd say you're both going to be stuck here for a few more days, which should give you enough time to make peace with each other."

the STRUGGLE

—⁓—

Paradise, Pennsylvania

"How's Johnny doing?" Naomi asked when Sally entered her store shortly after it had opened.

"He's still in quite a bit of pain." Sally frowned. "He's also cranky and impatient."

"A back injury can cause a person to be out of sorts. I hope it didn't ruin your Christmas."

Sally shrugged and picked up a shopping basket. "Our sons and their families came over for a while on Christmas Day, so that helped, but I wish we could have gone to Kentucky like we'd planned."

"I talked to my daed earlier this morning, and he said they're having blizzard-like conditions in Christian County right now, so maybe it's a good thing you had to stay home."

"Is everyone okay there?" Sally questioned, feeling concern.

"Dad said everyone's fine, but if the weather doesn't improve, they may end up having to stay a few days longer than they'd planned. He also mentioned that many people have been without power in the area, which is affecting quite a few of their English neighbors."

"If there's no power, how'd Abraham manage to call you this morning?"

"The power was on in Samuel's phone shanty, but Dad said with the wind blowing like crazy, there was a good chance they might lose power there, too."

"I'd better do my shopping in a hurry so I can get home and call Samuel's number. I want to check on Hannah and be sure she and the others are okay." Sally started down the notions aisle and nearly bumped into Phoebe Stoltzfus. "What are you doing here?" she asked.

"I came in to get some sewing supplies for my mamm," Phoebe replied with a smile.

"Shouldn't you be at the bulk food store right now? You can't expect Anna to handle things by herself, you know." Sally hoped Phoebe wasn't the kind of person who shirked her duties.

"I don't expect that at all." Phoebe's face turned red. "Since the store doesn't open for another half hour, I figured I'd have time to make a quick stop here before going to work."

"Oh, I see." Sally didn't know why, but she didn't quite trust Phoebe. She remembered how a few years ago the rebellious young woman had been going out with Titus Fisher but broke things off and headed for California with a friend. If Phoebe hadn't done that, Titus would still be living in Pennsylvania because the only reason he'd moved to Kentucky was to start a new life and try to forget about Phoebe.

Maybe that's why I don't care much for Phoebe, Sally thought. *Her foolish actions set the wheels in motion for three of the Fisher men to move to Kentucky. If Phoebe had stayed put in Lancaster County, she'd probably be married to Titus by now, and none of the brothers would have moved away, so Hannah would still be here, too.*

Turning her attention back to the issue at hand, Sally said to Phoebe, "Well, just see that you're not late for work today. Johnny and I don't want any of our employees sloughing off on the job."

"No, I won't be late," Phoebe mumbled before hurrying down the aisle.

———

Pembroke, Kentucky

Hannah glanced out the living-room window at the swirling snow and frowned. She hated being cooped up in the house—especially with so many people. Why couldn't Fannie and Abraham have stayed with Titus and Suzanne the whole time? Having them here was just a reminder that her folks were at home and Dad was down with a sore back. With the exception of the bird feeder Timothy had given Hannah, it had not been a very good Christmas. And now this horrible weather only made her feel worse. She knew it had upset Timothy that the bird feeder he'd given her would remain in the box until they got a place of their own. But she didn't want the feeder put up in Samuel's yard, even if temporarily. Hannah wanted the feeder in her own yard, not someone else's.

Then, to give her one more thing to fret about, this morning after breakfast, Samuel and Timothy had taken off with Samuel's horse and buggy for Hopkinsville, because they hadn't been able to get ahold of Allen and were worried about him. Hannah had tried talking Timothy out of going, reminding him that the roads were bad and it was hard to see. But he'd been determined to go, and nothing she'd said made any difference. It seemed as though whatever Hannah wanted, Timothy was determined to do just the opposite. Or at least that's how it had been since they'd moved to Kentucky.

"I think I'll go out to the phone shanty and see if there are any messages from my mamm," Hannah said to Fannie, who sat in the rocking chair by the fire with Jared and Mindy in her lap.

"It's awfully cold out there," Fannie said. "Abraham said so when he went out to help Samuel clean the barn this morning."

"I'll be fine." Hannah stepped into the hall and removed her heavy woolen shawl from a wall peg. After wrapping it snugly around her shoulders, she put on her outer bonnet, slipped into a pair of boots, and went out the door.

The snow was deeper than she'd thought it would be, and

she winced when she took her first step and ended up with icy cold snow down her boots. By the time she reached the phone shanty, her teeth had begun to chatter, and goose bumps covered her arms and legs. To make matters worse, Hannah's feet were soaking wet and fast getting numb from the snow that kept falling inside her boots.

I should have thought to put on some gloves, she told herself as she stepped inside the shanty and turned on the battery-operated light sitting on the small wooden table beside the phone. She blew on her fingers to get the feeling back in them, took a seat in the folding chair, and wiggled her toes, hoping to get some warmth in her boots before punching the button to listen to their voice-mail messages. There was one from Mom, saying she'd heard about the bad weather they were having and asking if everyone was all right. Hannah picked up the phone and dialed her folks' number, but since no one was in the phone shack, she had to leave a message. "Hi, Mom, it's Hannah. I wanted to let you know that we're all fine here, but the weather's awful, and I really miss you. I wish we could have been in Pennsylvania for Christmas instead of here."

Hannah hung up the phone, and with a feeling of hopelessness, she trudged back to the house, trying not to get more snow in her already-soaked boots.

—◊◊—

Hopkinsville, Kentucky

Allen shivered as he pulled a blanket around his shoulders and made his way to the kitchen. He couldn't believe he'd been without power for twenty-four hours, and with no phone or battery for his truck, it looked like he would be stuck here until the power came on and he could call someone for help.

"Man, it's sure cold in here! Guess this is what I get for building my home where there are no neighbors close by," he grumbled. If he had, he could have asked one of them to give him a ride into town where he could buy a new battery for his truck.

"Let's see now, what do I want to eat?" he asked himself, peeking into the refrigerator, which had stayed plenty cold despite the loss of power. A peanut butter and jelly sandwich would be real good about now, but he knew there was no peanut butter. It was on his grocery list. There was no jelly either, but he did find a package of cheddar cheese, a bottle of orange juice, two sticks of butter, and a carton of eggs. He wasn't in the mood for raw eggs, so he took out the cheese and orange juice, got down a box of crackers from the cupboard, and took a seat at the table. "Dear Lord," he prayed, bowing his head, "bless this pitiful breakfast I'm about to eat, restore power to the area soon, and be with my family and friends everywhere. Amen."

Allen's thoughts went to Bonnie. Did she have power at her place? Was she doing okay? He wished he could just jump in the truck and head over there now—or at least call to check up on her. "I'm such a fool," he muttered. He regretted the way he'd left on Christmas Eve and knew he needed to apologize for not showing up yesterday, too, although that was completely out of his control. Things had sure changed from when he had fretted over not flubbing up his proposal to Bonnie. He wished now her answer was all he had to worry about. One thing for sure: he needed to talk to Bonnie soon.

Allen had just eaten his second cracker when a knock sounded on the front door. He jumped up and raced over to the door to see who it was. Timothy and Samuel stood on his porch dressed in heavy jackets and straw hats.

"We've been trying to call and became worried when we didn't get an answer," Samuel said, his brows furrowed. "When Esther mentioned that Bonnie said you never showed up for Christmas, we decided we'd better come and check on you."

"How'd you get here?" Allen asked, looking past their shoulders.

"Came with Samuel's horse and buggy." Timothy motioned to where they'd tied the horse to a tree near Allen's garage.

"Wow, it must have taken you awhile to get here," Allen said. "Especially in this horrible weather."

Samuel nodded. "Took us over an hour, but there weren't any cars on the road, so we moved along at a pretty good clip."

"I'm glad you're here," Allen said, "because the power's out, and to top it off, the battery in my truck is dead. Since yesterday morning, I've been stranded with no heat, and I can't find my cell phone, so I haven't been able to call anyone for help."

"You left your cell phone at Bonnie's on Christmas Eve," Samuel said. "She told Esther that, too."

"Oh, I see. I kind of figured that might be the case." Allen opened the door wider. "You two had better come inside. It's not much warmer in the house than it is outside, but at least it's not snowing in here," he added with a chuckle.

"Why don't you gather up some clothes and come home with us?" Samuel suggested after they'd entered the house.

"I appreciate the offer, but I wouldn't want to impose."

"It's not an imposition," Samuel said. "Besides, if you stay here and the power doesn't come on soon, you'll either freeze to death or die of hunger."

"You've got that right. Although, I guess I could have tromped through the snow and pulled my barbecue grill out of the garage." Allen's nose crinkled. "But I don't have much food in the house, and even if I did, I don't relish the thought of bein' out in the cold trying to cook it."

"I can't blame you there," Timothy said.

"Give me a minute to throw a few things together, and then we can head out." Allen started for his room but turned back around. "Say, I have an idea."

"What's that?" Samuel asked.

"Instead of taking me to your place, how about dropping me off at Bonnie's? That way I can get my cell phone, and if she's still speaking to me, maybe I can talk her into letting me have one of her rooms at the B&B for the night."

"Why wouldn't she be speaking to you?" Timothy questioned.

"It's a long story. I'll tell you both about it on the way."

Samuel nodded. "If it doesn't work out and you still need a place to stay, you're more than welcome to come home with us."

"Thanks. Depending on how things go with Bonnie, I may need to take you up on that offer."

CHAPTER 24

Pembroke, Kentucky

It looks like Bonnie must have a guest," Allen said when Samuel pulled his horse and buggy up to the hitching rail. A small blue car, mostly covered in snow, was parked near the garage.

"That's right, she does," Samuel said. "Esther mentioned that the woman is from California and she arrived here late on Christmas Eve."

"I thought the B&B was closed for the holidays," Allen said, climbing down from the buggy.

"It was, but Bonnie made an exception because the woman couldn't find her way to Hopkinsville in the snow and needed a place to stay."

Allen smiled. That sounded like Bonnie. She was a good person, and they really did need to talk.

"Maybe you'd better come inside where it's warmer and wait until I see if Bonnie will rent me a room," Allen said, looking first at Timothy and then Samuel.

"Sure, we can do that," Samuel said, "but I doubt that

Bonnie would turn you out in the cold."

Allen wasn't so sure about that. He'd walked out Christmas Eve without a word of explanation or even telling her good-bye. No doubt, Bonnie's dad had told her about the conversation they'd had regarding Bonnie's past, so by him not showing up for dinner yesterday, she probably thought he was angry with her.

Well, I was at first, he admitted to himself as he tromped through the drifts of snow in the yard. *I was angry and hurt, but I'm going to fix things now if I can.*

After the three men stepped onto the porch, Samuel knocked on the door. A few seconds later, Bonnie opened it, and she looked at them in disbelief. Then her gaze went to the yard, where the horse and buggy stood. "I'm surprised to see you out in this horrible weather." She glanced over at Allen. "Did you come here in Samuel's buggy?"

He nodded.

"Where's your truck?"

"At home with a dead battery. I've been stranded there since Christmas morning, with no electricity, no vehicle, and no cell phone."

"Your cell phone is here. We found it on the chair you sat in on Christmas Eve." Bonnie opened the door farther and moved aside. "Come in, everyone, where it's warmer."

As they stepped into the entryway, Allen caught a glimpse of a middle-aged woman sitting in front of the fireplace in the living room to his right. He figured she must be Bonnie's unexpected guest.

"Let's go into the kitchen," Bonnie suggested. "I'll pour you some coffee, and how about a piece of pumpkin pie or some chocolate cheesecake to go with it?"

Allen's mouth watered. "Mmm. . .that sounds really good."

"Same here," Samuel and Timothy said in unison.

"Which one do you want—the cheesecake or the pie?" Bonnie asked.

"Both," Allen replied with a grin. "I've had very little to eat in the last twenty-four hours, and I'm just about starved to death."

"No problem. I have pie and plenty of leftovers from yesterday's Christmas dinner."

Allen grimaced. If he'd been there yesterday to eat with them, there wouldn't be so many leftovers, and he wouldn't feel as though he was close to starvation right now.

"Is your dad still here?" Samuel asked as he removed his jacket and took a seat at the table, along with the others. "I was hoping I'd get the opportunity to meet him."

"Yes, he's in his room right now, but I'll call him down before you leave." Bonnie poured them all coffee, and then she took a delicious-looking pumpkin pie from the refrigerator, cut three slices, and gave them each a piece. Following that, she placed a dish of chocolate cheesecake on the table and said they could help themselves.

"Dad was planning to leave today, but with the weather turning bad, he called the airlines and canceled his flight," Bonnie said. "He doesn't want to go until the weather improves, because he's concerned about me driving him to the airport on snowy roads."

"My truck has four-wheel drive, so I'd be happy to take him," Allen offered as he helped himself to a generous slice of pumpkin pie. "As soon as I get a battery for it, that is."

"I appreciate the offer, but I'm sure I can manage to get him there." Bonnie smiled, but it appeared to be forced.

She is upset with me, and I need to talk to her about my actions on Christmas Eve, but I can't very well say anything with Timothy and Samuel sitting here. Allen blew on his coffee and took a drink. "Uh...the reason we came over is, I was wondering if I could rent a room from you for the night."

She shook her head.

"You won't rent me a room?" He couldn't believe she would turn him out in the cold.

"No, but I will let you stay in a room free of charge." Her smile softened, reaching all the way to her eyes this time.

Allen relaxed and released a deep breath. "Thanks. I appreciate that very much."

They sat quietly for a while as the men drank their coffee and ate the pie. Then, when they were just finishing up, Bonnie excused herself and left the room. When she returned several minutes later, she had Allen's cell phone, and her father was with her.

"Dad, I'd like you to meet Samuel Fisher," she said, motioning to Samuel. "And this is his brother Timothy."

"It's nice to meet you both," Ken said, shaking their hands. "You did some real nice work on this old house," he added, looking at Samuel.

Samuel motioned to Allen. "I can't take all the credit. My good friend here did some of the work."

Ken looked at Allen and smiled. "It's good to see you again. We missed you on Christmas Day."

Allen explained his situation and why he was here right now. What he didn't admit was that even if he hadn't been stranded, he might not have come for Christmas dinner. He'd really needed the time alone to spend in thought and prayer. So at least something good had come from him being alone on Christmas Day, sad as it was.

"I'm sorry you were stranded but glad you're here now," Ken said, clasping Allen's shoulder. "I think you and my daughter need to talk."

Before Allen could respond, Samuel pushed his chair aside and stood. "Since Allen has a place to spend the night, I guess Timothy and I will be on our way. We've been gone quite awhile, and we don't want Esther, Hannah, or our mom to start worrying about us."

"Knowing Hannah, she's probably been worried since the moment we left," Timothy said.

"I'll walk you to the door," Ken offered.

Timothy and Samuel said their good-byes and started out of the kitchen.

"We'll be back to check on you tomorrow, Allen," Samuel called over his shoulder.

"Okay, thanks."

"Would you like another cup of coffee?" Bonnie asked Allen as the other men left.

He nodded. "That'd be nice. I hadn't had anything hot to drink since I lost power at my place."

"Oh, and would you like something more than just the pie to eat? I can fix you some eggs and toast."

"That does sound good, but if you don't mind, I'd like to talk to you first." He glanced toward the door to see if Ken might come back to the kitchen and was relieved when he heard footsteps clomping up the stairs.

"What did you want to talk about?" Bonnie asked, taking a seat across from him.

Allen cleared his throat a few times. "First, I need to apologize for rushing out of here on Christmas Eve without saying good-bye."

Bonnie sat staring at him.

"And second, I want you to know the reason I left."

"I think I already know," she said. "Dad told you about the baby I had when I was a teenager, and you were upset by it, so you went home."Tears welled in her eyes. "You probably think I'm a terrible person now, don't you?"

He shook his head. "We all make mistakes, Bonnie. You were just a confused teenager with no mother to guide you and a father who was struggling to raise you on his own."

She nodded slowly. "But that's still no excuse for what I did. I'd been brought up with good morals, and—" She stopped talking and reached for a napkin to wipe the tears that had dribbled onto her cheeks.

"Beating yourself up about the past won't change anything," Allen said. "And just so you know—the fact that you had a baby out of wedlock wasn't really why I left."

"It. . .it wasn't?"

"No. The main reason I left was because I couldn't deal with you having kept it from me—especially when I'd thought we'd been drawing so close."

"I was planning to tell you, Allen. I just couldn't seem to find the nerve or the right time to say it."

"How come? Did you think I wouldn't want to marry you if I knew about your past?"

"That's exactly what I thought." Bonnie blew her nose on the napkin. "I was afraid you might not want me if you knew what I'd done."

Allen left his chair and skirted around the table. Gently pulling Bonnie to her feet, he whispered, "I love you, Bonnie Taylor, and if you'll have me, I want to be your husband."

"Oh yes, Allen. I'd be honored to marry you," she said tearfully.

A wide smile spread across his face. "I was hoping you'd say that, and I'm also hoping you'll accept this." Allen reached into his jacket pocket and pulled out a small velvet box. When he opened it, Bonnie saw the beautiful diamond ring inside and gasped.

"Oh Allen, it's perfect!"

He removed it from the box and slipped it on her finger then pulled her into his arms.

They stood together for several minutes, holding each other and whispering words of endearment. Then, when Allen's stomach gurgled noisily, Bonnie laughed and pulled away. "I think I'd better give you something more to eat before you starve to death."

Allen chuckled and patted his stomach. "That might be a good idea, because I feel kind of faint. Of course," he quickly added, "it probably has more to do with the excitement I feel about you accepting my proposal than it does with my need for food. It isn't exactly how I wanted to propose; I had this big long speech I'd practiced for days that I was gonna give on Christmas Eve."

She gave him a quick kiss on the cheek. "Your proposal was perfect—simple and sweet. Now, take a seat and relax while I get some bacon and eggs cooking, and then I'll tell you about the woman who showed up here after you left on Christmas Eve."

—⁂—

"The one good thing about being snowed in like this is that it's given us more time to spend with the *kinskinner*," Abraham said to Fannie as they stood in front of the window in Samuel's guest room, looking out at Marla and Leon, who were in the yard tossing snowballs at each other and giggling.

"You're right about that," she said with a nod. "And even though I miss our grandchildren at home, I've enjoyed being here with Samuel's four kinner and Timothy's little Mindy." She sighed deeply. "It's just too bad they have to live so far away, which means we can't see them very often."

Abraham grunted. "Now, don't waste time on trivial matters."

"It's not a trivial matter to me. I miss my boys and their families."

"I understand that, because so do I, but it won't do any good for you to start feeling sorry for yourself. We'll come here to visit whenever we can, and I'm sure that our boys will bring their families to Pennsylvania as often as they can, too."

"Humph!" Fannie frowned. "I doubt that'll happen too often. With Suzanne most likely expecting a *boppli*, she and Titus will probably stick close to home. And as busy as Samuel seems to be, I'll bet we won't see him before he and Esther are married—whenever that's going to be." She folded her arms. "Then there's Timothy, who might never come back to Pennsylvania to see us."

"What makes you say that?"

"Think about it, Abraham. He moved here to get his wife away from her interfering mamm. If he takes his family home for a visit, Hannah will want to stay, and then Timothy will have an even bigger problem on his hands."

Abraham quirked an eyebrow. "Bigger problem?"

She nudged his arm. "He already has a problem with a wife who does nothing but complain and doesn't want to be here. To tell you the truth, I don't think she wants us here either."

"Now, Fannie, you shouldn't be saying things like that."

"Why not? It's the truth. Hannah's just not accepting of me the way our other daughters-in-law are. She rarely makes conversation, and when she does say something to me, it's usually a negative comment or she's expressing her displeasure with something I've done."

"Now what could you possibly have done to upset Hannah?" he asked.

"For one thing, just a little while ago she became upset

when I was about to give Mindy some Christmas candy." Fannie sighed deeply. "It's not like I was going to give her the whole box or anything; it was just one piece."

"Well, Hannah is the child's Mudder, and it's her right to decide when and if Mindy should have candy."

"But it's not fair that Mindy's cousins got to have a piece of candy and she didn't." Fannie moved away from the window. "I wish Timothy had never married Hannah. She's selfish, envious, and too overprotective where Mindy's concerned. She even wanted me to convince Timothy to move back to Pennsylvania."

Abraham's brows shot up. "Really? What'd you say?"

"Told her I couldn't—that Timothy wouldn't appreciate it." Fannie sighed. "You know, Abraham, Timothy and Hannah's marriage is already strained, and it makes me wonder if things will get worse in the days ahead." She clasped Abraham's arm. "I just have this strange feeling about Timothy and Hannah. Of all our Kinner, he's the one I'm the most worried about. Timothy and Hannah certainly need a lot of prayer."

CHAPTER 25

For the next several days, the bad weather prevailed. But by Monday, the snow had finally stopped and the roads were clear enough to drive on, so Abraham, Fannie, and their driver left for home. Hannah felt relieved, because Fannie was beginning to get on her nerves. Not only that, but Samuel's kids had been noisier than usual with their grandparents here, always vying for their attention and begging Abraham for candy, gum, and horsey rides. Mindy had also been whiny and often begged for candy and other things Hannah didn't want her to have. If that wasn't bad enough, it had sickened Hannah to see the way Esther acted around Fannie—so sweet and catering to her every whim. Was she trying to make an impression, or did she really enjoy visiting with Fannie that much?

Maybe it's because Esther's folks live in Pennsylvania, Hannah thought as she stared out the living-room window. *Is it possible that Esther misses her Mamm as much as I do mine?*

"As much as I hate to say this," Timothy said, slipping his arm around Hannah's waist, "Samuel and I have a paint job in Oak Grove this morning, and our driver just pulled in, so I need to get going."

Hannah squinted at the black van. "That doesn't look like Allen's rig."

"You're right; it's not. We won't be working for Allen today. This house is one Samuel lined up on his own, so he called Bob Hastings for a ride because his vehicle is big enough to haul all our painting equipment."

"Oh, I see." Hannah turned to look at Timothy. "Do you have any idea how long you'll be working today?"

He shrugged. "It'll probably be seven or eight before we get back home. Since we've been hired to paint the whole interior of the house and the owners would like it done by the end of the week, we'll need to put in a long day."

Hannah sighed. "It's my turn to cook supper this evening, so would you like me to fix it a little later than usual?"

He shook his head. "You and the kids should go ahead and eat. Maybe you can keep something warm in the oven for Samuel and me, though."

"Sure, I can do that."

When Timothy went out the door, Hannah headed for the kitchen, where Esther was doing the breakfast dishes.

"Would you like me to dry?" Hannah asked.

Esther turned from the sink and smiled. "That'd be nice."

Hannah grabbed a clean dish towel and picked up one of the plates in the dish drainer. "It seems quiet in here with Fannie and Abraham gone, Samuel and Timothy off to work, and Samuel's two oldest kinner at school," she said.

"Jah, but I kind of miss all the excitement."

Hannah couldn't imagine that. She preferred peace and quiet over noise and chaos. She was actually glad Christmas was over.

They worked quietly for a while; then Hannah broke the

silence with a question that had been on her mind. "Do you miss not living close to your mamm?"

"Of course I do." Esther placed another clean plate in the drainer. "But I know Mom and Dad are needed in Pennsylvania so they can help my brother and his family. I also know that my place is here."

"How can you be sure of that?"

"Because this is where Samuel lives, and I love him very much."

"So love is what's keeping you here?"

"Jah. That, and the fact that this is my home. I mean, I like it here in Kentucky, but if Samuel wanted to move back to Pennsylvania after we got married, I'd be willing to move there, too."

"So I guess that means I should have been willing to move here because it's what Timothy wanted?" Hannah couldn't keep the sarcasm out of her voice.

"A wife's place is with her husband," Esther said. "It's as simple as that."

Hannah cringed. Maybe a wife's place was with her husband, but wasn't the husband supposed to care about his wife's needs and wishes, too?

—⁓—

"Are you sure you don't mind taking me to the airport this afternoon? I feel bad asking you to drive after the snowy weather we've had these last few days," Bonnie's dad said as the two of them sat in the living room enjoying the warmth of the fireplace.

"Of course I don't mind, and since the roads are pretty well cleared, I'm sure we'll be fine."

"Excuse me," Trisha said, entering the room with her

suitcase in hand. "I wanted to let you know that I'm ready to head out, so if you'll print out my bill, I'll settle up with you now."

"Where will you be going from here?" Bonnie asked, leading the way to her desk in the foyer.

"Since my friend and her husband from Bowling Green are still away, I won't be stopping there. So I'll probably head for Virginia and check out some of the sights that I've read about."

"This sure isn't a good time of year to be traveling anywhere by car," Dad called from the other room. "Maybe you should head back to California."

Trisha looked at Bonnie and rolled her eyes. "He always did like to tell me what to do," she whispered.

Bonnie smiled. That didn't surprise her one bit, because Dad was a take-charge kind of guy.

Once Trisha's bill had been taken care of, she stepped into the living room and said good-bye to Dad.

"Have a safe trip," he mumbled.

Trisha hesitated a minute. Then she moved closer to him and said, "It was nice seeing you again, Kenny, and I'm truly sorry for whatever hurt I may have caused you in the past."

"It's Ken, not Kenny," Dad mumbled.

Trisha stood a few seconds, as if waiting for some other response, but when Dad said nothing more, she picked up her suitcase and opened the front door.

"It's been nice meeting you. Feel free to stop by if you're ever in this area again," Bonnie said, stepping onto the porch with Trisha.

Trisha turned and smiled. "I appreciate the offer, but if I do come back this way, I'll be sure and call first. I wouldn't want to be here if your dad's visiting, because it's obvious that

I make him feel uncomfortable."

"Well, he needs to get over it and leave the past in the past—forgive and forget. Life's too short to carry grudges, and I plan to talk to him more about that. You just call, no matter what, if you should ever come by this way again."

Trisha gave Bonnie a quick hug then started down the stairs. She was almost to the bottom when her foot slipped on a still-frozen step and down she went.

"What did I go and do now?" Trisha wailed. She tried to get up but was unsuccessful. "Oh, my ankle. . . . It hurts so much!"

Bonnie, being careful not to slip herself, made her way down the porch stairs and knelt beside Trisha. After a quick look at Trisha's already swollen ankle, she determined that it could very well be broken. "Stay right where you are," Bonnie said when Trisha once more tried to stand. "I'll get Dad's help, and we'll carry you into the house."

CHAPTER 26

I can't begin to tell you how much I appreciate you letting me stay here while my ankle heals," Trisha said to Bonnie as she hobbled into the kitchen with the aid of her crutches.

"It's not a problem," Bonnie said. "Since you broke it after falling on my slippery steps, the least I can do is offer you a room free of charge." She motioned to the table. "Now if you'll take a seat, I'll fix you some breakfast."

Trisha still felt bad about imposing on Bonnie like this, but she really did appreciate all she had done for her since she'd fallen two days ago. Bonnie had even gone so far as to call her fiancé, Allen, and ask that he take her dad to the airport so she'd be free to take Trisha to the hospital to have her ankle x-rayed. And when they'd learned that it was broken, Bonnie had stayed with Trisha at the hospital and brought her back here to care for her. It was definitely more than she had expected.

Being with Bonnie was a taste of what it might have been like if Trisha had been able to have children. She'd always longed to be a mother and had wanted to adopt, but Dave wouldn't even discuss that option. He'd said on more than one occasion that if they couldn't have children of their own, then he didn't want any at all. Trisha thought it was selfish of him to feel that way—especially when there were children out there who needed a home. But out of respect for her husband, she'd never pushed the issue. Besides, she'd always felt that a child needed love from both parents.

"Would you like a bowl of oatmeal and some toast this morning?" Bonnie asked, breaking into Trisha's thoughts.

"Yes, thank you; that would be fine." Trisha seated herself at the table and watched helplessly as Bonnie made her breakfast. "I feel like I ought to be doing something to earn my keep," she said.

Bonnie shook her head. "It's no bother, really. I have to fix breakfast for myself, anyway."

"But you've done so much for me already—even giving up your room downstairs and moving into one of your upstairs guest rooms.

"I'm happy to do that. After all, you can't be expected to navigate the stairs with your leg in a cast and having to use crutches."

"I'm just not used to being waited on or pampered," Trisha said. "I've always been pretty independent, and after Dave died, I really had to learn how to fend for myself."

"I understand. Dad was the same way after Mom passed away from a brain tumor."

"How old were you when she died?"

"Thirteen."

"That must have been hard for both you and your dad."

"It was." Bonnie went to the cupboard and took out a box of brown sugar, which she placed on the table. "Mom was a very good cook, and she didn't like anyone in her kitchen, so I never learned to cook well. After she died, Dad and I just kind of muddled by."

"But you obviously learned how to cook somewhere along the line, because that Christmas dinner you fixed was delicious."

Bonnie smiled. "I had a good teacher."

"Who was that?"

"Esther Beiler. When I moved into Grandma and Grandpa's house and decided to open the B&B, Esther came to work for me. At first she did most of the cooking, but then she took the time to teach me." Bonnie moved back to the stove to check on the oatmeal. "Of course, I'll probably never be as good a cook as Esther, because she just has a talent for it."

"Guess everyone has something they're really good at," Trisha said, reaching for two napkins from the basket on the table. She folded them and set them out for the meal.

"That's true. Where do you feel your talents lie?" Bonnie questioned.

"I don't know if I'm as good a cook as Esther, but I used to be the head chef for a restaurant in Fresno, and the customers often raved about some of the dishes I created. So I guess if I have a talent, it's cooking."

"Oh my!" Bonnie's cheeks turned pink. "I had no idea there was a chef who could no doubt cook circles around me sitting at my table on Christmas Day. If I'd known that, I probably would have been a complete wreck."

Trisha laughed. "I've never considered myself anything more than someone who likes to cook, so you really don't need to worry about whether anything you fix measures up."

"That's good to know, because the oatmeal's a little too dry. I probably didn't put enough water in the kettle."

Trisha waved her hand. "Don't worry about that. It's funny, but whenever someone else does the cooking, no matter what it is, the food always tastes so much better. I used to tell my husband that his toast was the best-tasting toast I'd ever eaten. Anyway, a pat of butter and some milk poured over the top, and I'm sure the oatmeal will be plenty moist."

"I know exactly what you mean about someone else's cooking. It's kind of like eating outdoors. When does the food taste any better than that?" Bonnie set two bowls on the table and took a seat. "No wonder my dad fell so hard for you when you were teenagers. You're a very nice woman, Trisha Chandler."

Trisha smiled. "Thanks. I think you're pretty nice, too."

—⁂—

When breakfast was over and Trisha was resting comfortably on the living-room sofa, Bonnie did the dishes. She'd just finished and was about to mop the kitchen floor when Esther showed up.

"I'm surprised to see you," Bonnie said. "I figured you'd be over at Samuel's by now."

"I told Hannah last night that I'd be coming over late because I had some errands to run," Esther said. "To tell you the truth, I think she was glad."

"Are things still strained between you two?"

"A bit, although I believe they are somewhat better. We've been talking more lately, and I think that's helped."

Bonnie smiled. "I'm glad. You should bring Hannah and the little ones over to see me again. Maybe Suzanne would like to come, too."

"That sounds like fun. And speaking of Suzanne, I found out yesterday that she and Titus are expecting a baby. She's due sometime in August."

Bonnie squealed. "Now that is good news! I'm sure everyone in Suzanne's family must be very excited."

"They are, and so are Titus's parents. We suspected it when they were here for Christmas, and when Titus called his folks and told them the official news, they were delighted."

"I'm sorry I didn't get to see Abraham and Fannie while they were here this time," Bonnie said. "I enjoyed meeting them when they came for Titus and Suzanne's wedding. They seem like a very nice couple."

"They are, and I look forward to having them as in-laws."

"How soon will that be?" Bonnie asked, taking a seat at the table and motioning for Esther to do the same.

Esther lowered herself into a chair. "I don't know. Samuel would get married tomorrow if it was possible, but I really think we should wait until Hannah and Timothy have found a place of their own."

"I understand, but what if it's a long time before they find a place? Will you change your mind and marry Samuel anyway?"

Esther shrugged. "I don't know. Guess I'll have to wait and see how it all goes." She reached over and touched Bonnie's arm. "Speaking of weddings, have you and Allen set a date for your wedding yet?"

"Not a definite one, but we're hoping sometime in the spring."

"I've never been to an English wedding before, so I hope I'll get an invitation."

"Would you be allowed to go? I mean, it's not against your church rules or anything, is it?"

Esther emitted a small laugh. "No, it's not."

"Then you'll definitely get an invitation. In fact, I'm sure Allen will want to invite all our Amish friends."

"Will Allen sell his house and move here to the bed-and-breakfast, or will you sell this place and move into his house with him?"

"We haven't actually discussed that. And you know, until

this minute, I hadn't even given it a thought." Bonnie's forehead wrinkled as she mulled things over. "I sure would hate to give up this place, and I do hope Allen doesn't ask me to."

"I don't think he will. He knows how much you enjoy running the B&B."

"That may be so, but some men expect their wives to do things they don't really want to do. Take Hannah, for instance. She didn't want to move to Kentucky, but Timothy insisted."

"And with good reason," Esther said. "He had to get Hannah away from her mother in order to make her see that her first priority was to him."

Bonnie's lips compressed. "Hmm. . . I wonder if Allen will make me choose between him and the bed-and-breakfast."

—⁓—

Hannah had just sent Marla and Leon off to school when she looked out the kitchen window and spotted Suzanne's horse and buggy pull into the yard. A few minutes later, there was a knock on the door.

"Brr. . . It's cold out there," Suzanne said after Hannah opened the door and let her in.

"Do you think it's going to snow again?" Hannah asked.

"I don't believe so. The sky's clear with no clouds in sight, so that's a good thing."

"After that blizzard we had, I don't care if I ever see another snowflake," Hannah said.

Suzanne laughed. "I'm with you, but I think the kinner might not agree."

"So what brings you by here this morning?"

"I need to go to the store to pick up a few things, and since Samuel's place is right on the way, I decided to stop by and see how you're doing."

Hannah could hardly believe Suzanne would ask how she was doing. No one else seemed to care—least of all Timothy. "I'm okay," she murmured. "How about you? I heard you've been having some morning sickness."

"That's true, and I felt nauseous when I first got up today, but after I ate something and had a cup of mint tea, it got better." Suzanne removed her shawl and black outer bonnet then placed them on an empty chair before taking a seat.

"Would you like something to drink?" Hannah asked. "There's some coffee on the stove, or I could brew a pot of tea."

"No thanks. I'm fine."

Hannah was tempted to start washing the dishes but figured that could wait. The idea of visiting with Suzanne a few minutes seemed appealing, so she also took a seat. "I remember when I was expecting Mindy, for the first three months I felt nauseous most of the day. After a while, it got better though."

"Speaking of Mindy, where is she right now? She's so sweet. I was hoping I'd get to see her today."

"She's still sleeping, and so are Jared and Penny."

"Now, that's a surprise. I figured they'd all be up, running all over the house by now."

Hannah frowned. "Those kids of Samuel's are just too active."

"They do have a lot of energy," Suzanne agreed. "But then I guess most kinner do." She placed her hand against her stomach. "I know I have seven more months until the boppli is born, but Titus and I can hardly wait for our little one to get here."

"Are you hoping for a *bu* or a *maedel*?"

"I think Titus would like a boy, but I don't really care what we have; I just want the baby to be healthy."

Hannah cringed, remembering the miscarriage she'd had last year. *I wish the baby we lost would have gone to full-term and been healthy. I wish I was pregnant right now.*

CHAPTER 27

"Get your coat; there's something I want to show you," Timothy said to Hannah one Saturday morning toward the end of January, when he entered the kitchen and found her doing the dishes.

"What is it?" she asked, turning to look at him.

"It's a house I want you to look at."

"Is it for sale?"

He nodded. "Samuel and I spotted the FOR SALE sign yesterday on our way home from work."

"How come you didn't mention it last night?"

"Because I knew we couldn't look at it until this morning, and I didn't want you bombarding me with a bunch of questions I couldn't answer till I knew more about the house."

She flicked some water at him. "I wouldn't have bombarded you with questions."

"Jah, you would." He dipped his fingers into the soapy water and flicked some water back in her direction, enjoying the playful moment—especially since things were so up and down between him and Hannah.

She moved quickly aside. "Hey! Stop that!"

He chuckled. "I figured if you wanted me to have a second shower of the day, then you'd probably want one, too."

"I don't think either of us needs another shower, but I do want to see that house. So let me finish up here, and we can be on our way." She paused, and tiny wrinkles formed across her forehead. "Will Samuel be able to watch Mindy, or do we need to take her along?"

"I've already talked to him about it, and he said he's fine with watching her, since he'll be here with his kinner anyway."

"Okay, great. I'll just be a few more minutes."

Timothy leaned over and kissed Hannah's cheek. She'd been so sullen since their move. It was good to see her get excited about something. He just hoped she wouldn't lose her enthusiasm once she saw the house he was interested in buying.

—⁓—

Bonnie had just finished feeding the chickens when she spotted Allen's truck coming up the driveway. She'd spoken to him on the phone several times but hadn't seen him for a while because he'd been so busy with work and bidding new jobs. It was amazing that he'd have so much work to do at this time of the year, but she was glad for him, as she knew many others were out of work.

"It's good to see you," she said when he stepped out of the truck and joined her near the chicken coop.

He leaned down and gave her a kiss. "It's good to see you, too. Are you busy right now? I'd like to talk to you about something."

"I've got the time, but let's go inside where it's warmer."

He smiled and took her hand. "That sounds like a plan, but I'd like to talk to you in private, and I know Trisha's still with you right now, so I thought maybe we could go for a ride."

"Trisha came down with a cold and is in her room resting."

"Sorry to hear she's not feeling well." Allen flashed Bonnie a look of concern. "I hope you don't get sick, too. You've been doing extra duty taking care of her since she broke her ankle, so your resistance might be low right now."

"I'm fine," she said as they strode hand in hand toward the house. "I take vitamins, eat healthy foods, and try to get at least eight hours of sleep every night."

He squeezed her fingers gently. "That's good to hear."

When they entered the house, the smell of something burning greeted them.

"Oh, no. . .my cookies!" Bonnie raced into the kitchen and opened the oven door. The entire batch of oatmeal cookies looked like lumps of charcoal. "That's what I get for thinking I could multitask," she muttered. "I figured I'd be finished feeding the chickens in plenty of time before the cookies were done."

Allen stepped up behind Bonnie and put his arms around her waist. "It's my fault for keeping you out there so long."

"It's okay. I have more cookie dough in the refrigerator, but I'll wait until after our talk before I make any more." Bonnie turned off the oven and took the burned cookies out. "I think I'll set these on the back porch so they don't smell up the house more than they already have. I can crumble them up later for the birds. I'm sure they'll eat them."

"Here, let me do that." Allen picked up another pot holder, took the cookie sheet from her, and went out the back door. When he returned, Bonnie had a cup of coffee waiting for him, and they both took seats at the table.

"So what'd you want to talk to me about?" she asked.

He reached for her hand. "Now that we're officially engaged,

I think it's time we decide on a wedding date, don't you?"

She smiled. "Yes, I do."

"So how about Valentine's Day?"

Her eyebrows shot up. "Oh Allen, I could never prepare for a wedding that soon. Valentine's Day is just a couple of weeks away."

His shoulders drooped. "I figured you'd say that, but I'm anxious to marry you, and you can't blame a guy for trying."

She giggled. "I'd really like to have a church wedding and invite all our friends—Amish and English alike. Of course, my dad and your folks will also be invited, and we'll need to give them enough time to plan for the trip."

"That's true. So how long do you think it'll take for us to plan this wedding?"

"How about if we get married in the middle of May? The weather should be pretty nice by then, and we could have the reception here—maybe outside in the yard."

"That would mean a lot of work for you, making sure everything looks just the way you want it."

"I'm sure some of our Amish friends will help me spruce up the yard, and I'll ask Esther to make the cake and help with all the other food we decide to have."

He leaned closer and kissed the end of her nose. "Sounds like you've got it all figured out."

"Not really, but I'm sure it'll all come together as the planning begins." She paused and moistened her lips, searching for the right words to ask him a question. "There's something else we haven't talked about, Allen."

"What's that?"

"Where we're going to live once we're married."

"Oh, that." He raked his fingers through the ends of his thick, dark hair. "I'm guessing you don't want to give up the B&B?"

She shook her head. "This place has come to mean a lot to me. But I suppose if you don't want to live here—"

He put his finger against her lips. "I have no objections to living in this wonderful old house with you. After all, I did have a little something to do with making it as nice as it is." He winked at her.

"Yes, you sure did." Bonnie tapped her fingers along the edge of the table. "But what about your house? I know you built it to your own specifications, and—"

"It's just a house, Bonnie. I can be happy living anywhere as long as I'm with you."

She gently stroked his cheek, not even caring that it felt a bit stubbly. "I'm a lucky woman to be engaged to such a wonderful man."

"No, I'm the lucky one," he said before giving her a heart-melting kiss.

—❧—

"How far away is this place?" Hannah asked when she stepped outside and found Timothy standing beside their horse and buggy. "I figured we'd have to hire a driver to take us there."

"Nope. It's just a few miles from here."

"That's good to hear." Hannah wasn't thrilled with the idea of living too far from Timothy's brothers and their families. She figured Timothy would be excited to hear that from her, but for some reason she wasn't ready to share those new feelings just yet. She had to admit, if only to herself, that since she'd gotten to know Esther and Suzanne better, she wanted to be close enough so they could visit whenever they wanted to.

"We'd better get going," Timothy said, helping her into the buggy. "I told the real estate agent we'd meet him there at nine o'clock."

With a renewed sense of excitement, Hannah leaned back in her seat and tried to relax. If they could get this house, they might be able to move out of Samuel's place within the next few weeks.

As they traveled down the road, Timothy talked about how much he was enjoying painting with his brother, and then he told Hannah that the place they'd be looking at had fifty acres, which meant he could do some farming if he had a mind to.

Hannah knew he'd enjoyed farming with his dad in Pennsylvania, but if he was going to keep working full-time for Samuel, she didn't see how he'd have time to do any farming. Maybe they could lease some of the land and only farm a few acres for themselves. She kept her thoughts to herself though. No point in bringing that up when they didn't even know if they'd be buying the house.

A short time later, Timothy guided the horse and buggy down a long dirt driveway with a wooden fence on either side. A rambling old house came into view. It looked like it hadn't been painted in a good many years, but Hannah knew Timothy could take care of that. What concerned her was that the shutters hung loose, the front porch sagged, the roof had missing shingles, and several of the windows were broken. If that wasn't bad enough, the whole yard was overgrown with weeds.

"Ach, my!" she gasped. "This place is an absolute dump! Surely you don't expect us to live here!"

CHAPTER 28

Timothy's mind whirled as he groped for something positive to say about the house before Hannah insisted that they turn around and head back to Samuel's place.

"Listen, Hannah," he said, clasping her arm, "I think we need to wait till we've seen the inside of the house before drawing any conclusions. Let's try to keep an open mind—at least for now."

She wrinkled her nose. "If the inside looks even half as bad as the outside does, then I'm not moving here."

"Well, let's go inside and take a look. I see the agent's car over there, so he's probably in the house waiting for us."

Hannah sighed. "Okay, but where are you going to tie the horse? I don't see a hitching rail, which probably means this house belongs to an Englisher."

"That may be, but if we buy the place, we can put up a hitching post, and of course we'll have to remove the electrical connections." He directed Dusty over to a tree. "I'll tie my horse here, and he should be fine for the short time we'll be inside the house."

When they stepped onto the porch a few minutes later,

Timothy cringed and took hold of Hannah's hand. There were several loose boards—the kind that looked like if you stepped on them the wrong way, they'd fly up and hit you on the back of the head. The porch railing was broken in a couple of places, too.

"I know this porch looks really bad right now, but imagine if the boards and railing were replaced and it was freshly painted," Timothy said with as much enthusiasm as he could muster. "And look, the front of the house faces east. Think of all the beautiful sunrises we can watch from here on warm summer mornings."

"I guess that's one way of looking at it," Hannah said in a guarded tone.

Timothy was about to knock on the door when it swung open. Tom Donnelson greeted them with a smile. "It's good to see you both again. Come on in; I'm anxious to show you around."

As they entered the living room, where faded blue curtains hung at the window, Tom explained that the elderly man who'd owned the house had recently passed away, and his children, who lived in another state, had just put the place on the market. He then took them upstairs, through all five bedrooms, each needing a coat of fresh paint, and pointed out that there was an attic above the second story that would give them plenty of storage. The wide woodwork around the floor base, as well as the frames around the doors, were impressive, but they were badly scratched and needed to be sanded and restained.

When they got to the kitchen, Hannah's mouth dropped open. Timothy was sure she was going to flee from the house in horror. Not only did it need to be painted, but the sink was rusty from where the faucet had been leaking, the linoleum was torn in several places, the counter had multiple dings, and some of the hinges on the cabinet doors were broken. An old electric stove and refrigerator sat side-by-side and would need to be replaced. Most of the rooms had been wallpapered with several layers that had been put on over the years. So before any painting could be done, the walls would have to be stripped clean.

"I think this old house has some potential," Tom said. "It just needs a bit of a face-lift."

"A bit of a face-lift?" Hannah exclaimed with raised brows. "If you want my opinion, I'd say it needs to be condemned." She turned to Timothy and frowned. "Don't you agree?"

He shrugged his shoulders. "I know it's hard to see, but if you could just look past the way the house looks right now and imagine how it could look with some remodeling—"

"But that would take a lot of time, and probably a lot of money, too," she argued.

"I'll bet with the help of Samuel and Titus we could have this place fixed up and ready to move into by spring."

"The beginning of spring or the end of spring?" she questioned.

He turned his hands palms up. "I don't know. Guess we'd have to wait and see how it all goes."

Hannah's dubious expression made Timothy think she was going to refuse to even consider buying the house, but to his surprise, she turned to him and said, "If you really think you can make this place livable, then let's put an offer on it."

"Are you sure?"

She nodded.

"All right then." Timothy looked at Tom. "Can we do that right now?"

Tom gave a nod. "There's no time like the present. Let's head over to Samuel's house, and we can discuss a fair offer, and then you can sign the papers."

That afternoon after Timothy and Hannah got back to Samuel's house and shared the news that they hoped to buy the house they'd looked at, Samuel decided to head over to the B&B and tell Esther. This was not only good news for Timothy and Hannah, but for him and Esther, as well, because it meant they could be married soon.

"Can we go with you, Daadi?" Leon asked as Samuel took his horse out of the barn. "We haven't gone over to play with Cody in a long time."

"And since Esther didn't come over here today, she's probably busy bakin' cookies," Marla added as she joined her younger brother. She licked her lips. "Sure would like some of those."

"I suppose you can go along, but Jared and Penny will probably want to go, too, and if they both go, then Mindy will want to be included, and I'm not sure Hannah will go for that."

"Can we at least ask?" Leon looked up at Samuel with pleading eyes. "If Aunt Hannah says Mindy can't go, then just the four of us will go with ya, okay?"

"Jah, and then Mindy will cry. You know she will." Marla frowned. "She's a whiny baby, and besides that she's spoiled."

Samuel reached under the brim of his hat and scratched his head. "You think so?"

"Sure do," Marla said with a nod.

"Hmm. . . Seems to me that Hannah's always telling Mindy no about something or other," Samuel said. "So I wouldn't call that spoiled."

"Mindy may not get everything she wants, but she's a big mama's baby, and Aunt Hannah's always fussin' over her," Leon interjected.

For fear that whatever he said might get repeated, Samuel didn't agree with the children, but he didn't disagree either. Truth was, he got tired of watching the way Hannah doted on Mindy, but if Timothy didn't say anything to his wife about it, then it wasn't Samuel's place to comment. He'd watched Esther with his children many times and was glad she didn't smother them with too much attention. He knew she loved them very much and felt sure that she'd make a good wife and mother.

"I'll tell you what," Samuel said, looking at Leon. "You run into the house and tell Aunt Hannah that you, Marla, Penny, and Jared are going over to see Esther with me, and if she doesn't mind, Mindy is welcome to come along."

"Okay. I'll be back soon!" Leon raced across the yard and into the house.

Samuel bent and gave Marla a hug. "You can get in the buggy if you want to."

"Okay, Daadi." Without waiting for Samuel's assistance, Marla climbed into the buggy and took a seat in the back.

He smiled. His oldest daughter was such a sweet little girl. In many ways she reminded him of Elsie. How glad he was that Marla and Leon had both been old enough when their mother died so they would have some memories of her as they grew up. Penny might remember some, too, but little Jared would only know whatever he was told about his mother. At least the children had Esther, and in fact, Jared and Penny often called her "Mama." Samuel had no problem with that.

Hearing the sound of laughter, Samuel glanced toward the house. Leon, Penny, and Jared, wearing straw hats, jackets, and scarves, pranced like three little ponies across the lawn. When they reached the buggy, they grabbed hold of Samuel's legs and squeezed.

"We can head out now, Daadi," Leon said. "Hannah said Mindy can't go."

"I figured as much," Samuel mumbled before lifting Penny and Jared into the buggy. *It's a shame Mindy couldn't join us,* he fumed. *Hannah is way too protective of that child.*

Leon climbed in last and took a seat up front on the passenger's side. "Hold the reins steady now while I untie my horse from the hitching rail," Samuel told the boy.

When Samuel took his seat on the driver's side, Leon handed him the reins and smiled. "Sure can't wait to play with Cody!"

Paradise, Pennsylvania

As Sally meandered up their driveway after getting the mail, she decided to stop at the phone shack and see if there were any new messages. She'd just stepped inside when she heard the phone ring, so she quickly grabbed the receiver. "Hello."

"Hi, Mom. This is a pleasant surprise. I wasn't expecting anyone to pick up the phone."

"Hannah, it's so good to hear your voice! How are you? How are Mindy and Timothy doing?"

"We're all fine. Mindy's taking a nap, and Timothy's in the house with our real estate agent, going over the paperwork we need to sign."

"Paperwork?"

"Jah. We found a house today, and we're going to put an offer on it."

"Wow, that was quick."

"Jah, quick as dew."

"I guess that means you'll be staying in Kentucky?" Sally

couldn't keep the disappointment she felt out of her voice.

"That's what Timothy wants, so I suppose we are."

Sally had expected Hannah to say she didn't want to stay in Kentucky, like she had so many other times when they'd talked. Maybe she'd resigned herself to the idea, knowing it was the only way to keep her husband happy.

"So tell me about the house. Is it close to where Timothy's brothers live?" Sally asked.

"It's just a few miles down the road from Samuel's place and not far from Titus's home either."

"Is it nice and big?"

"It's big, but. . .well, not so nice. In fact, it needs a whole lot of work."

Sally grimaced. "If it needs a lot of work, then why are you buying the place?"

"Because it's reasonably priced, and Timothy thinks he can have it fixed up enough so we can move in sometime this spring. With him and his brothers doing most of the work, it will save us a lot of money, too."

"I see."

"You and Dad will have to visit us after we get moved in. There are five bedrooms, so there's plenty of room for us to have company."

"Jah, we'll have to do that."

"How's Dad's back? Is he doing a lot better now?"

"He's working a few days a week at the store again but still has to be careful not to overdo. He had quite a siege with his back this time."

"I'm glad he's doing better." Hannah paused. "It's been good talking to you, Mom, but I'd better hang up now. I need to check on Mindy and see if the paperwork is ready to sign."

"Okay. Take care, Hannah, and please keep in touch."

"I will. Bye, Mom."

When Sally hung up the phone, a sick feeling came over her. Now that Timothy and Hannah were buying a house, she was almost certain they would never move back to Pennsylvania. If only there was something she could do to bring her daughter back home where she belonged. But what would it be?

With the mail in her hand and a heavy heart weighing her down, Sally trudged wearily toward the house. When she stepped inside, she found Johnny sitting in the recliner with a fat gray cat in his lap.

"You know I don't like that critter in the house," Sally snapped. "She gets hair everywhere!"

"I'm not letting her run all over the place, Sally. As you can see, I'm holding Fluffy in my lap."

Sally ground her teeth together, not even bothering to mention that there was cat hair clinging to her husband's pants, and tossed the mail onto the coffee table in front of the sofa. "I just spoke with Hannah on the phone, and guess what?"

"I have no idea." Johnny stroked the cat behind its ears and stared up at Sally with a smug expression. It only fueled her anger, watching more cat hair fly each time Johnny petted the feline.

"Hannah and Timothy are buying a house."

"That's good to hear. Samuel's been nice in letting them stay with him, but they really do need a place of their own."

Sally stepped directly in front of Johnny, her hands on her hips. "Don't you realize what this means?"

"Jah. It means they'll have a place of their own where we can stay when we go to visit."

She clenched her teeth so hard her jaw started to ache. "It

means they aren't moving back to Pennsylvania. They wouldn't be buying a house unless they planned to put down roots and stay in Kentucky."

"I think you're right about that, and it's probably for the best."

"What's that supposed to mean?"

"It means Timothy moving his family to Kentucky was the best thing he could have done for his marriage." Johnny stared at Sally over the top of his glasses, as if daring her to argue with him. "We've been through all this before, but I'm going to remind you once more that the Good Book says when a couple gets married, they are to leave their parents." Johnny let go of the cat and spread his arms wide. "And they are to cleave to each other. Leave and cleave!" He brought his hands together quickly and made a tight fist. "And that's the end of that, no matter what you may think."

CHAPTER 29

Pembroke, Kentucky

As soon as Samuel pulled his horse and buggy into Bonnie's yard, Cody leaped off the porch and darted into the yard to greet them. The children were barely out of the buggy when the dog was upon them, yapping excitedly and leaping into the air.

"Calm down, Cody," Samuel scolded, snapping his fingers at the dog. He remembered how once last year Cody had gotten his horse riled up and the critter ended up getting kicked pretty bad. The end result was a broken leg for the dog. Samuel sure didn't want anything like that to happen again.

"Take the dog over there to play," Samuel told Marla as he pointed to the other side of the yard. "That way he won't get kicked by the horse like he did last year."

She bent down and grabbed Cody's collar then led him across the yard. The other children quickly followed.

Samuel secured his horse to the hitching rail and hurried up to the house. He was about to knock when the door opened and Bonnie stepped out.

"Oh, it's you and the children. I heard Cody barking and wondered what all the commotion was about."

Samuel chuckled. "Yeah, that critter can get pretty worked up sometimes—especially when my kids come around."

Bonnie smiled. "Maybe the kids would like to come in for some cookies and hot chocolate."

"I don't know about the kids, but I'd like some." Samuel jiggled his eyebrows playfully, which was easy to do because of his good mood. "I'd like to talk to Esther first, though. Is she here or at the guesthouse?"

"She's upstairs right now, cleaning one of the rooms. I have some guests checking in later today." Bonnie motioned to the stairs. "Feel free to go on up if you'd like to talk to her, and then when you're done, you can join me and the kids in the kitchen for a snack."

"Sounds good to me." Samuel hung his jacket and hat on the coat tree in the entryway and sprinted up the stairs, hearing his kids squealing with delight as Bonnie called them in for a snack. He found Esther in one of the guest rooms sweeping the floor.

"Guder mariye," he said, stepping into the room.

Esther jumped. "Ach, Samuel, you startled me! I didn't realize you were here."

"Sorry about that. I'm surprised you didn't hear my noisy boots clomping up the stairs," he said.

"Well, I did, but I thought it was Bonnie."

"Bonnie has loud-clomping boots?"

Esther giggled, and her cheeks turned a pretty pink. "Her snow boots are a bit loud, but since we don't have any snow right now, I guess she wouldn't have been wearing any boots."

Samuel grinned. Esther looked so sweet when she looked up at him, almost like an innocent little schoolgirl. His heart ached to marry her, but he was trying to be patient.

"So what are you doing here?" she asked, setting her broom aside.

"Came to see you, of course." He took a few steps toward Esther. "I wanted to share some *gut noochricht*."

"What's the good news?"

"Timothy and Hannah are buying a house. Their real estate agent's at my place right now, and they're signing papers to make an offer on the place. If their offer's accepted, they hope to be moved in by spring." He moved closer and took Esther's hand. "So you know what that means?"

"I guess it means Hannah will be happy to be living in a place of her own, where she won't have to share a kitchen or worry about anyone giving Mindy too much candy."

"That's probably true, but what it means for us is that once they're moved into their own home, we can get married."

"But what if their offer's not accepted?"

"I think it will be. It's a fair offer, and Tom Donnelson told Timothy that the owner of the house has passed on, and his adult children are anxious to sell the place."

"If they're so anxious to sell, then why would it take until spring before Timothy and Hannah can move in?" Esther questioned.

"The place is pretty run-down, and it's going to take a few months to get it fixed up so it's livable." Samuel gave Esther's fingers a gentle squeeze. "But if Titus and I help with the renovations, I think we can have it done in record time."

"I believe you could. It didn't take long for you and Allen to fix this old place up, so I'm sure with three very capable brothers working on Timothy's place, it could be done in no time at all." Esther's eyes sparkled as she smiled widely. "Oh Samuel, after all these months of waiting to become your wife, I can hardly believe we could actually be married in just a few months." Her face sobered. "I think it's best if we don't set a definite date yet, though—just in case the owners of the house don't accept Timothy and Hannah's offer."

Samuel pulled Esther into his arms and gave her a hug. "I'm sure it'll all work out, but we can wait to set a date until we know something definite. Now, why don't you take a break from working and come downstairs with me? Bonnie's promised to serve hot chocolate and cookies to me and the kids, and I'd like you to join us."

"I'm almost done here. Just let me finish sweeping the floor, and I'll come right down."

"Okay, but you might want to hurry. The kinner are in the kitchen with Bonnie, already enjoying those kichlin, and I'm going down now and make sure there are some left for us." Smiling, and feeling like a kid himself, Samuel gave her a quick kiss and hurried from the room.

Esther smiled as she finished sweeping the floor. Did she dare hope that she and Samuel could be married in a few months—or at least by early summer? Of course, she'd need a few months to make her wedding dress and plan for the wedding. Since Samuel was a widower, they wouldn't have nearly as large a wedding as younger couples who'd never been married. But there would still be some planning to do.

Oh, I wish Mom could be here to help me prepare for the wedding, Esther thought wistfully. *But it wouldn't be fair to ask her to come when she's needed to help Sarah care for Dan.*

Esther knew she could probably count on Suzanne to help with wedding details, but with Suzanne being pregnant and possibly not feeling well by then, she might not be able to help that much.

I could ask Bonnie, but then she has her own wedding to plan for, and I'm sure that's going to take up a lot of her time. Then there's Hannah, but I'm not sure she'd even want to help—especially now that they may be buying a house that needs a lot of work.

Even though Hannah had been a bit friendlier to Esther lately, she still kept a little wall around her—like she didn't want anyone to get really close. Esther hoped that wall would come down someday, because she still wanted to be Hannah's friend.

I'd better wait and see first if Hannah and Timothy get that house. Then I can begin planning my wedding and decide who to ask for help.

Once Esther finished sweeping, she emptied the dustpan into the garbage can she'd placed in the hall and went downstairs to join everyone for a snack. She didn't realize how hungry she'd gotten.

She'd just stepped into the kitchen, where Samuel and his children sat at the table, when the telephone rang.

"Hello. Bonnie's Bed-and-Breakfast," Bonnie said after she'd picked up the receiver. There was a pause; then she said, "As a matter of fact, Esther is right here. Would you like to speak with her?" She handed Esther the phone. "It's your mother."

With a sense of excitement, Esther took the phone. "Mom, I was just thinking about you. I wanted to tell you that—"

"Esther, your daed's in the hospital." Mom's voice quavered. "They've been treating him for a ruptured appendix, and now he's in surgery."

Esther gasped. "Ach, Mom, that's *baremlich*! I'll either hire a driver or catch the bus, but I'll be there as soon as I can."

"What's terrible?" Samuel asked when Esther hung up the phone.

She relayed all that her mother had said and then asked Bonnie if she could have some time off.

"Of course you can," Bonnie was quick to say. "Other than the guests coming in later today, I have no one else booked until Valentine's Day."

Esther looked at Samuel. "Do you think Hannah would be willing to take over full responsibility of your kinner and all the household chores until I get back from Pennsylvania?"

"I'm sure she will," Samuel said. "And if she's not, then I'll find someone else to help out. Your place is with your family right now."

Esther smiled, appreciating the understanding of both Samuel and Bonnie. She felt sick hearing about Dad's ruptured appendix, knowing how serious something like that could be. She closed her eyes and sent up a quick prayer. *Lord, please help my daed to be okay.*

CHAPTER 30

A ray of sunlight beckoned Hannah to the window in Marla's bedroom, where she'd been cleaning. Esther had only been gone a week, and already Hannah was exhausted. Samuel's children were a handful—especially Jared, who was a lot more active than Mindy. Hannah never knew what the little stinker might get into, and she had to stay on her toes to keep up with him. Jared was also a picky eater, often refusing to eat whatever she'd fixed for meals. Esther had usually made him something he liked, but Hannah felt that Jared could either eat what was on his plate or do without. She figured in time he'd learn to eat what the others ate, even if he didn't particularly like it.

Then there was all the extra cleaning she had to do. It seemed that no matter how many times she got after the children to pick up in their rooms, they just ignored her. Penny and Jared were the worst, often scattering toys all over the place. It was either nag them to clean up or do it herself, which was what she was doing today. She was glad Marla and Leon were both in school, and she'd put the three younger ones down for a nap. It was easier to get things done when they weren't underfoot. Hannah often found herself wishing

Esther hadn't gone to Pennsylvania, because she now realized that it had been much easier to share the work.

Hannah sighed and bent to pick up one of Marla's soiled dresses that should have been put in the laundry basket. The only good thing that had happened this week was that the offer she and Timothy had made on the old house had been accepted. So she could now look forward to the day when they'd be able to move in. As soon as the deal closed, which should happen in a few weeks, Timothy would begin working on the interior. He and his brothers would take care of exterior work as well, but most of those renovations could be done once they were moved in.

Samuel had heard from Esther a few days ago, giving him an update on her dad's condition. Even though he'd made it through surgery okay, there'd been a lot of infection in his body, and he was still in the hospital being carefully watched and getting heavy doses of antibiotics. The family had been told that he'd probably be there at least another week. After that, he would need a good four to eight weeks for a full recovery. So Esther had decided that she would stay and take over the stands her dad had been managing at two of the farmers' markets in the area. The stands really belonged to Esther's brother, but with Dan's MS symptoms getting worse, he certainly couldn't manage them anymore. Esther's mother probably could have taken over the stands, but she felt Dan's wife needed her help to care for their home and two children, as well as Dan.

As Hannah moved across the room to make Marla's bed, her thoughts went to Bonnie. *I wonder how she's managing without Esther's help.*

Hannah knew the woman from California was still at the B&B because her ankle wasn't completely healed. No doubt, having her there created more work for Bonnie. She probably felt as overwhelmed as Hannah did right now.

—⁂—

"I was wondering if you've heard anything from Esther," Trisha said when Bonnie joined her in the living room in front of the fireplace.

"Her father is still quite sick, and Esther plans to stay in Pennsylvania and take care of the stands he's been running. It could be up to eight weeks before she returns to Kentucky," Bonnie said.

"So who will take her place helping you here at the bed-and-breakfast?"

Bonnie shrugged. "I don't know. If things get too busy, I'll probably have to place a help-wanted ad in the local newspaper."

"I could help. I'm getting tired of sitting around so much, so it would give me something meaningful to do."

Bonnie's eyes widened. "But your leg's still in the cast, and once you get it off, you'll need physical therapy. I sure can't expect you to climb the stairs and service the guest rooms."

"I could do some of the cooking. I'm pretty good at that, even if I do say so myself."

Bonnie folded her arms and leaned against the bookcase behind her. "That's right. Since you used to work as a chef, I'll bet you could create some pretty tasty dishes for my B&B guests."

Trisha nodded. "I could make them as fancy or simple as you like. I'd even be happy to work for my room and board."

Bonnie shook her head. "If you're going to work for me, then I insist on paying you a fair wage, as well as giving you room and board. I was doing that for Esther, you know."

Trisha smiled as a sense of excitement welled in her chest.

Maybe God had sent her here on Christmas Eve for a reason. She might even end up staying in Kentucky permanently. Of course if she did, she'd no doubt be seeing Bonnie's dad again.

Would I mind that? she asked herself. *Maybe not.*

CHAPTER 31

By the middle of February, Timothy and his brothers had done a lot of work on the house. If things went well, they hoped to have it fixed up enough so that Timothy, Hannah, and Mindy could move in by the middle of March, even if some things still needed to be done. Hannah thought she could live with that—as long as it didn't take too much time to finish the house after the move. She was so anxious to have her own place.

On this Saturday, Timothy and Titus were working at the house while Samuel went to Hopkinsville to run some errands. Hannah, tired of being cooped up in Samuel's house with five active children, decided to bundle the kids up and go over to her house to see how things were progressing. She'd also made the men some sandwiches because they'd left early this morning before she'd had a chance to fix them anything for lunch.

"You're the oldest, so I want you to keep an eye on the other children and wait here in the house while I get the horse and buggy ready," Hannah told Marla.

Marla looked up at her with a dimpled grin. "Okay, Aunt

Hannah. I'll watch 'em real good."

Hannah patted Marla's shoulder. Of all Samuel's children, Marla was the easiest to deal with. She was usually quite agreeable and seemed eager to please. She was also the calmest child, which Hannah appreciated, because Samuel's other three could think of more things to get into than a batch of curious kittens. She did notice, though, that Marla had a funny habit. Every so often, the child put her hand inside the opposite sleeve of her dress, as if hiding it or maybe trying to warm it up. No one else mentioned this or seemed to take notice, and Hannah didn't spend much time wondering about it herself. *After all, I used to chew my fingernails when I was a girl.* Fortunately, she gave up the habit before she reached her teen years, so she figured Marla would probably do the same.

"I shouldn't be too long, but give me a holler if you need anything," Hannah said before going out the back door.

Since the buggy was already parked in the yard, all she had to do was get her horse. When Hannah entered Lilly's stall, the horse flicked her ears and swished her tail.

"Would you like to go for a ride, girl?" Hannah patted the horse's flanks. "You need the exercise, or you'll get fat and end up in lazy land." She smiled to herself, remembering how Mom had often used that term to describe someone who didn't want to work.

Lilly whinnied in response and nuzzled Hannah's hand. She was glad they had been able to bring both of their horses when they'd moved. Having them here was a like a touch from home. Hannah glanced at the other side of the barn where all their furniture had been stacked under some canvas tarps. Once they could bring their belongings to the new house, she hoped it would help her feel closer to the home she used to know and love in Pennsylvania. Starting over was difficult, but it would be a bit easier when they could use their own things again. While Samuel's house was comfortable enough, nothing in it belonged to Hannah, and she still felt out of place—like a stranger at times.

Hannah was about to put the harness on Lilly when a little gray mouse darted out of the hay and zipped across her foot. Startled, she screamed and jumped back. There were a few critters she really didn't like, and mice were near the top of her list.

Hearing Hannah's scream must have frightened Lilly, for she reared up and then bolted out of the stall. Hannah chased after the horse, and realized too late that she'd left the barn door open.

"Come back here, Lilly!" Hannah shouted as she raced into the yard after the horse.

Around and around the yard they went, until Hannah was panting for breath. She knew she had to get Lilly back in the barn or she'd never get her harnessed and ready to go. And if the crazy horse kept running like that, she might end up out on the road, where she'd be in jeopardy of getting hit by a car.

"Whoa! Whoa, now!" Hannah waved her hands frantically, but it did no good. Lilly was in a frenzy and wouldn't pay any attention to her at all.

Hannah heard someone shout, and when she turned her head, she was surprised to see Leon running out of the house, waving his arms and hollering at Lilly. While the boy might be young, he must have known exactly what he was doing, because it wasn't long before he had Hannah's horse under control and running straight for the barn.

Hannah hurried in behind them and quickly shut the door. "Whew! Lilly gave me quite a workout! Danki for coming to my rescue, Leon."

The boy looked up at her and grinned. "I've helped Daadi chase after his horse before, so I knew just what to do. And if our pony ever gets outa the barn, bet I can get him back in, too." Leon's face sobered. "Marla said I wasn't supposed to go outside, but when I saw your horse runnin' all over the place, I had to come out and help. Sure hope that's okay."

She smiled and gave his shoulder a gentle squeeze. "I'm glad you did. Would you like to help me put the harness on Lilly?"

"Jah, sure."

A short time later, Hannah's horse was hitched and ready to go. Now all she needed to do was load the children into the buggy, and they could be on their way.

—⁂—

"Could you give me a hand with this drop cloth?" Timothy called to Titus, who was on the other side of the living room, removing some old baseboard that needed to be replaced.

"Sure thing." Titus stopped what he was doing and picked up one of the drop cloths. "Do you want to cover the whole floor or just this section for now?"

"If you're about ready to paint your side of the room, we may as well cover the entire floor," Timothy said.

"I will be as soon as I put the new baseboard up."

"Okay then, let's just cover the floor on my side for now. Sure am glad we both know how to paint," Timothy said as they spread out the drop cloth.

"Jah, but you've done more painting than I ever have, so your side of the room will probably look better than mine. Think I'm better at carpentry than painting."

"You are good with wood," Timothy agreed, "but your painting skills are just fine. I think you sell yourself short sometimes."

Titus shrugged. "That's what Suzanne says, too."

"Speaking of Suzanne, how's she feeling these days?"

"She's still havin' some morning sickness, but at least it doesn't last all day like it did at first." Titus's forehead wrinkled. "Since we've only been married a few months, we weren't expecting a boppli this soon. But then God knows what we need and when we need it, so we've come to think of it as a blessing."

Timothy thought about his brother's remark. He'd always felt that God knew what he needed and when he needed it, but he wasn't so sure Hannah shared that belief. Sometimes her faith in God seemed weak, and she usually had little to say about the sermons they heard at church. He felt that this move to Kentucky had been God's will, but he didn't think Hannah had come to accept it just yet. They still quarreled a lot, and Hannah often nagged him about little things. But since they'd bought this house, her outlook seemed a bit more positive. He hoped after they moved in and she arranged things to her liking she'd feel more like Kentucky was her home.

The brothers worked quietly for a while, until Timothy heard a horse and buggy pull in. Thinking it was probably Samuel coming to help, he didn't bother to look out the window.

A few minutes later, the front door opened, and Hannah stepped into the room carrying a wicker basket. Marla, Leon, Penny, Jared, and Mindy traipsed in behind her.

That's just great, Timothy thought. *The last thing we need is the kinner here getting in the way.* He was about to ask Hannah what they were doing when Mindy rushed over to Titus, who was crouched down with his back to them, and threw her little arms around his neck. "Daadi!"

With a look of surprise, Titus whirled around, nearly knocking the child off her feet. Mindy took one look at Titus's face and started howling. She'd obviously mistaken him for her daddy, but after seeing his beard, which was much shorter than Timothy's because he hadn't been married as long, she'd realized her mistake.

Hannah placed the basket on the floor, hurried across the room, and swooped Mindy into her arms. "It's all right, little one. That's your uncle Titus. Don't cry. Look, daadi's right over there." She pointed to Timothy.

Hannah set Mindy down, and the child, still crying, darted across the room toward Timothy. In the process, she hit the bucket of paint with her foot and knocked it over. Some of the white paint spilled out, but at least the drop cloth was there to protect the floor. When Mindy saw what she'd done, she started to howl even louder—like a wounded heifer.

Timothy, grabbing for the paint can and more than a bit annoyed, glared at Hannah and said, "What are you doing here, and why'd you bring the kinner? This is not a place for them to be when we're tryin' to get some work done!"

Hannah pointed to the basket she'd set on the floor. "You left so early this morning that I didn't get a chance to make your lunch, so I decided to bring it over to you." She motioned to the children, who stood wide-eyed and huddled together near the door. "I could hardly leave them at home by themselves, now, could I?"

"Of course not, but—"

"And I wanted to see how you're doing and ask if there's anything I can do to help," she quickly added.

"Jah, there is," Timothy shouted. "You can just leave the lunch basket and head back home with the kinner while I clean up the paint that got spilled!"

Hannah's chin quivered, and even from across the room he could see her tears. "Fine then," she said, bending to pick up Mindy. "I guess that's what I get for trying to be nice!" She ushered the kids quickly out the door, slamming it behind her.

"Hey, Timothy, you need to calm down. You caught the paint before too much damage was done, so did you have to yell at Hannah like that?" Titus asked, moving over to the basket. "I'm hungerich, and I'm glad she brought us some lunch."

"It was a nice gesture," Timothy agreed, "but she should have left the kinner in the buggy while she brought the lunch basket in here. She ought to know better than to turn five little ones loose in a room that's being painted." He shrugged his shoulders. "But what can I say? Sometimes my fraa just doesn't think."

"No one is perfect, Timothy. Maybe you're just too hard on Hannah. It might help if you appreciated the good things she does, rather than scolding her for all the things she does that irritate you."

A feeling of remorse came over Timothy. He didn't know why he'd been short on patience lately. Maybe it was because he wanted so badly to get this house presentable enough so they could move in. Even so, that was no excuse for him losing his temper—especially in front of the children.

"You're right, and I appreciate the reminder. I should have handled it better," Timothy said, watching out the window as the buggy headed down the road. "Guess it's too late now, but as soon as I get home, I'll apologize to Hannah and try to make things right." He dropped his gaze to the floor. "Guess I'd better say I'm sorry to the kinner, too—especially my sweet little girl, who probably thinks her daadi's angry with her."

CHAPTER 32

Trisha had just taken a loaf of banana bread from the oven when the telephone rang. Knowing Bonnie was outside emptying the garbage, Trisha picked up the receiver. "Hello. Bonnie's Bed-and-Breakfast."

"Bonnie, is that you?"

"No, this is Trisha." Then, recognizing the voice on the other end, she said, "How are you, Kenny?"

"I'm okay, and if you don't mind, it's Ken, not Kenny." There was a pause. "How's your ankle doing?"

"It's better. I got the cast off a week ago, but now I'm doing physical therapy."

"How much longer will you be staying at Bonnie's?" he asked.

"I don't know. I guess that all depends on when Esther returns from Pennsylvania."

"What's she doing in Pennsylvania, and what's that got to do with you?"

Trisha explained about Esther's dad and then told Ken that she'd been doing the cooking for Bonnie and that Bonnie was taking care of servicing the rooms. "I thought Bonnie would have told you that," she added.

"Nope. She never said a word."

Hmm. . .that's strange, Trisha thought. *I know Bonnie's talked to her dad since Esther left. I wonder why she didn't mention any of this to him.*

"She probably didn't mention it because she thought I wouldn't approve," Ken said, as though anticipating the question on the tip of her tongue.

"And would you?" she dared to ask.

"The B&B is Bonnie's to do with as she likes, so whomever she hires to work there is her business, not mine."

"So you're okay with me working here?"

"I didn't say that. Just said—"

The back door opened suddenly, and Bonnie stepped in. "It's your dad." Trisha held the receiver out to Bonnie. "I'm sure he'd rather talk to you than me."

After Bonnie took the phone, Trisha left the room, wondering once again if things would ever be better between her and Ken. She hoped they would, because over these last several weeks, she and Bonnie had become good friends. She'd gotten to know Allen, too, and appreciated the way he always included her in the conversation whenever he came to see Bonnie, although Trisha usually tried to make herself scarce so he and Bonnie could have some time alone.

I wish I could be here for Bonnie and Allen's wedding, Trisha thought as she entered the living room and took a seat in the rocker. *Maybe when Esther comes back I can find another job somewhere in the area and rent an apartment in Hopkinsville—at least until after Bonnie and Allen are married.*

If she and Ken hadn't broken up when they were teenagers, would she have visited him at this house? What if she had married Ken instead of Dave? Would they have ended up living in Kentucky instead of Oregon?

"Shoulda, woulda, coulda," she murmured, leaning her head back and closing her eyes. "There's always more than one direction a person can take. I guess there's no point in pondering the 'what if's.'"

———

It had taken Hannah awhile to get the children settled down after they'd gone back to Samuel's. They'd clearly been upset by Timothy's outburst. After they'd had silent prayer before lunch, Leon looked up at Hannah and said, "How come Uncle Timothy's mad at us?"

"I don't think he's mad at you," Hannah assured him. "He was just upset because we went over to the house when he was really busy, and when the can of paint got spilled, he was left with a mess to clean up. I think he was more upset with me than anyone," she added.

"When we first moved to Kentucky, Daadi used to yell at us like that," Marla spoke up, putting her hand inside the sleeve of her dress.

"He did?"

"Jah. Esther said it was because he missed our mamm so much, but we thought he didn't love us."

"But you know now that he loves you, right?" Hannah questioned.

Leon bobbed his head. "Daadi got better after I ran away from home. Maybe you oughta run away, too, Aunt Hannah. Then when ya come back, Uncle Timothy might be nicer to ya."

Hannah smiled despite her sour mood. "Sometimes I do feel like running away, but it probably wouldn't be the answer to our problems."

"What is the answer?" Marla asked.

Hannah shrugged. "I'm not sure. I guess I just need to let your uncle Timothy work on the house and not bother him when he's there." She reached over and wiped away a blob of peanut butter Mindy had managed to get on her chin.

Truth was, when Timothy snapped at her like he had today, it made her long to be back in Pennsylvania, where she'd have Mom's love and support. That wasn't likely to happen, though—especially now that they'd bought a house. Hannah figured she'd better make the best of things and try to stay out of Timothy's way when he was busy working on the house. That would be easier than quarreling all the time or being hurt when he said something harsh to her, which seemed to be happening a lot lately. She knew Timothy didn't like to argue either, but they seemed to do it frequently.

Maybe he thinks I'm hard to live with, Hannah thought.

The children had just finished their lunch, when Hannah heard the sound of horse's hooves coming up the driveway. When she went to the window, she was surprised to see Timothy's horse and buggy pull up to the hitching rail. *I wonder what he's doing back so early. Maybe he forgot a tool. Or maybe he came to lecture me some more.*

Fearful that Timothy might say something to upset the children, Hannah told them to go upstairs to their rooms.

"What about our *schissel?*" Marla asked. "Don't you want us to clear them first?"

Hannah shook her head. "That's okay. I'll take care of the dishes." She lifted Mindy from her stool and told her to go upstairs to play with Marla and the others.

When the children left the room, Hannah started clearing the table. She'd just put the last dish in the sink when Timothy entered the kitchen.

"What are you doing here?" she asked over her shoulder. "I thought you planned to work at the house all day."

"I do, but I had to come home for a few minutes." He stepped up to Hannah and placed his hands on her shoulders. "*Es dutt mir leed.*"

"You're sorry?"

"That's right. I shouldn't have gotten so angry about the spilled paint and spouted off like I did. Will you forgive me, Hannah?"

She nodded, feeling her throat tighten. "I'm sorry, too," she murmured. Hannah couldn't believe he'd come all the way home just to say he was sorry, but it softened her heart. She felt more love for her husband than she had in a long time. Did she dare hope that things would be better between them from now on?

CHAPTER 33

By the middle of March, Timothy and Hannah were able to move into their home. Not everything had been fixed, but at least it was livable. Since Esther was still in Pennsylvania, Hannah had agreed to watch Samuel's children at her house, which meant he had to bring them over every morning, but he seemed to be okay with that.

One sunny Monday, Hannah decided to take advantage of the unusually warm weather and hang her laundry outdoors, rather than in the basement. As she carried a basket of freshly washed clothes out to the clothesline, she wondered if they'd made a mistake in buying this old house. So much remained to be done. Several upstairs windows needed new screens. Some screens were broken, and some were missing altogether. The barn needed work, too, which was important because it not only housed their horses, but also Timothy's farming tools, painting supplies, and many other things, including hay and food for the animals. Then there was the yard. Hannah didn't know if she'd ever get the weeds cleared out in time to plant a garden this spring. The fields behind the house looked like they hadn't been cultivated in a good many years, and they'd need to be plowed and tilled before Timothy could plant corn. It was all a bit overwhelming, and having to take care of Samuel's children during Esther's absence only made it worse for Hannah. However, she'd agreed to do it, and the money Samuel insisted on paying her was nice for extra expenses.

Hannah shifted the laundry basket in her arms. On a brighter note, soon after they'd moved in, Timothy had mounted the covered-bridge bird feeder he'd given her for Christmas on a post in their backyard. Hannah glanced at the feeder and smiled when she saw several redheaded house finches eating some of the thistle seed she'd put out. She found herself humming and enjoying the joy spring fever always brought.

Redirecting her thoughts, she set the laundry basket on the ground and turned to check on the children. Penny, Jared, and Mindy sat on the porch steps, petting the pathetic little gray-and-white cat that had wandered onto their place the day they'd moved in. The kids had named the cat Bobbin because he bobbed his head whenever he walked. The poor critter had trouble with his balance and sometimes fell over when he tried to run. Hannah figured he'd either been injured or been born with some kind of a palsy disorder. One thing for sure, the cat had been neglected and was looking for a new home. While Hannah wasn't particularly fond of cats, she couldn't help feeling sorry for Bobbin, so she'd begun feeding him, which of course meant the cat had claimed this as his new home. For the sake of Mindy, who'd latched on to the cat right away, Hannah had allowed Bobbin to stay. But she'd made it clear that he was not to be in the house. She didn't want to deal with cat hair everywhere, not to mention the possibility of fleas.

As Hannah hung a pair of Timothy's trousers on the line, she thought about how hard he and his brothers had worked on the house. Looking around, she had to admit they really had accomplished a lot in a short amount of time.

She giggled to herself, thinking back to the day when their new propane stove had been delivered. When they were moving the appliance into place, part of the floor gave way, and the stove became wedged halfway between the kitchen floor and the basement ceiling. Everyone stood with looks of shock until someone had the good sense to suggest that they secure the stove before it fell any farther through the floor. Then they worked together to get the stove hoisted back up in place. Apparently, the wood floor had weakened in that area from a leaky pipe, because originally the sink was located there. It wasn't funny at the time, and it set them back a few days, but Timothy, Samuel, and Titus managed to get the floorboards replaced and a nice square area inlayed with brick for the stove to set on. Except for a few scratches on her new stove, which Hannah wasn't happy about, it had all worked out.

"Frosch schpringe net."

Hannah looked down, surprised to see Jared standing beside her, and wondered what he meant about a frog not jumping. She was about to ask when he pointed to her laundry basket. A fat little frog sat looking up at her.

Hannah screamed. She hated frogs. Even the sight of one sent chills up her spine. "Get that frosch out of there!"

Jared looked up at her like she was a horse with two heads as he picked up the frog.

"Put it over there," she said, pointing to a clump of weeds near the barn. She would have told him to take it all the way out to the field, but she didn't want him going that far from the house.

As Jared walked off, Hannah shook her head and continued to hang up the laundry. *That boy is really something,* she thought with a click of her tongue. *I hope Esther knows what she's getting herself into by marrying Samuel.*

She'd just finished hanging the last of the towels when she spotted a car coming up the driveway. When it pulled up next to the barn, she realized it belonged to Bonnie.

"Guder mariye," Bonnie said as she joined Hannah by the clothesline. "That is how you say *good morning,* isn't it?"

Hannah nodded, surprised that Bonnie knew some Pennsylvania-Dutch words.

"It's so nice out today, and I decided to take a ride and come by to see your new house. Oh, and I brought you a few housewarming gifts." Bonnie motioned to her car. "They're in there."

"I'd be happy to show you the house, but you didn't have to bring me anything," Hannah said.

Bonnie smiled. "I wanted to welcome you to the neighborhood. You know, my B&B isn't too far from here, so feel free to drop by any time you like."

"Thanks." Hannah bent to pick up the empty laundry basket. "Let's go inside, and I'll show you around."

"Sounds good. I'll get your gifts from the car and follow you up to the house."

Hannah skirted around the weeds and stepped onto the porch. "You all need to come inside now," she said to the children.

"Can't we stay out here?" Penny asked in a whiny voice. "We want to pet the katz."

"You can pet the cat later. I need you inside where I can keep an eye on you."

Penny's lower lip jutted out, and when Mindy started

to howl, Jared did, too. Their screams were so loud Hannah feared their nearest neighbor might call the police, thinking something horrible had happened. She held the laundry basket under one arm and against her hip then put her finger to her lips. "Hush now, and come inside, *schnell.*"

But the children didn't come quickly, as she'd asked them to do. Instead, they sat on the porch step, with Mindy still holding the cat, and all three of them crying.

Just then, Bonnie showed up carrying a wicker basket. She placed it on the little wooden table on the porch, reached inside, and handed each of the children a chocolate bar. Even though Hannah didn't normally allow Mindy to have candy—especially so close to lunchtime—she offered no objections, because Bonnie's gift to the children was all it took to stop their crying.

"You can eat the candy, but only if you come inside," Hannah said, opening the door. The children put the cat down, and as he bobbled off to chase after a bug, they followed Bonnie and Hannah inside.

Once inside, Hannah instructed them to go to the kitchen to eat their candy bars, while she gave Bonnie a tour of the house.

"This is a nice-sized home," Bonnie said when they stepped into one of the bedrooms upstairs. "Plenty of room for a growing family and extra room for any company you may have."

"Our family's not growing at the moment," Hannah said. "Unless you count Bobbin, the cat."

"I assume you and Timothy will want other children?" Bonnie asked.

Hannah nodded. "I had a miscarriage last year, but I haven't been able to conceive since then. Timothy says it's because

I'm always stressed out, but I think my womb might be closed up."

Bonnie gave Hannah's arm a gentle squeeze. "I'll pray for you."

"Thanks, I appreciate that." Hannah was surprised to see such compassion on Bonnie's face. It made her think maybe Bonnie might want children, too.

"The men did a good job painting all the rooms," Bonnie said, as they moved on to another bedroom.

"Yes, they did. It took them awhile to strip off the wallpaper, but it turned out nice. There's still some work that needs to be done up here, though." Hannah motioned to the windows. "Some of the screens are missing, and some are old and loose, so they'll all need to be replaced. But considering the repairs that have been done since we bought this place, we're fortunate that we could move in so quickly."

"There were a few missing screens at the B&B when I first moved in," Bonnie said. "But between Samuel and Allen, those were taken care of before the warm weather arrived last year."

"Hopefully, Timothy will get all the screens replaced here soon. With nicer weather on the way, it will be good to have fresh air circulating through the house."

Hannah left the room and stepped into the hall. "I think we should go downstairs now and see what the kids are up to in the kitchen."

"Oh yes, and I want to give you my housewarming gifts, too."

When they entered the kitchen, the children were gone. Hannah checked the living room and found them sitting on the floor with a stack of books. "Go to the bathroom and wash up," she instructed. "You probably have chocolate on your hands, and I don't want that getting on any of Mindy's books."

The children did as she asked, but they didn't look happy about it.

Hannah turned to Bonnie and said, "Those kids of Samuel's can sure be stubborn."

Bonnie chuckled. "I guess all kids can be that way at times."

The two women continued on into the kitchen, and Bonnie removed a carton of eggs, a cookbook, several dish towels, and a loaf of homemade bread from the wicker basket she'd set on the table. "The eggs are from my layers," she said. "Oh, and Trisha made the bread, I made the dish towels, and the cookbook was put together by some of the women at my church. I have one, too, and all the recipes I've tried so far have been very good."

"Thank you for everything," Hannah said as they both took a seat at the table.

Hannah thumbed through the cookbook and stopped when she came to a recipe for Kentucky chocolate chip pie. "You know, I was planning to make this pie for Christmas, but I didn't feel like doing any baking. I really do need to try it sometime though. Timothy likes anything with chocolate chips in it, and I bet he'd enjoy the pie."

"It does sound tasty," Bonnie agreed. "If you try it, let me know how it turns out. I could even be your guinea pig," she added with a gleam in her eyes.

"I might just do that." Hannah laughed. "Would you like a cup of tea?" She offered, feeling cheerful. "It won't take long to get the water heated."

"That sounds nice, but I really should get going. I need to drive Trisha to her physical therapy appointment this afternoon, and if we get an early start, I may try to get some shopping done while we're in Hopkinsville."

Bonnie was just starting for the door when a fat, little frog hopped out of the sink onto the counter, then leaped onto the floor by Hannah's feet. She screamed and jumped up. "Jared Fisher, did you bring that frosch into the house?"

Wearing a sheepish expression, Jared shuffled into the kitchen. Hannah pointed at the frog. "Take it outside, right now!"

Hannah was relieved when the child did as she asked but embarrassed that she'd made a fool of herself in front of Bonnie. "I've had a fear of frogs ever since my oldest brother put one in my bed when I was a little girl," she explained. "And I sure never expected to see a frog this early in the year."

"It must be the warm weather that brought it out." Bonnie smiled. "And believe me, I understand about your fear. I think we all have a fear of something."

"Not Timothy. I don't think he's afraid of anything."

"Most men won't admit to being afraid because they want us to think they're fearless." Bonnie chuckled and moved toward the door. "It was nice seeing you, Hannah, and thanks for giving me a tour of your new home."

"Thank you for stopping by and for all these nice things."

Hannah stood at the door and watched as Bonnie walked out to her car. It had been nice to have an adult to visit with for a while. Even though Hannah kept busy watching the children, she often felt lonely and isolated. Oh, what she wouldn't give for a good visit with Mom.

CHAPTER 34

As Esther's driver, Pat Summers, turned onto the road leading to Pembroke, Esther's excitement mounted. Here it was the first Saturday in April, and she could hardly believe she'd been gone two months. But her help had been needed in Pennsylvania, and she'd stayed until Dad was well enough to take over working the stands at both farmers' markets. It had been good to spend time with her family, but as hard as it was to leave, she knew her place was here in Kentucky with Samuel and his children. She would stop by the B&B first to drop off her luggage and let Bonnie know she was back, and then she would head over to see Samuel and the children.

"I hope the woman you work for at the bed-and-breakfast will have a room available for me to spend the night," Pat said as they neared Bonnie's place. "If there are no vacancies, I'll have to look for a hotel in Hopkinsville. I've done enough traveling for one day and need to rest up."

Esther smiled at her. "When I spoke to Bonnie on the phone a few days ago, she said she didn't have any guests coming until next weekend. So unless things have changed, I'm sure she'll have a room for you."

"I'm anxious to see the B&B," Pat said. "From what you've told me, it sounds like a real nice place."

Esther nodded. "It is now, but you should have seen the house before Samuel and Allen fixed it up. Both men are good carpenters, and Samuel's an expert painter, so Bonnie was very pleased with how it turned out." Esther motioned to the B&B sign on her right. "Here we are. Turn right there."

Pat drove up the driveway and parked her van on the side of Bonnie's garage. When they got out of the van, Cody leaped off the porch and ran out to greet them.

"Oh, I hope he doesn't bite," Pat said when the dog jumped up on Esther.

"No, he's just excited to see me." Esther told Cody to get down; then she bent over and stroked his head. "Good boy, Cody. Have you missed me?"

Woof! Woof! Cody wagged his tail.

"I've missed you, too," Esther said with a chuckle. "Now be a good dog and go lie down."

Cody darted over to Pat and sniffed her shoes before making a beeline for the porch, where he flopped down near the door.

Esther found the front door open, so she didn't bother to knock. They'd just entered the foyer when Bonnie stepped out of the kitchen. "Oh, it's so good to see you!" she said, giving Esther a hug. "I knew you were coming back today, but I wasn't sure what time you'd get here."

"We spent last night in a hotel in Louisville and got an early start this morning," Esther explained. She turned to Pat and introduced her to Bonnie.

"I was wondering if I might be able to rent a room for the night," Pat said after shaking Bonnie's hand.

Bonnie nodded. "I have no other guests right now, so you

can take your pick from any of the rooms. Shall we go upstairs and take a look right now?"

"Sure, that'd be great."

While Bonnie took Pat upstairs, Esther meandered into the kitchen. She found Trisha baking cookies. "Ah, so that's the source of the wonderful aroma," she said, motioning to the cookies cooling on racks.

"It's nice to see you, Esther," Trisha said. "I'm sure you're glad to be back."

Esther nodded. "Yes, I am. I've missed seeing all of my friends here."

"How soon will you want to start working at the B&B again?" Trisha asked.

"I'm not sure. I'll need to talk to Bonnie about that." Esther motioned to the cookies. "If those taste as good as they smell, I'd say any B&B guests who might get to eat them are in for a real treat."

"I hope so."

"I hope you'll stay here for a while," Esther said. "At least until I know what my plans are going to be."

Trisha quirked an eyebrow. "What do you mean? Are you saying you might not continue to work for Bonnie?"

"I'm not sure. It'll depend on how soon Samuel and I get married, and whether he wants me to keep working or not." Esther leaned on the edge of the counter. "I probably shouldn't have said anything until I've talked to Samuel, so I'd appreciate it if you didn't mention this to Bonnie."

"I won't say anything."

"If I should decide to quit, would you stay to help Bonnie?" Esther asked.

Trisha shrugged. "Maybe. I do like it here, and Bonnie and I have become quite close. In fact, I've begun to feel like she's the daughter I never had."

Esther smiled. "I'm glad."

Just then Bonnie and Pat entered the kitchen. "You were right. This place is wonderful," Pat said, looking at Esther.

"Which room did you choose?" Esther asked.

"The one with the Amish theme. I love that Log Cabin quilt on the bed."

"It is nice," Esther agreed. "But then I like most Amish quilt patterns."

"Why don't we all take a seat?" Bonnie motioned to the table. "We can have some of Trisha's delicious cookies and a cup of hot tea."

—⟋∿⟍—

A crisp afternoon breeze brushed Hannah's face, and she shivered. It might be officially spring, but the chilly weather said otherwise.

I wish Timothy didn't have to spend the day plowing the fields, Hannah thought as she hitched Timothy's horse to the buggy. She'd wanted to spend the day as a family—maybe hire a driver and do some shopping in Hopkinsville—but Timothy said he didn't have time. It seemed like whenever he wasn't painting with Samuel, he had work to do here. Hannah kept busy during the week, taking care of Samuel's kids and keeping up with things around the house, but when the weekend came, she was ready to do something besides work. Since Timothy wasn't available today, she'd decided to take Mindy and go over to see Bonnie for a while. Hannah's horse, Lilly, had thrown a shoe, so Hannah knew if she wanted to go anywhere, she'd have to take Dusty. She hoped he would cooperate with her and take it nice and easy, because there had been times when she'd ridden with Timothy that he'd had to

the STRUGGLE

work hard to keep the horse under control. Since Dusty had
been let loose in the pasture this morning and had a good run,
Hannah figured he might be ready for a slower pace.

As she guided the horse and buggy down the lane, Hannah
saw Timothy out in the field. He must have seen her, too, for
he lifted his hand in a wave. Hannah waved back and stopped
the horse at the end of the lane to check for traffic. Seeing no
cars coming, she directed the horse onto the road. They'd only
gone a short ways when Dusty started to trot, but it quickly
turned into a gallop. Hannah tightened her grip on the reins
and pulled hard, but that didn't hold the horse back. "Whoa!"
she hollered, using her legs to brace the reins. "Whoa, Dusty!
Whoa!"

Dusty kept running, and the foam from his sweat flew
back on Hannah, but she was concentrating so hard, she
barely took notice. As the horse continued to gallop, the buggy
rocked from side to side. If she didn't get Dusty under control
soon, the buggy might tip over.

The sound of the horse's hooves moving so fast against the
pavement was almost deafening as Hannah struggled to gain
control. Dusty clearly had a mind of his own.

*This is what I get for taking a horse I really don't know how
to handle,* Hannah fumed. *Guess I should have stayed home today
and found something else to do.*

The buggy swayed, taking them frighteningly close to a
telephone pole, and Mindy, sitting in the seat behind Hannah, began to cry.

"It's gonna be okay, Mindy," Hannah called over her
shoulder. "Hang on tight to your seat, and don't let go!"

CHAPTER 35

Hannah's fingers ached as she gripped Dusty's reins and pulled with all her strength. Why wouldn't the crazy horse listen to her and slow down? If she wasn't able to get control of him soon, she didn't know what would happen.

Another buggy was coming from the opposite direction. As it drew closer, she realized it belonged to Titus and Suzanne. They must have known she was in trouble, for as soon as they passed, Titus whipped his rig around and came up behind Hannah's buggy. A few minutes later, his horse came alongside hers. Grateful for the help, but fearful a car might come and hit Titus's buggy, all Hannah could do was cling to the reins and pray.

Titus's horse was moving fast, and he managed to pass and move directly in front of Hannah's horse and buggy. Hannah knew if Dusty kept running he'd smack into the back of Titus's rig, but thankfully, the horse slowed down. When Titus pulled over to the side of the road, she was able to pull in behind him. Titus then handed Suzanne the reins, hopped out of his rig, and came around to Hannah's buggy. "Are you okay?" he asked with a worried expression.

Out of breath and barely able to speak, she nodded and said, "Dusty got away from me, and I couldn't slow him down."

"Well, slide on over and let me take the reins," Titus said. "I'll drive your horse and buggy, and Suzanne can follow us in my rig."

"Danki. I appreciate your help so much," Hannah said, blinking back tears and grateful that nothing serious had happened—especially since she had Mindy with her.

"Where were you heading?"

"I was going to visit Bonnie, but I've changed my mind. I just want to go home."

Titus climbed into the buggy and took a seat beside Hannah. Then glancing into the backseat, where Mindy was still crying, he said, "It's okay, Mindy. Everything's gonna be fine."

Hannah was so relieved that Titus had come along and taken control of Timothy's horse. One thing she knew for sure: she'd never take Dusty out again by herself!

—⟨⟩—

Esther's heart raced as she neared Samuel's house. Rather than taking the time to hitch her horse to the buggy, she'd ridden over on her scooter. Since Samuel's place wasn't far from Bonnie's, it hadn't taken her long to get there.

Esther parked the scooter near the porch and hurried up the steps. Just then the door opened and Samuel, as well as all four of his children, rushed out to greet her.

Samuel gave Esther a hug. "It sure is good to see you!"

She smiled. "It's good to see all of you, too."

The children began talking at once, asking Esther questions and vying for her attention.

"All right now," Samuel finally said, "you can visit more

with Esther later on. Right now I'd like some time to visit with her alone. Why don't you all go to the kitchen and eat a snack? There's some cheese and apple slices in the refrigerator."

"I'm not hungerich." Penny pointed to her stomach. "My silo's still full from lunch."

"So your silo's still full, is it? Didn't know my little maedel had a silo right there." Samuel gave Penny's stomach a couple of pats; then he leaned his head back, and the sound of his laughter seemed to bounce off the porch ceiling.

Esther and the children laughed, too. It was good to be back with Samuel and his family. She'd missed them all so much. These children had become like her own, and she couldn't wait to become their stepmother.

When the laughter subsided, the children gave Esther another hug and bounded into the house.

As Esther and Samuel sat on the porch visiting, she studied the man with whom she'd fallen so hopelessly in love. Samuel's light brown hair, streaked with gold from the sun, was thick and healthy-looking. His dark brown eyes, so sincere, spoke of his love for her.

"Now that you're back," Samuel said, reaching for Esther's hand, "can we set a date for our wedding?"

She smiled. "I'd like that."

"How about next month?"

Esther shook her head. "Oh Samuel, as much as I would like that, it's just a bit too soon. I'll need some time to make my wedding dress, and with Bonnie and Allen getting married soon, and then going on a two-week honeymoon, I'll also need to help at the B&B. Could we get married the last Tuesday in June?"

"I'd sure like it to be sooner, but I guess June isn't that far off," he said.

"No, it's not, and we do need to give our folks some advance notice so they can plan for the trip." Esther's face sobered. "I hope Mom and Dad will be able to come. With my brother not doing well, they may feel that they can't leave Sarah to care for him on her own."

"I'm sure they can get someone else to help with Dan's care for a few days," Samuel said. "I don't think your parents would miss your wedding."

"I hope not. I'd really like to have them here."

"Speaking of your parents, maybe when they come for the wedding I can ask about buying this house. I've appreciated being able to rent the place from them, but I'd really like to have a house I can call my own."

Esther nodded. "It's good that you mentioned it, because that topic came up while I was in Pennsylvania. Mom and Dad said they'd be willing to sell the house to us for a reasonable price, and I'm sure Dad will discuss the details with you soon."

Samuel grinned. "Now, that's good news!"

"There's something else we need to discuss," Esther said.

"What's that?"

"I was wondering if you'd like me to quit my job at the B&B after we're married."

Samuel pulled his fingers through the ends of his beard and sat quietly as he contemplated her question. Finally, he smiled and said, "It's really your decision, but if it were left up to me, you'd quit working for Bonnie and be a full-time wife and mother."

"I feel that way, too," Esther said. "And I think Trisha might be willing to stay on and keep working for Bonnie. She seems really happy there. In fact, if she agrees, then I can quit even before we get married."

"That's good to hear. Sounds like it will all work out."

"As I said, I'll need to help out at the B&B while Bonnie and Allen are on their honeymoon. If things get busy, Trisha will need some help."

"That's fine with me." Samuel smiled widely. "I can't wait to share the news with my family that you and I will be getting married in June."

CHAPTER 36

"Are you getting nervous yet?" Trisha asked when Bonnie came down to breakfast two days before her wedding.

Bonnie nodded. "I'd be lying if I said I wasn't."

"I understand. My stomach was tied in knots for two full weeks before my wedding."

"I think I'll feel better once I get busy around here. Since Allen and I will be going to Nashville tomorrow to pick up my dad and his folks at the airport, I need to get as much done today as I can in preparation for the reception."

"I'll do everything I can to help, and don't forget, Esther will be coming over."

"I'm sure Dad and Allen's folks will help when they get here, too." Bonnie opened the refrigerator and took out a boiled egg. "Guess I'd better hurry and eat so I can get going."

"You'd better have something more than an egg to eat, or you'll run out of steam before you even get started." Trisha placed a plate of toast on the table and poured Bonnie a glass of orange juice and a cup of coffee.

"Thanks." Bonnie smiled. "You certainly do take good care of me."

A lump formed in Trisha's throat. "You've become very special to me, and it gives me pleasure to do things for you."

"You're special to me, too," Bonnie said as she took a seat at the table. "Are you going to join me for breakfast?"

"I already ate, but I'll have a second cup of coffee and visit while you eat."

After Trisha joined her at the table, Bonnie said a prayer, thanking God for the food and for her and Trisha's friendship. When the prayer ended, she reached for a piece of toast and spread some strawberry jam on top. "Are you sure you can manage on your own for the two weeks Allen and I will be in Hawaii?" she asked Trisha.

"Esther will be helping as much as she can, so between the two of us, we'll manage just fine."

Bonnie placed her hand on Trisha's arm. "I'm so glad you've decided to stay here permanently."

"I'm happy about it, too; although some of my friends in California weren't too thrilled when I called and gave them the news."

"I'm sure that's only because they're going to miss you and had hoped you might be returning to California soon."

"I suppose." Trisha pursed her lips. "I just hope your dad won't mind when he hears the news."

"Why would he mind?"

Trisha shrugged. "He might not like the idea of his ex-girlfriend working for his daughter."

"Dad already knows you're working for me, and he hasn't said anything negative about it."

"He may not have said anything to you, but when I spoke to him on the phone the last time, he made it pretty clear that he wasn't thrilled about me being here." Trisha's forehead wrinkled. "He probably didn't say anything to you because he assumed my working at the B&B was temporary. He may have figured by the time he came here for your wedding, I'd be long gone."

"I think you're worried for nothing. I'll bet when Dad gets here he won't say a negative thing about you working for me." Bonnie gave Trisha's arm a little pat. "Now, I'd better finish my breakfast, because this is going to be a very long day."

———⁓———

The slanting afternoon sun glared in Hannah's face as she gripped the hoe and chopped at the weeds threatening to overtake her garden. Weeding was no fun, but it needed to be done. She'd planted several things a few weeks ago, and already the weeds looked healthier than the plants coming up. Maybe what they needed was more water. They'd had a dry spring so far, and Hannah had to water her vegetable garden, as well as the flowers she'd planted close to the house, by hand. Oh how she wished they would get some much-needed rain.

Mo-o-o! Mo-o-o! A brown-and-white cow in their neighbor's pasture peered across the fence at Hannah with gentle-looking eyes but a forlorn expression that matched Hannah's mood. She would much rather be doing something else, but if she didn't stay on top of the weeds, she wouldn't have any homegrown food to can in the fall.

Of course, she thought ruefully, *all the homegrown food in the world won't stave off the loneliness I've often felt since we moved to Kentucky.* In Pennsylvania she'd had some friends, and Hannah's mother had always been available whenever she'd needed help. *If Mom were here right now, she'd be helping me with the weeding.*

Hannah knew she should quit dwelling on the same old thing. After all, she was making some new friends here in

Kentucky, and things had been a little better between her and Timothy since they'd moved into their new home.

Hannah's thoughts were halted when she heard buzzing to her left. Three hummingbirds fluttered around the glass feeder she'd hung on a shepherd's hook in one of her flower beds. It was always fun to watch the tiny birds skitter back and forth between the trees and the feeder. If more hummingbirds came, she'd need to put up a second feeder.

Just then the van belonging to Timothy's driver came up the lane. Hannah smiled. Timothy was home early today. Maybe he'd get those screens put in the window like he kept promising to do. Or maybe they could spend some time together this afternoon and do something fun with Mindy.

After Timothy told his driver good-bye, he joined Hannah by the garden. "Looks like you've been busy," he said.

She nodded. "It's a lot of work to keep up a garden."

"Jah, but it'll be worth it when we have fresh produce to put on the table, not to mention whatever you're able to can for our use during the winter months."

"I'm surprised to see you back so early," she said, changing the subject.

"Samuel and I finished our job in Clarksville sooner than we thought, and he figured it was too late in the day to start something else, so he said I should go home."

"I hope you won't have to work this coming Saturday," Hannah said. "It's Bonnie and Allen's wedding day, remember?"

"Don't worry. Neither Samuel nor I will be working that day, and Titus won't be working at the woodshop either, so we'll all be free to go to the wedding."

"I've never been to an English wedding," Hannah said. "I wonder what it'll be like."

"We'll find out soon enough, but right now I'm going to

get some work done around here."

"Are you going to be able to replace those screens for the windows today?" she asked.

He shook his head. "I need to get some more planting done in the fields, but I'll get to the screens as soon as I can."

"But it's hot and stuffy upstairs, and it's only going to get worse as the weather gets warmer."

"So open the windows awhile."

"Flies and other nasty insects will get in."

"If you can't stand the flies, just keep the doors and windows downstairs open during the day, and that should help."

"It seems like you never finish anything when I ask," Hannah mumbled. "At least not since we moved here."

"I'll get the screens done as soon as I can. Right now, though, I'm going into the house to get something to eat before I head out to the field."

"Don't eat too much," she admonished, "or you'll spoil your supper."

"Well what can I say?" he said with a sheepish grin. "I'm a hardworking man, and I need to eat a lot in order to keep up my strength. You wouldn't want me to waste away to nothing, would you?"

"No, of course not."

He started to walk away, but she called out to him, "Don't make a bunch of noise when you go inside. Mindy's taking a nap. Oh, and please don't make a mess in the kitchen. I just cleaned the floor this morning."

He grunted and strode quickly up to the house.

Hannah sighed. Since Timothy seemed in a hurry to get out to the fields, she hadn't even bothered to mention them doing anything fun together this afternoon. What was the point? She was sure he would have said no. Between Timothy's paint jobs and his work in the fields, they rarely spent any quality time together anymore. And what time they did spend, Timothy either had work on his mind or ended up talking about Samuel and Titus. With the exception of church every other Sunday, they hardly went anywhere as a family. They'd talked about going to see the Jefferson Davis Monument, which wasn't far from where they lived, but they hadn't even done that. Hannah was beginning to wonder if all Timothy wanted to do was work. Maybe he thought she would be happy working all the time, too. As it was, she kept busy doing things she didn't really enjoy in order to keep from being bored. She'd all but given up on the idea of buying and selling antiques. The last time she'd mentioned it to Timothy, he'd repeated his objections.

Timothy has his brothers and Allen for companionship, Hannah thought. *But who do I have? Just Mindy most of the time, and of course that dopey little cat who likes to lie on the porch with his floppy paws in the air. Bonnie and Esther are busy planning their weddings, and Suzanne only comes around once in a while.*

Hannah knew she was giving in to self-pity, but she couldn't seem to help herself. Her resolve to make the best of things was crumbling. *Maybe I should join Timothy for a snack. I could really use something cold to drink, and at least it would give us a few minutes to visit before he heads out to the fields.*

She set the hoe aside, stretched her aching limbs, and hurried toward the house. When she stepped into the kitchen, she halted, shocked to see Timothy sitting on a chair with Mindy over his knees, giving her a spanking.

"What do you think you're doing?" Hannah shouted over Mindy's cries.

Timothy looked at Hannah, but he didn't speak to her

until he'd finished spanking Mindy. Then he set the child on the floor and told her to go upstairs to her room.

Mindy looked at Hannah with sorrowful eyes, tears dribbling down her cheeks. Hannah reached out her arms, but Timothy shook his head. "She's a *nixnutzich* little girl and deserved that *bletsching*." He pointed to the door leading to the stairs. "Go on now, Mindy, schnell!"

Alternating between sniffling and hiccupping, Mindy ran out of the room.

Hannah placed her hands on her hips and glared at Timothy. "Now what's this all about, and why do you think Mindy is naughty and deserved to be spanked?"

"When I came in to get a snack, I figured Mindy was still taking a nap," Timothy said. "But what I found instead was our daughter with a jar of petroleum jelly, and she was spreadin' it all over the sofa. When I told her to come with me to the kitchen, she wouldn't budge—she just looked up at me defiantly. So I picked her up and carried her to the kitchen. After she started kicking and screaming, I'd had enough, so I put her across my knees and gave her a well-deserved spanking."

"She shouldn't have been playing with the petroleum jelly," Hannah said, "but she's only a little girl, and I think you were too harsh with her." Irritation put an edge to Hannah's voice, but she didn't care. As far as she was concerned, Timothy had punished their daughter in anger, and that was wrong.

"I may have been angry, but I didn't spank her that hard. I just wanted Mindy to learn that it's wrong to get into things and make a mess, and that her disobedience will result in some kind of punishment."

"It doesn't have to be a bletsching." Hannah's tone was crisp and to the point. "There are other forms of punishment, you know."

"Sometimes a spanking's the best way to teach a child as young as Mindy that there are consequences for disobedience."

Hannah's mouth quivered as she struggled not to give in to the tears pricking the back of her eyes. *I won't let him see me cry. Not this time.*

Timothy stood and pulled her gently into his arms. "Let's not argue, Hannah. I love you, and I love Mindy, too."

"You have a funny way of showing it sometimes."

He brushed a kiss across her forehead. "I'm doing the best I can."

Hannah shrugged and turned away.

"Where are you going?" he called as she headed for the stairs.

"Upstairs to comfort Mindy!" Hannah raced from the room before he could say anything else. Timothy might think he was doing his best, but at the moment, she wasn't the least bit convinced.

CHAPTER 37

Hopkinsville, Kentucky

When Allen stepped out of his bedroom, he heard his parents' voices coming from the kitchen. Hearing his name mentioned, he paused and listened, even though he knew it was wrong to eavesdrop.

"I can't believe our son is finally getting married," Mom said. "I was about to give up."

Allen rolled his eyes. Mom could be so dramatic about things.

"I know," Dad agreed. "This is a very special day for him, and for us, too."

"Maybe there's some hope of us becoming grandparents."

"That would be nice. Think I'd enjoy having little ones to buy Christmas gifts and birthday presents for."

"I wonder if Allen and Bonnie are planning to start a family right away."

"Are you two talking about me behind my back and planning my future to boot?" Allen asked, stepping into the kitchen. He wasn't really irritated—just surprised by their conversation.

Mom smoothed the lapel on Allen's white tuxedo. "You and Bonnie do want children, don't you?"

Allen nodded. "Yes, Mom, we do."

She smiled. "You know, when I came here last year to help out after you'd injured your back, I had a hunch you and Bonnie would get together."

He tipped his head. "Oh, really? What made you think that?"

"I could see the gleam in your eyes whenever you spoke of her. After spending time with Bonnie yesterday when you two picked us up at the airport, I could see how well you complement each other."

"I agree with your mother," Dad said. "Bonnie's a great gal, and I do believe she was worth waiting for, son."

Allen smiled. "You're right about that. Bonnie is all I could ever ask for in a wife, and I hope we have as good a marriage as you two have had."

—⁂—

Fairview, Kentucky

"Dad, there's something I've been wanting to talk to you about," Bonnie said after she'd pulled into the church parking lot and turned off the car.

"What's that?" he asked, turning in the passenger's seat to face her.

"Trisha plans to make Kentucky her permanent home. She'll be working for me at the B&B full-time."

His mouth dropped open. "How come?"

"Because Esther will be getting married toward the end of June, and she won't be working for me any longer."

He folded his arms and stared straight ahead. "I see."

"I have a complaint." Bonnie readily listened to the

complaints of others, but rarely spoke of her own. Today she would make an exception.

"What's the gripe?" he asked.

"I'm not happy about the way you give Trisha the cold shoulder."

"I don't do that."

"Yes you do. I have a hunch you're still angry with her for breaking up with you when you were teenagers. You know, you shouldn't think negative thoughts about someone until you have all the facts."

Dad frowned deeply. "Facts about what? Trisha broke up with me; I blamed my parents; and I can't go back and change any of it—end of story."

"But you're still angry about it."

"So?"

"So, you need to forgive Trisha as well as yourself. And remember, what lies behind us and what lies before us are small matters compared to what lies within us."

Dad rubbed his forehead, as though mulling things over.

"Remember when you asked what I'd like for a wedding present?"

He nodded.

"Well, the one thing that would give me the greatest pleasure would be for you to make peace with Trisha. Is that too much to ask?" She sat quietly, hoping he'd take her words to heart.

He turned his head and gave her a faint smile. "I'll give it some thought."

———

Pembroke, Kentucky

As Samuel stood in front of the bathroom mirror combing

his hair, he smiled. Two of his good friends were getting married today, and he couldn't be happier for them. He was glad Allen and Bonnie had invited him and the kids to attend the wedding, but he was a bit nervous about going. He'd never been to an English wedding before and wasn't sure what to expect. The ceremony would be quite different from Amish weddings, and he hoped the kids wouldn't say or do anything to embarrass him.

They usually behave themselves during our church services, he reminded himself. *So, hopefully they'll be on their best behavior today.*

Setting his comb aside, Samuel opened the bathroom door and was surprised to see Penny standing in the hallway.

"I smell peppermint candy," she said when Samuel stepped out of the bathroom. "Were you eatin' candy in there, Daadi?"

Samuel chuckled and patted the top of her head. "No, silly girl. Daadi washed his hair with some new shampoo that smells like peppermint."

Penny stuck her head in the bathroom and sniffed the air. "Are ya sure 'bout that?"

"Of course I'm sure. Now go tell your brothers and sister that it's time for us to pick Esther up. We don't want to be late for Allen and Bonnie's wedding."

Penny looked up at him with a serious expression. "I wish it was you and Esther gettin' married today."

"I wish that, too, but just think. . .by the end of June, Esther will be my fraa, and your new mamm."

Penny offered him a wide grin. "I can hardly wait for that!"

Samuel smiled and nodded. "No more than I can, little one."

CHAPTER 38

Fairview, Kentucky

"Y ou make a beautiful bride," Trisha said as she helped Bonnie set her veil in place. "And your dress is absolutely gorgeous!" She gestured to the hand-beaded detail on the bodice and hem of the long, full-gathered skirt made of an off-white satin material.

"You don't think it's too much, do you?"

Trisha shook her head. "Absolutely not. Your wedding gown is as lovely as the woman wearing it, and you deserve to look like a princess today."

Bonnie smiled. "You're a pretty matron of honor, too."

Tears pooled in Trisha's eyes. "I'm honored that you would ask me to stand up with you."

Bonnie gave Trisha a hug. "You've become a good friend."

"But Esther's your friend, too, and I figured you'd want her to stand up with you."

"You're right, Esther's a very special friend, but I'm fairly sure that her church wouldn't allow her to be part of my bridal party, so I only asked you." Bonnie readjusted her lacy veil just a bit. "I'm glad most of my Amish friends will be able to attend the wedding, however."

"Will you be invited to Esther and Samuel's wedding?" Trisha questioned.

"Oh yes. I went when Titus and Suzanne got married, so I'm sure I'll get an invitation to Esther and Samuel's wedding, too."

"Are Amish weddings much different than ours?"

"They definitely are." Bonnie smiled at Trisha. "Since you and Esther have gotten to know each other quite well, I'm almost sure you'll get an invitation to her wedding."

"I hope so. That would truly be an honor for me."

A knock sounded on the door of the little room in the church where Bonnie and Trisha had gone to get ready.

"Would you like me to see who that is?" Trisha asked.

Bonnie nodded. "If it's Allen, I don't want him to see me until I walk down the aisle, so please don't let him in."

"Don't worry. I won't." When Trisha opened the door, Bonnie's dad walked in. He stepped up to Bonnie and stared at her as though in disbelief.

"Doesn't your daughter look beautiful in that dress?" Trisha asked.

"Yes, she's stunning." Dad smiled and gave Bonnie a hug. Then he turned to Trisha and said, "You look very nice, too."

Trisha's cheeks flushed. "Why, thank you, Kenny—I mean, Ken. You look pretty spiffy yourself."

Bonnie smiled. For the first time, she felt the barrier between Dad and Trisha come down a wee bit. *Thank You, God, for this answered prayer.*

"I believe it's time for me to walk you down the aisle," Dad said, extending his arm to Bonnie. "Your groom is waiting for you and probably growing anxious."

"No more than I am," Bonnie said, blinking back tears.

They followed Trisha from the room, and when they reached the back of the sanctuary, Trisha turned and gave Bonnie's dress and veil a quick once-over. After offering Bonnie a reassuring smile, she made her way slowly down the aisle in time to the soft organ music.

Bonnie clung to Dad's arm as they followed Trisha down the aisle. Just as all the wedding guests stood, an explosion of sunlight spilled through the stained-glass windows. The light seemed to guide Bonnie down the aisle, where her groom waited beside his cousin, Bill, whom he'd chosen to be his best man. Every fiber of Bonnie's being wanted to be Allen's wife. He was like a magnet drawing her to him.

Bonnie glanced to her left and spotted Esther sitting with Samuel and his children. In the pew next to them sat Titus and Suzanne, along with Timothy, Hannah, and little Mindy. To the right, she saw Allen's parents, and behind them Allen's friend, Zach, with his wife, Leona. They'd come from Pennsylvania for this special occasion and would be staying at Titus's place. Others from Bonnie's church and some from the community had also come to witness the wedding. It was wonderful to know she and Allen had so many good friends.

When Bonnie and Dad joined the wedding party at the altar, Pastor Cunningham smiled and said, "Who gives this woman to be wed?"

"I do," Dad answered in a clear but steady voice. When he kissed Bonnie's cheek and hugged her before taking a seat in the first pew, Bonnie noticed tears in his eyes.

—ᴍ—

Hannah sat straight as a board as she watched this very different wedding ceremony and recalled her own wedding day. She wondered what it would have been like to wear a long white gown with a veil and walk down an aisle in a church with people sitting on both sides of the sanctuary watching her every move. At least in an Amish wedding, the bride and groom were able to sit throughout most of the service. They didn't stand before the minister until it was time to say their vows.

"Dearly beloved," the pastor said, capturing Hannah's attention, "we are gathered together in the sight of God and the presence of these witnesses to join this man and this woman in holy matrimony, which is an honorable estate instituted by God in the time of man's innocence, signifying unto us the mystical union that exists between Christ and His Church. It is, therefore, not to be entered into unadvisedly, but reverently, discreetly, and in the fear of God. Into this holy estate these persons present now come to be joined."

The pastor's expression was solemn as he continued: "Allen and Bonnie, I require and charge you both as you stand in the presence of God, to remember that the commitment to marriage means putting the needs of your mate ahead of your own. The act of giving is a vivid reminder that it's all about God and not you. Be an encourager to your mate. The more you bless each other, the more God will bless you."

Hannah cringed. She had fallen short when it came to encouraging Timothy—especially when he'd decided to move to Kentucky. She rarely put his needs ahead of her own.

"Remember, too, that it's a privilege to pray," the pastor continued. "Turn your thoughts toward God in the morning, and you'll feel His presence all day. Make each day count as if it were your last, and forget about the *if onlys*, for they can only lead to self-pity. Tell yourself each morning that this day is what counts, so you may as well make the most of it. Finally, don't harbor bitterness toward God or your marriage partner."

Hannah shifted uneasily in her seat. She'd been harboring bitterness toward Timothy ever since they moved to Kentucky, and when he'd spanked Mindy the other day, it had fueled her anger.

She turned her head and smiled at Timothy and was glad when he smiled in response. Maybe they could start over. Maybe if she tried harder to be a good wife, things would go better between them.

CHAPTER 39

Paradise, Pennsylvania

Sally had just finished washing the supper dishes when she looked out the kitchen window and spotted a horse and buggy coming up the driveway. When the driver stopped near the barn, she recognized who it was.

"Abraham Fisher is here," she called to Johnny, who sat at the table reading the newspaper.

"He must have come to look at the hog I have for sale." Johnny left his seat and hurried out the back door.

A few minutes later, Sally saw Fannie standing near the buggy, so she opened the back door and hollered, "You're welcome to come inside if you like!"

Fannie waved and started walking toward the house.

"Let's go into the kitchen and have a glass of iced tea while the men take care of business," Sally suggested when Fannie entered the house.

Fannie smiled. "That sounds nice. It's been hot today—too hot for the first day of June, if you ask me."

"I agree. Makes me wonder what our summer's going to be like."

Sally poured them both a glass of iced tea, and they took seats at the table.

"I haven't heard from Timothy in a while," Fannie said. "Have you heard anything from Hannah?"

"No, not for a week or so."

"The last I heard from Timothy, he mentioned that he and Hannah were going to Allen Walters's wedding."

"Hannah mentioned that, too, but I haven't heard anything from her since," Sally said. "To tell you the truth, I haven't been phoning Hannah as often as before."

"How come?" Fannie took a sip of iced tea.

"Johnny pointed out that I need to give our daughter some space." Sally sighed. "I still miss Hannah something awful, and it's hard having her living so far away."

"I understand," Fannie said. "Try as I may, it's still hard to accept the fact that three of my sons have moved to Kentucky. I'd always hoped and believed that when Abraham and I reached old age we'd have all our kinner and kinskinner living close to us. But I've learned to accept that it's not meant to be."

"The problem for me," Sally said, "is that I'm not as emotionally close to our sons and their wives as I am to Hannah. That's made it doubly hard for me since she moved away."

"I understand, but you can still be close to your daughter without her living nearby." Fannie smiled. "Just be there for her, if and when she needs you. That'll count for a lot."

—◦◦◦—

Pembroke, Kentucky

Trisha couldn't believe how lonely she'd felt since Bonnie and Allen had left on their honeymoon. She'd become used to fixing supper and sharing it with Bonnie and didn't enjoy eating all her meals alone. She didn't have any guests at the B&B right now, either, so things had been unusually quiet.

"Now quit feeling sorry for yourself," Trisha mumbled as she entered the kitchen. "You've been living alone since Dave died and managed okay, so why's this any different? Besides, you should be enjoying this little rest before things start to pick up again."

Resolved to make the best of the situation, Trisha took a container of leftover soup from the refrigerator and poured the contents into a kettle. She was about to turn on the stove when the telephone rang. She quickly picked up the receiver. "Hello. Bonnie's Bed-and-Breakfast."

"Trisha, this is Ken."

"Oh, hi. How are you?"

"I'm doing okay, but I was wondering if you've heard any-thing from Bonnie lately. I'm worried about her and Allen."

"How come?"

"I just heard on the news that one of those tour helicopters from Kauai went down, and I know they were planning to go up in one, so I'm wondering if—"

"Did you try calling them, Ken?"

"Yes, I did, and I had to leave a message on both of their cell phones. I'm telling you, Trisha, this has me really worried."

"I'm sure they're fine. If Bonnie and Allen were involved in that crash, I'm certain you would have heard about it by now." Trisha cringed. *Oh, I hope they weren't in that helicopter. What a tragedy that would be.*

"You know, I never used to worry so much, but the older I get, the more I fret about things."

Trisha gave a small laugh, hoping to reassure him. "I know what you mean. I'm the same way."

"How are things going there?" he asked. "Have you been really busy since Bonnie and Allen left?"

"No, not really. Actually, business has been kind of slow, but I'm sure it'll pick up now that summer's almost here. I guess I should enjoy this little break before it gets busy again."

Trisha jumped as a gust of wind blew against the house, causing the windows to rattle. Rain pelted down on the roof. When the lights flickered, she said, "I hate to cut this short, Ken, but I'd better hang up. It's raining really hard, and the wind's howling so much that I'm afraid the power might go out. I need to get out some candles and battery-operated lights, just in case."

"Okay, I'll let you go. Oh, and Trisha, if you hear anything from Bonnie, would you please ask her to give me a call?"

"Yes, of course I will." The lights flickered again then went off, leaving Trisha in total darkness.

—m—

Exhausted after a hard day's work, Timothy flopped onto the sofa with a groan. He'd put in a full eight hours painting in Clarksville then come home and worked in the fields until it had started raining real hard. Every muscle in his body ached.

He leaned his head against the back of the sofa and closed his eyes, allowing his mind to wander. Things had been better between him and Hannah lately—ever since Allen and Bonnie's wedding, really. They hadn't argued even once, and Hannah seemed much sweeter and more patient with him. She hadn't nagged when he'd left his shoes in the living room the other day or complained because he'd tracked dirt into the house. Timothy didn't know the reason, but Hannah had definitely changed her attitude and actually seemed more content.

He smiled. Hannah was in the bathroom right now giving

Mindy a bath. He'd promised when she was done and had put Mindy to bed that the two of them would share a bowl of popcorn while they relaxed. He looked forward to spending time alone with his wife but wasn't sure he had the strength to stand in front of the stove and crank the lever on the corn popper. He figured Hannah would probably be awhile, so if he rested a few minutes, he might feel more like popping the corn by the time she was done bathing Mindy.

Timothy was at the point of nodding off when Mindy bounded into the room wearing her long white nightgown and fuzzy slippers. She climbed onto the sofa and put her little hands on both sides of his face. "*Gut nacht*, Daadi."

"Good night, little one." Timothy's heart swelled with love as he kissed her forehead. "Sleep tight."

Hannah smiled. "I'm taking her up to bed now, and I shouldn't be too long, so if you want to start the popcorn, I'll pour the lemonade as soon as I come down."

"Okay." How could he say no when Hannah was being so sweet?

As Hannah and Mindy headed up the stairs, Timothy pulled himself off the sofa and ambled into the kitchen. He glanced out the window. It was pitch dark, and the rain pelted the house so viciously it was almost deafening. It was hard to believe a day that had begun so sunny and warm could turn into such a stormy night.

Sure hope it'll be better by morning, he thought. *Samuel and I won't be able to finish the outside of that house we started on today if it's still raining tomorrow.*

By the time Hannah came downstairs, Timothy had made the popcorn and drizzled it with melted butter.

"That smells wunderbaar," she said, sniffing the air. "If you'll take it into the living room, I'll join you there in a few minutes with some lemonade."

"Sounds good."

A short time later, Timothy and Hannah were on the sofa with a large bowl of popcorn between them and glasses of cold lemonade.

"It sure is a stormy night," Hannah said. "A lot different than today was, that's for sure."

"You're right about that." Timothy frowned. "I'm afraid if the rain doesn't quit, I might lose my corn. It's coming down pretty fierce out there."

"I know how hard you worked planting that corn," she said. "I hope you don't lose it."

He nodded. "Working with the land reminds me that it's the Lord's creation, and it makes me feel at one with nature. We need that corn for our own use, and it would also be nice to have some to sell."

She gave him an encouraging smile. "My daed once said that disasters often bring a person back to what really matters. And if you have to replant, then there's no shame in asking your friends and family to help."

"Your daed's a wise man." Timothy's gaze came to rest on the faint smattering of freckles on Hannah's nose that had been brought out by the sun. He leaned over and nuzzled her cheek. "And as my daed always says, 'If we let God guide, He will provide.'"

—∞—

The house was quiet, and the kids had gone to bed some time ago. Samuel removed his reading glasses and rubbed his eyes then put his Bible on the table. He was wide awake and had the house all to himself—a rare opportunity for him these days.

"Guess if I'm gonna be any good tomorrow, I better get

some sleep." he murmured, slowly rising from the chair in the corner of the living room. Quietly, he walked down the hall to his room, so as not to waken anyone. His body was weary from putting in long days, but he was thankful Allen had several jobs lined up for him and Timothy. It was a blessing to have steady work, especially in these hard economic times.

When Samuel entered his bedroom, he didn't bother to turn on the battery-operated light; he just got undressed and crawled into bed. Outside the wind was blowing so strong it made the window sing. The heavy rain sounded like pebbles being thrown against the side of the house. In an effort to drown out the noise, he grabbed his pillow and put it over head. But it was no use.

Samuel groaned and stretched, trying to get the kinks out of his muscles. It was going to be one of those nights where sleep would not come quickly. True, he was bone tired, but maybe he was just too tired to sleep. Normally the rain would have lulled him to sleep, but for some reason, it had the opposite effect on him tonight. Maybe he ought to go back to the living room and read more from the Bible. Or a glass of warm milk might help him become drowsy enough to fall sleep.

Stepping into the kitchen a short time later, Samuel was surprised to find Marla sitting at the table in the dark.

"What are you doin' in here, sweet girl?" he asked, turning on the gas lantern overhead.

Marla sighed. "Oh, just thinking is all. I woke up and couldn't get back to sleep."

"I couldn't sleep either. That's some storm out there, isn't it?"

She nodded.

"The wind's blowing so hard it made my windows sound like they were singing." Samuel smiled, thinking Marla might get a chuckle out of that, but then he noticed tears glistening on her cheeks. "What's wrong? Are you afraid of the storm?" he asked.

She shook her head. "Daadi, do you think Mama would mind that you're gonna marry Esther, and that Penny and Jared have already started callin' her 'Mamm'?"

Samuel studied Marla's face and was reminded again how much she was like her mother. The child was kind and always concerned about others—just the way her mother had been. His little girl seemed to have grown up right before his eyes. She seemed more like a young lady than the nine-year-old that she was.

"Is there a reason you're thinking about this, Marla?" Samuel asked. "I thought you liked Esther."

"Oh I do, Daadi. In fact, I like Esther a lot. I just hope if Mama's lookin' down from heaven that she's not upset."

Before Samuel could respond, Marla continued. "I had a dream tonight before I came down, and it got me to thinkin'."

"Was it a bad dream?" he asked.

She shook her head. "It was kind of a nice dream, but somethin' strange happened."

"What was that?"

"I was dreamin' that we were all back in Pennsylvania, like it used to be before. . ." Marla looked down as if struggling for the word.

"Before what, Marla?"

"Before Mama died. We were sittin' by this pond, havin' a picnic. All of us were eatin' and laughin' and havin' a good time. Then, just like that, we were back in Kentucky, still sittin' by a pond havin' a picnic—only Mama's face disappeared, and it was Esther's instead." Marla sniffed. "Then the dream ended, and when I woke up, it made me wonder if Mama would be sad about Esther comin' into our lives."

Samuel's heart almost broke for his daughter's concern. She was such an innocent child with grown-up feelings. He decided right then and there to be honest with her.

"You know, Marla, I used to ask myself that same question. And before I go on, let me say that it's important for you to know that Esther is in no way replacing your mamm. No one could ever do that. You also need to know that I was torn about letting Esther into my heart when we started to have feelings for each other. I prayed about it and almost moved us back to Pennsylvania because I thought it was wrong." Samuel noticed that Marla seemed to be hanging on his every word.

"Then, while I was struggling with what to do, your mamm spoke to me in a very special way," he continued.

"She did? How'd she do that, Daadi?" Marla questioned.

Samuel didn't want to reveal just yet about Elsie's journal, because one day when Marla was an adult, he planned to give her the diary on a special occasion. He would know when the time was right.

"Well, it's kind of personal to me right now, and one day I'll share with you how I know." Samuel smiled and tousled his daughter's hair. "Believe me when I tell you that your mamm did let me know that it was okay for me to love Esther."

Marla grinned, and Samuel was glad to see her relax. They sat together in silence awhile, until he noticed that Marla was holding something and kept wrapping it through her fingers.

"What have you got there?" he asked.

"It's one of Mama's hankies." Marla's voice grew shaky. "I. . .I hope you don't mind, Daadi, but last year on my birthday when you gave me Mama's teacup and it broke, I knew you went out to the barn. So I left my room and was gonna ask Esther if you were okay, but when I walked past your room,

I saw a box sittin' on the floor. I knew it was wrong, but I went into your room to see what was in the box. When I saw Mama's hankie with the butterfly on it all folded up nice and neat with all the other things, I took it." Tears gathered in the corners of Marla's eyes. "I'm real sorry, Daadi. I shouldn't have done that, but I've taken good care of the hankie. Ever since that night, I keep it with me under the sleeve of my dress. Then at night, I put it under my pillow to keep it close. It makes me feel like Mama's right here with me. When I'm hurtin', I can just reach my hand into my sleeve and hold the hankie, and it's like Mama's holdin' my hand and makin' me feel better."

Samuel was so choked up it took a moment before he could speak. "Ach, Marla," he whispered, taking her into the comfort of his arms and rocking her as he'd done when she was a baby. "It's okay; don't you worry now. Keep your mamm's hankie close and never let it go, and do whatever you have to so that you won't forget her."

Samuel paused a minute, trying to keep his emotions under control. "Your mamm left wonderful memories behind for me, you, and your brothers and sister. They were so young at the time, but someday when Penny and Jared are older, they'll be coming to you and Leon and wanting to hear all that you remember about their mamm. Never be afraid to talk about her, even to Esther. That's what keeps her memory alive—remembering our time with her."

Samuel sat with his arm around Marla a few more minutes, enjoying this tender moment. Then, when she said good night and headed to her room, he remained at the table and bowed his head. *Thank You, Lord, for special moments like this and a memory that will be with me forever.*

CHAPTER 40

When Timothy came in from doing his chores the following morning, he wore a sorrowful look. "Sometimes I just want to give up." He flopped into a chair at the table with a groan. "Why is it that a person can feel so good about things one day, and a day later everything just comes tumbling down?"

"What's wrong?" Hannah asked, feeling concern as she handed him a cup of coffee.

"It's the corn crop," he said with a slow shake of his head. "Almost all of it's ruined, and of course after all that rain we had, it's hot and muggy now."

"I'm sorry," she said. "Did the rain cause the damage, or was it the high winds that came up last night?"

"I think it was mostly the wind, because much of the corn is lying flat. I'll either have to forget about having a corn crop this year or replant and hope the warm weather stays long enough for all the corn to grow and mature." Timothy groaned. "It's a shame, too. The corn was looking so good before the storm blew in and ruined it."

"What are you going to do now?" Hannah asked, joining him at the table.

"I don't know. What do you think about all of this?"

Hannah blew on her coffee as she contemplated the situation. She was tempted to tell Timothy that this might be a sign that they shouldn't have moved to Kentucky but knew that would probably make him all the more determined to stay. Besides, after hearing what the pastor had said during Bonnie and Allen's wedding, Hannah had resolved to be a more supportive wife. And lately she'd been thinking that living here might not be so bad after all.

"Well," she said, "since you're so busy painting right now and really don't have the time to replant, maybe you ought to forget about trying to grow corn this year. We could plant some in the garden for our own personal use and see how that does. We could always lease some of the land and keep a few acres for our own use. That way it won't be so much for you to handle."

He offered her a weak smile and reached for her hand. "I think you might be right about that."

Hannah smiled, too. It felt good to be making a decision together.

—⁂—

The phone rang, and Trisha hurried into the foyer to answer it. "Hello. Bonnie's Bed-and-Breakfast."

"Hi, Trisha, it's Ken."

"Oh, I'm surprised you're calling so early." She glanced at the clock on the mantel in the living room. "It's eight o'clock here, so it must only be six in Oregon."

"Yeah, it's early yet, but I had a hard time sleeping last night and got up at the crack of dawn."

"How come? Are you still worried about Bonnie and Allen?"

"Yes, I am, but I'm also worried about you."

Now that's a surprise. "Why are you worried about me?" she asked.

"When we talked last night, you said the weather was bad and you might lose power."

"The electricity was out for several hours, and we had pounding rain with harsh winds most of the night. But the weather looks much better this morning. The sun's out now, and it's warming up fast, so I think things will dry fairly quickly this morning."

"That's good to hear. I'm glad you're okay. But I don't think it's good for you to be in that big house all alone."

Trisha smiled. She could hear the concern in Ken's voice, and it made her feel good that he might care more for her than he was willing to admit. Or maybe it was just wishful thinking. Even if he did feel something for her, with him living in Oregon and her in Kentucky, it wasn't likely that they'd ever begin a relationship.

They talked awhile longer, until Ken said, "I'd better let you go. I'm going to keep trying to get ahold of Bonnie, and I'd appreciate it if you'd let me know if you hear anything from her or Allen."

"I certainly will. You take care and try not to worry. Goodbye, Ken." Trisha hung up the phone and leaned against the doorjamb with a sigh. She knew it was silly, but talking to Ken on the phone reminded her of when they were teenagers and used to spend hours talking to each other. Part of her missed those carefree days, yet she really wouldn't want to go back to being a teenager again.

"It's time to get some breakfast and begin my day," she told herself as she headed for the kitchen.

———

"You look kind of down in the dumps this morning," Samuel said when Timothy showed up at his house. "Did you and Hannah have a disagreement?"

"Nope. We've been gettin' along much better lately," Timothy said. "But that nasty weather we had last night completely ruined my corn crop."

"I'm sorry to hear that. It's supposed to be dry the rest of this week, and there's even going to be a full moon. Would you like me to help you plant more corn?"

Timothy shook his head. "You're busy enough, and so am I. After talking things over with Hannah, I've decided to forget about trying to grow more corn this year. Might even consider leasing some of the land next year so I don't have so much to take care of. For now, though, I think I'll just concentrate on our jobs and on getting the rest of the things done at my house that still need to be taken care of."

"Are you sure? I'd be happy to help if you want me to."

"No, that's all right. You and Esther will be getting married in a few weeks, and you're gonna be busy preparing for that."

"I can't believe it's finally going to happen." Samuel grinned and thumped Timothy's back. "Won't it be great to have most of our family here for the wedding?"

Timothy nodded. "It'll be good to see everyone again."

"Esther talked with her folks the other day, and they're planning to be here, too. It's going to be a great time."

———

Hannah swatted at a pesky fly. She'd been working in the garden all morning while keeping an eye on Mindy, who was squatted in the grass nearby, picking dandelions. It was hot and humid, but the rustle of grass gave Hannah some hope that the wind might bring relief from the muggy weather. She guessed this kind of weather was better than the awful storm they'd had last night. As much as they'd needed some rain, they hadn't wanted that much. Hannah knew how hard Timothy had worked planting the corn, and she felt bad when he'd told her that it had been ruined. Well, some things couldn't be helped. They'd just have to try again next year or think about leasing some of the acreage out like they'd discussed.

Maybe this afternoon I'll bake that Kentucky chocolate chip pie I've been wanting to try, she decided. *It might cheer Timothy up when he comes home to a dessert that I'm almost sure he'll enjoy.*

Hannah glanced at Mindy, who had moved closer to the house. *My little girl is growing so much, and she's so full of curiosity. I hope Mom and Dad can come for a visit soon. They're missing so much by not being able to see all the little things Mindy does.*

Hannah leaned her hoe against the fence and headed for the house. Like it or not, it was time to start lunch. Her bare feet burned as she hobbled across the gravel but found relief as soon as she stepped onto the cool grass.

"It's time to go in for lunch," Hannah said to Mindy. "After that, Mama's going to bake a pie."

Mindy looked up with a sweet expression and extended her hand, revealing one of the dandelions she'd picked earlier. *"Der bliehe."* Apparently she didn't care about pie today.

"Jah, I see the flower. Leave it on the porch and come into the house with me now." Hannah opened the door and held it for Mindy. The child, still clutching the dandelion, trotted into the house.

Hannah washed her hands at the kitchen sink and took out a loaf of bread for sandwiches. While she was spreading peanut butter, a fly buzzed noisily overhead. It was hot in the kitchen, and Hannah fanned her face with one hand while swatting at the bothersome insect with the other. Would she spend the whole summer killing bugs and trying to find a way to stay cool? Of course, the reason there were flies in the house was because she'd opened the upstairs windows this morning, trying to get some ventilation.

Mindy tromped into the kitchen and tugged on Hannah's apron. "Der bliehe," she said, showing Hannah the dandelion she still held in her hand.

Hannah, feeling a bit annoyed, said, "Mindy, I want you to go to the living room and play until I call you for lunch."

Mindy gave Hannah's apron another tug. "Der bliehe."

"Not now, Mindy! Just do as I say and go to the living room."

Mindy's lower lip protruded as she turned and left the room.

Bzz. . .bzz. . . Hannah gritted her teeth as the irksome fly kept buzzing around her head. Finally, in exasperation, she grabbed the newspaper Timothy had left on the counter last night, waited until the fly landed on the table, and gave it a good whack.

"That's one less thing I have to deal with right now," she said, scooping the fly up with the paper and tossing it in the garbage can.

Hannah went to the sink and wet a sponge. Then she quickly wiped the table where the fly had landed and went back to finishing the sandwiches she'd started.

When their lunch was ready, Hannah went to the living room to get Mindy. The child wasn't there. She opened the front door and looked into the yard but saw no sign of Mindy there either.

I wonder if she went upstairs to her room.

Hannah hurried up the stairs, and when she entered Mindy's bedroom, she spotted the child's favorite doll lying on the floor under the window. Then her gaze went to the open window. Now, the once-broken screen was no longer there.

With her heart pounding, Hannah moved slowly forward, while her brain told her to stop. She felt cold as ice as she approached the window. She held her breath as her gaze moved from the horizon, down to the yard below. She already knew what she would see but prayed it wouldn't be so. Mindy lay on the ground in a contorted position. She wasn't moving.

Hannah dashed down the stairs and out the front door, her fear mounting and making it hard to breathe. When she reached Mindy, she noticed that her daughter still held the shriveled-up dandelion she'd tried to give Hannah only a short time ago.

Hannah dropped onto the grass and checked for a pulse, but there was none. Stricken with fear such as she'd never known, Hannah raced for the phone shanty to call for help, while whispering a desperate prayer, *"Please, God, don't let our precious Mindy be dead."*

CHAPTER 41

Trisha had just started baking some bread when the telephone rang. She wiped her floury hands on a clean towel and picked up the receiver. "Hello. Bonnie's Bed-and-Breakfast."

"Hey, Trisha. It's Bonnie."

"Oh, it's so good to hear from you!" Trisha sighed with relief. "Your dad and I have both tried calling you and Allen, but all we ever got was your voice mail. We've been worried about you two ever since we heard about a helicopter crash on Kauai. Your dad was afraid you might have been on that 'copter, but thank goodness, you obviously weren't, and I'm so relieved."

"Yes, it's been all over the news, and it was a terrible tragedy. Allen and I might have been on the helicopter had we not decided to go on a boat cruise instead. I'm so sorry we made you worry. I lost my cell phone on the beach, and the battery in Allen's phone was dead and wouldn't recharge. So he got a new battery this morning. And I never did find my cell phone but decided to wait until we get home to buy a new one."

"Oh, that's too bad. Have you called your dad yet to let him know you're all right?"

"Yes, I did, and he was thankful to hear from me."

"The last time Ken and I talked, I told him that I was sure we'd have heard if something tragic had happened to you and Allen." Trisha took a seat at the desk that held the phone. "Speaking of tragedies, we had one in this community three days ago."

"What happened?" Bonnie asked.

Even though she'd only known the people in this community for a short time, Trisha struggled to convey the news and explain about Mindy's death without breaking down.

"Oh no, that's terrible! I can't imagine how Timothy and Hannah must feel." Bonnie paused before continuing. "Have they had the funeral yet? I wish we could be there for it."

"Her funeral is today, but I'm not going because I don't know the family that well and wasn't sure if I'd be welcome."

Trisha could hear Bonnie sniffling.

"I hope this hasn't ruined your honeymoon," Trisha said. "I thought you should know so you can be praying for Mindy's family."

"Yes, we'll definitely do that."

"Oh, and some of Timothy's relatives are staying here at the B&B since there wasn't enough room at all the brothers' homes for everyone who came."

"I'm glad you had the rooms available. Oh, and Trisha, please let them know that there will be no charge for the rooms. It's the least I can do to help out during this difficult time."

"That's very generous of you. I'll let them know." Trisha paused then quickly added, "Try to relax and have a good time during the rest of your honeymoon, okay?"

"Yes, we will, though it won't be easy. It's so hard to believe Mindy is dead, but thank you so much for letting us know."

—⁓—

Hannah, dressed in black mourning clothes, stood in front of a small wooden coffin in shock and disbelief. The body of the little girl inside that box just couldn't be her precious daughter. It wasn't possible that they were saying their final good-byes. Hannah's eyes burned like hot coals. She wished this was just a horrible nightmare. But as hard as she tried to deny it, she knew Mindy was gone.

Over and over, Hannah had replayed the horrible event that had taken place three days ago. Looking out Mindy's bedroom window and seeing her daughter's body on the ground below had nearly been Hannah's undoing. After she'd gone to the phone shanty to call for help, she'd returned to Mindy and stayed there until the paramedics came. Hannah, though clinging to the hope that it might not be true, had known even before help arrived that Mindy was gone. Yet in her desperation, she'd continued to pray for a miracle— asking the Lord to bring Mindy back to life the way He had the little girl whose death was recorded in Matthew 9.

If God could do miracles back then, why not now? Hannah asked herself as she gazed at Mindy's lifeless body. But Hannah's pleas were for nothing. Mindy was dead, and God could have prevented it from happening—and so could Timothy. *If only he had put in those screens when I asked him to.* A deep sense of bitterness welled in Hannah's soul. *If Mindy hadn't fallen through that broken screen, she would still be alive— running, laughing, playing, picking dandelions.*

Her stomach tightened as she thought about the comment their bishop's wife had made when she and the bishop had come to their house for the viewing. "I guess our dear Lord must have needed another angel."

He shouldn't have taken my angel! I needed Mindy more than He did. Hannah lowered her head into the palms of her hands and wept.

"It's time for us to go the cemetery now," Timothy said, touching Hannah's arm.

Hannah didn't budge. *I don't want to go. I don't want to watch as my only child is put in the cold, hard ground.*

Hannah's mother stepped between them and slipped her arm around Hannah's waist. "Everyone's waiting outside for us, Hannah. We need to go now."

Hannah, not trusting her voice, could only nod and be led away on shaky legs. How thankful she was for Mom's support. Without it, she would have collapsed.

Outside, a sea of faces swam before Hannah's blurry eyes— her brothers and their families, Timothy's parents and most of his family, as well as many from their community. Most were already seated in their horse-drawn buggies, preparing to follow the hearse that would take Mindy's body to the cemetery. A few people remained outside their buggies waiting to go.

Hannah shuddered. She'd attended several funerals, but none had been for a close family member. To lose anyone was horrible, but to lose her own child was unbearable—the worst possible pain. Hannah feared she might die from a broken heart and actually wished that she could. It would be better than going through the rest of her life without Mindy. Yes, Hannah would welcome the Angel of Death right now if he came knocking at her door.

Once Hannah's parents had taken seats in the back of the buggy, Hannah numbly took her place up front beside Timothy. She blinked, trying to clear the film of tears clouding her vision, and leaned heavily against the seat. Oh, how her arms ached to hold her beloved daughter and make everything right. If only there was some way she could undo the past.

As the buggy headed down the road toward the cemetery, the hooves of the horse were little more than a plodding walk. Even Dusty, who was usually quite spirited, must have sensed this was a solemn occasion.

When they arrived at the cemetery, Hannah sat in the buggy until the pallbearers removed Mindy's casket from the hearse and carried it to the grave site. Then she and all the others followed.

After everyone had gathered around the grave, the bishop read a hymn while the coffin was lowered and the grave filled in by the pallbearers. With each shovelful of dirt, Hannah sank deeper into despair, until her heart felt as if it were frozen.

Even though Hannah hadn't actually spoken the words, Timothy knew she blamed him for Mindy's death. Truth was, he blamed himself, too. If only he'd taken the time to replace the screens, the horrible accident that had taken their child's life would not have happened. If he could just go back and change the past, they wouldn't be standing in the cemetery right now saying their final good-byes.

A lump formed in Timothy's throat as he tried to focus on the words of the hymn their bishop was reading: "*Ah, good night to those I love so; Good night to my heart's desire; Good night to those hearts full of woe; Out of love they weep distressed. Tho' I from you pass away; In the grave you lay my clay; I will rise again securely, Greet you in eternity.'*"

Timothy glanced at his parents and saw Mom's shoulders shake as she struggled with her emotions. Dad looked pale as he put his arm around her.

Timothy looked at Hannah's parents and saw Sally sniffing as she swiped at the tears running down her cheeks. Johnny stood beside her with a pained expression.

Nearly everyone from Timothy and Hannah's families had come for the funeral, and each of their somber faces revealed the depth of their compassion and regret over the loss of Mindy. *Do they all think I'm responsible for Mindy's death?* he wondered. *I wouldn't blame them if they did.*

Timothy's gaze came to rest on Hannah. Her face looked drawn, with dark circles beneath her eyes. She hadn't slept much in the last three days, and when she had gone to bed, she had slept in Mindy's room—probably out of a need to somehow feel closer to her. Timothy missed having Hannah beside him at night, for he desperately needed her comfort. If she could just find it in her heart to forgive him, perhaps he might be able to forgive himself.

The bishop's reading finally ended, and everyone bowed their heads to silently pray the Lord's Prayer. Timothy noticed how the veins on Hannah's hands protruded as she clasped her hands tightly together and bowed her head. He suspected she was only going through the motions of praying, because that's what he was doing. What he really wanted to do was look up at the sky and shout, "Dear God: How could You have taken our only child? Don't You care how much we miss her?"

When the prayer ended, most of the mourners moved away from the grave site, but Hannah remained, hands clasped, rocking back and forth on her heels.

"Hannah, it's time for us to go now. We must return to the house and spend time with our guests," Timothy said, gently touching her shoulder.

Hannah wouldn't even look at him. Finally, Hannah's mother and father led her slowly away.

Timothy stayed at the grave site a few more minutes, fighting to gain control of his emotions. He knew he had to find a way through the difficult days ahead, but he didn't know how. Worse yet, he feared that his wife, who'd been so close to their daughter, might never be the same.

CHAPTER 42

Paradise, Pennsylvania

I'm worried about Timothy and Hannah," Fannie told Abraham as they ate breakfast a week after they'd returned from Kentucky.

"I know you are, Fannie, but worrying won't change a thing." Abraham rested his hand on her arm. "We're told in 1 Peter 5:7 to cast all our cares on Him."

"I realize that, but it's hard when you see a loved one hurting and know there's nothing you can do to ease their pain."

"There most certainly is. We can pray for them, offer encouraging words, and listen and be there when they want to talk."

"You're right." Fannie sighed. "I just wish we could have stayed in Kentucky longer. I really think Timothy and Hannah need us right now."

"But remember, Fannie, Hannah's folks are still there, and I think it might have been too much if we'd stayed, too."

"But we could have stayed with Samuel," she argued.

"There's plenty of room in that big house of his, and we would have been able to go over often and check on Timothy and Hannah."

Abraham stroked Fannie's hand. "We'll be going back in a few weeks for Samuel and Esther's wedding. I'm sure Hannah's folks will be gone by then, and it'll give us a chance to spend more time with Hannah and Timothy."

"That's true, but how can we celebrate what should be a joyous occasion when our son and his wife are in such deep grief?"

"While there will be some sadness, it'll be good for everyone to focus on something positive," he said. "Samuel went through a lot when he lost Elsie, and he deserves to be happy with Esther."

Fannie nodded. "You're right. And since I've come to know Esther fairly well, I believe she's the right woman for Samuel and his kinner."

"I agree, and I hope Timothy and Hannah are able to be at the wedding, too, because I'm sure Samuel would be disappointed if they didn't come."

"Do you really think Hannah will be up to going? You know how upset she's been since Mindy died." Fannie paused, feeling the pain of it all herself. "Abraham, it about broke my heart to see the way she shut Timothy out. She barely looked at him the day of Mindy's funeral."

"I know."

"Timothy thinks she blames him for Mindy's death." Fannie's forehead wrinkled. "Do you think our son is responsible for the tragedy?"

Abraham shrugged. "Guess there's a little blame on everyone's shoulders. Timothy for not putting in new screens; Hannah for not keeping a closer watch on Mindy; and even little Mindy, who shouldn't have been playing near the window." He sighed. "But as I told Timothy when I spoke to him on the phone last night, blaming himself or anyone else will not bring Mindy back."

Fannie nodded slowly. "You're right, of course, but it's a hard fact to swallow."

"I also reminded our son that in order to find the strength to press on, he needs to spend time alone with God."

"That was very good advice," Fannie said. "I just hope Timothy will heed what you said."

———※———

Pembroke, Kentucky

"You really need to eat something," Sally said, offering Hannah a piece of toast.

Hannah shook her head. "I'm not hungry."

Sally frowned. She was worried sick about her daughter. Over the last week, a number of women from the community had brought food, but Hannah wouldn't eat anything unless she was forced to. She simply sat quietly in the rocking chair, holding Mindy's doll.

If all I can do is offer comfort and sit beside Hannah, then that's what I'll do, Sally thought, taking a seat beside Hannah. "You can take comfort in knowing that Mindy is in a better place," she said, placing her hand on Hannah's arm.

"Better place? What could be better for my little girl than to be right here with me?" Hannah's eyes narrowed into tiny slits. "It's Timothy's fault Mindy is dead! If he'd just put new screens in the windows like I asked—"

"Kannscht ihn verge ware?" Johnny asked as he entered the room.

290

Hannah slowly shook her head. "No, I don't think I can ever forgive him."

Johnny stood beside Hannah and placed his hand on her shoulder. "If there's one thing I've learned over the years, it's that we don't get to choose our fate. We can only learn how to live through it."

Hannah just continued to rock, staring straight ahead.

"God doesn't spare us trials," Sally said. "But He does help us overcome them."

Hannah made no reply.

"Maybe we should leave her alone for a while." Johnny nudged Sally's arm and motioned to the kitchen. "Let's go eat breakfast. Timothy's finishing his chores in the barn, and I'm sure he'll be hungry when he comes in."

Sally hesitated. She really wished Hannah would join them for breakfast but didn't want to force the issue. Maybe Johnny was right about Hannah needing some time alone; she had been hovering over her quite a bit this week. With a heavy sigh, Sally stood and followed Johnny to the kitchen.

When Timothy joined them a few minutes later, Sally couldn't help but notice the tears in his eyes. He was obviously as distressed about Mindy's death as Hannah was, but at least he continued to eat and do his chores. Yet Timothy spoke very little about his feelings. Maybe he thought not talking about it would lessen the pain. Sally knew otherwise.

The three of them took seats at the table, and after their silent prayer, Sally passed a platter of scrambled eggs and ham to Timothy. He took a piece of the ham and a spoonful of eggs; then after handing the platter to Johnny, he said, "I appreciate all that you both have done, but you've been here almost two weeks now, and I think it's time for you to go home."

"But Hannah's not doing well, and she needs me," Sally argued. She couldn't believe Timothy would suggest that they return to Pennsylvania right now.

With a look of determination, Timothy shook his head. "Hannah and I need each other in order to deal with our grief. As long as you're here, she'll never respond to me."

Sally winced, feeling as if he'd slapped her face. Did Timothy honestly believe that Hannah, who hadn't said more than a few words to him since Mindy's death, needed him more than she did her own mother? She was about to tell him what she thought about that when Johnny spoke up.

"I believe you're right, Timothy. Sally and I will leave in the morning."

CHAPTER 43

Timothy leaned against Dusty's stall and groaned. It had been three weeks since Mindy's death, and things seemed to be getting worse between him and Hannah. He'd figured once Hannah's parents went home, Hannah would return to their own room at night, but she'd continued to sleep in Mindy's bedroom. To make matters worse, whenever Timothy spoke to Hannah, she barely acknowledged his presence. Didn't she realize how horrible he felt about Mindy's death? Didn't she know that he missed their daughter, too?

Despite his grief, Timothy knew he needed to get back to work or they wouldn't have money to pay their bills and buy groceries. Yet he couldn't leave Hannah by herself all day—not in the state she was in. So he'd called and left a message for Suzanne last night, asking if she'd be willing to come and sit with Hannah. He hoped that either she or Titus had checked their voice mail, because Samuel and his driver would be coming by in an hour to pick him up. If Suzanne didn't come over by then, there was no way Timothy could go off to work. He couldn't ask Esther to stay with Hannah. Between taking care of Samuel's kids and doing last-minute things for her upcoming wedding, she had her hands full. Thankfully, Bonnie and Allen had returned from their honeymoon a few days ago, so Esther's help wasn't needed at the B&B anymore.

Forcing his thoughts aside, Timothy finished feeding Dusty and Lilly then went back to the house. Hannah was sitting in the rocking chair with Mindy's doll in her lap.

"We need to talk," he said, kneeling on the floor in front of her.

Hannah kept rocking, staring straight ahead, with no acknowledgment of his presence. If her pale face and sunken eyes were any indication of how tired she felt, she hadn't slept much since the accident, but then, neither had he. How could he get any quality sleep when his wife stayed two rooms away and wouldn't even speak to him? He longed to offer Hannah comfort and reassurance, but it wouldn't be appreciated. Hannah had shut him out, and he wasn't sure she would ever let him into her world again. Her brown eyes looked so sorrowful behind her tears, yet she wouldn't express her feelings.

Timothy was even more worried because he'd noticed that Hannah had lost a lot of weight since the accident. She ate so little, and then only when someone practically forced her to do so. Did she think that not eating would dull her pain, or was she trying to starve herself to death? He hoped she wasn't so depressed that she wanted to end her own life. He couldn't deal with another tragedy—especially one of that magnitude. He'd just have to try harder to get through to her.

"I love you, Hannah. Please talk to me." Timothy's fingers curved under her trembling chin.

She winced and pulled away as if she couldn't stand the sight of him. Her reluctance to look at him or even speak his name was so strong he could feel it to the core of his being. Even his gentle touch seemed to make her cringe. If only there was something he could do to bridge the awful gap between them.

"Why are you shutting me out?" he asked, trying once again. "Don't you think I miss Mindy, too?"

Hannah turned in her chair, refusing to make eye contact with him.

Timothy swallowed around the lump in his throat. It hurt to know she didn't love him anymore.

A knock sounded on the back door, and he went to answer it.

"I got your message," Suzanne said when he found her standing on the porch. "I'd be happy to stay with Hannah while you go to work today."

Timothy breathed a sigh of relief, trying to stay composed. "Let's go into the kitchen so we can talk," he said.

When they entered the kitchen, Timothy shared his concerns about Hannah. "I know it's only been a few weeks since Mindy died, but Hannah's still grieving so hard it scares me. What if she doesn't snap out of it? What if—"

"I'll try talking to her," Suzanne said. "Maybe she'll open up to me."

"You might be right. Since she doesn't blame you for our daughter's death, she probably won't give you the cold shoulder the way she does me. I can't get her to respond to me at all."

Suzanne offered Timothy a sympathetic smile and patted his arm. "Things will get better in time; you'll see."

Timothy sighed. "I hope so, because the guilt I feel for not putting in new window screens is bad enough, but having my wife shut me out the way she has is the worst kind of pain."

"I can only imagine."

A horn honked, and Timothy looked out the window.

"Samuel and his driver are here, so I'd better go. Thanks again for coming, Suzanne."

"You're welcome."

—✳—

As Hannah continued to rock, her shoulders sagged with the weight of her depression. She almost felt paralyzed with grief and was sure that her life would never be normal again.

When she'd refused to talk to Timothy, she'd seen the pained expression on his face, but she didn't care. Because of him, she was miserable. Because of him, she'd never see her precious little girl again.

Hannah stopped rocking, lifted Mindy's doll, and studied its face. *If Mindy had lived and been crippled, that would have been better than her dying,* she thought. Then she remembered a conversation she'd had with Esther some time ago about her brother, Dan, who was struggling with MS. Hannah had mentioned that she didn't think she could take care of someone like that. If she could have Mindy back, she'd gladly make the sacrifice of caring for her, even if she was disabled.

Suzanne stepped into the living room, disrupting Hannah's thoughts. "I'm here to spend the day with you," she said, handing Hannah a cup of hot tea.

Hannah shook her head. "I don't want anything to drink, and I don't need you to babysit me."

Suzanne set the teacup on the small table near the rocking chair and took a seat on the sofa across from Hannah. "Timothy is really worried about you."

Hannah said nothing.

"We're all worried, Hannah."

Hannah started the rocker moving again. *Creak. . . Creak. . . Creak. . .* It moved in rhythmic motion.

"I know you're going through a hard time, but if you ask God for strength, He will give it to you. When you're hurting, He will give you comfort in ways that no one else can."

Hannah's throat constricted, and a tight sob threatened to escape. "God doesn't care about me."

"He most certainly does. God loves and cares about all His people."

"Then why'd He take Mindy?"

"I don't know the answer to that, but I do know that accidents happen, and—"

Hannah's face contorted. "It was an accident that shouldn't have happened! God could have prevented it, and so could Timothy. He should have put new screens on the windows when I asked him to. Now our daughter is gone, and she's never coming back!"

—∽—

Hopkinsville, Kentucky

"Are you sure you're ready to begin working again?" Samuel asked Timothy as he set a ladder in place inside the doctor's office they'd been hired to paint.

"Whether I'm ready or not is beside the point. I have to work. We need the money, and I need to keep busy so I don't think too much," Timothy said after he'd opened a bucket of paint.

"It's good to be busy, but I'm concerned that you might not have given yourself enough time to heal before returning to work," Samuel said. "You look like you haven't been sleeping well."

"I haven't. It's kind of hard to sleep when I know it's my fault that my daughter is dead. And knowing Hannah blames me for the accident makes it even worse." Timothy clenched his fingers tightly together. "When I look in the mirror these days, I don't like what I see."

"That's *narrish*. Blaming yourself will only wear you down."

"It might seem foolish to you, but that's the way I feel." Timothy dropped his gaze as he continued. "I keep hearing Hannah that day, asking me to fix the window screens upstairs. But I was too worried about planting the field. I kept putting it off and finding other things to do. Now in hindsight, I keep asking myself, *What was I thinking?* Replacing those screens, especially in my daughter's room, was far more important than the corn crop that ended up getting destroyed. Same goes for the rest of the projects I did instead of taking care of the screens. Mindy's life was at stake, and now I'm paying the price for being so stupid."

Samuel moved across the room and clasped Timothy's shoulder. "It takes a strong person to deal with hard times, and you're a strong person. So with God's help, you can choose to forgive yourself and go on with your life. And never forget that you have a family who loves and cares about you. We're all here to support you through this difficult time. Remember, Timothy, I was in a similar situation over a year ago when I lost Elsie. I know it's not exactly the same, but the pain is just as strong. In time, good things will happen again in your lives. I never would have believed it myself, but good things have happened for me."

"I appreciate hearing that, and I know as time passes it might get easier. I couldn't get through this without my family's support, but I sure wish I had Hannah's. She won't even speak to me. In fact, she avoids looking at me." Timothy groaned. "I really don't know what to do about it."

"Would you like me to talk to her? With all I went through

after Elsie died, I might be able to help Hannah through her grief."

"You can try if you like. Suzanne said she'll attempt to get through to Hannah, too, but I doubt it'll do any good." Timothy picked up his paintbrush. "Guess we'd better get to work, or this job will never get done."

Samuel nodded. "Just remember one thing: I'm here for you, day or night."

CHAPTER 44

Pembroke, Kentucky

Mom, Dad, it's so good you could be here for my wedding today," Esther said as she sat with her folks eating breakfast at Bonnie's dining-room table. Mom and Dad had arrived yesterday afternoon and would be staying for a few days after the wedding. Esther's brother James and his family, who lived in Lykens, Pennsylvania, had also come. But due to Dan's failing health, he and his family had remained in Pennsylvania.

"We're glad we could be here, too," Mom said, smiling at Esther. "There's no way we could miss our only daughter's wedding."

Dad bobbed his head. "Your mamm's right about that."

Esther glanced across the table at Samuel's sister Naomi. She and her husband, Caleb, as well as some other members of Samuel's family, were also staying at the bed-and-breakfast. Esther appreciated the fact that Bonnie had graciously agreed to let them all have their rooms at no cost. They'd set up a cot for Trisha in the guesthouse, and she'd slept there last night, since they needed all the extra rooms for their guests. Trisha would be living in the guesthouse full-time after Esther was married.

"I can't believe this day is finally here," Esther murmured. "I just feel a bit guilty getting married when Timothy and Hannah are still grieving for Mindy. Samuel and I had thought about postponing the wedding for another month or two, but Timothy wouldn't hear of it."

"One thing I've always thought was special about you is that you can't look the other way when someone you know is hurting," Mom said, smiling at Esther. "But postponing your wedding won't bring Timothy and Hannah's little girl back, and I'm sure they would want you to go ahead with your plans."

Esther nodded. "That's exactly what Timothy told Samuel."

"Life goes on even when people are hurting. Maybe going to the wedding will help them focus on something else, if only for a little while," Naomi spoke up. "I remember when my little brother Zach was kidnapped. Nothing seemed right. But we forced ourselves to keep on with the business of living despite the pain we felt over losing him."

"That's right," Naomi's sister Nancy said. "It was hard going on without our little brother all those years, but God helped us get through it."

"And He will help Timothy and Hannah, too," Allen said. "They just need to stay close to Him and rely on others for comfort and support."

"Do you think they'll attend the wedding?" Bonnie asked, turning to look at him.

"Well, Timothy's back working with Samuel again, and when I spoke to him yesterday, he said he was planning to go and that he hoped Hannah would feel up to it."

—∾—

When Timothy entered the kitchen, Hannah was standing in front of the stove making a pot of coffee. That was a good sign, because ever since Mindy died he'd had to make his own coffee in the mornings.

"I'm just going to have a bowl of cereal, and then I'll need to get ready for the wedding," he said, stepping up beside her.

No reply. Not even a nod.

"Hannah, are you planning to go Esther and Samuel's wedding with me?"

She slowly shook her head.

"Maybe I shouldn't go either, because I don't want to leave you here alone."

"Just go on without me; I'll be fine," she mumbled. Well, at least she was talking to him again.

"Are you sure you won't go? It might do you some good to get out of the house for a few hours."

She whirled around and glared at him. "You can't expect me to put on a happy face and go to the wedding when I feel so dead inside!"

Normally, Timothy preferred to listen rather than talk, but something needed to be said, and he planned to say it. "You know, when we first made plans to move to Kentucky—"

Her eyes narrowed. "Your plans, don't you mean? You never considered whether I wanted to move. All you thought about was yourself!"

"I wasn't just thinking of me. I was thinking of us and our marriage."

She folded her arms. "Humph!"

"We can make this work, Hannah, but it's going to take both of us to do it."

"It's never going to work, and I don't see how you can expect it to," she said. "If we were still in Pennsylvania, none of this would have happened. Don't you realize that the day our daughter died, a part of me died, too? You took her from me, Timothy. You took our precious little girl, and she's never coming back!" Hannah turned and rushed out of the room, leaving him staring after her, eyes wet with tears.

It had been hard for Timothy to hitch his horse to the buggy and go over to Samuel's for the wedding, but out of love and respect for his brother, he'd made himself do it. Now, after turning his horse loose in the corral and starting in the direction of the house, he was having second thoughts. Maybe he should have stayed home with Hannah. She was terribly upset when he left. But if he couldn't get through to her in the kitchen this morning, it probably wouldn't have mattered if he'd stayed there all day and talked to Hannah. Suzanne had tried, Samuel had tried, and Esther had tried, but no one could get through to her. Hannah blamed Timothy for Mindy's death, and she obviously wasn't going to forgive him. Short of a miracle, nothing he could say or do would change the fact that she no longer loved him. He feared that for the rest of their married life they'd be living in the same house, sleeping in separate bedrooms, with Hannah barely acknowledging his presence. That wasn't the way God intended marriage to be, but Timothy didn't know what he could do about it.

As he neared the house, he spotted Bonnie and Allen on the front porch talking to Trisha. He wasn't surprised that they'd been invited, since Allen and Samuel were good friends and so were Bonnie and Esther. And since Trisha and Esther had been working at the B&B together for the last several weeks, it was understandable that she'd received an invitation to the wedding as well.

"It's good to see you," Allen said, clasping Timothy's shoulder as soon as he stepped onto the porch.

"Thanks. It's good to see you, too."

"How's Hannah doing?" Bonnie asked. "I was hoping she might be here today."

Timothy shook his head. "Hannah's still not doing well. She didn't feel up to coming."

"That's too bad. I've been meaning to drop by your place and see her," Bonnie said. "I was busy getting ready for the out-of-town wedding guests, and I'm sorry I didn't take the time to check on her. I'll try to do that within the next day or so."

Timothy forced a smile. "I appreciate that, and hopefully Hannah will, too." He motioned to the house. "Guess the service will be starting soon, so I'd better get inside."

When Timothy took a seat beside his dad, he noticed that Samuel and Esther had already taken their seats, facing each other. They fidgeted a bit, an indication that they were nervous, but their eager smiles let him know how happy they were. They'd both been through a lot, so they deserved all the happiness of this special day.

Timothy glanced to his right and saw his other five brothers sitting beyond his dad. On the benches behind them were his three brothers-in-law. His sisters sat together on the women's side of the room with his sisters-in-law. Many of his nieces and nephews had also come to the wedding, making quite a large group from Pennsylvania. They'd hired several drivers with vans to make the trip.

As the first song began, Timothy thought about how this was the second of his brothers' weddings he'd attended alone. Last October, Timothy had left Hannah and Mindy in Pennsylvania when he'd come to Kentucky to attend Titus and Suzanne's wedding. Hannah had used the excuse that her mother needed help because she'd sprained her ankle, so she'd insisted on staying home. Now Timothy was at Samuel and Esther's wedding, and he was alone once again. This time he understood why Hannah hadn't wanted to come. It had been difficult for him to come, but he was happy Samuel had found love again, and Timothy wanted to witness his brother's marriage.

As the service continued, Timothy thought about his own wedding. He'd loved Hannah so much back then—and still did, for that matter. But things had changed for Hannah. Even before Mindy's death, she'd often been cool toward him. He'd shrugged it off, figuring she was still upset with him for making them move to Kentucky. But there had been times, like the week before Mindy died, when he thought Hannah was beginning to adjust to the move and had actually warmed up to him. Just when he'd felt there was some hope for their marriage, Mindy's tragic death had shattered their world. Timothy was convinced that Hannah's love for him was dead. Their tragedy was so huge, nothing short of a miracle could mend their relationship.

Timothy's thoughts were halted when Bishop King called Esther and Samuel to stand before him. Their faces fairly glowed as they each answered affirmatively to the bishop's questions. When the vows had been spoken, the bishop took Esther and Samuel's hands and said, "So go forth in the name of the Lord. You are now husband and wife."

I hope they will always be as happy as they are right now, Timothy thought. *And may nothing ever drive them apart.*

—⟶

As Hannah entered the cemetery to visit Mindy's grave, she spotted a lone sheep rubbing its nose on one of the headstones. At least she thought it was a sheep. Due to the tears clouding her vision, she wondered if she might be seeing something that wasn't actually there.

Hannah moved forward and stopped when she heard a loud *baa*. There really was a sheep by that headstone. But why would the creature be in the cemetery, and who did it belong to?

Hannah heard another *baa* and glanced to her left. Several sheep grazed in the field on the other side of the cemetery. Apparently one had found a way out and ended up over here. Well, the sheep could stay right where it was, for all she cared.

Hannah ambled slowly through the cemetery until she came to the place where Mindy's body had been buried. The simple granite headstone inscribed with Mindy's name, date of birth, and date of death had been set in place, making the tragedy even more final. Tears welled in Hannah's eyes, and she swayed unsteadily. The anguish that engulfed her was so great she felt overcome by it. She dropped to the ground and sobbed. "Oh Mindy, my precious little girl. . . How can I go on without you?"

CHAPTER 45

After Hannah returned home from the cemetery, she sat on the porch awhile, holding Bobbin and hoping the cat would offer her some comfort. He didn't. She just felt worse because she was reminded of how Mindy had enjoyed playing with the animal. One time Bobbin had lost his balance and rolled down the stairs like a sack of potatoes. Mindy had been so concerned and looked so relieved when she'd seen that the cat wasn't hurt.

Even with the memories she had left of Mindy, Hannah didn't think anything would ever bring her the comfort she so badly needed. She barely noticed the birds singing in the trees and refused to look at the flowers she'd planted in the spring. She thought about the dandelions Mindy had picked on the morning of her death and winced. It was such a bittersweet memory.

Bobbin rubbed his nose against Hannah's hand and purred, as though sensing her mood; yet Hannah felt no comfort.

When the sun became unbearably hot, Hannah set the cat on the porch and went inside for a glass of water. She took a seat at the table and sat staring at the stool Mindy used to perch on during their meals. This house was way too quiet without the patter of Mindy's little feet and the sound of her childish laughter bouncing off the walls. She'd been such a happy girl—curious, full of energy, so cute and cuddly. Hannah's arms ached to hold her and stroke her soft, pink skin.

Giving in to her tears, Hannah leaned forward and rested her head on the table. She'd been on the brink of tears every day since Mindy died, and often let herself weep, as she was doing now.

"Oh how I wish I'd had the chance to say good-bye, kiss my precious girl, and tell her how much I love her," Hannah sobbed. Overcome with fatigue and grief, she closed her eyes and drifted off.

Sometime later, Hannah was awakened when Timothy entered the kitchen, touched her shoulder, and said, "How come you're sitting here in the dark?"

Hannah sat up straight and rubbed her eyes. "I must have dozed off."

Timothy lit the gas lamp above the kitchen table. "Sorry I'm so late. There were lots of people from my family at the wedding, and I wanted to visit with them."

Hannah glanced at the clock on the far wall. It was almost seven o'clock. Had she really been asleep nearly two hours?

"Mom and Dad said to tell you hello. They'll be over to visit in the next day or so. I think tomorrow they're going to help Esther and Samuel with the cleanup from the wedding."

Hannah shrugged. She didn't care whether Fannie and Abraham came over to see her. She wasn't good company and really had nothing to say to either of them.

"Have you eaten supper yet?" Timothy asked.

She shook her head. "I'm not hungry."

"Hannah, you need to eat. I'm worried because you've lost so much weight, and it's not good for your health to skip meals like you do."

"Why'd the Lord bring us here, only to forsake us?" she wailed.

"God hasn't forsaken us, Hannah. He knows the pain we both feel." Timothy rested his hands on her trembling shoulders, and for just a minute, Hannah's pain lessened a bit.

"Why don't the two of us go for a ride?" he suggested. "It'll give us a chance to enjoy the cool evening breeze that's come up, and I think it would be good for you to get out of the house for a while."

She shrugged his hands away. "I don't want to go for a ride. I just want to be left alone."

"Not this time, Hannah. You need me right now, and I...I need you, too."

Hannah just stared at the table, fighting back tears of frustration.

"Don't you love me anymore?" he asked, taking a seat beside her.

His question burned deep in her heart, and she shifted in her seat, unsure of how to respond.

He leaned close and moaned as he brushed his lips across her forehead. "I love you, Hannah, and I always will."

Overcome with emotion, she took a deep breath and forced herself to look at him. His eyes held no sparkle, revealing the depth of his sadness. When he pulled her into his arms, she felt weak, unable to resist.

As Timothy's lips touched Hannah's, a niggling little voice in her head said she shouldn't let this happen, yet her heart said otherwise, and she seemed powerless to stop it.

Finding comfort in her husband's embrace, Hannah closed

her eyes and allowed his kisses to drive all negative, hurtful thoughts from her mind.

—⁂—

When Timothy awoke the following morning, he glanced over at his sleeping wife and smiled. She looked so peaceful with her long hair fanned out on the pillow and her cheeks rosy from a good night's sleep. He decided not to wake her. After all, he'd been fixing his own breakfast for the last few weeks, so he could do it again this morning.

He grabbed his work clothes, bent to kiss Hannah's forehead, and slipped quietly out of the room. There was extra pep to his step because, for the first time in weeks, he actually felt hopeful.

As Timothy fixed a pot of coffee in the kitchen, he thought about last night and thanked God that he and Hannah had found comfort in each other's arms. Timothy was certain her response to him had been the first step in helping them deal with the pain of losing Mindy. He felt hopeful that they could now face the loss of their daughter together and find the strength they both needed to go on.

When Timothy walked out the door to wait for his driver, he leaned against the porch railing. Watching the sunrise, he thought it had never looked more beautiful.

—⁂—

Hannah yawned and stretched her arms over her head. Her brain felt fuzzy—like it was full of thick cobwebs. She must have slept long and hard.

When Hannah sat up in bed and looked around, she felt as if a jolt of electricity had been shot through her. She was in her own bedroom, not Mindy's! *How in the world did I end up here?*

Hannah rubbed her forehead. Then she remembered Timothy's kisses and words of love. She'd needed his comfort and let her emotions carry her away.

"What was I thinking?" Hannah moaned. She hadn't forgiven Timothy for causing Mindy's death and didn't think she ever could. One night of being held in his arms wouldn't bring Mindy back to them, and it may have given Timothy false hope.

Hannah pushed the covers aside and crawled out of bed. With tears blinding her vision, she stumbled across the room. She couldn't stay here anymore. She had to get away.

As Hannah packed her bags in readiness to leave, pain clutched her heart. If they hadn't moved to Kentucky, none of this would have happened. Mindy would still be with them, and they'd be living happily in Pennsylvania.

After Hannah got dressed, she opened the bedroom door, set her suitcase in the hallway, and headed for Mindy's room. When she stepped inside, she stared at her daughter's empty bed. She hadn't even changed Mindy's sheets since the tragic day of her death. A deep sense of sadness washed over Hannah as she sat on the bed and buried her face in Mindy's pillow. She took a deep breath, trying to keep her daughter's essence within her. But sadly, she was reminded once again that Mindy was never coming back. Hannah wouldn't see her little girl's sweet face again—not in this life, anyhow. The only way she could deal with this unrelenting pain was to leave this place, where painful memories plagued her night and day, and return to Pennsylvania. At least there she would have Mom and Dad's love and support. Yes, that's what she needed right now.

With one last glance, Hannah spotted Mindy's favorite doll. She picked it up and carried it, along with her suitcase, down the stairs. Upon entering the kitchen, she found a notepad and pen and quickly scrawled a note for Timothy, which she left on the table.

Hannah pushed the screen door open and stepped onto the porch. A blast of warm, humid air hit her full in the face, yet she still felt chilled. She heard a pathetic *meow*. Looking down, she saw Bobbin lying on his back on the porch, paws in the air. Did the poor cat know she was leaving? Did he even care?

Shoulders slumped and head down, Hannah stepped off the porch and made her way down the lane, where she would stop at the phone shanty to call her driver for a ride to the bus station in Clarksville.

As she ambled slowly past the fence dividing the lane from the pasture, Mindy's doll slipped from her hand, unnoticed. Squinting against the morning sun, blazing like a fiery furnace, Hannah kept walking and didn't look back. It was best to leave all the painful memories behind.

—⁓—

When Timothy's driver dropped him at the end of their lane that evening, Timothy winced with each step he took. He hurt all over—even the soles of his feet. He and Samuel had worked on a three-story house in Hopkinsville today, and he'd been up and down the ladder so many times he'd lost count. It had been easier to work, however, knowing things were better between him and Hannah and that she'd be waiting for him when he got home. He hoped she'd have supper ready and that they could sit outside on the back porch after they ate and visit while they watched the sun go down and listened to the crickets sing their nightly chorus.

As Timothy continued his walk up the lane, he kicked

something with the toe of his boot. He looked and was surprised to see Mindy's doll lying facedown in the dirt.

"Now what's that doing here?" he murmured. Could Hannah have gone out to get the mail today and taken the doll along? She'd had it with her almost constantly since Mindy died and often rocked the doll as though it were a baby. Hannah had probably dropped it on the way back from the mailbox and just hadn't noticed.

Timothy picked up the doll and carried it under one arm. When he entered the house, all was quiet, and he didn't smell any food. It was a disappointment, but he was used to it because Hannah hadn't done any of the cooking since Mindy died. Timothy stepped into the utility room and put the doll on a shelf then went to the kitchen. Hannah wasn't there, and he was about to call for her when he spotted a note on the table. He picked it up and read it silently.

Timothy,

I'm sure you'll be disappointed when I tell you this, but I can't stay here any longer. Every time I look at you, I remember that you could have prevented our daughter's death, and it's too painful for me to deal with. I'm returning to Pennsylvania to be with Mom and Dad. Please don't come after me, because I won't come back to Kentucky, and I can no longer live with you. It's better this way, for both of us.

—Hannah

Timothy sank into a chair and groaned. He couldn't believe it. After last night, he was sure things were better between them. Why had she let him kiss her and then slept in their room if she hadn't forgiven him for being the cause of Mindy's death?

He shuddered and swallowed against the sob rising in his throat. He'd not only lost his daughter, but now his wife was gone, too. He didn't know if he'd ever see Hannah again. She hadn't even signed the note with love. Should he go after her—insist that she come home? Or would it be better to give her some time and hope she'd come back on her own? After so many weeks of trying to remain strong, Timothy could no longer hold in his grief. He leaned forward and sobbed so hard it almost made him ill. He didn't care anymore. He was exhausted from trying to be strong for Hannah, and now he had nothing left. How much more could a man take?

CHAPTER 46

Paradise, Pennsylvania

Sally had just entered the phone shack to make a call when the telephone rang. She quickly picked up the receiver. "Hello."

"Sally, is that you?" a male voice asked.

"Yes, it's me. Who's this?"

"It...it's Timothy."

"Is everything all right? You sound *umgerennt*."

"I am upset. I came home from work today and found a note from Hannah." There was a pause. "She said she was leaving me and returning to Pennsylvania."

Sally drew in a sharp breath. "Hannah's on her way here?"

"Jah. I'm not sure if she hired a driver or caught a bus." Another pause. "I thought maybe you would have heard from her."

"No, but then maybe she didn't call because she was afraid we would have told her she shouldn't come."

"Would you have?"

Sally sank into the folding chair, unsure how to respond. If Hannah had told her that she was coming, it would have

315

been hard to dissuade her. But she was fairly sure if Hannah had talked to Johnny about this, he would have told her to stay put—that her place was in Kentucky with her husband.

"Sally, are you still there?"

"Jah, I'm here."

"What are you gonna do when Hannah gets there?" Timothy asked.

Sally was glad he hadn't forced her to answer his previous question. She shifted the phone to her other ear.

"We'll make her feel welcome, of course."

Timothy grunted. "Figured as much."

"Hannah's obviously in great distress or she wouldn't have felt the need to leave Kentucky. Seriously, we can hardly ask her to go as soon as she gets here."

"No, I suppose not, but Hannah's place is with me."

"Maybe she needs some time away—time to think and allow her broken heart to heal."

"You might be right, but I'm hurting, too, and I think I should be the one to help Hannah through her grief."

"You may not realize this now, but a time of separation might be what you both need."

"It's not what I need, Sally. When Hannah gets there, will you please ask her to come home?"

"Pennsylvania has been Hannah's home since she was a baby."

"Not anymore," Timothy said forcefully. "Her home's here with me!"

"I can't talk anymore," Sally said. "I need to fix supper for Johnny. One of us will call and let you know when Hannah arrives so you won't worry about her. Good-bye, Timothy. Take care." Sally hung up the phone quickly, before he could respond.

She sat for several minutes, mulling things over. *So Hannah's coming home. I wonder what Johnny will have to say about this?*

—⚬—

Pembroke, Kentucky

When Timothy hung up the phone, he sat in disbelief. After his conversation with Sally, he was convinced that she had no intention of trying to persuade Hannah to return to Kentucky.

Needing some fresh air, he stepped out of the hot, stuffy phone shanty. He needed to talk to his brothers about this, and he'd start with Titus, since he lived the closest.

Timothy sprinted up to the barn to get his horse and buggy, and a short time later he was on the road. He let Dusty run, and as the horse trotted down the road, Timothy's thoughts ran wild. He remembered the day he'd told Hannah he wanted to move to Kentucky. She'd argued with him and begged him to change his mind. When she'd asked if he would be sad to leave Pennsylvania, he'd replied, "As long as I have you and Mindy, I'll never be sad." Little did he know then that less than a year later, he'd be sadder than he ever thought possible.

"Maybe Hannah was right about my decision to move here," he mumbled. "But if we'd stayed in Pennsylvania, Hannah would have continued to put her mamm's needs ahead of mine, and she'd have spent more time with her than she did me."

Who am I kidding? My marriage to Hannah is in more trouble now than it's ever been. I'd thought things were better last night, but I was wrong. Hannah obviously doesn't love me. She probably had a moment of weakness and, when she woke up this morning,

realized her mistake and wanted to get as far away from me as
possible. No doubt she'd rather be with her Mamm right now.

By the time Timothy pulled into Titus's place, he felt even
more confused and stressed out. He really did need to talk to
someone who'd understand the way he felt about things.

"What brings you by here this evening?" Titus asked,
stepping out of the barn. "Is everything okay?"

"No, it's not," Timothy said, climbing out of the buggy.
"Hannah's gone!"

"What do you mean?"

Timothy explained about the note he'd found and told
Titus about the conversation he'd had with Hannah's mother.

"Would you like my opinion?" Titus asked.

"Jah, that's why I came over here. I'd also like Suzanne's
opinion. Is she in the house?"

"No, she's feeding the cats in the barn. You want me to call
her, or should we go in there?"

"Let me secure my horse, and then we can go in the barn."

When they entered the barn a few minutes later, Timothy
spotted Suzanne sitting on a bale of hay with Titus's cat, Callie,
in her lap. Seeing Suzanne so large in her pregnancy reminded
him of Hannah when she was carrying Mindy. How long ago
that now seemed.

"Oh hi, Timothy," she said, smiling up at him. "Is Hannah
with you?"

He shook his head then quickly explained the situation.
"I can't believe she would just up and leave me like that,"
he said.

"She's been an emotional wreck ever since Mindy died,
and people like that don't think things through before they
act," Suzanne said. "If you want my opinion, I think you
should give her some time."

"So you don't think I should go after her?"

Suzanne shook her head. "That might make matters even worse."

Timothy looked at Titus. "What are your thoughts?"

"I agree with my wife. If you try to force Hannah to come back to Kentucky, she might resent you more than she already does. It could drive a wedge between you that will never break down."

"What if Hannah never gets over Mindy's death? She blames me for the accident, and I'm afraid—" Timothy stopped talking and drew in a shaky breath. "You don't think Hannah will divorce me, do you?"

Suzanne gasped. "That would be baremlich, and it goes against our beliefs."

"Jah, it would be terrible," Titus said, "but I really don't think Hannah would do such a thing."

"How do you know?" Timothy questioned.

"If she got a divorce, she'd have to leave the Amish faith. Can you really see Hannah doing something that would take her away from her family—especially her mamm—and in such a tragic way?"

"I hope not, but in Hannah's current state of mind, she might do anything." Timothy sank to a bale of hay and let his head fall forward into his hands. All he could do was wait and pray for a miracle.

CHAPTER 47

Paradise, Pennsylvania

Hannah sat in a wicker rocking chair on her parents' front porch, watching two of Dad's cats leaping through the grass, chasing grasshoppers. It made her think of Mindy and how she'd loved playing with Bobbin. Mindy had also liked playing with her doll, but a few days after she'd arrived at her folks', Hannah had realized that Mindy's doll must still be in Kentucky. She'd had it with her when she was walking down the lane to call for a driver, so she assumed in her grief, she must have dropped it along the way. It was probably just as well. Seeing it all the time would be a constant reminder of what Hannah had lost.

Tears sprang to her eyes. She remembered the time she'd entered the living room and spotted Mindy leaning against the wall, wearing Timothy's sunglasses and a grin that stretched from ear to ear. She'd been such a happy child—so spontaneous and curious about things.

"Mind if I join you?" Mom asked, joining Hannah on the porch.

"No." Hannah motioned to the chair beside her.

"Are you doing okay?" Mom asked, taking a seat. "You look like you're deep in thought."

"I was thinking about Mindy and how much fun she used to have playing with the cat." Hannah sniffed. "Thanks to us moving to Kentucky, you and Dad missed so many of the cute little things Mindy said and did. I wish. . . ." Her voice trailed off, and she stared down at her hands, clasped firmly in her lap.

Mom reached over and took Hannah's hand. "It's all right, Hannah."

"Would you like to hear about some of the things Mindy did?"

"Of course."

"One day Mindy and I were walking on the path leading from our house to the mailbox. She stopped all of a sudden and looked up at me with a huge smile. Then she said, 'I love you Mama.'"

Hannah stopped talking and drew in a shaky breath, hoping to gain control of her swirling emotions. "Another time, Mindy was picking dandelions and kept calling them 'pretty flowers.' She had a dandelion in her hand when she died, Mom." Hannah paused again, barely able to get the words out. "I. . .I will never forget the shock of seeing my precious little girl lying there so still, with a withered dandelion in her hand." Hannah nearly choked on the sob rising in her throat. "I don't think I can ever forgive Timothy for causing Mindy's death."

—⁂—

Pembroke, Kentucky

"Not long ago, Trisha and I were talking about how food always tastes so much better when it's eaten outside," Bonnie said as she and Allen sat on the front porch of the B&B eating supper. They'd invited Trisha to join them, but she'd declined, saying she wanted to give the newlyweds some time alone and would fix something for herself in the guesthouse.

"You're right about the food tasting good," Allen agreed, after taking a bite of fried chicken. "The only problem with eating outside is this hot July weather. Whew! It makes me glad for air-conditioning! I don't know how our Amish friends manage without it."

Bonnie smiled. "I guess one never misses what one's never had."

"That's true."

"By the way," she asked, "have you seen Timothy since he ate supper with us last week? I've been wondering how he's doing."

"Not very well. I saw him yesterday, and he's so despondent. It's a miracle he's been able to keep going at all."

"I wish Hannah hadn't walked out on him. She may not realize it, but she needs her husband as much as he needs her."

"I agree." Allen reached for Bonnie's hand. "If we ever had to go through anything like that, I'd want you right by my side."

She nodded. "I'd want you near me as well, but I hope we're never faced with anything like what Hannah and Timothy are going through right now."

━━━❦━━━

In the two weeks Hannah had been gone, it had been all Timothy could do to cope. He missed his wife so much and longed to speak with her. He'd called her folks several times and left voice messages for Hannah, but she never responded. He'd gotten one message from Sally the day Hannah got there, but it was brief and to the point. She didn't think Timothy should try to contact Hannah and said Hannah would contact him, if and when she felt ready.

"What a slap in the face," Timothy mumbled as he made himself a sandwich for supper. Since he wasn't much of a cook, he'd been eating sandwiches for supper every evening unless he ate at one of his brothers' homes. Both Esther and Suzanne were good cooks, so he appreciated getting a home-cooked meal. He'd eaten supper at Bonnie and Allen's one night last week, and that meal had been good, too.

If I could just talk to Hannah, he thought, *I might be able to convince her to come home.*

Timothy wanted to go to Pennsylvania and speak to her face-to-face, but Samuel and Titus had both advised him to stay put and give Hannah all the time she needed. Trisha, who had lost her husband a few years ago, had reminded Timothy that everyone was different and that it took some people longer than others to deal with their grief. Timothy understood that because he was still grieving for Mindy. He really believed he and Hannah needed each other during this time of mourning. He also feared that the longer they were apart, the harder it would be to bridge the gap between them.

Through prayer and Bible reading, Timothy had been trying to forgive himself, but it was difficult knowing Hannah might never forgive him or come back to Kentucky. How could he go on without her? Nothing would ever be the same if they weren't together as husband and wife.

Timothy set his knife down and made a decision. He would call his mother and ask her to speak to Hannah on his behalf. He just hoped Hannah would listen.

CHAPTER 48

On Monday morning, during the second week of August, Titus showed up at Samuel and Esther's house with a big grin. "Suzanne had the baby last night, and it's a boy!" he announced, after he'd entered the kitchen, where they sat with the children having breakfast.

Samuel jumped up and hugged Titus. "That's really good news! Congratulations!"

"How are Suzanne and the baby doing?" Esther asked.

"Real well, all things considered. Her labor was hard, but then I guess that's often the case with first babies. The boppli is healthy and has a good set of lungs. Oh, and he weighs nine and a half pounds, and he's almost twenty-two inches long."

"That's a pretty good-sized baby," Samuel said with a low whistle. "Much bigger than any of my kinner when they were born. I think Leon was the biggest; he weighed seven pounds, eleven ounces. The other three were all six and seven pounds."

"What'd ya name the boppli?" Marla asked.

Titus's grin, which had never left his face, widened. "Named him Abraham, after my daed. 'Course we'll probably call him Abe for short."

"I like that name," Leon spoke up. "It'll be nice to have another boy cousin."

"I'm sure Dad will be happy to hear you named the baby after him." Samuel motioned to the table. "If you haven't had breakfast yet, you're welcome to join us."

"I appreciate the offer, but I'm too excited to eat anything right now. I've gotta call the folks and leave 'em a message. And I want to stop and tell Timothy the news. Then I'll be heading back to the hospital to see how my fraa and boppli are doing."

"What about Suzanne's family?" Esther questioned. "Do they know about the baby?"

Titus bobbed his head. "Suzanne's mamm went with us to the hospital last night, so she was there when the boppli came."

"I'll bet she was excited," Esther said. "Especially since this is her first grandchild."

"Jah. Since Nelson seems to be in no hurry to find himself a wife, our little Abe will probably be the only grandchild for Suzanne's mamm to dote on for some time." Titus rolled his eyes. "Which means he'll probably end up bein' spoiled."

"We're really happy for you," Samuel said. "There's nothing quite like becoming a parent." He patted the top of Jared's head.

Esther smiled. She knew how much Samuel loved his children and hoped it wouldn't be long before they could have a child of their own to add to this happy family.

—∿∿—

Paradise, Pennsylvania

Fannie had just finished making french toast for breakfast when Abraham ambled into the kitchen with a smug-looking smile. "I've got some good news," he said, clasping Fannie's arm.

"Glad to hear it, because it'll be nice to get some good news for a change. Seems like there's too much bad going on in our world these days."

"I just came from the phone shack, and there was a message from Titus."

"Oh? What'd it say?"

"Suzanne had her boppli last night, and they named him after me."

Fannie smiled widely. "They had a boy?"

"Jah. A big, healthy boy, at that."

"That's wunderbaar! Just think, Abraham, this gives us forty-eight kinskinner, not counting dear little, departed Mindy. Oh, I wish we could go to Kentucky right now so we could see the new boppli."

"We'll go soon, Fannie—unless Titus and Suzanne decide to come here first."

She shook her head. "That's not likely to happen. From what Titus said the last time we talked, things are really busy in the woodshop right now, so I doubt he'll be taking time off for a trip anytime soon. Besides, it's a whole lot easier for us to travel than it would be for a young couple with a new baby."

"You're probably right, so we'll go there soon. But I think we should give 'em some time to adjust to being parents before we barge in, don't you?"

She nodded slowly. "I suppose you're right, and when we do go, it'll be nice to see Samuel and his family, as well as Timothy."

Abraham took a seat. "Speaking of Timothy, have you been able to talk to Hannah yet? You did promise him you'd try to talk her into going back to Kentucky, right?"

"Jah, I did, but every time I've gone over to the Kings' place, I've only seen Sally." Fannie sighed deeply. "She always gives me the excuse that Hannah's resting or isn't feeling up to company. Makes me wonder if I'll ever get the chance to speak to Hannah face-to-face."

"Well, don't give up. One of these days when you stop over there, Sally's bound to be gone, and then she won't be able to run interference for Hannah." Abraham grunted. "Wouldn't surprise me one bit if she doesn't do it just so she can keep Hannah all to herself. You and I both know that Hannah's mamm had such a tight hold on Hannah before Timothy moved them to Kentucky that it was choking the life out of their marriage. Now that Hannah's back home and livin' under her folks' roof again, Sally will probably do most anything to keep Hannah there."

"Oh, I hope that's not the case." Fannie set the platter of french toast on the table and took a seat beside Abraham. "As soon as we're done with breakfast, I'm going over to see Hannah again. Since I promised Timothy I would talk to her, I need to keep trying."

Hannah had just entered the kitchen when a wave of nausea ran through her. She clutched her stomach and groaned. This was the third day in a row that she'd felt sick to her stomach soon after she'd gotten out of bed. *Could I be pregnant?* she wondered. *Oh, surely not. I don't see how. . . .*

Hannah's thoughts took her to the last night she'd spent in Kentucky. She remembered how she'd allowed herself to find comfort in Timothy's arms and had awakened the next morning fearful that because of her willingness to be with him, he'd gotten the wrong idea. Had Timothy believed she'd forgiven him and that things were better between them? Well, he ought to know that just wasn't possible! Even if Hannah was carrying Timothy's child, she could never return to Kentucky and be the wife Timothy wanted and expected her to be. The only way Hannah could cope with Mindy's death was to stay right here in the safety of her parents' home.

Hannah had just put the teakettle on the stove when her mother entered the kitchen. "I'm going shopping as soon as we're done with breakfast, and I was hoping you'd come with me," Mom said.

Hannah shook her head. "I don't feel like it, Mom. I just want to stay here."

"Oh, but Hannah, you've been cooped up in this house ever since you came home, and I think it would be good for you to get out for a few hours."

"I can't. I might see someone from Timothy's family, and then they'd probably tell me I was wrong to leave Timothy and that my place is in Kentucky with him." Hannah leaned against the counter as another wave of nausea rolled through her stomach.

"Are you feeling all right? You look pale," Mom said with a worried frown. "Are you grank?"

"I'm fine. Just tired, is all."

"That's because you're not sleeping well. I think you should let me take you to the doctor and see if he'll prescribe some sleeping pills."

Hannah shook her head vigorously. "I don't want any sleeping pills. I sleep when I need to—sometimes during the day. I'm sure I'll feel better once I've had some breakfast."

Mom pulled Hannah into her arms for a hug. "I can't help but worry about you. Maybe I should wait until tomorrow to do my shopping."

"I'll be fine. Go ahead with your plans."

"All right, then. Is there anything you'd like me to pick up for you while I'm out and about?"

Hannah shook her head. "There's nothing I need." *Except a sense of peace I may never feel,* she added to herself.

—⁓—

Soon after Mom left, Hannah decided to sit on the porch for a while because it was so hot and stuffy in the house. With a cup of peppermint tea in one hand, she took a seat on the porch swing and tried to relax. Besides the nausea that still plagued her, the muscles in her back and neck were tense. She leaned heavily against the back of the swing and concentrated on the noisy buzz of the cicadas coming from the many trees in her parents' yard.

Hannah had only been sitting a few minutes when a horse and buggy pulled into the yard. Her first impulse was to dash into the house, but curious to see who it was, she stayed. When she saw Fannie Fisher climb down from the buggy, Hannah felt her heart pound. *Oh no! Not her! I can't deal with the questions I'm sure she's likely to ask.*

Hannah jumped up and was about to run into the house when Fannie called, "Stay right there, Hannah! I need to speak to you!"

Feeling like a defenseless fly trapped in the web of a spider, Hannah collapsed onto the swing. She supposed she couldn't avoid Timothy's mother forever, so she might as well get it over with. Maybe after she explained how she felt about things, Hannah wouldn't be bothered by Fannie again.

"Wie geht's?" Fannie asked as she joined Hannah on the porch.

"I'm surprised to see you," Hannah mumbled, avoiding

Fannie's question about how she was doing.

"I've come by several times to see you, but your mamm's always said you weren't up to company."

Hannah didn't say anything—just waited for the barrage of questions she figured was forthcoming.

Fannie shifted from one foot to the other; then without invitation, she took a seat in one of the wicker chairs. "I understand that you're hurting, Hannah. Losing Mindy was a horrible tragedy, and we all miss her."

Just hearing Mindy's name and seeing the look of compassion on Fannie's face made Hannah feel like crying.

"I also understand why you may have felt that you needed to get away from Kentucky for a while," Fannie continued. "But have you considered how much this is hurting Timothy? He's grieving for Mindy, too, you know."

Hannah's jaw clenched. "I'm sure he is, but it doesn't change the fact that it's his fault our little girl is dead."

A pained expression crossed Fannie's face. "Timothy blames himself, too, but all the blame in the world won't bring Mindy back."

"Don't you think I know that? When I discovered Mindy lying on the ground so still, I begged God for a miracle, but He chose not to give me one. Instead, He snatched my only child away when He could have stopped it from happening in the first place." Hannah couldn't keep the bitterness out of her voice, and it was a struggle not to give in to the tears pricking the back of her eyes.

"You know, even with a brand-new screen on a window, someone could still fall through if they ran into it too hard or leaned heavily against it. Screens are only meant to keep bugs out, not prevent people from falling out of windows."

Hannah offered no response. She was sure Mindy had

fallen out the window because the screen was broken, and nothing Fannie could say would change her mind.

"You're right that God could have prevented Mindy's death," Fannie said with tears in her eyes. "He could let us go through life protected from every horrible thing that could hurt us."

"Then why doesn't He?"

"I don't know all of God's ways, but I do know that whenever He allows bad things to happen to His people, He can take those things and use them for good." Fannie slipped her arm around Hannah's shoulder. "But we have to decide to let it work for our good and not allow bitterness and resentment to take over. We can choose to let God help us with the hurts and disappointments we must face."

Hannah's throat felt so clogged, she couldn't speak. What Fannie said, she'd heard before from one of the ministers in their church. But letting go of her hurt wouldn't bring Mindy back, and besides, she didn't think she could do it. Hannah felt the need to hold on to something—even if it was the hurt and bitterness she harbored against Timothy.

As though sensing Hannah's confusion and inability to let go of her pain, Fannie said, "The only way you'll ever rise above your grief is to forgive my son. Bitterness and resentment will hurt you more in the long run, and when you do the right thing, Hannah, God will give you His peace. Won't you please return to Kentucky and try to work things out with Timothy?"

Hannah looked away, tears clouding her vision. "I just can't."

Fannie sat for several minutes; then she finally rose to her feet. "I pray that you'll change your mind about that, for your sake, as well as my son's." She moved toward the porch steps but halted and turned to look at Hannah. "Oh, before I go,

I thought you might like to know that Suzanne had a baby boy last night. They named him Abraham, and I guess they're planning to call him Abe for short."

It took all that Hannah had within her, but she forced herself to say she was glad for Suzanne and Titus. Inside, however, just hearing about Suzanne's baby made her hurt even more. It was one more painful reminder that Hannah no longer had any children to hold and to love.

"We'll be going to Kentucky to see the boppli in a month or so. Maybe you'd like to go along," Fannie said.

Hannah shook her head. A wave of nausea came over her, and she thought she might lose her breakfast. "I don't mean to be rude, but I'm not feeling so well, and I need to lie down." Before Fannie could respond, Hannah jumped up and rushed into the house.

Pembroke, Kentucky

When Timothy arrived home from work that day, the first thing he did was head to the phone shanty to check for messages. He found only one—it was from Mom, and it wasn't good news. She'd spoken to Hannah but couldn't get her to change her mind about coming back to Kentucky.

With a heavy heart, Timothy dialed his folks' number to leave a message in return. He was surprised when Mom answered the phone.

"It's Timothy, Mom. I just listened to your message about seeing Hannah today. Is there anything else you can tell me about your visit with her?" he asked.

"Hannah isn't the same woman you married, Timothy,"

Mom said. "Losing Mindy has changed her. She's bitter and almost like an empty vessel inside. I fear she may never be the same."

"Does she still blame me for Mindy's death?"

"Jah, and she's not willing to return to Kentucky."

Sweat beaded on Timothy's forehead, and he reached up to wipe it away. "She didn't mention divorce, did she?"

"No."

"Well, that's a relief. Maybe it's for the best that she's not with me right now. Seeing her every day and knowing how she feels about me would only add to the guilt I already feel for causing Mindy's death."

"I think maybe Hannah needs more time, Timothy. We're all praying for her, and for you as well. You've got to stop blaming yourself, son, because all the blame in the world won't bring Mindy back, and it's not helping your emotional state, either."

"I know, Mom, but if I could, I'd give my life in exchange for my daughter's."

"That's not an option, and you need to find a way to work through all of this. You need to get on with the business of living."

"How can I do that when my wife hates me and won't come back to our home?"

"I don't think Hannah hates you, Timothy. I just think she's so caught up in her grief that she needs someone to blame. I also believe in the power of prayer, so let's keep praying and believing that someone or something will help Hannah see that her place is with you. I don't think you should try to force her to come back."

"I would never do that, Mom. If Hannah decides to return

to Kentucky, it has to be her decision of her own free will." Timothy blinked as a trickle of sweat rolled into his eyes. "And I. . .I want more than anything for Hannah to say that she's forgiven me and can love me again."

CHAPTER 49

"There's something I need to tell you," Bonnie said to Allen as they shared breakfast together one Saturday morning in mid-September.

Allen set his cup of coffee down. "You look so somber. I hope it's not bad news."

She shook her head. "It's good news. At least it is to me. I'm hoping you'll think it's good news, too."

He wiggled his eyebrows. "Then tell me now, because I can't stand the suspense."

Smiling and taking in a deep breath, Bonnie said, "I'm pregnant."

Allen stared at her like he couldn't believe what she'd just said. "Are. . .are you sure?" he asked in a near whisper.

"I took a pregnancy test earlier this week, and I saw the doctor yesterday afternoon. It's official, Allen. The baby's due the first week of April."

"How come you waited till now to tell me?" Allen's furrowed brows let Bonnie know he was a bit disappointed. Was it because she hadn't told him sooner, or was he upset about her being pregnant?

"I know we've only been married four months, and I'm sorry if you're disappointed because we didn't expect to start a family so soon, but—"

Allen placed his finger against her lips. "I'm not the least bit disappointed. I'm thrilled to hear such good news. You just took me by surprise, that's all." He smiled widely then leaned over and gave her a kiss. "Wow, I can't wait to tell my folks this news. Mom will be so excited when she hears that she's gonna be a grandma. Have you told your dad yet?"

"No, you're the first one I've told, and I would have given you the news last night, but you fell asleep soon after we ate supper."

"I don't usually conk out like that," Allen said, "but I've been working such long hours lately, and I can't seem to get enough sleep."

She smiled. "I understand. Things have been busier around the B&B recently, too, and it's keeping me and Trisha hopping."

"You should probably slow down now that you're expecting a baby. Maybe you ought to consider hiring someone else to help Trisha so you can take it easy and get plenty of rest."

"I promise I won't overdo it, but I can't sit around doing nothing. It's not in my nature."

He nodded. "Okay. I guess you know what you're capable of doing."

Bonnie finished eating her scrambled eggs then pushed away from the table. "I think I'll call my dad right now. After that, I'm going to share our good news with Trisha."

"Sounds like a plan. While you're calling your dad, I'll use my cell phone and give my folks a call." Allen grinned. "Something tells me that once the baby comes, they'll be making a lot more trips to Kentucky."

Bonnie nodded. "I'll bet Dad comes to visit us more often, too."

―⚬―

"You look like you're in a good mood this morning," Trisha said when she found Bonnie humming as she did the breakfast dishes.

Bonnie turned from the sink and smiled. "I sure am. In fact, I'm feeling very blessed and happy."

"Would you like to share some of that happiness with me?"

"That's exactly what I was planning to do." Bonnie motioned to the table. "Let's have a seat, and I'll tell you about it."

Leaning her elbows on the table, Bonnie smiled and said, "Allen and I are going to have a baby. I'm due the first part of April."

Trisha grinned and reached for Bonnie's hand. "Oh, that is good news! I'm so happy for you, Bonnie."

"I appreciate God giving me a second chance at motherhood since I was forced to give up my baby when I was sixteen."

"I know you'll make a good mom. I've seen how patient and kind you are with Samuel's kids. And Allen will make a good daddy, too."

"Yes, I believe he will." Bonnie tapped her fingers along the edge of the table.

"Is there a problem?" Trisha asked.

"Well, no, not for me, but you might not see it that way."

"What is it?"

"When I called Dad to give him the good news, he was very pleased."

"I imagine he would be."

"Well, the thing is. . ." Bonnie paused and moistened her lips. "He said something about quitting his job at the bank and moving here so he can be closer to me and the baby."

"I can understand him wanting to do that."

"How would you feel about it if Dad decides to move?"

Trisha shrugged. "Whatever Ken does is his business."

"I know there has been some tension between you two, and if he moves here, you'll be seeing him fairly often, so I thought—"

"It's not a problem, Bonnie. When your dad came to your wedding in May, things were better between us, so I don't anticipate any issues if he should decide to move here."

"That's a relief. I want having this baby to be a positive experience, and I was a little concerned that you might decide to leave if Dad moves to Kentucky."

Trisha shook her head. "As long as you want me to help at the B&B, I'm here for you."

"I'm glad to hear that, because my business has picked up since you came to work for me. Besides, you and I have become good friends, and I'd miss not having you around."

Trisha smiled. "I'll stay as long as you want me to."

Paradise, Pennsylvania

Hannah sat in the rocking chair inside her parents' living room and placed both hands against her stomach. It hadn't taken very long for her to realize that she was definitely pregnant. Due to the morning sickness, Mom had figured it out, too. Hannah was okay with her folks knowing, but she didn't want anyone else to know—especially not anyone from Timothy's family. If they knew she was expecting a baby, they'd tell Timothy. And if he knew, Hannah was sure he would come to Pennsylvania and insist she go back to

Kentucky with him. So Hannah had asked her folks not to tell anyone, and they'd agreed to keep her secret. But Dad had made it clear that he wasn't happy about it. He'd said several times that he thought Hannah's place was with her husband, no matter how she felt about him. "Marriage is for keeps, and divorce is not an option," Dad had said the other night.

Hannah grimaced. She'd never said she was going to get a divorce, but one thing she did know: she couldn't be with Timothy right now.

A tear trickled down her cheek as she thought about the baby she carried. She wasn't ready to be a mother again— wasn't ready to have another baby. She wasn't even sure she could provide for this child and wondered whether Mom and Dad would be willing to help her raise it.

—⁂—

Pembroke, Kentucky

"As time goes on, I become more worried about Timothy," Samuel said as he dried the breakfast dishes while Esther washed. "When Hannah left three months ago, Timothy hoped she would change her mind and come back to him, but the longer she's gone, the more depressed he's become. I really don't know how much longer he can go on like this."

Esther nodded. "It's sad to think of him living all alone in that big old house, feeling guilty for causing Mindy's death and longing for Hannah to come home."

"I've tried everything I know to encourage him, but nothing I've said has made any difference." Samuel reached for another plate. "My mamm tried talking to Hannah several weeks ago, but it was all for nothing. Mom told Timothy that Hannah wasn't very cordial and she isn't willing to forgive him or come back to Kentucky."

Esther slowly shook her head. "I've said this before, Samuel, and I'll say it again. All we can do for Timothy is pray for him and offer our love and support. What Hannah decides to do is in God's hands, and we must continue to pray for her, too."

CHAPTER 50

Paradise, Pennsylvania

Fannie had just entered her daughter's quilt shop when she spotted Phoebe Stoltzfus's mother, Arie, on the other side of the room by the thread and other notions. Fannie and Arie had been close friends when Titus and Phoebe had been courting, but after the couple broke up, the two women saw less of each other. Of late, Fannie hadn't seen much of Arie at all. She figured that was probably because Arie had been busy helping Phoebe plan her wedding, which would take place in a few weeks.

"It's good to see you," Fannie said when Arie joined her at the fabric table. "It's been awhile."

Arie nodded. "I've been really busy helping Phoebe get ready for her wedding, this is the first opportunity I've had to do some shopping that doesn't have anything to do with the wedding."

Fannie smiled. "I know how that can be. When Abby was planning her wedding, I helped as much as I could. Of course, the twins were still little then, so I couldn't do as much as I would have liked. But then, Naomi and Nancy helped Abby a lot, so that took some of the pressure off me."

"Speaking of your twins, I saw Timothy's wife the other day," Arie said.

"Oh, really? Did you pay her a visit?" Fannie was anxious to hear about it, because she wondered if Hannah had been more receptive to Arie than she had to her.

"I saw Hannah coming out of the doctor's office in Lancaster," Arie said.

"Has she been grank?"

"I don't know if she's sick or not. I didn't say anything to Hannah, because as soon as I approached her, she hurried away." Arie's forehead wrinkled. "That young woman, whom I remember as always being so slender, has either put on a lot of weight or else she's pregnant."

Fannie's mouth dropped open. "Are you sure it was Hannah?"

"Of course I'm sure. Her belly was way out here." Arie held her hands several inches away from her stomach.

Fannie frowned. "Hmm. . ."

"Have you seen Hannah lately?" Arie questioned. "Do you know if she's pregnant?"

"I saw her some time ago but not recently. She's been staying with her folks for nearly five months, so I don't see how she could be pregnant. Unless maybe. . ." Fannie set her material aside. "I've got to go. It was nice seeing you, Arie."

"Where are you off to?"

"I'm going to pay a call on Hannah," Fannie said before hurrying toward the door.

———※———

When Fannie arrived at the Kings' place a short time later, she found Sally on the porch hanging laundry on the line that had been connected by a pulley up to the barn.

"Is Hannah here?" Fannie asked, joining her.

"Jah, but she's not up to visiting with anyone right now," Sally said, barely looking at Fannie.

"She never is. At least not when I or anyone from my family has come by. What's going on, Sally?"

"Nothing. Hannah's just not accepting visitors right now."

"Why not?" Fannie's patience was waning.

"Well, you know how sad Hannah feels about losing Mindy, and she doesn't want anyone bombarding her with a bunch of questions. I thought you understood that she needs to be alone."

"Wanting to be left alone for a few weeks or even a month after losing a loved one might be normal, but this has gone on far too long, and it doesn't make sense."

Sally's eyes narrowed. "What are you saying, Fannie?"

"I'm saying that it isn't normal for a wife to leave her husband the way Hannah did and then stay cooped up in her parents' house and refuse to see anyone but them."

"Everyone grieves differently."

"That may be so, but most people know when they're going through a rough time that they need the love and support of their family and friends. That should include Hannah's husband's family, too, don't you think?"

Sally said nothing. She picked up a wet towel and hung it on the line. Then she bent down to pick up another one.

"Is Hannah expecting a boppli?" Fannie blurted out.

Sally dropped the towel and whirled around to face her. "What made you ask such a question?"

"Someone saw Hannah coming out of the doctor's office in Lancaster the other day, and they said she looked like she was pregnant." Fannie took a step closer to Sally. "Is it true? Is Hannah pregnant?"

Sally lowered her gaze. "Hannah's asked me not to discuss

anything about her with anyone."

Fannie tapped her foot impatiently. "I'm not just anyone, Sally. I'm Hannah's mother-in-law, and if she's carrying my grandchild, I have the right to know."

Sally lifted her gaze, and tears filled her eyes. "I really can't talk about this right now."

Fannie stood several more seconds then hurried away. Even without Sally admitting it, she was quite sure Hannah was expecting a baby. It wasn't right that she was keeping it a secret. Timothy deserved to know, and Fannie planned to call him as soon as she got home.

CHAPTER 51

"If Fannie suspects I'm pregnant and tells Timothy, I don't know what I'll do if he shows up here," Hannah said after her mother told her about Fannie's most recent visit.

"Now, you need to calm down and relax," Mom said, handing Hannah a cup of herbal tea. "Since I didn't admit anything to Fannie, she would only be guessing if she told Timothy you were expecting a boppli."

Hannah got the rocking chair she was sitting in moving harder and grimaced when the baby kicked inside her womb. This baby was a lot more active than Mindy had been when she was carrying her. It seemed like the little one was always kicking. Sometimes it felt as if the baby was kicking with both feet and both hands at the same time. When that happened at bedtime, it was hard for Hannah to find a comfortable position so she could sleep.

"Was that Fannie Fisher's rig I saw pulling out when I came in?" Dad asked, stepping into the living room.

Mom nodded. "She wanted to speak to Hannah, but I wouldn't let her."

"Any idea what she wanted to talk to her about?" he asked.

"Fannie suspects that I'm pregnant," Hannah said. "I. . .I'm afraid she may tell Timothy."

Dad crossed his arms. "That might be the best thing for everyone concerned. I never did think Timothy should be kept in the dark. I've been tempted to tell him myself, but I knew if I did, I'd have you and your mamm to answer to."

"You've got that right," Mom said with a huff. "If Hannah doesn't want Timothy to know, we need to respect her wishes."

"That's kind of hard to do when I think she's wrong." Dad's forehead wrinkled as he narrowed his eyes and looked right at Hannah. "I think you should forgive that husband of yours and go on back to Kentucky."

"I just can't." Hannah placed her hands on her swollen stomach, and even though she knew the next words were ridiculous, she couldn't seem to stop them. "Even if I could forgive him for causing Mindy's death, how could I trust him not to do something that could hurt this boppli, too?"

—⁂—

Pembroke, Kentucky

"How'd things go for you today?" Esther asked when Samuel came in the door around six o'clock.

"Okay. Timothy and I are almost done with the house we've been painting in Herndon. If all goes well, we should be able to start on another house in Trenton by the end of this week." Samuel slipped his arm around Esther's waist. "How was your day?"

"Good. Trisha and Bonnie picked me up, and the three of us went to see Suzanne and the boppli." Esther smiled. "Little Abe is so cute, and I really enjoyed holding him. Even Jared and Penny were taken with the little guy."

Samuel chuckled. "I'll bet those two would like to have a baby brother or sister of their own to play with."

Esther sighed. "Are you disappointed that I haven't gotten pregnant yet?"

" 'Course not," Samuel said with a shake of his head. "We haven't been married half a year yet, so there's plenty of time for you to get pregnant."

"But what if I don't? Maybe I won't be able to have any children."

Samuel gave Esther's arm a tender squeeze. "Try not to worry. It'll happen in God's time, and if it doesn't, then we'll accept it as God's will."

Esther smiled. She appreciated her husband's encouraging words. She was about to tell him that supper was almost ready when she heard several bumps followed by a piercing scream.

Esther and Samuel raced into the hall, where they found Penny lying at the foot of the stairs, red-faced and sobbing. Leon, Marla, and Jared stood nearby, eyes wide and mouths hanging open; they looked scared to death.

Samuel dropped to his knees. "Are you hurt, Penny?" he asked, checking her over real good.

"I. . .I'm okay, Daadi." Penny sniffed and sat up.

"What happened?" Esther asked. "Did you trip on the stairs?"

Penny turned and pointed to a small wooden horse.

Samuel's face flushed. "How many times have I told you kids not to leave your toys on the stairs? Now I hope you see how dangerous that can be!"

The children nodded soberly.

Esther knew Samuel's first wife had died after falling down the stairs, so she could understand why he would be upset, but she thought he was being a little too hard on the children.

"I'm sorry, Samuel," she said. "I should have kept a closer watch to make sure that nothing was left on the stairs."

"It's not about things getting left on the stairs," Samuel said, shaking his head. "The toy horse shouldn't have been there in the first place."

"You're right." Tears welled in Esther's eyes. "I guess I'm not doing a very good job with the kinner these days."

"That's not true," Marla spoke up. "You take real good care of us."

All heads bobbed in agreement, including Samuel's. "Marla's right, Esther. You've done well with the kinner ever since you started taking care of them, but you can't be expected to watch their every move." He gave each of the children a stern look while shaking his finger. "It's your job to watch out for each other, too, and that includes keeping the stairs and other places free of clutter so you'll all be safe." He smiled at Esther. "And I want you to be safe, as well."

—⁓—

"I talked to my dad today," Bonnie told Allen as they sat at the dining-room table, eating supper that evening.

"What's new with him?"

"He'll be moving here next week."

Allen's eyebrows shot up. "Here, at the B&B?"

"Only for a little while—until he finds a place of his own. If it's okay with you, that is."

"Sure, I have no problem with that."

"He got word that he'll be managing one of the banks in Hopkinsville."

"That's all good news." Allen grinned. "Does Trisha know about this?"

Bonnie nodded. "To tell you the truth, I think she was rather pleased."

"Well, who knows? There might be a budding romance ahead for those two."

Her eyebrows arched. "You really think so?"

"Would you be okay with it?"

Bonnie smiled. "Most definitely. I think Dad and Trisha would be perfect for each other."

"Hmm...you might be right about that." Allen reached for his glass of water and took a sip. "So tell me about your day. Did you get some rest?"

"I didn't work, if that's what you mean. Trisha and I took Esther over to see Suzanne's baby, and holding little Abe made me even more excited about having our own baby."

Allen grinned. "I'm looking forward to that, too."

Bonnie handed him the bowl of tossed salad. "And how was your day?"

"Busy. I bid two jobs in Hopkinsville and then stopped at the house Samuel and Timothy have been working on this week."

"How's Timothy doing?" she asked, reaching for her glass of water.

"Not very well, I'm afraid. He doesn't look good at all, and he's pushing himself way too hard. He probably believes working long hours will help him not think about Hannah so much." Deep wrinkles formed across Allen's forehead. "If Timothy's not careful, though, he'll work himself to death."

CHAPTER 52

On Friday afternoon after Timothy got home from work, he fixed himself a sandwich. Then he headed for the barn to feed the horses, muck out their stalls, and replace a broken hinge on one of the stall doors.

Ever since Hannah had left, he'd worked on some unfinished projects—including new screens for all of the windows in the house. His most recent project was the barn. So far, he'd reinforced the hayloft, replaced a couple of beams, and fixed a broken door. Tomorrow, with the help of Samuel, Titus, and Allen, he planned to re-roof the barn. It felt good to keep busy and get some of the projects done that he'd previously kept saying he would do later. It was the only way he could keep from thinking too much about Hannah and the guilt he felt for causing Mindy's death.

It was dark by the time Timothy finished up in the barn, and he was so tired he could barely stay on his feet. He shook the grit and dust from his hair and headed for the house, not caring that he hadn't gone to the phone shanty to check for messages. Stepping onto the porch, he barely noticed the hoot of an owl calling from one of the trees.

When Timothy entered the house, he trudged wearily up

the stairs, holding on to the banister with each step he took. After a quick shower, he headed down the hall toward his room. But as he neared Mindy's bedroom, he halted. Other than the day he'd replaced the screen in her window, he hadn't stepped foot in this room. For some reason, he felt compelled to go in there now.

Timothy opened the door, and a soft light from the moon cast shadows on the wall.

"Oh Mindy girl, I sure do miss you," he murmured. "Wish now I'd spent more time with you when you were still with us. If I could start over again, I'd do things differently." Tears coursed down Timothy's cheeks as a deep sense of regret washed over him. "If I'd just put a screen on your window when your mamm asked me to, you'd be here right now, sleeping peacefully in your bed, and your mamm would not have left me."

Timothy moaned as he flopped onto Mindy's bed and curled up on his side. With his head resting on her pillow, he could smell the lingering sweetness of his precious little girl. After Hannah had left, he'd thought about changing Mindy's sheets but hadn't gotten around to it. Right now he was glad.

Mindy. . .Mindy. . .Mindy. . . Timothy closed his eyes and succumbed to much-needed sleep.

---ᨠ---

"Daadi. . .Daadi. . .I love you, Daadi."

Timothy sat up and looked around. Had someone called his name? The voice he'd heard sounded like Mindy's, but that was impossible—she was dead.

"Daad–i."

Timothy blinked, shocked to see Mindy standing on the other side of her bedroom. Her clothes glowed—illuminating the entire room.

351

"I...I must be seeing things!" Timothy rubbed his eyes and blinked again. Mindy was still there, moving closer to him. Her golden hair hung loosely across her shoulders, and her cherubic face glowed radiantly.

"I'm sorry, Daadi," she whispered, extending her hand to him.

"Sorry for what, Mindy?"

"I shouldn't have been playin' near the window that day. Don't be sad, Daadi. It's not your fault. You work so hard and just got busy and forgot about the screens."

Timothy drew in a shaky breath, struggling to hold back the tears stinging his eyes. He reached out his hand until his fingers were almost touching hers. Mindy looked like a child, but she sounded so grown-up. "Mindy, my precious little girl. Oh, I've missed you so much."

"Don't cry, Daadi. I'm happy with Jesus, and someday you and Mama will be with us in heaven."

Timothy nearly choked on a sob as he lifted his hand to stroke her soft cheek. Then she was gone, and the room lost its glow.

"Mindy, don't go! Come back! Come back!"

———

Feeling as though he were in a haze, Timothy pried his eyes open and sat up. Sunlight streamed in through the bare window, and he knew it was morning.

Timothy glanced down at himself and realized he must have fallen asleep on Mindy's bed. He sat for several minutes, rubbing his temples and trying to clear the cobwebs from his brain. He'd seen a vision last night. Or was it a dream? Mindy had spoken to him and said he shouldn't blame himself for the accident. She was happy in heaven, as he knew she must be, and that gave him a sense of peace.

Timothy rose to his feet and ambled over to the window. "Thank You, God," he murmured with a feeling of new hope. "I believe You gave me that dream last night so I would stop blaming myself. Now if Hannah would only forgive me, too."

—⁓—

Paradise, Pennsylvania

"Mama. I love you, Mama."

"Mindy, is that you?" Hannah sat up in bed with a start, rubbing her eyes in disbelief.

"I'm over here, Mama."

A bright light illuminated the room, and Hannah gasped. Mindy stood by the window, dressed all in white with golden flecks of sunlight glistening in her long hair.

"Mindy! Oh, my precious little girl!" Hannah gulped on a sob, grasping the quilt that still covered her.

"Don't cry, Mama. Don't be sad. I'm happy livin' in heaven with Jesus. Someday you and Daadi will be with us, too."

Hannah couldn't speak around the lump in her throat. All she could do was hold out her hands.

"Don't blame Daadi anymore, Mama. He just got busy and forgot about the screens. Daadi needs you, Mama. Go back to him, please."

Hannah sniffed deeply as tears trickled down her cheeks. She was unable to take her eyes off her precious angel.

"Go soon, Mama. Tell Daadi you love him."

Hannah blinked. Then Mindy was gone.

—⁓—

Hannah's eyes snapped open when she heard the clock ticking beside her bed. It was early—not quite five o'clock. She'd had a restless night, trying to turn off her thoughts and find a comfortable position for her sore back. "I had a dream about Mindy," she murmured. The dream had been so real, Hannah wondered if it hadn't been a dream at all. If it was a dream, could it have been God's way of getting her attention—making her realize that she needed to forgive Timothy and return to Kentucky?

Hannah swung her legs over the side of the bed and ambled across the room. Then she lowered herself into the rocking chair near the window. *You must forgive Timothy,* a voice in her head seemed to say. *Mindy wants you to.*

Hannah thought about a Bible verse she'd learned as a child and quoted it out loud: " 'If ye forgive men their trespasses, your heavenly Father will also forgive you,' Matthew 6:14."

A sob tore from Hannah's throat, and in the dimness of the room, she bowed her head and closed her eyes. "I forgive him, Father," she prayed. "Forgive me for feeling such resentment and anger toward my husband all these months."

Hannah opened her eyes and gently touched her stomach. "Timothy and I can be one again. Together we can welcome this miracle into the world," she whispered.

Bracing her hands on the arms of the chair, Hannah stood and gazed out the window, watching the light of dawn as it slowly appeared in the horizon. It was almost December, and mornings were chilly in Pennsylvania this time of the year, but feeling the need for a breath of fresh air, she opened the window. Taking in a few deep breaths, Hannah felt as if a heavy weight had been lifted from her shoulders. "I need to return to Kentucky. I need to go now."

CHAPTER 53

Sally had just starting making breakfast when Hannah came into the room, looking bright-eyed and almost bubbly. It was the first time since her daughter had been home that Sally had seen a genuine smile on her face.

"You look like you're in a good mood this morning," Sally said. "Did you sleep well last night?"

Hannah nodded. "I had a dream, Mom. It was a dream about Mindy."

"Oh? Was it a good dream?"

"Jah, it was a very good dream. Mindy said I shouldn't blame her daed for the accident. She also said she was happy in heaven." Hannah took a seat at the table. "Mindy was right, Mom. My unwillingness to forgive Timothy was wrong."

Mom touched Hannah's shoulder. "Perhaps God gave you that dream so you would realize the importance of forgiveness."

"I need to return to Kentucky," Hannah said. "Timothy needs to know that I've forgiven him. I also want to tell him about the boppli I'm carrying."

Sally was quiet for a few minutes as she processed all of

this. She knew Hannah's place was with her husband, but she would miss her daughter. *I can't say or do anything to prevent her from going,* she told herself. *Timothy wishes to make his home in Kentucky, and even though I'm going to miss her, I know that's where my daughter belongs.*

Sally was about to voice her thoughts when Johnny entered the room. "Is breakfast ready yet?" he asked. "I need to get to the store and open it, 'cause neither of my helpers can come in till ten this morning."

"I think I ought to start working in the store again, and then we can let those two young women go," Sally said. "Once Phoebe gets married, she'll probably want to stay home and start raising a family, anyway."

"You're welcome to work in the store if you want to," Johnny said, "but I thought you liked staying at home."

"I do, but now that Hannah's going back to Kentucky, I'll be alone and will need something meaningful to do."

Johnny's eyebrows shot up. "Hannah's returning to Kentucky?"

"That's right, Dad." Hannah repeated the dream she'd had and told him about the decision she'd made to be reunited with her husband.

"Well all I've got to say is it's about time you saw the light." Johnny shook his head. "I never did think you should have left Timothy, and not telling him about the boppli wasn't right, either."

"Hannah doesn't need any lectures this morning," Sally was quick to say. "What she needs is our love and support."

Johnny bobbed his head and smiled at Sally, obviously happy to hear her say that. "She definitely has my support, and I think I know a way she can head for Kentucky today."

"How's that, Dad?" Hannah asked.

"Abraham Fisher came by my store yesterday, right before

closing time. He mentioned that he'd hired a driver to take him and Fannie to Kentucky to see Titus and Suzanne's baby. He said he'd arranged it without Fannie knowing, and that he was going to surprise her with the news this morning. Guess the plan is for them to leave sometime this afternoon, and they'll get to Titus's place tomorrow." He grinned at Hannah. "I'm sure their driver would have room for one more if you'd like to go along."

Hannah's eyes brightened. "I definitely would! It's like this was meant to be."

"Great! I'll stop by Abraham's place on my way to work and set it all up." Johnny clapped his hands together. "Now I think we'd better have some breakfast so I can get going and you can pack."

―⁓―

Pembroke, Kentucky

"This roof is even worse than I thought," Timothy called to Samuel, who stood on the ground below picking up the shingles his brother had already thrown down to him.

Samuel cupped his hands around his mouth and shouted, "When Titus and Allen get here, one of 'em can go up there and help you!"

"Okay, whatever!" Timothy gave a quick wave and continued to almost frantically tear off more of the shingles.

Samuel was still worried about his brother. Timothy had been driving himself too hard. Truth was, he probably shouldn't be working on the barn roof at all today. But the weather had been nicer than usual for this time of year, and Timothy had insisted on getting the roof done before bad weather set in. Samuel had suggested that Timothy rest

357

awhile and let him take over the job of removing shingles, but Timothy wouldn't hear of it. Samuel was afraid if Timothy didn't slow down soon, he'd keel over from exhaustion. Maybe when Allen and Titus showed up, one of them could talk some sense into him.

———

As Hannah rode in Herb Nelson's van, along with Fannie and Abraham, all she could think about was her dream. She'd shared the details of the dream with Fannie and Abraham and thanked them for allowing her to travel to Kentucky with them. Now, as they neared Pembroke, Hannah felt compelled to tell Fannie something she hadn't shared with anyone yet.

"All this time, I've been blaming Timothy for Mindy's accident, but I really think I'm the one to blame," Hannah said.

Fannie's eyes widened. "Wh–what do you mean?"

"When Mindy came into the kitchen that day, she held a dandelion in her little hand that she wanted to give me. But I sent her away—told her to go out of the room and play." Hannah swallowed hard. Just thinking about it made her feel sad. "If I hadn't done that, she wouldn't have gone upstairs to her room, and if I'd kept her in the kitchen with me, she'd still be alive."

Fannie reached across the seat and took Hannah's hand. "It was an accident—perhaps one that could have been avoided— but if it was Mindy's time to go, then she could have died some other way."

Hannah nodded slowly. "One thing I do know is that Mindy's happier in heaven than she ever could be here on earth, and the dream I had gave me a sense of peace about things."

Fannie smiled. "I'm glad, and I'm also pleased that you're going back to Timothy. I know he will be so happy to see you."

"He'll also be glad about the boppli you're expecting, just as we are," Abraham said from the front passenger's seat.

Hannah looked down at her growing stomach. "I'm grateful God's given us another chance to be happy, and I pray that we'll do a good job raising this baby."

"You'll do fine, Hannah," Fannie said. "I just wish we'd known about the boppli sooner."

"I didn't feel like I could tell anyone. I was afraid if Timothy found out, he'd insist that I go back to Kentucky. Until I had that dream about Mindy, I just wasn't ready to go back. Now this van we're riding in can't seem to get me there fast enough."

As they turned onto the road near her house, Hannah leaned toward their driver and said, "Would you mind dropping me off by the mailbox? Then I can walk up to the house and surprise Timothy. I'd like a few minutes alone with him before you all join us," she added, looking at Fannie.

"I have a better idea," Abraham said. "How about if after we drop you off, we head over to Suzanne and Titus's place to see their new boppli? Then in a few hours, we'll go over to your house and surprise Timothy, because he has no idea we're coming."

"That'll be fine," Hannah said with a nod. "After I've greeted Timothy and we spend some time together catching up, I plan to make him something special. It seems like ages ago now, but I've been wanting to bake Timothy a Kentucky chocolate chip pie. We can all have some when you come over later on."

Abraham grinned. "Sounds good to me. Never have been known to turn down a piece of pie. Isn't that right, Fannie?"

"Absolutely!" Fannie reached over the seat and gave his shoulder a pat.

When their driver pulled over by the mailbox a few minutes later, Hannah got out of the van, took her suitcase, and said, "I'll see you in a few hours." Then she turned and headed down the lane with a sense of confidence, letting her hand bounce between the boards on the fence. Her heart picked up speed as the path curved, taking her closer to the house. She could hardly wait to see Timothy.

Just as Hannah stepped into a clearing, she spotted a red-and-blue ambulance with its lights flashing. She tensed. Something terrible must have happened. Clutching her stomach, she let the suitcase drop to the ground. Her breath came hard as she ran the rest of the way. *Please, God, I pray that nothing's happened to Timothy.*

When Hannah got closer to the house, she spotted Samuel, Titus, and Allen near the ambulance. "Wh—what happened?" she panted. "Where's Timothy?"

"Hannah?" Titus looked stunned. "What are you doing here?"

"I'll explain later. Please tell me what's going on. Has someone been hurt? Is. . .is it Timothy?"

Samuel clasped Hannah's shoulders. "Jah. Timothy was working on the barn roof, and he slipped and fell."

Hannah swayed unsteadily, and Titus reached out to give her support. "Oh, dear Lord, no!" she cried, looking toward the sky. "Please, don't take my husband from me now, too!"

CHAPTER 54

Would you mind if I skip out on you for an hour or so while I run a few errands?" Bonnie asked Trisha as she finished putting some bread dough into two pans.

"Of course not. I've never minded when you run errands without me," Trisha said.

"Well, since my dad will be arriving sometime later today, I don't want you to worry that I might not make it back before he gets here. He's driving instead of flying this time, so there's no way I can be sure what time he'll arrive. When I spoke to Dad on the phone last night, he said he thought it would probably be later this afternoon, so I'm sure I have plenty of time."

Trisha put the loaves of bread in the oven and closed the door. "If for some reason you're not, I'll show him which of the guest rooms you have reserved for him."

Bonnie smiled. "What would I ever do without you, Trisha?"

"You'd be fine. Just like you were before I showed up at your door last Christmas."

"I was managing okay," Bonnie said, "but things have gone

even smoother since you started working here. I never thought anyone could cook better than Esther, but I think you're a pro."

Trisha's face heated with embarrassment. "I appreciate the compliment, but the only reason I cook as well as I do is because I've had a few more years' experience than Esther. For a young woman in her twenties, she's not only a good cook, but a very capable wife and mother to Samuel's four lively children."

"That's true, and I don't know how she does it all." Bonnie patted her protruding stomach. "When this little one makes his or her appearance, I hope I can be even half as good a mother as Esther is to those kids."

"I'm sure you will be."

Bonnie slipped into her jacket and grabbed her purse. "I'd better get going, or Dad will definitely be here before I get home." She hugged Trisha and hurried out the door.

For the next two hours, Trisha kept busy cleaning the kitchen, mixing cookie dough, and answering the phone. She'd just taken a reservation from a couple who would be staying at the B&B in a few weeks when she heard a car pull into the yard. She figured it must be Bonnie but was surprised when she glanced out the kitchen window and saw Ken getting out of a black SUV. Her heart skipped a beat. Even in his late fifties, he was as handsome as he had been in his teens.

Now stop these silly schoolgirl thoughts, she reprimanded herself. *I'm sure Ken doesn't feel all giddy inside every time he sees me.*

Drawing in a deep breath to compose herself, Trisha wiped her hands on a paper towel and went to answer the door.

"It's good to see you," she said cheerfully when Ken entered the house. "How was your trip?"

"Long and tiring, but at least there were no problems along the way."

"That's good to hear. Bonnie's out running errands at the moment, but I can show you to your room if you'd like to rest awhile," Trisha offered.

He shook his head. "If I lie down, I'll probably conk out and won't wake up till tomorrow morning. Think I'll just sit in the living room and wait for Bonnie to get home. I'm anxious to find out how she's feeling."

"She's doing real well," Trisha said. "Not much morning sickness and not as tired as I figured she'd be."

"That's because she comes from hardy stock," he said with a chuckle.

Trisha laughed, too, and felt herself begin to relax. "Would you like a cup of coffee, Ken?"

"Sure, that'd be great."

"I was just making some cookies when you pulled in," she said. "If I put a batch in the oven now, you can have some of those to go with the coffee."

He smacked his lips. "Sounds good. I'm always up for cookies."

Ken followed Trisha into the kitchen, and after he'd taken a seat at the table, she handed him a cup of coffee.

"Why don't you join me?" he asked. "The cookies can wait a few minutes, can't they?"

"Sure." Trisha was pleased that he wanted her to sit with him. "So when will you be starting your new job?" she asked after she'd poured herself some coffee.

"Monday morning. I'll need to start looking for a house pretty soon, too, because I don't want to take up a room here that Bonnie could be renting to a paying customer."

"I'm sure Bonnie won't mind you staying here for however long it takes to find a place."

"That may be so, but I'm not going to take advantage of

my daughter's good nature."

Trisha smiled. "Oh, I have something I'd like to show you."

"What is it?"

Trisha went to the desk and removed a manila envelope from the bottom drawer. "Bonnie found this in the attic a few days ago. It's full of pictures—some of you and me when we were teenagers." She handed Ken the envelope and sat down across from him.

Ken pulled out the pictures and smiled. "We made a pretty cute couple, didn't we?"

Trisha nodded, looking at the photos again. "We had a lot of fun together back then."

"Have you ever wondered how things would have turned out if you'd married me instead of Dave?" he asked, surprising her.

"Yes, I have," she answered truthfully. "But if you'd married me, you wouldn't have Bonnie for a daughter."

"You're right. We would have had some other child, or maybe we'd have several."

Trisha slowly shook her head. "No, Ken. We wouldn't have any children."

"How do you know?"

"Because I'm not able to have children of my own." Tears welled in Trisha's eyes, blurring her vision. "I wanted to adopt, but Dave wouldn't hear of it. Since I'm an only child, and so was Dave, I don't even have any nieces or nephews to nurture and enjoy. So to help fill the void in my life and because I love kids, I taught the preschool Sunday school class at our church for several years, and I volunteered once a month for nursery duty during worship services."

"Trisha, I'm so sorry," he said sincerely. "I know not having children or being able to adopt must have been hard for you."

She nodded, swallowing around the lump in her throat.

Ken left his chair, and taking the seat beside Trisha, he pulled her into his arms.

His kindness was her undoing, and she dissolved into a puddle of tears.

———

When Bonnie drove into her yard, she was surprised to see Dad's SUV parked alongside the garage. She really hadn't expected him this soon.

After she turned off the engine and gathered up her packages, she quickly headed for the house, anxious to greet him. When she stepped into the kitchen, she halted, surprised to see Dad sitting at the table hugging Trisha. She stood in disbelief, and when she cleared her throat, they both quickly pulled away.

"Sorry," Bonnie apologized. "I didn't mean to startle you." Seeing the tears in Trisha's eyes, she said, "Is everything all right? You look upset, Trisha."

Trisha reached for a napkin and dried her eyes. "It's nothing to worry about. I was just telling your dad about my inability to have children, and I got kind of emotional."

"I. . .I was comforting her." Dad's cheeks were bright red, and Bonnie was sure he was more than a little embarrassed. Could something be happening between Dad and Trisha? Maybe some sparks from their teenage years had been reignited. She hoped it was true, because they both deserved a second chance at happiness.

"Come here and give your old man a hug." Dad stood and held his arms out to Bonnie.

"It's so good to see you," she said after she'd set down her packages and given him a hug. "I didn't expect you so soon, though. How was your trip?"

"I made good time, so I can't complain, and the trip was fine." He gave her stomach a gentle pat. "How's that little grandson of mine doing?"

Bonnie shook her head. "Dad, that's wishful thinking on your part. We don't know if it's a boy or a girl."

"Well you ought to find out. I thought most pregnant women were doing that these days."

"Not me. Allen and I want to be surprised when the baby comes."

Dad grunted. "But if I knew for sure it was a boy, I could start buying things for the little fellow."

"You can decide what to buy after the baby gets here, and it might end up being girl toys and pretty pink dresses."

He nodded. "Guess you're right about that. I'll try to be patient, and I want you to know, I'll be just as happy if the baby's a girl."

Bonnie smiled. Like Dad had ever been patient about anything.

"Why don't you sit down and visit with your dad while I bake some cookies?" Trisha suggested. "I was getting ready to do that when he arrived."

"Thanks. I'm kind of tired, so I think I will take a seat."

Bonnie talked with Dad about his trip until he changed the subject. "So where's that son-in-law of mine?" he asked. "Is Allen working today?"

"Not his usual job, but he is helping Timothy re-roof his barn. Samuel and Titus are supposed to be there helping, too."

Dad smiled. "I've said this before, and I'll say it again: that man of yours is a keeper."

Bonnie nodded vigorously. "You're right about that, and I love him very much."

Just as Trisha took the first batch of cookies from the oven, Allen showed up.

"Look who's here," Bonnie said, motioning to Dad. "He arrived earlier than expected."

Allen smiled and shook Dad's hand. "I'm glad you made it safely." Then he turned to Bonnie and said, "I have some bad news."

"Oh dear. What is it?"

"Timothy fell off the roof of his barn, and he's in the hospital."

Bonnie gasped. "Oh no. Was he hurt badly? Is he going to be okay?"

"I don't know yet. After the ambulance came, I drove Hannah, Titus, and Samuel to the hospital, and then—"

"Hannah was there?"

Allen nodded. "She showed up unexpectedly, and you know what else?"

"What?"

"She's pregnant."

"Wow! Now that is a surprise!" Bonnie hardly knew what to say. She'd never expected Hannah to return to Kentucky, although she had been praying for that. And the fact that Hannah was expecting a baby was an even bigger surprise.

"I can't stay long," Allen said. "Timothy's folks are over at Titus and Suzanne's place, and I need to let them know what's happened. They'll no doubt want a ride to the hospital." He touched Bonnie's arm. "Do you want to go along?"

"Definitely," she said with a nod.

—⁓—

Hannah felt as if everyone in the waiting room was staring at her as she paced back and forth in front of the windows.

She was just too nervous and worried to sit still. Before Allen, Bonnie, Fannie, and Abraham got there, she'd explained to Titus and Samuel what made her decide to return to Kentucky. Then when the others arrived, she'd told Bonnie and Allen.

After that, Hannah hadn't said much because all she could think about was Timothy. What could be causing them to take so long in finding out the extent of his injuries? What would she do if Timothy didn't make it? How would she find the strength to go on? She'd exhausted her storehouse of endurance.

"Lord, we need Your help," Hannah whispered tearfully. "Please be with Timothy, and let us hear something soon."

"Why don't you come and sit with us?" Bonnie said, gently touching Hannah's shoulder. "You look worn-out, and you're not doing yourself any good by pacing."

Hannah couldn't deny her fatigue, but just sitting and doing nothing made her feel so helpless. "I wish we'd hear something," she said, fighting tears of frustration. "It's so hard to wait and not know how Timothy is doing. I. . .I'm so afraid he won't make it."

"I understand, but I'm sure you'll hear something soon." Bonnie took hold of Hannah's arm. "You must never give up hope. Just put your trust in the Lord, Hannah."

Trust. It was hard to trust when her future was so uncertain, but Hannah knew that she must. Reluctantly, she allowed Bonnie to lead her to a chair.

"Is it all right if I say a prayer out loud for you and Timothy right now?" Allen asked.

Hannah nodded and bowed her head. She knew they needed all the prayers they could get.

"Heavenly Father," Allen prayed, "we come to You now, asking that You'll be with the doctors and nurses as they examine and care for Timothy. Give them wisdom in knowing what to do for him, and if it be Your will, we ask that Timothy's injuries are not serious. Be with Hannah, and give her a sense of peace as she waits to hear how her husband is doing. We thank You in advance for hearing our prayers. In Jesus' name we ask it, amen."

Hannah had just opened her eyes when a middle-aged man entered the room and walked over to her. "Mrs. Fisher?"

Hannah nodded and swallowed hard. She didn't know if she could stand hearing bad news. *Help me, Lord. Please help me to trust You.*

"I'm Dr. Higgins," he said, offering Hannah a reassuring smile. "I wanted you to know that your husband has suffered a mild concussion. He also has several nasty bruises, a few broken ribs, and a broken arm. But as bad as that might sound, he's not in serious condition and should be able to go home in a day or so."

Hannah breathed a sigh, almost fainting with relief. "Oh, I'm so thankful. Can I please see him now?"

The doctor nodded. "Certainly. Follow me."

Hannah looked at Timothy's family members. "Would you mind if I go in alone and speak to him first?"

"Of course not," Fannie spoke up. "You're his wife, after all."

Hannah smiled and gave Fannie a hug. Then, sending up a prayer of thanks, she followed the doctor down the hall.

When she entered Timothy's room, she found him lying in the hospital bed with his eyes closed. Quietly, she took a seat in the chair beside his bed. It scared Hannah to see her husband all bandaged up and his arm in a cast, but she knew it could have been so much worse. She'd only been sitting there a few seconds when Timothy opened his eyes and turned his head toward her.

"Am I seeing things, or am I dreaming? Is that really you,

Hannah?" he asked, blinking as he gazed at her with disbelief.

Hannah's eyes burned as she thought of how close she'd come to losing him. Jumping up and reaching for his hand, she blinked against the tears that sprang to her eyes. "Yes, Timothy, it's really me—you're not dreaming. The doctor said you're going to be all right, and it's the answer to my prayers."

"But how'd you get here? When did you arrive? Wh–what made you come?"

Hannah explained everything to Timothy, including the dream of Mindy that she'd had.

"That's really strange," he said, "because I had a dream about Mindy, too." Hannah placed her hand gently on Timothy's arm. "I want you to know that I've forgiven you, and I. . .I need to ask your forgiveness, too. It was wrong of me to leave the way I did, and I'm sorry for putting all the blame on you for Mindy's death. I've had a long time to think about things, and I know now that I'm also at fault for what happened to our daughter."

"Wh–what do you mean?"

"I should have been watching her closer that day, and I never should have sent her out of the kitchen because I thought I was too busy and couldn't be bothered."

Tears pooled in Timothy's eyes. "It's okay, Hannah. I forgive you, and I'm grateful that you've found it in your heart to forgive me. Now we both need to forgive ourselves."

She nodded solemnly. "There's. . .uh. . .something else you should know."

"What's that?"

Hannah pulled her coat aside.

Timothy's eyes widened as he stared at her stomach. "You. . .you're expecting a boppli?"

"Jah." She seated herself in the chair again, feeling suddenly quite weary. "It'll be born next spring."

"Oh Hannah, what an unexpected blessing! Even in our grief, God has been so good to us."

"And He was watching out for you today," she said. "Falling off the barn roof could have ended in tragedy. How grateful I am that your injuries aren't life-threatening."

"I'm thankful for that, too, and from now on, whenever I'm working up high, I'll be a lot more careful than I was today."

"I don't know what I would have done if something had happened to you." Hannah leaned close to him, and despite her best efforts, she couldn't hold back the tears.

"I love you, Hannah," Timothy said as he reached out his hand and wiped away the tears trickling down her cheeks. "Oh, how I've prayed for this moment!"

"And I love you," she murmured. "Forever and always."

EPILOGUE

Six months later

Hannah hummed as she placed one hand on each of her twins' cradles in order to rock the babies to sleep. Little Priscilla Joy was the first to doze off, but Peter John wasn't far behind.

Hannah sighed. God had surely blessed them with these two precious bundles, and she was ever so grateful—not just for the privilege of raising these special babies, but for the opportunity to be Timothy's wife. She loved him so much and knew with assurance that he loved her, too.

Once Hannah was sure the babies were asleep, she stopped rocking their cradles and moved to the living-room window to look out at the beautiful spring day. The birds were singing so loud she could hear them from inside the house. To her, they'd never sounded more beautiful. A multitude of flowers had popped up in the garden, and the grass, which had recently been mowed, was lush and green. Their home looked beautiful. *Yes, our home,* she thought. It had been a long time in coming, but Hannah knew without a doubt that this was where she belonged.

Hannah's gaze went to the field where Timothy had been working all morning. She didn't see any sign of the horses or plow, so she figured he must have stopped to take a break. She glanced toward the kitchen and chuckled. Even the scratches on her new stove made her smile, remembering how it had happened all those months ago. She'd been upset about it at the time. Now Hannah couldn't believe she had let something so trivial bother her. She saw the mishap with the stove as a reminder of how hard her husband and his brothers had worked to turn this house into a real home. It had also become a good conversation topic when friends or family came to visit. The story of how the stove fell halfway through the floor always gave everyone a good laugh.

Hannah's thoughts took her back to the day they'd brought Timothy home from the hospital, two days after he'd fallen from the roof of their barn. Hannah had seen that he was settled comfortably on the sofa and then gone to the kitchen to prepare something for supper. Going into the utility room to get a clean apron, she'd been surprised to discover Mindy's doll on a shelf. When she'd asked Timothy about it, he'd explained that he had found the doll lying on the path leading to the mailbox. Hannah couldn't have been more relieved. After that, she'd taken the doll and tucked it safely away. One day she would give it to Priscilla Joy and let her, as well as Peter John, know all about their sister, Mindy.

Hannah had struggled with discontentment and bitterness when they'd first moved to Kentucky, but now she saw the Bluegrass State for its beauty and peacefulness and was happy to call it her home. She was thankful for English friends like Bonnie, whose baby girl, Cheryl, had been born two weeks before the twins. Things were going well for Trisha, too.

She'd sold her condo in California and was planning to marry Bonnie's dad in June. Hannah had also established a closer bond with Suzanne and Esther. Suzanne's baby, Abe, was growing like a weed, and Esther had told her the other day that she and Samuel were expecting a baby in October. The Fisher family in Christian County, Kentucky, was definitely growing, and Hannah was happy to be part of their clan.

Hannah sighed contently. Everything seemed right with the world.

"Are you wishin' you were outside working in the garden on this nice spring day?"

Hannah smiled at the sound of her husband's deep voice as he came up behind her. "I guess you are taking a break. I didn't think I'd see you until suppertime."

"The horses needed a break more than I did, but I used it as an excuse to come up to the house."

Hannah heard the laughter in Timothy's voice and knew even before she turned around that there must be a smile tugging on his lips. "I'm glad you came in."

"Me, too. I decided while the team rested I'd spend a few minutes with my fraa and bopplin, which is where I'd rather be, anyway."

Hannah gently squeezed his arm. "The babies are sleeping right now, but you're just in time to have a piece of the Kentucky chocolate chip pie I baked this morning."

"Mmm. . .that sounds good." He wiggled his eyebrows playfully. "But aren't you worried that it'll spoil my appetite for supper?"

She shook her head. "Supper won't be ready for a few hours yet. By then, I'm sure you will have worked off that piece of pie and will be good and hungry."

He grinned and nuzzled her cheek with his nose. "You

know me so well, Hannah."

"That's right, I do. I know and love you, Timothy Fisher. And you know what else?" she asked, tipping her head to look up at him.

"What's that?"

"Despite any struggles we may encounter, I know in my heart that we can make it through them because we'll have each other." She stepped into her husband's embrace. "And most importantly, we'll have the Lord."

"That's right," he agreed, brushing his lips across her forehead. "For as we are reminded in Psalm 71, He is our rock and our fortress."

Hannah's Kentucky
Chocolate Chip Pie

Ingredients:
1 stick butter or margarine, melted
2 eggs, beaten
1 cup sugar
1 teaspoon vanilla
1 cup chocolate chips
1 cup nuts, chopped
1 (9 inch) unbaked pie shell

Preheat oven to 325 degrees. In small kettle, melt the margarine and set aside. In bowl, beat eggs, sugar, and vanilla. Add chocolate chips and nuts and stir. Add margarine and beat well. Put in unbaked pie shell. Bake for 50 minutes or until done.

DISCUSSION QUESTIONS

1. Hannah had a hard time accepting her husband's decision to move from Pennsylvania to Kentucky because she knew she would miss her family, especially her mother. What are some things people can do to accept a move and adjust to their new surroundings?

2. Was there anything, other than moving, that Timothy could have done to improve his marriage and help Hannah realize that she was too close to her mother?

3. What are some things that parents can do to help their grown children who are married not to be so dependent on them and to cleave to their mates?

4. When Timothy and Hannah were forced to live with Timothy's brother Samuel for a time, it put further strain on their marriage, and it became difficult for Samuel and his future wife, Esther, to continue with their plans to be married. What are some ways a family can deal with having other people living with them for a time?

5. When a tragedy occurred in this story, Hannah blamed her husband and pulled away from him emotionally as well as physically. What are some ways we can work through a tragedy without blaming someone else?

6. Bonnie felt guilty for something she'd done when she was a teenager and was afraid to tell Allen about it. Is there ever a time when we should keep information about our past from a loved one?

7. Allen had a hard time forgiving Bonnie for not telling him about her past. He not only felt betrayed but wasn't sure he could trust her anymore. How can being unwilling to forgive others affect our relationship not only with that person, but also with God? What does the Bible say about forgiveness?

8. The Amish believe strongly that once they are married, God wants them to stay together until death separates them. What impact do you think it would have on an Amish community if one of their members left their spouse and perhaps even got a divorce?

9. What differences did you see in this story between the Amish in Lancaster County, Pennsylvania, and the Amish who live in Christian County, Kentucky?

10. What verses of scripture did you find the most helpful in this story? In what ways might you apply them to your own life?

ABOUT THE AUTHOR

Wanda E. Brunstetter is a *New York Times* bestselling author who enjoys writing Amish-themed, as well as historical, novels. Descended from Anabaptists herself, Wanda became deeply interested in the Plain People when she married her husband, Richard, who grew up in a Mennonite church in Pennsylvania. Wanda and her husband now live in Washington State but take every opportunity to visit their Amish friends in various communities across the country, gathering further information about the Amish way of life.

Wanda and her husband have two grown children and six grandchildren. In her spare time, Wanda enjoys photography, ventriloquism, gardening, beach-combing, stamping, and having fun with her family.

In addition to her novels, Wanda has written two Amish cookbooks, two Amish devotionals, several Amish children's books, as well as numerous novellas, stories, articles, poems, and puppet scripts.

Visit Wanda's website at www.wandabrunstetter.com, and feel free to e-mail her at wanda@wandabrunstetter.com.

Other Books by Wanda E. Brunstetter

KENTUCKY BROTHERS SERIES
The Journey
The Healing
The Struggle

INDIANA COUSINS SERIES
A Cousin's Promise
A Cousin's Prayer
A Cousin's Challenge

BRIDES OF LEHIGH CANAL SERIES
Kelly's Chance
Betsy's Return
Sarah's Choice

DAUGHTERS OF LANCASTER COUNTY SERIES
The Storekeeper's Daughter
The Quilter's Daughter
The Bishop's Daughter

BRIDES OF LANCASTER COUNTY SERIES
A Merry Heart
Looking for a Miracle
Plain and Fancy
The Hope Chest

SISTERS OF HOLMES COUNTY SERIES
A Sister's Secret
A Sister's Test
A Sister's Hope

WHEN A YOUNG AMISH COUPLE FACES INSURMOUNTABLE ODDS,

Will Their Love Be Strong Enough to Endure?

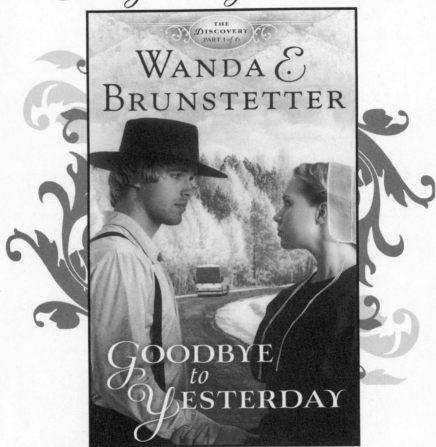

Wanda E. Brunstetter is back and better than ever with an exclusive 6-consecutive-month release of her brand-new Amish serial novel, The Discovery.

COMING FEBRUARY 2013

The Discovery

Will the faith and love shared by this Amish couple be enough to bring them back together again, against all odds? You'll need to read all 6 serial novels to discover if Meredith and Luke's love will survive.

 **STARTING FEBRUARY 2013**

The Discovery: Part 1 – Goodbye to Yesterday

Instead of experiencing newlywed bliss, Meredith and Luke Stoltzfus are faced with the hardest challenge of their young lives. Financial struggles. Arguments. A confirmed pregnancy. A last-minute trip to South Bend, Indiana. A drug addict on the run. A deadly encounter at a Philadelphia bus station... is only the beginning of the story.

THE STORY OF THE DISCOVERY CONTINUES WITH...

The Discovery: Part 2 – The Silence of Winter
Available March 2013

The Discovery: Part 3 – The Hope of Spring
Available April 2013

The Discovery: Part 4 – The Pieces of Summer
Available May 2013

The Discovery: Part 5 – A Revelation in Autumn
Available June 2013

The Discovery: Part 6 – A Vow for Always
Available July 2013

Go to www.facebook.com/TheDiscoverySaga to learn more!